STOLEN ENGLISH

MEDITERRANEAN SERIES

TASHA BOYD

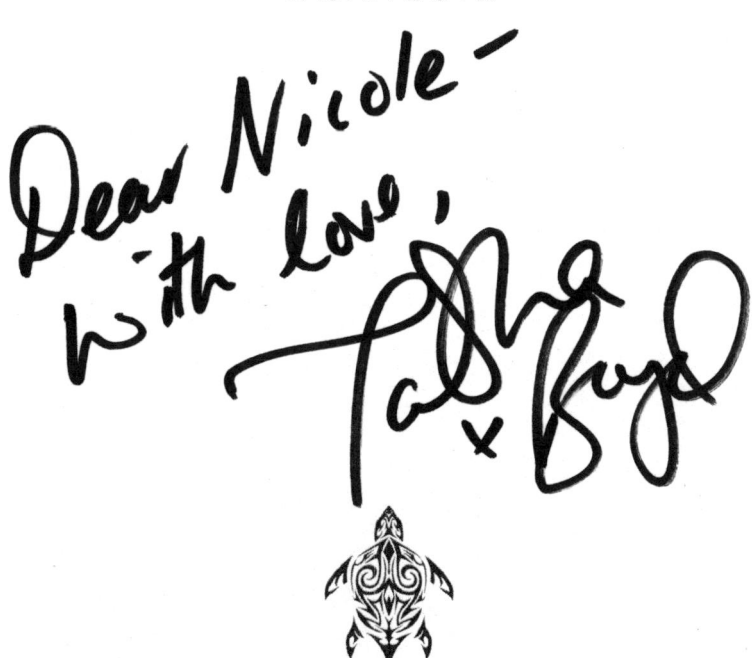

*Dear Nicole —
with love,
Tasha Boyd
x*

Dear Nicole -
with love,
Lola ♥

STOLEN
English

I believe you.
And it's not your fault.

Copyright © 2022 by Natasha Boyd, writing as Tasha Boyd

All rights reserved.

No part of this book may be reproduced in any form or by any electronic or mechanical means, including information storage and retrieval systems, without written permission from the author, except for the use of brief quotations in a book review.

All characters and situations in this book are entirely fictional, and any parallel to real life is entirely accidental. There are some real places mentioned, and any mistakes in their description is entirely the fault of the author.

Content edit: Judy-Roth.com

Proofread: karinaasti.com

Cover Design: hearttocover.com

First Paperback Edition November 2022

Updated Version June 2023

ISBN 9798364061140

ONE

Andrea

"DOES THAT ALIEN HAVE AN ERECTION?"

I jumped at the brusque, amused, male voice behind me. I knew that voice. I narrowed my eyes and turned around, tucking my notebook down at my side.

Sure enough, the morning sun dappling through the elm trees in the statue garden illuminated the last person I'd expected to see here. And not today, of all days. Evan Roark, thorn in my side, and my boss' chief of security. At one time I'd thought we were good friends but these days not so much. Not since I'd apparently mistaken our flirting and high tension for something a little more, and Evan had very quickly disabused me of the notion. Our banter and energy was ... off. Or I was off. I honestly didn't know.

"Evan. Didn't I leave you on a boat far, far, away this morning?"

He tucked his hands into his black pants that molded to his muscular legs. His tanned bare forearms revealed by his short-sleeved white polo he wore for work on the boat, flexed. "That's not a very welcoming greeting."

"What are you doing here?" I asked, annoyed that I always noticed things like his stupid muscles and dimpled grin. He was total eye candy. My type. Broad shoulders, muscly arms and thighs, not too big, but big enough, looking like he could bench press me without breaking a sweat. But going for my type was not a thing I was willing to repeat. Not after what I'd been through. Besides ... friend zone. We'd been in it for an awfully long time. "I didn't know you were into art," I said breezily, like his presence was neither here nor there.

He looked around, no doubt taking in the odd and bizarre assortment of bronze avant-garde artwork, and coming back to, he was right, a fully erect penis. "This is art? Okay. Why am I looking at an alien erection?"

"Assuming it is an alien," I said, adopting my professional docent voice, or what I presumed a docent might sound like as they dragged gawking tourists around the museum. "And that aliens have erections." Turning to face the creature, I took in the large black eyes and thick rotund body that almost looked like it would be pulled forward by the size and length of the weighty appendage disproportionately protruding out from its midsection. "Perhaps it's just an extra limb, like an arm." I bit down on my inner cheek to keep a straight face.

"But what's the meaning behind it?" He bent closer, taking it very seriously, and I tried not to laugh. Months of summer sun had shot his brown hair through with gold, and though short, it curled around his nape.

"I don't know, Evan. The very famous and celebrated artist Joan Miró is no longer around to ask."

"Is it supposed to make me feel something?" he asked.

"Why? *Does* it make you feel something? Tingly, perhaps? You know," I dropped my voice, "down there."

He pressed his lips together, refusing to react. "It's rather big."

"For an arm or an erection?"

"I guess it could be the spare arm he uses to, I don't know, like, eat? Or open things—letters? Cans?"

"You think it might be a can opener?" I deadpanned.

He straightened and locked his annoyingly gorgeous hazel eyes on me. "I think we both know what it is." He dragged his twinkled gaze from mine and looked at the sculpture again with a somber expression. "The question is ... why?"

I pitched my voice with sympathy and tilted my head. "Are you envious?"

"I've never had any complaints, thank you. And I don't need to wear a stabilizing weight belt to avoid throwing my back out when it's erect. Though, maybe ..." He cupped his chin in mock serious thought, looking back at the piece. "My lower back has been giving me some issues."

"That's because you're getting old." And he was lying. The man was in peak physical shape. And I did not want to think about his erect penis. I did not.

I did.

No!

"Speak for yourself," he said, giving me a side-eye.

My mouth dropped open. "Wow. You are really charming it up this morning." I scowled. He didn't have to know I was feeling every bit of thirty-three today. It was my birthday, my real birthday, and I'd woken up this morning before the sky had even lightened and suddenly it was like I really *woke up*. The main question that had plagued me as I sat bolt upright was what was I doing with my life?

I'd immediately requested a meeting with Lilian, the head curator, and made an appointment with a lawyer whose card I'd been dog-earing for months. Waking up and having a who-am-I-and-what-am-I-doing-here moment may have also been precipitated by what had happened, or not happened, between Evan and me.

It wasn't like I'd even been sure I was ready, but to be so soundly rejected had been humiliating. It was my friend Josie's fault anyway. And champagne. It had happened in a nightclub in Saint-Tropez, and Josie had just convinced me she thought Evan had a thing for me. And I was feeling so free and brave that night. It was the first time in so long I'd allowed myself to really let go. Evan had been all growly and speaking in whispers in my ear, ordering me around, and I couldn't help it, I'd turned my head and tried to catch his mouth. You'd think I'd slapped him by the way he went ramrod straight and set me coldly away from him. God, it had been utterly humiliating. And then the asshole had avoided me for days, so I couldn't even address it, before acting like it had never even happened. Josie must have been in her loved-up lust phase with Xavier, seeing heart-eyes everywhere, to have ever thought Evan had a thing for me.

I focused hard on the statue. Art. Right. Sure enough there was a bronze belt-like thing around the creature. "Huh. I guess he is wearing a weight belt." I pulled up my notebook and pretended to make a quick note about it.

"And what are *you* doing out here?" Evan asked, acting innocent. "Why are you taking notes on alien erections?"

"I'm—" I dropped my hand, holding the notebook to my side again to hide it. My main job was chief steward on Xavier Pascale's mega yacht—a yacht I lived and worked on for only five months out of the year before volunteering at the art foundation. And Evan, as Xavier's head of security, body guard, and I guess, best friend, had to be freaking everywhere I turned all summer long. And apparently in off-season too. And I wasn't interested in telling Evan a damned thing about why I was here a full month earlier than usual. "I asked you what you were doing here first, and you haven't responded." Then a thought occurred to me, and I couldn't help grinding my teeth together in irritation before I continued. "You followed me again, didn't you?"

A faint wince crossed his face. "It's a total coincidence. Look, I had some errands to run. You were gone. With the party coming up next week, security is paramount. My team—"

"Security is always paramount," I snapped with an eye roll.

He raised his hands. "I swear, I tried to call you. You weren't answering. Then I was running over to pick up some stuff at the Valbonne house, and you weren't there either. Just so happened I needed to come here anyway."

"Not true."

"True. And if you'd answered your phone, you would have saved me a trip."

"Evan," I said, my voice dripping with irritation.

"Andrea," he responded smoothly. Unruffled.

"Just … stay out of my business." I hugged my notebook to my chest as I tried to cross my arms. Ugh. I swung around, turning my back to him, and picked my way around a reflecting pool. The pool had a mosaic and yet more statues rising from its waters. They really should have a pathway around it, I grumbled inside my head as I almost tripped on a gnarly root. Ahead of me the glass door to the inner gallery spaces opened, and Lilian, the head curator, waved. I lifted an arm to wave back. I was due to find her for our meeting at ten thirty. I glanced at my watch. Shit, it was ten twenty-nine. Evan had almost made me late.

"Lil—" I started.

"Oh, Evan," she called over my head. "There you are! I have the pieces ready for you in my office."

I turned to Evan in confusion.

He gave me a tight but self-satisfied smirk. "Like I said, I had an errand to run. But you could have done it for me since you were already here—if you'd answered your phone." He made to brush past me and head toward Lilian, but then stopped, standing far too close. His damn citrus and pine scent tickled my nose, and fine, his nearness tickled something lower too. I gritted my teeth.

"But also, knowing where Xavier's employees are when they go MIA is kind of my job," he added. "So yes, I looked up your phone's location."

I growled in the back of my throat. "I'm not MIA, I work here every off-season. Which you obviously already know, *you stalker*."

He dipped his head next to my ear, and the growl died, my pulse hammering. "I like that sound. I should piss you off more often."

I froze, rigid. Damn, but that sounded sexual. Why did he

toy with me like this? It was very similar to what he'd done that night in Saint-Tropez. No wonder I got confused and irritable.

Evan immediately pulled back and something crossed his features, just like it always seemed to. He straightened. "Next time, when I text you and ask where you are, let me know."

And that was why my stupid crush was utterly misplaced. Should I ever date again, not that he was remotely in to me, Evan and I would never work. I might find him physically attractive, but that need to control everyone and everything around him was ice-cold water on my libido.

At least, it used to be. It should be.

"Ugh." I rolled my eyes and shook my head to break the spell. I looked toward Lilian, ready for an apology.

Lilian had already retreated inside, waiting for him. Or me.

Evan chuckled, low and deep, a rumble that sprinkled goose bumps in its wake, and headed inside too. Then he stopped. "Oh, before I forget. Meg and Sue asked me to invite you out for drinks tonight."

"I can't."

He narrowed his eyes. "Can't or don't want to?"

"Will you be there?"

"Yes."

"Then I don't want to." I did want to. I adored Meg and Sue and was so happy they'd agreed to come back on crew after Xavier had pared down the boat staff after his wife passed away. I loved their energy. They were easy to work with and had become really good friends. And it was my birthday. My old-self birthday. But no one knew that. Did Evan?

Evan's mouth twisted sideways, his eyes narrowing as if he

could hear my thoughts, and he seemed about to say something else. But then he shrugged and turned back inside.

That was the thing with Mr. Unflappable—because he never seemed to react to me, I'd found myself saying more and more things that would sound probably mean to any bystander. I didn't know whether I was pushing to see how far I could go or covering up my stupid crush. Probably a bit of both. It was a crush I didn't understand. Not at all. Why him? Apart from the obvious—he was hot, and one of the only men I was around half the time.

He didn't even care when I tried to annoy him. He was literally immune to me.

Now I was left feeling miserable and bereft in the wake of his presence and guilty about what I'd said. He really did seem to bring out the worst in me. Another strike against ever entertaining the idea of us together.

I blew out a breath and lifted my face to the sky. Despite the interruption, I was ready for my meeting with Lilian. I was going to rock this, and it would be the first step to a new life. The next step would happen at noon, in just an hour and a half, when I'd meet my new landlady. And tomorrow, a lawyer.

But not before I turned off the location permissions on my phone. Evan Roark, Mr. Safety Patrol himself, was going to have a conniption, but he was going to have to suck it up.

∽

AFTER MY MEETING WITH LILIAN, which had gone exceedingly well, I drove my rented Smart Car, which let's face it, felt like driving a piece of Lego through the winding roads of the French Provençal countryside toward my next destination.

Approaching the village, I parked nose out in between two mopeds in a space that looked as though it wouldn't fit a discarded olive pit. Smart Car for the win. I was lucky it was after the summer tourist rush, and I was even able to park this close to the village gate. The parking spot was perched on a rocky outcrop with a steep drop-off overlooking a green valley below and rolling hills dotted with other small medieval towns in the distance.

I craned my neck forward to look up the imposing town walls next to me. The town had been a fortress. It *looked* like a fortress. If a fortress was now a cute ramshackle cobblestoned and artsy mecca. The medieval village of Saint-Paul de Vence had been home to artists, writers, and poets for hundreds of years. You couldn't see the enclosed village from here, but I'd visited once before and knew not only that I needed to come back, but that if I ever got to this stage of life, this would be where I would come to figure things out. A sting of excitement coursed through me, and I climbed out of the car, locking it behind me.

I slung my favorite woven bag I'd picked up at a market this summer over my shoulder, glad I'd changed into my running shoes after my meeting, as I set off to the archway in the wall ahead of me.

The air was warm but with a touch of chill autumn breeze nipping my bare arms in the shady areas, a chill that would be gone by midafternoon. It would be at least a month or two until the final remains of summer ebbed away.

The entry to the village was an opening between two offset

outer walls so ancient invading armies in the valley couldn't see the exact place the entrance was from most angles. The town felt protected.

Once through the four foot thick stone walls and iron turnstiles, I was presented with two options—a road to my left, passing a restaurant called *Le Tilleuil*, and one narrower cobbled road straight ahead that climbed up a slope between the buildings. The restaurant had a few patrons, but the lunch rush wouldn't pick up for a couple of hours. I pulled up the address I'd been sent and headed into the narrow street. There was a step up every ten feet or so to help with the incline. There were shop fronts and art galleries either side of me, most doors already closed for the season, but some open and I glanced in, making notes about which ones I wanted to pop into as soon as possible. A sooty cat shot across the road in front of me, and the smell of baking bread permeated my senses as I approached a corner. Up ahead an old woman swept her front stoop with a straw broom.

Around another bend to the left, the road split two ways, up the hill between more buildings and down the hill to the road that hugged the town wall, and right in the middle was a narrow townhouse with a blue front door and single front window with sturdy, but pretty, wrought iron bars over it and front stoop. There were vines covering most of chipped stucco, which revealed the original stone it was built with.

The house was shabby and utterly charming. And it looked safe. The door swung open.

TWO

"*Bon*, you are here! Andrea? *Oui?*" A smiling young woman came out of the small village house, her dark curls piled on her head, and a faded red peasant sundress with tiny white flowers that would have looked like a sack on me, molded to her curves and hit just below the knee.

"Marianne?" I asked. "Nice to meet you."

We shook hands.

She was made even more alluring by her French accent and the huskiness in her voice.

"You are lucky, or perhaps it is me who is lucky. I only put up the advertisement last evening. I was so sad to lose my winter rental, and I thought no one would want to come now. And *bon*. Here you are!"

I *had* been lucky to rent this place. It was a hugely popular short-term rental for five months over the summer and rented long-term over the winter. I'd seen it before during my searches and never lucked out. Then I'd seen it online this morning and called immediately. It felt like fate. "It is definitely me who's lucky. I have been wanting to rent your place for years, but the timing was always off."

"You have no luggage?"

"Oh, not yet. I'll bring it as soon as my other job finishes for the season."

"Here is your parking permit for the lower gate." She handed me a vinyl car hanger, and I put it in my bag. "The lot is just to the right as you enter."

That had been another plus to choosing Saint Paul de Vence. There were only two ways in and out of the central village. The way I'd come, on foot, and a service road that had more iron turnstiles, which only lowered for permitted vehicles and deliveries. I hated that I had to think like that, but it was better safe than sorry.

"Come in." She swept an arm to the door in welcome. "But also, you can park in the public parking outside the gates so you can come and go more easily."

"I'll probably do that most of the time."

"The walk can be tiring, but you get used to it."

Inside, the front door opened to a cozy living area with a corner fireplace and a single comfortable love seat sofa, a scarred wooden farm table that did double duty as eating and kitchen island, and a short bank of kitchen cabinets against the back wall that had a cute robin's egg blue fridge, a sink, and a two top stove. A narrow set of stone stairs disappeared up into the left wall next to a padlocked wooden door.

Marianne gestured to the door. "That is for access to the other small apartment, but since the rental has cancelled and it is just you, it is locked off."

"Will you let me know if you rent it?" The last thing I needed was for some creep to end up next door.

"Of course! But it has no kitchen and this late in the year, it is not worth turning on the heating and gas for a few short term rentals, you understand." She waved her hand. "Here is the living room."

The compact space had high ceilings, and everything was light and airy, from the creamy ecru stucco on the walls and floor to the gauzy curtains that filtered light through a side window. An antique olive oil jar in pale green glass sat on the deep sill, holding a couple of olive branches.

"I hope you are used to small spaces," Marianne said after she showed me where everything was in the compact open kitchen area.

"I live on a boat most of the time, so yes. And this is divine. You have beautiful taste."

She beamed. "Thank you. I've always found it best to keep things simple."

Upstairs was a bedroom the same size as the living room with a window overlooking the front entrance and a larger side window that had a wooden writing desk in front of it. Marianne walked over to the bigger window and swept open the pale linen to reveal a blast of sun. "This is the best part. This window is above the height of the town wall. Look."

I joined her as she cranked the window lever and breathed in crisp air and the sight of rolling bucolic fields green and glowing in the autumn sun. In the mornings, I imagined they glistened with morning dew and wisps of mist that sparkled as the sun came up. Inhaling again, I felt my chest taking one of the deepest breaths it had in years, ribbons of tension loosening. "What a view to wake up to."

"You may not want to sleep with the curtains open though, unless you like a sunbeam to the eye first thing." She laughed and stepped back. "Bathroom is small but ..."

I looked around at the king-sized bed and the bathroom. "It's perfect. I honestly won't know what to do with all this space. Do I get a discount for only taking up twenty-five percent of the bed?" I teased.

Marianne laughed. "You'll have to learn to roll around. Perhaps with a lover?"

I shook my head vigorously. "Oh no."

"No? *Pourquoi non?* You are young, you are beautiful."

I waved a hand awkwardly at the compliment and not sure how to quickly get us past the turn in the conversation. "It's ... complicated." Like perhaps there were cobwebs all up in there and things of that nature. But I was pleased to be called young on a day I'd woken up feeling anything but.

"Ha. *Bien sûr.* When is love not complicated?" She laughed. "Well, perhaps you will meet someone. Not in this town though. Definitely avoid the artists, they will break your heart because they are tortured and hate themselves. And also they don't stay very long. And I know everyone else who lives here, and they are all grumpy and old. I'm glad I live and work down in Nice."

My stomach sank a bit. I'd been hoping she lived closer, it might be nice to have a friend or someone my own age to have a drink with every now and again. I had Meg and Sue and the rest of the crew before they all went off to other pastures for the winter months, but a lonely winter once again loomed ahead of me.

"I try to come up often though, my parents live close by. Perhaps when I am back we can go for a glass of wine, and I will tell you about all the village characters? There are some fun stories about people you will probably come to know."

"That would be great. I'd like that."

"And maybe you can come down to the city instead of hiding up here, and I can find you a lover."

I smiled wanly. I didn't want to protest again and have it become a thing. I probably should have rented in a city that was more vibrant and filled with people my age, but ... safety ... and quiet, and ... baby steps.

"*Alors*, why are you holed up in my little poet's house? You must love to get quiet and bored," Marianne asked with a charming bluntness I'd become used to living in Europe. It was like she'd read my thoughts as I followed her back down the stairs. "Are you writing a book?" she asked.

"God, no." I shuddered at the thought of sitting down and letting words come out unchecked. God knew what would happen if I did that. "No."

At the bottom of the stairs, she took down two small coffee cups from a hook on the wall, and I peered over her shoulder as she showed me how to use the espresso machine. But the pregnant silence seemed to be waiting for me to fill since I hadn't answered her question.

I took a breath. "I'm going to be working up at *Fondation Maeght*. Normally I volunteer, but now it's becoming a real job. I was an art history student, a long time ago. This is close to the gallery. And ... I also need some time and space to figure out the next part of my life."

"The complicated love life?" she asked, handing me a black coffee and showing me the basket of starter supplies she'd prepared for her guests that included a mini creamer.

"That's part of it." A huge part of it, if I wanted to be honest with myself, which I was most definitely not ready to be. "But I'm here because I need to make some decisions about other areas of my life too. I need space and quiet to think. And for the last five months I've been living in a tiny cabin that's not big enough to even change my mind."

Marianne cackled.

"Also, I've been working a lot for the last few years, and there are some things I want to do."

"Like?"

I tilted my head as I thought about things I longed for when I was cooped up on the boat. "I want to hike, and I think I want to go camping since I never have. I want to figure out what I like to do. Honestly, am I even interested in art or art history anymore? I used to cook. Do I still like to do that? I think I want to find out who I am really. Who I want to *be*, maybe. And read." I blew out a breath. "I want to read a ton of books. I never get a chance to read when I'm on the boat, so I like to catch up when I'm off. Sorry, that was a lot of personal stuff." And it wasn't even the half of it.

She waved her hand with a sympathetic smile, indicating it was fine. "That's a lot to figure out. Maybe like an early midlife crisis?" We moved to the front door and sat at a two-person bistro table on the tiny front patio. She watched me over the rim of her cup as she took a sip. Her deep brown eyes were kind and thoughtful. "You are lucky. None of us really ever have the privilege to take that time. It's good that you are. I thought most boat people go and work in the ski chalets for the winter months."

"My boss pays us well, so we don't have to work when he doesn't need us." I evaded the obvious question she was asking about why I didn't leave the area in the off-season.

"Who is your boss?"

"Oh, I'm actually not allowed to say." I cringed. "Sorry. I mean he's not a criminal or anything, but his head of security makes all of us sign agreements that we don't even mention his name."

Marianne whistled. "Wow. He must be a big deal. I apologize. I am a curious person. I love to wonder about other people. You can always tell me to mind my own business. My boyfriend tells me to all the time. Affectionately, of course." She rummaged in a pocket in her dress and pulled out a cigarette and a lighter. I shook my head when she offered, and she lit hers up, taking a deep inhale.

I still never got used to how many French people smoked. It was as though the tobacco backlash just never reached this country.

"I will quit soon, I promise. I am down to one a day. But with coffee, it is hard to resist." She angled her face toward the street and exhaled a plume of smoke. "My boyfriend and I, we love to go and camp near *Les Gorges du Verdon*. I will let you know when we plan our trip, and perhaps you can come too? Then you will do your camping and also hiking."

"Oh, I wouldn't want to impose."

"It's no fun alone anyway. We normally invite a few friends

along. You can come solo, or maybe you will have a lover by then." She waggled her eyebrows.

I laughed. "You really want me to have a lover, don't you?"

"But of course. Life is better with a lover. A good one anyway. We all need to sleep, to eat, and to fuck. The French have perfected all three."

I snorted a shocked giggle and she laughed along with me. Only someone as pretty and with a sexy French accent like Marianne could say that with a straight face and not sound the least bit crass. I had a bit of a girl crush. "It's on my list. At some point," I grudgingly admitted.

"Ha!" She smacked her knee with a big grin.

After our coffees, we went back inside and she showed me how the TVs worked and what the Wi-Fi was and we made sure we had each other's phone numbers since I'd mostly communicated with her via email.

After she left, I stood in the middle of the living room and closed my eyes. Breathing deeply and counting to five, I tried to hang on to the loosening feeling in my chest, but I couldn't stop the bonds tightening back up a bit. It was eerily silent and still. For months and months every year, I lived with the ground moving beneath my feet and constant sounds of the ocean and the sounds of a boat echoing around me even when we had no guests—every lap of a wave, every creak, and rock, and engine sound.

I breathed in again, my eyes still closed. Slowly the sounds of life, and a tweeting bird, permeated the stone walls, or perhaps the window we'd left open upstairs. My eyes snapped open. I walked to the front door. It was a keypad entry on the outside Marianne had shown me. I turned the inside knob, which meant it would automatically lock when closed. Then I tried the deadbolt, and my shoulders eased as I felt it slide across, oiled and smooth. The front window didn't open and had those pretty wrought iron trellis bars over it.

Moving to the side window, I inspected the crank and locking mechanism similar to the ones upstairs. They looked sturdy. I made sure the lock was in place. Looking out, I could see the angle of the descending road made it so only someone very tall walking past would be able to see in, and then they'd probably only be able to see the ceiling. I backed away and looked out the window from the kitchen and also from the couch, satisfied I could only see the top of the village wall, which meant only someone actually *on* the wall could see me.

I went through the same check upstairs in the bedroom. The frosted bathroom window wasn't big enough for a person to fit through. I'd feel safe here.

My phone buzzed from my bag I'd left on the bed. There was lots to do today. I hurriedly pushed aside the legal envelope taking up all the space in my bag and pulled my phone out. *Safety Patrol* flashed green—Evan's silly moniker I'd saved him as in my phone. My pulse spiked. Think of the devil.

Safety Patrol: *Where are you?*

Running another errand. I'll be back in about two hours. Everything okay?

Safety Patrol: *Your locations are turned off.*

He'd noticed already. I swallowed a grain of guilt. I could either play dumb or come clean. Ish. He was going to be pissed.

A girl needs some privacy sometimes. I'll turn it back on in a bit.

Or maybe I wouldn't. I hadn't decided.

Three dots popped up, then disappeared, then came up and disappeared two more times.

I lowered to sit on the bed and chewed the side of my thumbnail, waiting. Finally my phone buzzed. Yep. He was pissed.

Safety Patrol: *the fuck, Andrea. How am I supposed to do my job when you deliberately put yourself in danger?*

I inhaled deeply and frowned at the words he'd written.

I'm not in danger. And I'm not your job.

Safety Patrol: *Everyone who works for Xavier is my job.*

Well, relax, Dad. I am in fact very, very safe right now. If only he could see my eye roll.

Safety Patrol: *Turn them back on.*

My pulse clogged my throat. *No.*

Then I bit back a smile. Honestly, the guy was so expressionless and hard to rile up that the idea of ruffling his feathers was always absurdly appealing. He was such a control freak.

At that thought, my smile vanished. I'd definitely had my share of a control freak. Enough of one to last a lifetime in fact. I was beginning to wonder if I had a subconscious "type" I was drawn to. And that was unacceptable.

I stood and trotted back downstairs. I had lots to do this week. For the hundredth time, I wished Josie were still here. Meg and Sue were amazing, but they were besties and three was a crowd. And I wished I could talk to Josie, or anyone, about what I was about to do.

THREE

Back on the boat after returning from my second meeting with my new lawyer in Nice, I hurried past the catering team who'd been called in for the event so the crew could all enjoy the end of season party. It had been a busy but exhilarating week, and tomorrow I'd move into my new place in Saint Paul de Vence.

In my small cabin, I took extra care with my appearance. After showering and blow-drying my hair, I spent a long time putting on some really pretty natural looking makeup I'd bought out shopping with Josie a few months ago. Normally I never wore anything apart from a tinted SPF moisturizer and lip balm, but tonight felt different. I followed a social media tutorial and was really pleased with the results. I wasn't working with much, but at least I would look as if I'd made a proper effort. Then I slipped on a gray silk dress and paired it with high heeled sandals that had straps around my ankles. Dressing up this much was ridiculously out of my comfort zone, especially as I'd put on some weight recently like I did every summer on the boat with no work-outs and Chef's incredible cooking. It was becoming harder every year to shed the pounds, but everyone dressed up for the end of season party, especially since we hadn't had one the last couple of years, so I had to make the effort. And since Xavier had expressly forbidden any of us to work this evening, I didn't need to worry about wearing anything practical. Deep down I knew this desire to wear a knock 'em dead outfit was part of the restlessness I'd been feeling recently and wanting to test myself to see if I had enough confidence these days to pull off a sexier look. My hand shook a little with nerves as I finished my mascara and checked the time, satisfied I was ready before the party officially began and would have time to start the next phase of my plan.

I pulled open the narrow dresser drawer and took out the plain white envelope I'd stuffed in with my underwear earlier. I took a deep breath, and pasting a smile on my face, headed for my meeting.

Hurrying up the stairs and through the galley, I made it to the master cabin. The door was closed. As I raised my knuckles to knock, it opened, and I was skewered by the green and brown scowling gaze of Chief of Security, *aka Safety Patrol*, and pain in my ass, Evan Roark. And of course he was dressed for the party in a dark suit that looked made for him, blue shirt open at the collar, and the smell of soap and a woodsy cologne I knew but could never place, subtly lacing the air. I gulped. Did he have to actually present like my kryptonite? It was bad enough on a regular day in close quarters. I really needed to get out and meet some new people so this stupid situational fixation would evaporate.

Evan's eyes raked down from the top of my head to my shoes, a muscle twitching in his jaw, another scowl forming.

Great. Maybe I hadn't pulled the knock-'em-dead outfit off after all. Heat swept up my skin until my face throbbed, adding to the lingering feelings of rejection I still harbored. He looked vaguely disturbed. Or disgusted, I couldn't tell. His hand went to his tie and then his midsection like he was holding down bile. Nice.

I glared at him. "Stomach issues?"

He shook his head subtly. "Did you need something?" he asked in a clipped voice, his gaze not missing the envelope I clutched in my hand. I lowered it to my side.

"I have an appointment with Xavier." I tried not to sound dejected he hadn't even complimented my outfit. Not that I should expect it. Frost crept into my tone. "Can you excuse us?"

He looked over his shoulder as Xavier Pascale came into view, busying himself with sorting out some papers on his desk.

"Where did you go today after I saw you?" Evan asked me, not getting out of my way.

"Why do you always need to know? Where was Chef? Rod, for that matter?"

"I—" He paused. "They were here."

"And if they hadn't been?"

He let out a low growl. "They wouldn't have turned their fucking location permissions off."

I started to brush past him. I should have held my breath so I didn't smell anymore of him, but I tortured myself instead and inhaled his woodsy and citrus scent as I tried to get by. My eyes almost rolled back in my head.

Xavier waved a hand, beckoning me inside. "I'm sorry, Andrea. You are quite right. Our meeting slipped my mind. Come in." He glanced at Evan. "I'll see you out there, Evan."

"We haven't finished our discussion," Evan protested.

"*I've* finished. You disagreed. But I'm not changing my mind."

I stepped back, feeling awkward. "I can come back."

"No," Xavier said. "You stay. Evan, see you later."

Evan looked back at me. "You look ... nice," he gritted out like he was chewing glass, then moved past me.

Finally. Though it had hardly sounded sincere. "Thanks. So do you," was all I said.

"Turn them back on," he whispered from behind me.

My skin pebbled, but I gave him the finger over my shoulder before the door closed behind me. Imagining his scowl, I let a grin tug my lips. Now that I knew keeping location permissions off on my phone drove him so batshit, I was likely to never turn them back on.

A string of under the breath curse words came from behind me as the door closed.

Xavier was watching our interaction with amusement.

"I'm so sorry to interrupt you two," I started.

"You weren't interrupting, you were saving me from arguing until I was blue in the face. We disagree on a security issue. He's lucky he's my oldest friend as well as my head of security. Maybe if I hadn't made him such a large shareholder, he'd actually listen to me for once. I've created a monster. Have a seat." He motioned to the seating area and came to join me. His cabin spanned the entire width of the boat and had a desk and seating area as well as a massive king-sized bed. "What can I do for you?" He was dressed in gray pants and a crisp white button down shirt. It felt bittersweet to notice after he'd broken Josie's heart, but he really was the most ridiculously handsome man.

Josie was devastated on the other side of the world, and I only wished Xavier would wake up and go get her.

Before sitting, I stepped forward and handed him the envelope.

"What's this?" he asked.

I pressed my lips together, suddenly nervous. "Um, it's uh ... it's my resignation."

Xavier Pascale froze and blinked at me before quickly recovering. "Does Evan know?"

I frowned at the unexpected response. "No?"

"I see. Can I ask why you're resigning?"

I nodded at the envelope. "I tried to explain—"

"I'd like you to tell me."

My knees weakened, and I sank onto the edge of the couch and wiped my sweaty palms together, wishing I could wipe them on my dress, but I'd probably leave marks on the silk. "Well, I, uh. I've been here a long while ..."

"You have."

"And it's been wonderful. Truly. I came here during a pretty dark time, and if I'm being honest, your job didn't just change my life, it saved my life ..." I paused, drawing on a deeper reserve of strength. I'd rehearsed this so many times, knowing the day would finally come. "The thing is, I'm stronger now, and I think I've been using this job as a shield. In the beginning, it was protecting me, I know that." I gulped a breath. "And I appreciate that. It probably still is."

Xavier cocked his head, waiting for me to continue.

My pulse thumped. "Before I continue, have you heard anything new about my husband?"

"No. Nothing new that I know of. But this is a question for

Evan. I'm sure Evan would have told us if he'd heard your husband had located you. You know you can speak to Evan anytime you are concerned?"

I nodded, though I hated that Evan knew so much. It made me feel like a wounded bird he had to protect. "Well," I bravely battled on, wondering why I'd bothered to write this all down in a resignation letter if I was a going to have to go through it verbally anyway. "In recent years, being here has felt less like protection and more that I've been ... hiding." Not to mention a little bit suffocating. But I kept that observation to myself.

"Did something change? I thought it was a good thing you're hiding."

"It is. It has been. But I've decided I—I'm going to finally try to get divorced. I mean, it's been nine years. I can't give him any more of my life."

Xavier gave a slow nod, eyebrows raised in mild surprise. "I really wish you'd let Evan be a part of this conversation."

"Why? It's nothing to do with him." Apart from the fact my burgeoning attraction to Evan was a small part of the reason this all had to happen immediately, before I turned into a pathetic fool.

"I disagree. Don't you think you should stay within our protection if you are going to try to get divorced? *Especially* if you are going to."

My gut twisted. He was right, but I'd already set things in motion. My lawyer was obscuring my address so I still had some anonymity. And now that I'd made the decision it was like I was fighting my way out to breathe and hadn't realized how long I'd been under water.

"I, yes. But I feel like I finally woke up and realized how

much time has passed. And now that I have, I don't want to waste a single second. I don't even know who I am anymore apart from chief stew. And that has been wonderful. I'm truly grateful. But I've kind of lost track of who I am. And I want to ..." I paused. This was the tough one to talk about. "I think I'm ready to date again. I want a family, I think. I don't know. Maybe I want kids. I'm thirty-three. I may even be too late for all I know, but I can't let my husband steal another year of my life. I saw you and Josie this summer, and—"

A shadow flashed across Mr. Pascale's face, and he swallowed and looked away from me, stuffing his hands in his pockets.

"I'm sorry." I cut myself off.

He inhaled deeply. "No need for apologies. But I'd hardly hold us up as an example," he said, a bite in his tone.

"No. I understand. I think it was just meeting Josie. She was so ..." How did I even begin to describe the sunshine she'd brought to everybody?

"Are you in touch?" His voice was calm, but I detected a slight edge to it.

"A little. Anyway, meeting Josie made me realize how much of life I was missing out on—a career, *choices*," I swallowed, "love, even. I've been acting like my life is almost over. Like I'm seventy-three, not thirty-three."

His mouth hooked up at the side. "She had a similar effect on me."

"I think you could win her back." I rushed the words out on a whim and to reassure him after that discomfort I'd seen. "I *know* you can. She's crazy in love with you, and with Dauphine. You should go get her. Sorry, I know it's not my place. But—"

"I appreciate you saying that. But I have a lot to apologize for. Besides, let's get back to why you're here." His tone invited no further discussion on that subject. "I think you know how much you are valued in my organization. Let me at least keep you on staff through the off-season. I'd offer you a pay raise to stay, but somehow I don't think that would change your mind."

I shook my head. "It won't. Besides, you already pay generously. And no, I'd like to resign now."

"Are you sure it's safe?"

"I—" I deflated a little. "No. I'm not sure. But I'm doing as much as I can to keep my whereabouts hidden. And I'm not the same person I was back when I started working for you."

"You need to tell Evan."

I sucked a lip between my teeth. I didn't want to tell Evan. I didn't want to *need* Evan.

Xavier crossed to his desk and perched against it, crossing his ankles and his arms. "Andrea." He paused. "No. *Merde*. It's not my place to have this conversation with you. If you want to resign, I would never stop you. But you and Evan need to have a serious conversation."

"I don't understand. What has Evan got to do with whether I work here or not?"

He picked up a paperweight, hefting its weight and then tossing it from hand to hand. "Evan is my chief of security. Not just for me and my family but my whole business and everyone who works for me."

"I know that."

"That means he does a lot of digging and keeps an eye on a lot of potential threats. Threats to people who work for me are also threats to me. Anywhere there is a weakness, there's a place to get to me or Dauphine."

Just this summer an unscrupulous family member had exploited a weakness with one of the crew, and we'd almost lost Dauphine. I swallowed heavily at the reminder. "I know that." And Evan Roark had drummed the weakest link theory into all of our heads over the years, but even so it wasn't an infallible way to protect the family. It had already failed once, after all. "That's why I don't think I should be working for you when I do this. I don't want to be the weakness."

"You should talk to him."

As much as I'd found having to tell everyone my background in the beginning humiliating, thinking about Evan constantly looking into my past felt worse. I always knew on some level, but hearing it said out loud drove it home.

"Can *you* do it?"

"I think he'd rather hear it from you. Why do you not want to trust Evan with this?" Xavier pressed.

"It's not ... he's ..." I took a fortifying breath. "He's ... I don't know. Of course I trust him." I had trusted him with my life after all. I had no good reason beyond the fact I didn't want to be some weak, helpless damsel to Evan, and I didn't want him so entwined in my life anymore. I also wanted to date again. And it was hard to do that when a) a bodyguard was all over your every move, and b) you perhaps had an ill-advised crush on said bodyguard that made other men pale in comparison. I mean, would he even let me date? I almost laughed out loud at the fact I was asking myself the question.

"What's so amusing?"

I hadn't realized I'd actually let the strangled sound leave me. "That's why I have to resign now and not try to date while he still thinks he's responsible for my safety. Would Evan let me date without background checking everyone I even think of talking to? It would be a nightmare."

Xavier's eyebrows drew together even while his mouth told me he found that utterly amusing. "I can see your point. But you won't lose our concern for your safety just because you no longer work for me." He paused and seemed to weigh his next words. "Evan ... cares for you. All of you," he added. "So do I. You are all like a family to me."

My throat felt thick. "Thank you. That means a lot."

He glanced out the window, seemingly in thought. Then his eyes narrowed as if he'd had an idea, and he turned back to me. "What about someone who's already background checked?"

I tilted my head.

He shook his. "I cannot believe I'm doing this. Do you know one of my executives, Christian Felice? He spent some time on board a few weeks ago with the finance team."

I knew who he was talking about. He was an executive with Pascale Company, super smart, and insanely good looking. He kind of knew it too. He'd been sweet and flirty with me nonstop the week he'd been on the boat with a group of finance people. I nodded. Far too young for me to even look at that way obviously, but—

"He asked me if I had any objection to him asking you out."

My head bobbed back. "What? He did?"

"Yes, he did. And I hope you don't mind me saying, even if I'd said I had a problem, I doubt I'd be able to stop him once he sees you this evening. You do look lovely."

My cheeks and the skin on my chest prickled with self-conscious heat. "Thank you," I forced out. I was very aware of my shortcomings. My curviness. And Christian Felice was *way* out of my league. "But isn't he way too young for me?" I'd honestly thought he was just one of those guys that flirted with all women regardless of age, shape, and size. So I hadn't even let myself think of him that way.

"He didn't seem to think so. And he's a good guy. Extremely smart. No skeletons in the closet or he wouldn't be working for me. And for an added bonus, Evan will absolutely hate it," he added with a delighted chuckle. "*Alors.*" Xavier stood upright before I could ask what he meant by that and then tapped a finger on the envelope on his desk containing my resignation. "I will read this tomorrow morning. We have a party to get to. Shall we?"

FOUR

Evan

XAVIER'S WORDS TO ME, and our subsequent disagreement, keep ricocheting around my brain as I step out onto the teak entertainment deck of the yacht where the cocktail party is almost in full swing. *You are not coming with me to America.*

The tinkle of laughter and merriment dances over a husky lounge singer crooning the blues in a corner of the lower deck. It's the annual end-of-season get-together where everyone who has worked on the yacht during the summer in one capacity or another, as well as people from Pascale Company, are invited to cocktails on deck, followed by a spectacular dinner in town at a restaurant of Chef's choosing. It's been three years since we've had one of these events, ever since the late Mrs. Pascale passed away.

There are people from up at the house in Valbonne

attending as well as some of the top executives and their wives from the company, including some of the Pascale Company security team I've built up over the years. My second-in-command, Pete, is trustworthy and has the team well in hand, and he's on duty for me tonight. For the guests, the party is half work, half play. It's a season ender for some and a welcome back for others. I find it one of the most stressful times of the year. We're sitting ducks—all of Pascale Company's executives in one place. Luckily I make Xavier hold the cocktail party portion of this evening at a berth in Cannes since the city is used to high security situations like the film festival every year.

Rod, the main deckhand, and Andre, Xavier's long-time chef, who goes simply by "Chef," wave me over. A server offers me a glass of champagne on the way, and I take it, even though I probably won't drink it.

"It's a party, mate. Cheer up," Rod says good-naturedly as I stroll over to them. I realize my argument with Xavier followed by the gut punch of how gorgeous Andrea looks tonight must have put my scowl face on a permanent setting. I'd almost swallowed my tongue when I opened the door and saw her outside Xavier's office. And she's pissing me off with her lax security and caginess the last couple of days. That's the real reason I'm so annoyed. Last week, knowing it was her birthday, I'd deliberately invented a reason to check on her. As I suspected, she seemed extra prickly. Still does.

I shake my head and try a smile. "Rod," I greet. "Chef."

Rod leans in. "What do you think my chances are?" He nods over to Meg and Sue who have rejoined our crew. Luckily for us their contract on another mega yacht was abruptly cancelled, their previous boss having had their yacht impounded for tax evasion. The French didn't fuck around. We took them back on to help Andrea out after Xavier left the boat for the summer and let his executive team and their families take the boat out for the rest of the season. "If you don't know what your chances are by now, Rod, I have to say they are probably quite slim."

His face falls, and I feel bad. I always forget teasing Rod is like accidentally kicking a puppy. I set a hand on his shoulder. "Sorry, mate. Maybe, I'm wrong. Which one do you have your eye on?" I ask to be friendly.

"Meg is super fit. I've always been in to brunettes. But Sue makes me laugh."

"Frankly," piped in Chef grumpily, "I keep getting their names mixed up."

Rod elbows him in annoyance. "No, you don't. You just do it to annoy them."

"Maybe." Chef is shaking his head with a laugh.

Rod turns back to us. "Honestly, they are both so nice. I'm so glad we're getting back up to capacity. Feels like the band has gotten back together." He lets out a long wistful sigh.

"What's the sad sighing for then?" asks Chef.

Rod shrugs, looking forlorn all of a sudden. "I just want a girlfriend. You know? Sorry, maybe this makes me sound like a sentimental old tosser. But I want someone to love and want someone to love me back. Is that so much to ask?"

Both Chef and I burst out in a chorus of, "Awww," as Chef adds, "But *I* love you."

I press my lips together to tamp down a chuckle. "What brought this on?" I ask.

"I think everyone has love fever after being around Mr. Pascale and the American nanny," scoffs Chef.

"Speak for yourselves," I say. "So, where have you guys decided to spend the off-season?" I listen as they discuss options and rentals. Normally the crew settles sort of close to each other if they stay in the area. It makes my job easier of keeping an eye on everyone. Eventually I have to ask, "Has Andrea mentioned where she might be staying?"

"No. Some village, but I don't know which one. She's kept very mum on that count. Being quite shady actually," said Rod. Suddenly he lets out a low whistle, and Chef and I swing our gaze back to Meg and Sue just in time to see Andrea joining them.

"Goddamn, she scrubbed up well for tonight, didn't she?" Rod gushes. "Holy hell. I could be into an older woman, just saying."

I grimace. Andrea's objectively stunning. I've always thought so. Glancing down at my drink, I wish I wasn't on self-assigned duty and that it was scotch and not a tiny little drink of bubbles. "Thirty-three is not old. And that's enough gawking," I manage in a low tone. "And don't even let it cross your mind, Rod. She's off limits."

Chef gives me a look.

I give him one right back.

Rod shrugs. "She doesn't date as far as I can tell. Men or women. What a waste. Why is that again, anyway?" he asks.

"What about you, Evan?" Chef interrupts. "No love fever for you? Anyone on your radar?" he asks pointedly, clearly disregarding the shut-up-and-don't-ask-questions look I just gave him.

Xavier steps out onto the deck at that moment and catches my eye. I grab the diversion. "I'd love to stand around and gossip about who likes who like a group of teenage girls," I tell Chef and Rod, "but I need to speak to our host." And find out what his meeting with Andrea was about. I hate being left in the dark.

Xavier holds out his glass for me to clink as I approach. "I'm done arguing about the American trip, so don't bring it up again," Xavier says as I join him. "Besides, I have bigger news to share."

I give my boss and best friend my full attention as his words register. "Bigger than you informing me you are leaving the country and don't want a security detail?"

He's leaving in three days to go and win Josie's heart once and for all. I'd finally seen my best friend break open to let love in this summer, only to lose it again, fool that he is. I'm confident he'll win his girl back. But he and his daughter traveling without security? "It's unacceptable. Especially after what happened with Dauphine. You just sprung this harebrained idea on me, and I haven't had time to organize a proper security detail if I don't go. Pete can't go either. I *have* to come with you."

"Evan, I really appreciate it, but no one apart from you knows I'm even going. Nobody there knows me. No one can galvanize any kind of presence that would be a threat to me or Dauphine so quickly. I'll concede to you sending someone in a week or two. But for the love of God, let it not be you."

"Trying not to be offended here." I scowl. "So, what you're saying is, I have to stay behind in France and not protect the person I've actually been hired to protect."

"I hired you as my head of security for my entire company.

The fact you like to be my personal bodyguard during the summer months is great. I'm under no illusions as to why. It's not because you want to spend your summers with *me*. You want to spend them on my yacht, and mostly because of who's on it." Xavier slides his glance toward Andrea.

My gaze follows. "What are you even talking about?"

Andrea's still talking to Meg and Sue, holding her glass of champagne, but Rod and Chef have ambled over to join them.

Andrea tilts her head back and laughs at something Rod says and the setting sun catches her hair. She's left it down tonight. It's always pulled into a tight bun when she works as chief steward of the yacht. Which is pretty much every day for five months straight. She's wearing a dove silk dress that slips over her curves and is held up by the tiniest, thinnest straps possible. Xavier clears his throat, and I whip my gaze back to him.

"As I was saying ..." He grins and takes a sip of champagne.

I growl in the back of my throat. "Asshole," I grumble. "She looks great, so what?"

"Something tells me the idea of you having to come all the way to America to watch *my* ass, and not hers, is causing you a serious amount of stress," he adds. "Why don't you consider it a favor that I'm ordering you not to come with me."

I swallow, not responding. He's right. I've been extremely torn since he told me. In the last nine years she's been under my watchful eye, most all of the crew, and particularly Andrea, have stayed close. It's been easy to do my job as head of security for Xavier as well as making sure she stays safe. Traveling with Xavier means I won't be able to keep an eye on her. Or anyone else.

"Has she told you where she's renting yet?" I ask.

"No, did she tell you?" Xavier asks.

I set my jaw. "No. And she turned her damn location permissions off a few days ago. What was your meeting with her about?"

I see the hesitation before he speaks. "Well, that is the bigger news I wanted to tell you about. She's going to be looking for another job." His tone is off. Cryptic. He's either feeling me out or fishing for my reaction.

"I thought you paid her enough she didn't have to work in the offseason."

"I do," says Xavier, "as well you know. But sometimes a job is not about the money, it's about self-worth. And about identity. And living again. Haven't you noticed? She seems different recently ... lighter. Determined."

My fingers tighten around the stem of the champagne glass I haven't taken a sip of yet. "What are you not saying?" And yes, I have noticed. Every year she's been away from that son of a bitch, she's healed a little bit more. And there's definitely something about her since this summer when she and Josie, the nanny, became friends. She even went out to a nightclub for God's sake. I had never seen her in that kind of environment. I was so proud of her and so fucking terrified at the same time. I was probably a bit of a brute to her that night, if I was honest. It's amazing how with everyone else, I can be lighthearted and fun and chatty, and with Andrea I just want to growl all the time. At least it's become more so recently.

I can't forget what almost happened that night at the nightclub either. Thank God I had my wits about me because when she leaned in all tipsy and soft and doe-eyed, the faint smell of her light floral scent punching straight down to my groin, I'd almost given in and kissed her. Jesus, that would have freaked her out. I needed her close and trusting me, not taking advantage of her after she downed five champagnes. Yes, I'd been counting.

And of course I *want* her to live again and have some freedom. I do. But that means putting herself in danger.

Xavier's words cut in. "I think you and she need to talk."

"Of course we will."

"No. I mean really talk. You'll be too late if you're not careful." He tilts his head toward a couple of his finance team members, and I turn in time to see Christian Felice trailing his sticky gaze all over Andrea.

I lower my voice as much as possible and lean in. "Firstly, it's not like that. I just care. Like I do about everyone. And secondly, anyone from Pascale Company dating her would be a massive conflict of interest—"

"She just resigned, Evan. She no longer works for Pascale Company."

My next words die in my throat.

The stem of my glass snaps in my fingers and the flute full of champagne tilts and hurtles to the deck beneath me with a high pitched shatter, drawing everyone's gaze. There's a beat of silence. I'm frozen.

FIVE

Everything snaps back into real time, and I give a fake apologetic smile and drop to a crouch to pick up the larger shards of glass. Xavier crouches next to me even as a server is hurrying in our direction.

"Well, that's more of a reaction than I've ever seen from you. You need to talk to her," Xavier says. "Before you lose her."

"I have no idea what you are talking about." I sear him with a look that musters every ounce of shut-the-fuck-up I have in me. "I need to clean this up."

Andrea is suddenly at my side as I go through the door, instantly back in chief steward mode, problem solver, server. "Here, let me—"

"I've got it," I snap and shrug her hand off my elbow. Then I stop and close my eyes, breathing out a long breath, and turn to her. She's hurt. I've hurt her. Shit. Her normally blue eyes look gray and they're wide and surprised. And wary. I hate that look. It's the look she always had in the beginning after she left him. And I've done it to her twice today. "I'm sorry. I didn't mean to snap at you. Xavier just pissed me off. It's no excuse."

She glances back over her shoulder at Xavier. He's watching us even while Paco, the captain, has wandered over to engage him in conversation. "Why? What did he say?" she asks, chewing her bottom lip. She doesn't add anything else. Doesn't offer up the news. Just waits to see if I know.

I feel betrayed by her silence, which pisses me off even more.

"Just a security issue we disagree on," I finally evade, dropping the piece of glass I'm still holding in the trash and pop open a small cabinet to grab a dustpan and brush we keep close by for exactly this.

If she doesn't walk away, I'm going to lose my shit right here. My chest is suddenly so fucking tight I can't breathe. I know this feeling. Fuck. Haven't had it in years. Like a dread feeling I'd wake up with right before a dawn raid in Kandahar. Not knowing if today was the day my life would end, not being able to control someone else's mistakes that could get me or my team killed. Which doesn't make sense. It's not the same feeling obviously. And not the same situation at all. How could it be close? That was war. This is ...

A female server from the catering team comes in to help, and I hand her the dustpan.

Andrea is staring at me.

I take a long, slow breath, reeling in my thoughts. "Did you have something you wanted to say?" I manage steadily through the sound of loud silence rushing in my ears. I want to walk away right now and deal with whatever panic attack is happening inside me. Because I think that's what this is. Thank

God, on the outside, I know she sees nothing. "News you wanted to share?"

She shakes her head, but her throat moves heavily as she swallows. "He told you." Not a question.

I drop to my haunches to secure the cabinet door since I don't want to be rude and walk away, and I have to get out of the line of fire burning from her eyes. I don't trust myself to speak just yet.

"Evan," she says from somewhere over my head.

"Were *you* going tell me, or am I supposed to hear it second hand?" I throw it out casually as if it's neither here nor there. "Well?" I ask. The cabinet door is stiff on its rails, and it jams as I try to slide it closed.

She steps closer. Her jeweled wedge sandals bearing peek-a-boo pink painted toenails step right into my line of vision. "Your tone sounds like you don't care if I leave. For someone who's on my case and whereabouts every damned second, that's surprising."

I abandon the door and let my gaze wander past her ankles and up the smooth skin of her calf, past her knee length and sexy-as-hell dress, skimming her curves and up to her amused face looking down at me. Whatever I was about to respond gets lost in my throat as something, some reaction to seeing me on my knees in front of her, passes over her expression. Her breath catches, her smile falters. I wouldn't even notice it if I hadn't been studying her from behind my dark glasses for years. But I don't have them on now, do I? I snap my eyes closed and quickly look down. With pure brute force I slam the cabinet door closed and slowly get my feet far too close to her. She doesn't step back. She should be stepping back. I expected her to. She smells incredible. Candy floss ... or is it candy apple? She must have new body cream. I hate that I know this.

"Excuse me," I say as if I'm about to move past her, and that's the only reason for our proximity.

"Do you care?" she asks, throat bobbing.

"Of course," I snap. Then I sigh. "Do you think it's safe?" I ask because this is me, and this is the only thing I'm supposed to care about.

She looks disappointed in my answer. "That's a different question all together," she says. "One Xavier says I apparently need to discuss with you." She's never acknowledged that I keep an ear to the ground for news of her husband. I know she knows. Probably not *how* closely I do. Especially since I found out last week he's been MIA, which could mean he's on the move.

"So, I guess you should know, I'm filing for divorce too."

Panic hits my gut and a thousand questions burn on the tip of my tongue. Shit. I swallow it all down. Fuck. I need to go and process everything—process my reaction to her leaving. And now this. I know I should talk to her as a friend. This is huge for her. I should be responding as a good friend would to this. Normally I would be happy for her, right?

But I can't speak.

She huffs in frustration and probably a bit of hurt at my lack of response. "Did you even hear what I said? What's up with you tonight?"

"Nothing. I'm just stressed at these social events. You know how it is. Security and all that." I remain stiff.

"Security concerns," she says. "That's it?"

"I'll see you at the restaurant," I say and muster up a vague smile so I can disengage from her.

Her face falls at my obvious attempt to get away from her. "Evan. Please."

"I need to go check on something," I add. What can I say? *Don't put yourself out there, please, otherwise nine years of protecting you from him might be for nothing. And how will I protect you if you aren't part of my job?*

Her expression is conflicted and disappointed and worse ... resigned to my carefully projected indifference to her that I've been honing for years.

And that's when the meaning of what I just asked myself hits me, like someone just threw a five ton warhead at my chest and belatedly said, *catch*. But not before it completely knocks the wind out of me and lands me on my ass. *How do I protect her when she's not part of my job?*

Fuck.

She turns away, unaware of my self-inflicted crisis of realization, and heads out the open sliding door toward Rod and Chef and some of the staff from up at the Valbonne house. I stare after her as at the last minute she veers over to a small group from Xavier's office. It's the group of men including Christian Felice. He takes her hand and bows over it, giving it a kiss and blinking up at her through his lashes. He's a good looking motherfucker and unfortunately also a good guy. Not a single skeleton in his closet apart from a penchant from gambling on Formula 1, but it's peanuts and hasn't been flagged as a potential problem. *Yet*. A slice of acid burns through me, but I breathe deeply because she won't take him up on it if he asks her out. She's always politely rebuffed everyone who's ever asked her.

Then again she's never wanted to leave Pascale Company or file for divorce or ...

Oh.

I glance back to where Xavier is talking to his CFO who's just returned from a family trip to Thailand, and I can hear he's regaling everyone who will listen. And of course, despite Xavier's ears listening to Jean-Marc's vacation anecdotes, his eyes didn't miss a second of my exchange with Andrea or the current situation with her talking to Christian. He lifts an eyebrow.

Fucker.

He smirks at me and gives a small shake of his head, nonverbally calling me an idiot.

I snap out of my trance and take a deep breath to ease my chest and make a decision. I stalk over to Xavier. Giving a polite nod to the group, and a short apology, I pull my boss and best friend aside.

"Is there any chance you can *not* accept her resignation?"

"No."

"Offer her more money."

"Evan."

I breathe in and pinch the bridge of my nose. "Fine. Since you don't need me traveling with you, I'm taking a leave of absence," I say. "Starting tomorrow morning."

Xavier sucks his lips together to keep from grinning.

"Shut up," I tell him.

He lifts his palms up. "Did not say a word."

"It's got nothing to do with anything," I lie. "You've made

me rich enough over the years that maybe I can afford to take some time off now. Maybe I'll even retire," I add just to piss him off.

"And where will you be spending your time off? Or your maybe-retirement?" he asks, unwilling to rise to the bait, his eyes cutting back over to where Andrea and Christian stand closely, talking.

I eye him. "None of your business." I grit my teeth. "But if she tells you where she's moving to while she makes herself into a fucking target, let me know immediately."

My best friend barks a laugh and claps me on the shoulder. "Good luck. Don't fuck it up," he says and then turns back to his work colleagues.

This was about Andrea's safety. Nothing else. I'd do it for anyone.

SIX

Andrea

A WAITER APPROACHED as I left the conversation with Evan and came out onto the entertaining deck. I accepted another glass of champagne. I'd just made some of the most important decisions of my life in resigning and filing for divorce, and Evan had acted like an uncaring brute. I knew things had been tense between us recently, but to brush me off when I told him about getting the divorce had really hurt.

I swallowed the lump in my throat, shook his attitude off, and blinked, pasting on another smile.

I'd forgotten how stressed he got about this event every year when it used to be a regular thing. He'd told me once he'd begged Xavier not to have it at all because it was such a target if someone wanted to affect his business with an attack of some sort. I felt a twinge of guilt for adding to his stress today of all days. But then part of me wondered why I was the one who always stressed him out, and why he'd been checking up on me so much, like showing up at the art foundation when he had so much else to deal with.

I nodded greetings to some of the familiar faces and then sought out Xavier's chef and Rod, our main deck hand. They were in an animated discussion with Meg and Sue, who'd joined the crew for the last six weeks when we were at full capacity of guests. A group of men I didn't know who were obviously from the Sofia Antipolis office were chatting nearby. I caught the eye of a dark haired man, and recognition hit me. It was Christian. He gave me a smile and a slow head nod, lifting his glass of champagne. I felt a tiny thrill in my belly, even though I was sure he was just being polite despite what he'd told Xavier, but it felt good to be seen. And he was undoubtedly extremely hot. I returned his smile.

I did want to try to date again. I might as well start immediately. I veered toward him.

"Andrea." Christian bowed over my hand and then pressed his lips to my skin.

His kiss was soft and moist. I managed a polite smile and pulled my hand back, feeling mildly put off at the intimate gesture. I was so out of practice. "Christian," I said, belatedly remembering the basics of social interaction. "Lovely to see you again."

"May I say? You are looking very beautiful this evening."

"Thank you."

"I would be honored if you would accompany me at the restaurant this evening." He nodded over to some other men and women he'd been talking to. "You will see all my colleagues have their beautiful wives with them, but I would like the most beautiful woman here this evening to sit beside me."

I cleared my throat and suppressed my instinct to laugh at his over-the-top charm. How had I missed this cheesiness before? Or was he really sincere? I honestly had no idea these days how to even read my own instincts. Another reason to start getting out more.

"And that is you," he added, his eyes boring into me when my silence obviously made him concerned I hadn't understood.

"Oh, yes. Thank you. I—I hoped so?" Oh my God. I was making myself out to be a simpleton. How was I ever going to date anyone? I was so, so bad at it. "Thank you. That would be lovely."

There was a pause.

"Um," I tried, "how have you been? Did you recover from the sunburn you got when you were here on the boat?"

He set a hand on his chest, affecting a sad look on his face. "*Alors.* I am afraid since I had no one to help me put the cooling lotion on, it took me a long time to recover."

I cut my eyes away for a second to see if anyone was watching or listening. It was like I was on a sitcom. How was I supposed to act? Was I supposed to flirt and coo? Act like I wished I'd known? Offer to be there to put lotion on? "Oh." I stalled. "I'm so sorry." My mind scrambled. "But you look very athletic, I'm sure you could reach all those difficult places." I replayed what my words sounded like. Good God.

His gaze flared and he leaned in. "Yes, *ma chérie.* I can touch *all* the places." Then he lifted my hand and tucked it into the crook of his arm, causing my shoulders to tense.

I looked around and saw everyone was exiting toward the gangplank to go to the restaurant.

"Shall we?" he asked.

Maybe I was just being overly sensitive. I knew Christian was nice. Even if he was a bit cheesy. He was being very attentive.

Luckily my crew from the boat, Rod, Chef, Paco, Meg and Sue, merged with us as we turned to the back of the deck. I was able to disentangle from Christian's eager touch in the throng that moved from the boat down the gangplank and toward the quay and a series of vans that would take us a few hundred meters along the strip to the restaurant on the beach.

The van ride was crammed, and Meg ended up between Christian and me. As soon as we got out though, Christian took my hand in his clammy one and led me down toward the beach restaurant that had been booked out for us. I gritted my teeth as I decided I was *not* a hand-holding person. It was hot and close and clammy and just … no. I tried to remember if I'd ever been.

Lots more people were already at the venue as we arrived, chatting and seating themselves, accompanied by calypso music from a two man steel drum band. There were four long tables on a large square deck set on the sand, decorated with pale pink table cloths and candles glowing from within rattan baskets and nested with pink flowers, seating at least twenty each. I tried to stay with the crew group, and we at least ended up at the same table. Christian pulled out a seat for me and sat next to me.

There was a distracting motion on my other side and then Evan sat down, leaving a very put out lady standing over him who I didn't recognize but was maybe from the corporate office.

She had to move everyone down a place to get a seat by her husband after Evan took her spot.

Evan pretended not to notice. "You okay?" asked Evan, flapping open his napkin.

"Fine," I said, my eyebrows sky high. "Everything okay with *you*? I think you almost knocked that woman over."

He looked the other way and mumbled what I hoped was an apology. Then he turned back to me. "Sorry. I just saw a seat and went for it. Fancy being next to you."

I stared at him, perplexed. Then shook my head. "Uh, okay. Anyway," I leaned back and hitched a thumb, "do you know Christian?"

Christian was calling down the table to a colleague and unaware of our conversation.

"I do," Evan said as he pursed his lips into a disapproving line.

"What's that supposed to mean?"

"I just know a lot about everyone who works for Xavier. The skeleton keeper, if you will."

I huffed out a breath, thinking of my earlier thought in Xavier's office about Evan background checking my potential dates.

A waiter appeared over my shoulder, and I indicated I wanted white wine. As soon as he poured it, I grabbed up the glass. "Okay. We are *not* doing this," I said and took a sip of the cool, crisp liquid.

"Doing what?" asked Evan as he acknowledged the waiter. "*Rouge, s'il vous plaît.*"

"If you knew something bad, he wouldn't be working for Xavier."

Evan shrugged noncommittally, a smirk on his lips. He reached for his water glass rather than the red wine he'd just asked for.

Remembering my conversation with Xavier, I added, "And I also don't need you vetting my dates."

Evan's jaw flexed, and his piercing eyes cut to mine. "Is that what this is?"

"What?"

He sat forward. "A date?"

"Shut up." I glanced to my other side to make sure we weren't being overheard. "I don't know. And so what if it is?"

"I thought you didn't date."

"Maybe I'm ready to." I had no idea if I was ready, but I was willing to try.

He squeezed his eyes closed briefly. "Is that what you were doing today? Visiting an attorney?"

"No. I've done that already."

"Already. Shit. What address did you give to file?"

"It's none of your business, honestly. I really appreciate all you do to keep Xavier safe, and obviously I've benefitted from that, but you can just keep on keeping Xavier's family safe and not worry about me anymore. Okay?"

Evan's eyes flamed. "Do you think that just because I—"

"*Chérie,*" Christian cooed from my other side.

Evan glared at Christian, clearly forgetting himself for a moment.

I was shocked he was having any kind of reaction at all.

"Evan?" Christian asked, nonplussed. "Is everything okay?"

"Yes. It's fine," Evan gritted out. "Great to see you. How have you been?"

I stared ahead, irritated by Evan's bizarre attitude tonight while they talked over me. Meg caught my eye, her gaze cutting to Christian briefly as she waggled her eyebrows. "*So cute,*" she mouthed.

Across me, both men were discussing Max Verstappen winning his first Formula 1 championship.

I gave Meg what I hoped was a friendly "I know" smile. Objectively, Christian was gorgeous. Smooth. Sophisticated. Perfectly plucked eyebrows, clean shaven. So perfect, he could be a model. There'd probably even be no stubble burn from a make-out session. I glanced at his hands. They'd felt super soft when he held mine. I had no doubt he probably visited a manicurist and aesthetician every week.

And because I was a sucker for punishment, I glanced over at Evan's hands. One was wrapped around his water glass. His fingers were strong, not short, but a bit thick. His nails were clipped and clean, and I could see the palm of his left hand as it fiddled with his cutlery. His palm and fingers were slightly calloused from use. Men's hands.

I looked back at Christian's hands. They hadn't seen anything but a computer keyboard or a manicurist in his entire life. There was nothing wrong with that, but it was Evan's hands I wanted to stare at. They'd feel amazing on my skin. I shook my head. Or would they?

Angus had also had rough hands, like Evan's. They'd both spent time in the armed forces. But I knew that while Evan's hands were undoubtedly capable of violence, it would never be misdirected. I wasn't sure how I knew that for sure, but I did.

I shook off a sudden chill from the memory of the violence my husband's hands were capable of.

"Are you cold?" Evan asked.

"Here," said Christian immediately from my other side.

"Excuse me?" I asked, suddenly realizing they were talking to me just as Christian shrugged off his jacket and began to settle it around my shoulders. "Oh. No. I'm fine. Actually, it's quite warm." I managed to stop him.

Evan chuckled from my other side, and I saw he too had begun to take his jacket off.

Across from me, Meg's eyes were taking it all in with amusement.

I shook my head, letting her know that whatever she was thinking was ridiculous.

Servers arrived with trays full of *antipasti* and small salads with smoked salmon, and the rest of dinner was underway. Christian talked a lot about where he was from and his education and his weekend chalet in Gstaad he'd just bought with a group of friends, and of course, Formula 1. Always Formula 1.

Evan had been talking to the woman he'd bumped out of the way earlier, and clearly she'd forgiven him as I'd heard her husky laughter over Christian's nonstop chatter. Eventually Evan excused himself and mumbled something about doing something I didn't hear. It suddenly felt lonely on my left side.

"Do you ski?" Christian asked, surprising me with a question about myself, as dinner was cleared and little bowls of sorbet in five different fruit flavors were circulating around.

"I have a few times." I used to do a lot of things.

Christian launched into more words about himself that had me absently nodding and smiling blandly. My heart wasn't in this. I was tired. Now that Evan had left the table, my energy seemed to have left with him. Christian kept signaling the waiter to fill my glass, and after a while I had to keep putting my hand over it to refuse.

People were drifting over to a dance area and small tiki bar set up on the sand. Some were taking their shoes off and wandering down toward the darkness of the sea. The moon was a small sliver tonight. A new moon. Only the lights from the hotels and restaurants glittered onto the water. I excused myself and sought out Meg and Sue.

"This is an incredible party," Sue gushed, her blonde curls bouncing in the breeze. "In all the years and all the yachts we've worked on, no one ever has a gig like this that we get invited to except Mr. Pascale."

Meg nodded in agreement.

"It's pretty nice," I agreed. "We haven't done it for a few years so you didn't miss many. Do you think you'll apply to work for the boat again next summer?" I asked them. "It's been really great to have you both back."

Sue nodded. "Definitely."

"I'm not sure," Meg said. "I've been trying to get a chief steward position. I feel as though I've done my time, and I'm ready for more responsibility. The agency agrees."

I took a deep breath. "Well, here goes nothing. Let's hope I'm not groveling for a job back that's already been filled, but you should know I'm resigning. So there'll be a spot open for next year."

"Wow, really?" Meg whispered.

I nodded. "Yes. It's time. I've been with the *Sirenita* and the Pascale Company for almost ten years. Rumor has it he's selling *Sirenita* and buying a new boat. So I don't know what that means for other crew positions, but you know you'd have my recommendation."

Meg flushed. "Thank you. That means a lot."

Sue nudged her. "Meg! This is so exciting."

"Nothing is set yet." Meg shushed her, embarrassed. But I could tell she was pulsing with excitement.

"And Sue, you'd stay on too I hope, right?"

"And leave this duck?" She elbowed her best friend. "Not a chance. Of course!"

I filled them in on my cute last minute rental I lucked out on, and we commiserated about the lack of affordable but nicely furnished housing this year. Everyone, it seemed, had turned their places into Airbnbs, and it was hard to find seven to eight consecutive months anywhere.

"So, what's going on with you and that hot executive?" Meg asked.

"Yeah," Sue added. "He was on board a few weeks back, wasn't he? That was a nice view."

"Christian?" I responded. "He's ... nice. I don't know."

"I totally thought you and Evan had a thing," Sue said. "Tension was so thick I was choking on it. Shows how much I know. To think, Evan was free all this time, and I didn't make a move." She frowned.

"That tension was still alive and well tonight from where I sat," said Meg.

My gut twisted at the vision of Sue and Evan together. "No. I mean—no, we don't have a thing."

"But you wish you had a thing." Sue was grinning, her eyebrows high as she nodded. "Yep. I saw that jealousy flare for a second. Don't blame you."

It seemed dumb to deny it when, firstly, it was kind of true, and secondly, apparently I hadn't fooled anyone except the man himself. Thank God for small mercies. But I wouldn't confirm it either because what would be the point except to make it more real? "It's ... complicated."

Sue squealed. "See, Meg? I totally called it. We should have put money on it."

"But it's about to be uncomplicated now that I'm leaving," I added.

"Right. What will you do? Where are you going?" Meg asked.

"Actually, I normally volunteer at an art gallery, but I'm taking a paid position there. *Fondation Maeght*? Do you know it?"

"I do, actually. I remember you starting there when we had our last season. It's modern art, right?"

Sue giggled. "Oh my God, is that the one with the statue of an alien with an erect penis outside in the gardens?"

"It's a sculpture by Miró," I said with a laugh. "And yeah, that's the one everyone remembers."

"Well, cool," Sue said. "That should be interesting at least."

We chatted a bit longer. They promised to come take me out for wine a few times over the winter and extracted an insincere promise from me to visit them for some skiing in Chamonix. I hadn't quite built up to traveling in the off-season yet. I felt safe in my bubble. The idea of accidentally seeing someone from my old life that could report back to Angus was terrifying.

Christian arrived at my elbow, and Meg and Sue smirked and headed to the bar. He nodded toward the ocean. "Come and take a moonlight walk?" he asked.

I didn't want to point out there was hardly a moon. And I really didn't want to spend any more time with him. He was nice, but I wasn't sure I was ready to be alone with a guy I'd just met.

He moved us toward the sea and the darkness, his hand on my upper arm.

I wanted to yank it out of his grip. "Actually, I was hoping to call it a night." I pretended to stumble and kicked up a heel to adjust my shoe, at least to get my arm back. I'd have to remove my shoes if I was going to walk on the sand anyway.

Christian, insistent, took hold of my elbow, and my breath froze in my chest. "Only a few minutes," he said with a firm tug.

The panic came out of nowhere, hitting me hard, making me jerk back. Instantly I was embarrassed, but he didn't let go. Oh my God, he wasn't letting go. *Breathe.* I glanced behind me to see if there was someone I could pretend to want to talk to. Anything to get out of this without making more of a scene.

Suddenly there was Evan, across the decking. His gaze was firmly on me, or more particularly Christian's firm grip.

And his legs were already in motion in my direction.

SEVEN

"Andrea," Evan said calmly as he approached, his eyes fully trained on mine. I had the feeling he wanted to grab me himself and was physically holding himself back. "I was looking for you. You asked me to come get you when I was ready to leave." The lie tripped so easily from his lips, the tone deceptively casual.

"She was taking a walk with me." Christian tugged almost imperceptibly, but it could have been with a thousand times more force for the reaction it caused in me. My heart pounded heavily in my ears.

"No," I said and cleared my throat, pulling my arm free and forcing a smile. I had always been so good at pretending everything was okay, and the instinct came back flawlessly. "No, thank you. I had a lovely evening, but I'm ready to leave now."

"*Mais, ma chérie,* allow me to accompany you."

"I've got it," Evan said. He clapped Christian on the shoulder, jovially, not allowing him to argue and subtly keeping him in place as I slipped out of his reach. "Great to see you, Christian. Let's plan to go to a race soon."

"Bye, Christian," I said. "Oh, let me quickly run and say bye to Meg." I walked back to the main grouping of people. Seconds later, Evan was beside me. Wordlessly, and without saying goodbye to anyone, not even Meg, we both walked straight through the restaurant and up the concrete stairs to the beach walk along the strip. The street lights and the lights from the hotels and passing cars brought reality roaring back, and I took a deep inhale, letting the air whistle around my tight ribs. I didn't want to talk about what had happened, and I didn't want Evan to ask me either.

He was quiet and solid by my side as I breathed in deep lungfuls of air. He wordlessly hailed a taxi and gave him the quay number. The taxi driver looked put out to only be driving us a short distance, but Evan shoved twenty euros at him and the man nodded. Evan opened the door for me, and I climbed in and slid across the seat. Then Evan was in beside me and the door closed and we set off.

"You don't have come back with me." I glanced at him out of the corner of my eye and noticed the twitch in his jaw, even while the rest of his form seemed outwardly calm. "Thank you," I whispered when he didn't answer.

He nodded once, still staring ahead.

"How did you know?" What was I even asking? How did he know I'd panicked? Or did he know something about Christian I didn't?

He closed his eyes briefly and then looked at me. "You forget how long I've known you."

I felt my frown form. "I'm not sure I understand what you mean by that. And also I feel bad now. Christian seems like a good guy."

"He is."

"So then—"

"Let's leave it. Are you glad you left or not?"

I nodded.

"Great. We're here." He turned his attention outside, and he was right, we were pulling up at the quay gate. Evan spoke to the driver and we exited.

"Should *you* have left?" I asked. "I'm fine from here."

"My guys are there. Pete is running point tonight. Come on. It's late." He punched in our quay gate code, and it swung open on a whine.

"I can't wait to get these heels off," I said as I teetered. Despite my attempts to not drink so much wine, I'd clearly had more than I was used to. Expecting Evan to reach out, I was surprised when he didn't. He hadn't earlier when he'd rescued me from Christian either, though I'd gotten the sense he wanted to.

He thinks I'm afraid of being touched. My belly tightened with annoyance, and I thought back, trying to remember when the last time was that Evan had even reached out a steadying hand. Tonight with Christian had been unexpected, surprising even me because I'd thought I'd have been over that by now. I *was* afraid of being touched, not by Evan, but ...

Sadness and annoyance filled me, growing with each step I took. I bent down and undid the small buckles at my ankles and slipped my shoes off, giving a moan of relief, and darted along the gangplank onto the boat.

Evan swore under his breath.

"Are *you* okay?" I asked.

"Fine," he said as he followed me and unlocked the sliding glass door. It slid open without issue.

We padded through the living area and headed to the galley. The boat was quiet and dark, the caterers packed up and gone. The fact that Evan and I were utterly alone on it was strange. I was more aware of him tonight. How tall he was, how broad. How much space he took up. The way my attention always swung in his direction when he entered a room. Okay, I'd obviously had *way* more wine than I could handle.

I shook my head and turned on the galley lights. The sooner I went out there in the world and found some other interesting men, the better. Not Christian. Although, he'd seemed nice. Maybe I'd overreacted. Misunderstood his intentions.

"How about you? Are you okay?" he asked and snatched an apple from the fruit bowl.

"About what?"

"About tonight. Him ... touching you like that."

Shit. It had been so obvious. I winced. "I'm fine, Evan. What? You think I don't like being touched?" I snapped childishly.

His brow furrowed.

"Sorry." I blew out a breath. "No. You're right. But it's not about being touched. Or maybe it is. I don't know what that was. It kind of came out of nowhere. I want ... I ..." I craved touch. I hadn't been touched properly in years. My eyes prickled at the edges, and the truth bubbled its way forward. I'd been scared. My fears tonight had erupted out of the deepest parts of me I thought I'd dealt with.

His expression softened, his head cocked to the side. He was letting me talk. His hand was on the galley counter between us. Before I could think about it, I leaned forward and touched his fingers. His whole body stilled. I let my hand cover his, willing him to flip his hand over under mine and hold it. His skin was slightly rough even on top. I'd been right.

He was rigid.

What the hell was I doing? I snatched my hand back.

Shit. "I shouldn't have drunk so much wine," I said instead, forcing everything I was about to spill out back down into my gut. I hated him treating me like a wounded animal. I'd been thinking I'd make some chamomile tea before bed, but now I just wanted to get out of Evan's space. "Can I get by? I appreciate you getting me back here. Good night."

He reached out to stop me, and I flinched at the same time he yanked his hand back.

"Jesus. Sorry," he said.

I squeezed my eyes shut for a second. "You just took me by surprise." Dammit. "I'm fine," I gritted out.

"It seems like it," he said, and we stayed in a stare off. Finally, he sighed. "You drinking too much wine didn't have anything to do with what happened. Or with you feeling unsafe out there. I haven't seen anything in his background that would suggest—I could be wrong though—"

"Evan, just stop. It wasn't Christian. I think I overreacted. And I was blaming the wine more for loosening my tongue around *you* than anything that happened on the beach. I mean, *nothing* happened. It was harmless. He was harmless. I was balancing on one foot to adjust my heel. He was probably just steadying me. I got spooked. I'm just ..." I trailed off. *I just think I'm broken.* I couldn't do this, I made to turn away again before I begged him to hold me. To see if maybe Evan was my cure. Because I was about to.

"Please," Evan begged quietly. "You can talk to me."

"No. I can't. I don't want to be your problem to solve. I don't need you adding things I tell you into your mental personnel file anymore."

"That's not what I do."

"Yes. It is. It's your job. You're good at it. I'm not mad at you for it. But you can't control everything."

He raked his fingers through his soft hair. "I'm well aware of that fact, trust me."

"I'm really tired and recently, I never know if I've pissed you off or not. And I'm tired of you acting like you care about me when it's really just your job." Whoa. Damn wine. "Good night."

I spun away and left him alone as I hotfooted it down the steps to my cabin, embarrassed.

Inside, I closed the door and leaned against it, letting out a huge breath. After a few moments, I did my mental calming exercises and then peeled myself off the door and began to undress and remove my makeup. I got into my sleep shirt and slipped my last few belongings into the bags I was taking to the village in the morning.

There was a knock at my door.

"Just leave me alone, Evan." Before I said something stupid and made things even more awkward between us. "I'm tired." Thank God I'd quit. I wouldn't have to face him much longer. Though that thought itself brought a conflicting rush of emotions.

"I have tea."

I yanked the door open to him standing with a cup of steaming tea in one hand and his half eaten apple in the other. The sight of him bringing me a simple cup of tea made my chest tight. "Chamomile?" I asked.

He dragged his gaze up from my bare legs over my baggy sleeping shirt and to my face. "Of course. With a dash of apology. I'm sorry that I've seemed brusque recently, I'm under a ton of pressure right now. Of course, I care about you. I'm sorry you ever questioned whether I did. With Xavier going to America—"

"What? He's going to America? To Charleston? Is he going to win Josie back?" I whispered. I stepped back, inviting him into my tiny cabin without thinking, immediately realizing my mistake when his presence and scent surrounded me with nowhere for me to go. I cleared my throat. "Is he?"

"He's been an absolute shite since she left. So yeah. Finally. Here," he said, and I took the teacup carefully from him and set it down on my side table.

Xavier was going to win back Josie. I grinned and clapped my hands. "He has been grumpy without her. More so than usual." I'd hardly seen Xavier since he and Dauphine hadn't come back to the boat after the "incident" with her uncle, although the uncle was claiming it was a misunderstanding. In the panic of everything that had happened, I think Xavier blamed Josie, and it had broken them.

The thought that he was suffering from missing Josie was extremely satisfying. He shouldn't have let her go to begin with. "He didn't say a word to me about it tonight," I said. "But you're right, he's been a real bear recently. Even more than you," I added.

Evan's eyes narrowed and he looked around my cabin, noting the suitcase packed on the bed. "Why does him being a grumpy arse make you so giddy?" he asked.

"Because I was hoping he would go get her," I answered. "Why does it make you so scowly? Josie is one thousand percent in love with him, and he with her, and they both deserve happiness." I let out a quiet squeal. This was so great. I wanted to call her. "Does she know?"

"No. So don't call her yet. I never knew you to be such a romantic."

I scoffed lightly. "I never knew you to be such a love grinch."

"A love grinch?"

"Yes. Sometimes I think your heart is two sizes too small." I'd gone for a teasing tone but somehow missed as a strange look passed over his face. "I'm sorry," I said quickly. "That was a dumb thing to say. I definitely didn't mean it. And I don't think it. I just think everyone deserves happiness if they can find it. And not everyone can." I swallowed. I should know. "So—"

"Why do you think I wouldn't?"

"Do you?"

"Think everyone deserves happiness? Yes. What kind of person do you think I am?"

"I don't know actually. After nine years, you still confuse me. Some days you are like a cyborg. Utterly unflappable. Like right now. Your questions tell me I hurt your feelings, but," I waved my hand in front of his face, indicating his expression, "nothing."

Belatedly remembering the apple in his hand he brought it

up to his mouth, then seemed to think better of it. "You think I don't have feelings?"

"Do you?" I cocked my head.

He stared at me, his hazel eyes going through a kaleidoscope of greens and browns. His nostrils flared as he inhaled.

I held his gaze, wine making me braver, and it was like holding my hand to the fire.

"So fucking many," he said finally. He peeled his gaze off mine and turned to leave but paused at the door, looking once more at the suitcase on the bed. "Why are you really leaving?"

"What do you mean?"

"I mean, why now? Why after nine years do you suddenly feel like you have to go out there? And you haven't shared anything with me about your plans. Did something happen?"

I thought of my burgeoning attraction to Evan and couldn't stop my eyes straying to his mouth. It was always a straight line, hard jaw, faint stubble, a small scar on his upper lip. His bottom lip was full with a faint line indent. Sometimes when he was thinking, he'd pinch it between thumb and forefinger and leave it pinker and fuller. I licked my lips and felt my insides tighten. This was why I had to leave now, but I couldn't tell him. Because the attraction that had simmered in the background was suddenly singeing the edges of my sanity.

But it wasn't real. It was situational. My hormones were obviously raging and trying to get in a last party before my biological clock slowed down. I'd read about it today. Women in their early thirties were at their peak sexually. It wasn't Evan. It was science.

When I didn't answer him, a look of disappointment crossed his features. "Where are you moving to tomorrow?"

I twisted my mouth, not answering that either.

"I wish you would trust me." He sounded tired.

"I do. I—"

"Save it," he said and began to leave. "I'll find out soon enough."

"Over my dead body." I bristled.

"Don't joke. Turn your locations back on," he added over his shoulder. "Pascale Company issued your phone. Until you have a new one, you *will* comply. Goodnight, Andrea." And then he bit into his apple and left.

"Ugh." I slammed the cabin door behind him. Turning my locations off last week had been absolutely terrifying and felt utterly rebellious, but it was necessary if I was ever going to start living again. I was a grown up for God's sake. I needed to feel safe on my own and to rely on my own instincts and gut feelings. Especially now.

EIGHT

Evan

I'M NOT proud of myself for what I'm about to do, but Andrea has left me no choice. Sitting at my desk in my office on the security floor of our office in Sofia Antipolis, I log onto my terminal. Glancing out my open door, I see my second in command, Pete, step out of the elevator, and my shoulders sink. I should've closed my door. The guy's a bloodhound.

I quickly pull up the tier one list of mobile devices and go through the triple security authentication so I can access their satellite movements. Turning off location permissions just makes tracking harder but not impossible. Not these days.

Working fast, I swallow down the guilt, telling myself it's to keep her safe and make a promise to myself that as soon as she's completely safe, I'll tell her everything.

For now, though, she doesn't know what the threat is, I've made sure of that. But it's backfiring in the worst way possible, i.e., her thinking it's safe to reveal her whereabouts by filing for divorce.

"You look like you're trying to copy a term paper before the teacher catches you."

I jerk. "Jesus. Fuck." I lean back and blow out a breath, my hand smoothing my tie down as I meet Pete's cheerful face at my door frame. "Would it kill you to give a guy some warning? Your stealthy approach is not appreciated in noncombat spaces, Sneaky Pete." I add his extremely apt regiment nickname and shake my head. "You just took five years off my life."

He thumps the doorframe with the side of his fist. "Hard to believe. Nothing rattles you. Which begs the question," his eyebrow arched into his signature sharp arrow, "what are you up to that has you so jumpy?"

I slide my fingers through my hair as I contemplate how to answer.

He steps inside. "Ah no. We talked about this."

"What?"

"You said you wouldn't overstep the bounds when it comes to her."

I sit forward. "How do you always do that?"

"Know exactly what you're thinking, sometimes even before you? Honed in the desert of hell, my friend. As well you know."

"I know." I chuckle and shake my head.

He takes the seat opposite my desk. "So. Tell Uncle Pete where it itches."

I should throw something at him for being gross, but instead I tell him the truth because he'll know what it means. "She resigned."

His eyebrows fly up to his hairline. "Oh."

"Yeah. Oh."

"And Xavier let her?"

I give him a look.

"Right. So. Just that?"

"No." I suck air as deep as I can. "She also filed for divorce."

His expression remains still, but I know his brain is processing the same variables I've already been through. "Well, fuck. How many parameters do we know?"

I appreciate the "we" suddenly in his sentence. "None. I don't know where she filed, with whom, which address she used. I don't even know where she's going to live. She left the boat this morning."

"And you didn't follow her? I'm impressed."

"You have no idea. She made it clear she was beginning to find my presence ... overbearing. Controlling. That's the last thing I want her to see me as. Not—"

"Not after him. I know."

"Hence." I gesture to my screen.

Neither of us mention the glaring truth that this is not on company time or dime. Not anymore. Not now that she's resigned. Or that it's glaringly over the line of invading her privacy.

"Have you heard anything new on him recently?" I ask Pete.

"You know I'd have shared it with you. He's still independent, that's all I know." Which made him hard to track. Pete stands and comes round my desk. "I might as well be oversight then, to make sure you stay in bounds."

I smile. "Yeah." We both know I'm already so far out of bounds, I'm in the shadows. Her shadows. And not the good ones. The only thing I can do at this point is to stay there and make sure they never reach her.

I send the last month's geo location pings to the printer. Pete walks over and grabs it so we have a hard copy. He walks to my office door and after a quick look outside closes us in, then takes the list to my planning table. "I love this pricey gadget," he says. "Makes the office feel like a real situation room."

Joining him with an eye roll, I switch on the under-table light and select the closest geographic region. A satellite image of France appears as the table top. Then I select the locations my terminal is listing and small red dots ping all over Southern France. I zoom in.

I share a look with Pete then. We've only done this once in the last couple of years, and that was just over two months ago when Dauphine, Xavier's daughter, was in danger. Other times before that have been purely for random personnel issues if we got a whiff of corporate espionage. And none had ever been serious. It's a huge responsibility having access to this much data. We've never abused it.

"Are we doing this?" I ask him.

"I'll stop immediately if you tell me," Pete says.

"You're a good friend."

"Brothers in arms," he responds, his face somber. "This might tell us nothing. No harm, no foul."

I take a breath. "Okay. Go."

Pete reads out the first map coordinate that corresponds to a dot on the map. I zoom in and read off the location or nearest town, or street name and number if I can get close enough. Pete writes them in on the hard copy.

Most of the locations we know, there aren't many surprises.

Fondation Maeght would have been a surprise this early in the year if I hadn't seen her there myself. From there she'd driven to the small medieval village of Saint Paul de Vence. I zoom in as close as I can. There are several nearby addresses. But they all look residential or commercial. No business offices. There's unlikely to be a law office in the village. I zoom out and we go to the next addresses, working our way backward in time until the list is done.

"I hate to point out the obvious, but have you considered just asking her?" Pete says when I step back and clear the screen and the data and turn it all off.

"I'd say turning her location permissions off was a clear enough message on that subject."

"Fair." Pete rubs his chin. "You want me to start working on the list and corresponding businesses?"

"I just need the name and address of the lawyer so I can stick a detail on them and make sure there's no contact. In the meantime, I'll find out where she's moving."

"Done. So how was the rest of your summer?" Pete asks. "I didn't get to talk to you at the shindig last night since I was running point. I thought it went well, by the way. The party. I expected you to request the full report first thing this morning."

"Anything out of the ordinary?" I ask, ignoring the jab.

"All good. Everyone there was an invitee apart from a couple of friends of some execs who tagged along, but their IDs all checked out."

"Okay, thank you." I sit back down at my desk, straighten a few edges, and modulate my tone. "So, Christian Felice? I haven't looked at his file in a while. All good there?"

"Did you hear something?" Pete asks.

"No. More that I saw him get a little handsy."

Pete cocks his head and remains standing. "With who? Ohhh. Are you sure he was handsy, or were you jealous?"

"Pete," I warn.

"You seemed to leave in a hurry with a certain someone. You were playing the white knight again?"

"Remind me why we're friends again? You love to push my buttons."

"It's just too easy. We're friends because I know all your deepest secrets, and at this point it's probably mutually assured destruction. But no. There's never been an indication Christian has ever had to coerce anyone into his bed. They seem to fall in of their own volition. And often. Would you like me to dig a bit deeper?"

"No. I guess not. I'm already overstepping." I scrub a hand down my face. "Anyway, there's something else I need to talk to you about. I'm taking a break from things for a bit."

"I'm sorry, what? It sounded like you said Mr. Control Freak would be taking a break from work?"

I grimace. "I'd appreciate you not calling me that. But yes. You heard correctly. You're in charge."

"For how long?"

"I—for however long it takes."

He makes finger quotes. "'It' being?"

"I don't know."

"Coz you could be waiting until he's dead. Which reminds me, you know we know some people. All natural. No one the wiser."

"Pete. For fuck's sake."

"I'm just saying. If it were my woman, I wouldn't hesitate."

"But she's not—"

"Your woman. I know."

"We are friends. Nothing more."

"So you keep saying. But just for reference, I can mobilize and have it done within twenty-four hours. Super quick. No trail."

"Jesus. How did *you* pass my background check?" I shake my head.

Pete throws his back and laughs. "We know the same guys, you fool. And you know they'd love nothing more than to deal with this piece of shit. It could even be on the house."

"For the love of God, I'm glad we regularly sweep this place for bugs. You are certifiable. I already have to live with how I meddled. I can't also have murder on my conscience. Our past is bad enough."

"That was combat."

"My soul doesn't care about the difference."

Pete chuckles again, wheezing. It was actually more of a howl than a chuckle. "Your *soul*." He howls again. "You been reading those self-help books again?"

"What about you?" My jaw flexes. "Spoken to Millie recently?" I invoke his estranged wife's name out of sheer desperation.

Pete jerks back in affront. "Well, I can see we've reached the end of your humor. I shall take my leave." He heads for the door.

I feel guilty for half a second, then shake it off. "Hey, Pete. Thank you. It's good to know I can leave this place in the hands of someone I trust."

"Sweet talker. Now if you mention early retirement, then

you'll have my attention." He gives a salute as he leaves my office, the door unfortunately not hitting his ass on the way out.

I pick up my phone and dial.

"This is Meg."

"Hi Meg, this is Evan Roark."

"Evan! Great to hear from you. I was actually hoping to speak to you."

I sit up. "You were?"

"Oh, yes. I wanted to submit to whatever crazy security stuff you have, so I can put my name in for chief stew. I've passed practically every background check you can think of. But rumor is, you're a stickler." She chortles. "And Andrea said there might even be a different boat? Which is fine," she rushed on. "I have experience on practically everything at this point. But I know this is a coveted position and if it holds any sway, Andrea said she'd endorse me."

Her words all bleed together, but I have enough left in me to hear the last part. "She did?"

"She did. But, well, I don't know the details of her leaving, but she was pretty amazing in her role. Know they are big shoes to fill."

"Right. She was amazing. Is. She is amazing." I clear my throat.

"Right. So, it's okay if I put my name forward?"

I suddenly remember I was the one who called Meg and not the other way around. "Sure. You can put your name forward," I say, withholding any kind of endorsement of my own and feeling like a shit for it. "Can you do me a quick favor, though? I'm driving and can't access her file where she updated her off-season address. Would you mind texting it to me? I assume you know it. I couldn't get hold of the woman herself, and I need to run something by there." I wince at the lies, grateful Meg can't see me.

"Oh, uh. Let me look quick. Hang on. Yep, texted it to you now. She really lucked out with that cute rental."

"Thanks, Meg. And I think you'll be an amazing asset to the team and the family." My phone beeps with her incoming message. "Go ahead and forward me a formal request, and I'll run it up the chain." The chain just being me. "We certainly want to make sure no one else snaps you up before next season." I fucking hate myself right now. Thank God Pete, nor Xavier, can witness me manipulating employees in return for personal information.

"Thanks, Evan. You're the best."

We both hang up and I smack my palm on the desk. I am unhinged. What is fucking wrong with me? Haven't I meddled enough? The answer is clear, with her, there is no enough.

A few keystrokes later and I'm making another call. Never mind any lives taken, my soul is going to burn in hell for this particular misdeed I'm about to commit.

NINE

Andrea

"WHAT DO you mean you've rented out the place next door to me?" I asked Marianne as I clutched my phone tight. "I thought you said it was closed off and empty?" I guess the woman could do what she wanted, it was her place. But ugh. I had the phone under my chin as I jogged downstairs to glare at the offending connecting door. Thank God for the padlock.

"*Je sais.* I know. I'm sorry. But he was desperate. He seems very nice. He had an emergency at his home. And he will be very quiet."

"He?"

"*Oui.*"

"You said there was no kitchen."

"He doesn't need one, he says. It is just to sleep."

"Do you know him?" I asked her.

There was a pause before she answered. Shoot. So he probably just offered a shit ton of money. Too much to turn down.

"No," she admitted.

"It's your property, you can do what you like obviously. I'm very grateful it worked out for me to stay here. I'm just ... I'm a bit nervous to have a stranger so close. Where is he from?" I tried to sound reasonable.

"He is English. He seems very nice. I think he's even single. Yes? *Bon*, maybe you two will make a love story in our little village."

I barely heard her words as I processed an Englishman suddenly turning up and renting the place next door. My heart thumped erratically, and my breath came in straggles. *Shit*. I was going into full blown panic attack. There was no way my husband would find me so soon. Surely. I hadn't given this address. My lawyer was doing everything through her office.

"Andrea? Andrea? Are you still there? *Merde*."

"I'm still here," I managed weakly. The edges of my vision were darkening. I slumped into a wooden kitchen chair, sweat prickling at my hairline. "Do you have a name?" I asked. "A background check?" I couldn't believe it. I was going to have to call Evan. After being so devil-may-care, I was going to have to go crawling back and apologize and ask him to check out my new neighbor who'd conveniently shown up a few days after I filed for divorce. I'd been careful with who I'd told about this place. But then again I'd been careful once before, I'd thought. What had I been thinking doing this?

"Andrea?" Marianne's voice brought me back to the present.

"I'm here."

"I will come this afternoon and make sure to introduce you when I give him the keys. But you will probably never even know he is there. It will be okay."

"Okay." My voice wobbled. "Thank you for letting me know. I'm sure it will be fine."

I hung up and placed my palms on the kitchen table, trying to breathe through the panic. Thinking I'd been ready to be on my own was a joke. I was a mess.

~

A FEW HOURS LATER, after I'd showered, blown out my hair, and put on a pretty sundress and cardigan to wander around the village, I was starting to feel more positive about Marianne's call. I needed to keep things in perspective. The chances of the next door neighbor suddenly moving in had almost zero chance of being anything to do with me.

With the spur of mood and energy came the need to reach out. I was dying to call Josie, but not knowing when Xavier might get there, I didn't want to spoil the surprise. I settled for checking in with our crew group chat. After all, they'd become family over the last few years. And now included Meg and Sue and a couple of deckhands who were twin brothers we'd brought on for late season and in preparation for the new boat. I'd coded them Deck 1 and Deck 2 in my phone and really needed to get their names straight and saved at some point, even though I was no longer working with them.

As per usual, Chef had posted a thoughtful meditation for the week. No matter how much flack he got for it, he still did it every Sunday like clockwork. I'd come to really look forward to it. And it kept the group alive during the off-season, when the need to communicate as a group dwindled as people scattered toward their own lives that didn't revolve around the boat.

I'd been so cautious about sharing where I was going to be staying, mostly because I didn't want anyone talking me out of it or influencing my decision. Now though, after being here a few days, I felt a little on the outside of the group. Maybe I should open up about where I was staying. Not to Evan obviously. But I'd told Meg and Sue after all. I could even invite everyone over for dinner one evening before they left. I was looking forward to trying out some recipes and cooking again.

Today's quote from Chef was from Khalil Gibran.

I scrolled past the requisite static from the crew, including Rod asking him to stop passing along his Alcoholics Anonymous propaganda, and saw Evan's response.

Safety Patrol: *Wise words. It's all about mindset.*

Rod: *FFS. Did I accidentally subscribe to crypto bros manifestation techniques? If you mention a vision board, I'm leaving the group.*

Sue: **quietly packs up vision board that includes pic of dream job working on a mega yacht in the South of France**

Chef: *Don't believe in it, or believe in it. Either way you are right.*

Rod: *oh my god.*

Meg: *1000%*

I laughed out loud, and feeling better, gave a quick thumbs up on Chef's original quote. No one had mentioned my resignation, so clearly Meg and Sue hadn't told anyone yet. It just reinforced that they were trustworthy friends and crew members, and I was glad they were staying with us for next season.

I slung the leather handles of my basket bag over my shoulder to stroll into the village.

The door locked easily behind me, but I double-checked all the same, then stepped off the small stone front porch and breathed in deeply. It was the kind of weather where you didn't notice it—neither hot nor cold, but the air was fresh and the sky was vibrant blue.

The ancient stones of the thick and tall village wall to my left were a beautiful contrast. Ahead of me, I could see the lazy bustling of residents on Sundays.

I began to make out the aromas of bread and coffee, and as I rounded the corner a block over toward a *tabac* I'd seen on my way in, the village church bells began chiming. It took a bit of getting used to, but eventually, you realized there was no need for a watch or to check the time at all when you adjusted to the rhythms of village life. The bells chimed on the hour, every hour, and singly on the half hour as well. Now though, they announced the end of the morning service. Glancing down the cobbled street at the narrow crossroads, I saw the church doors open and villagers begin to stream out and clump together into small groups.

Maybe I'd start going to church too. I hadn't been since I'd left school, apart from once to get married and a handful of friends' christenings. I hadn't been to a funeral since my mother's at age twenty-three.

The grizzled old man who ran the *tabac* peeled away from church and began the walk up the hill toward me to reopen his shop. I loitered as he swung open the wooden doors and fastened them against the stone wall of the building and pulled out his chalkboard sign onto the sidewalk. Going back inside, he then emerged with the unwieldy postcard and magazine rack. I darted forward to help. "*Pardon, je peux vous aider,*" I said, earning a mutter and a nod. I smiled back, and he scowled as we worked together to set the rack upright on the sidewalk.

I waited a bit when he went back inside to make sure he wasn't bringing anything else out, then I ducked inside the tiny shop, stepping down. The smell of clove cigarillos and strong coffee was a hit to my brain, and behind the counter a small box TV was already playing a fuzzy soccer game, the commentator streaming in French, and somehow the old man had managed to fit a recliner behind the counter. I hated to make him get up when he'd obviously just sat down, but he immediately snapped his recliner upright and surprised me with a spry hop to his feet.

"*Bonjour,*" I greeted him as if he'd never seen me outside and ordered an espresso.

"You must be the English lady renting the poet house?" He surprised me by answering in heavily accented English.

"Oh. Yes." I let out a half laugh. "Uh, how do you know?"

He waved a hand as he turned and retrieved a small espresso glass and white ceramic saucer before setting them down at the machine to his left.

"Um, okay. Well, hello. I'm Andrea."

"Albert," he answered over his shoulder, pronouncing it, "Al-bear."

"Nice to meet you. I guess all the residents know each other?"

He huffed dismissively and handed me my cup with steaming dark liquid and set down a small white saucer with a receipt. "Two euros. In the summer? *Non.* It's a small village from now until next spring. You'll be coming to me for your espresso, *oui?*"

"Yes, why not." I fished out three euro coins from my purse and put them on the saucer. I took a sip of coffee and moaned aloud. "Mmm. What did you put in here?" I asked the smug looking man.

He rubbed his hands together in satisfaction, then snapped open his newspaper and plopped back into his recliner.

Dismissed, I shook my head with a quiet laugh, drained the small coffee, and said goodbye before I retraced my footsteps to the corner.

The next few hours were spent popping in and out of the few shops and galleries still open and then wandering toward the bottom edge of town where there was a more commercial looking supermarket so I could get some supplies. The village market with all the local producers was Wednesday and a larger one Friday mornings, and I couldn't wait for them. I hummed under my breath. I wanted much more of this provincial life.

My basket stuffed with groceries and weighing me down, I decided it was time to head home and drop them off. The delicious smells emanating from the *trattoria* in the square were making my stomach growl. The village square was busy with children running around while parents and grandparents sat on benches and soaked up time with friends and neighbors.

It felt like I was in a storybook village from *Beauty and the Beast*. I wanted to burst into song. I half expected to see Gaston with his barrel chest and cheesy smirk appear from around the corner.

Someone entering the lower village gate caught my attention, and I did a double take. What the hell?

Evan strolled in over the cobblestones, in faded jeans, hiking boots, and a rumpled white dress shirt rolled up at the sleeves. He wore dark sunglasses, and his burned caramel hair flopped forward over his forehead. On one shoulder a leather-watch-strapped wrist held one strap of a backpack. If it wasn't Evan, it was his doppelgänger. And his doppelgänger was sexy as hell. Ugh. I froze, unsure what to do. I didn't think he'd seen me. I could just slowly turn away and start walking back to my place. So much for spending the afternoon back down in the square. What the hell was he doing here?

I turned away, willing myself to look as inconspicuous as possible, taking a couple of casual looking steps.

"Andrea?"

Damn it. What were the odds? This day. Honestly. I glanced at the sky briefly, then pasted on a smile and turned. "Gaston. Fancy seeing you here."

TEN

My fake smile gave way to the glare I couldn't hold back as Evan walked into my village and toward me, sunglasses hiding his eyes. "Evan's twin brother, right?" I greet him. "Has to be. Because there's *no* way Evan would be here, right? I'm Andrea. If he's the evil one, I guess you're the good one?"

Evan chuckled. "Good to see you too. And who is Gaston?"

"A joke. What are you doing here?" I asked.

"I'm here for an appointment."

"Right. You tried that one last week at the foundation."

He chewed the corner of his mouth and folded his arms over his chest. "And did I, or did I not, have a legitimate appointment?"

I shifted my heavy shopping, looked forlornly at the *trattoria* and realized I was going to have to go back home and stay inside the rest of the day.

"Small towns, eh?" Evan said with a grin. "Can I help you with your bag? It looks heavy. Groceries?"

"No," I said, even as my baguette poked out of the top. "Why would I be buying groceries?"

"I guess you wouldn't unless you lived here. Do you?"

"I don't have to answer any more of your questions. But I should be going. Bye Evan's twin."

He laughed as I walked away.

"I thought you'd be happy to see a familiar face," he said from behind me a few seconds later as I walked up the hill.

"Are you following me?" I asked, swinging around. "Again?"

"I happen to be headed the same direction, I guess."

I huffed and turned back, aware of him easily striding up the steep road, not struggling for a moment, and probably not breaking a sweat. I just had to get to the corner then I could lose him in the maze that was the village and head home. I turned at the corner and he followed. Okay, so just a few more turns to home and he'd peel off. I tried not to sound out of breath. I really shouldn't have bought so much stuff and loaded up my bag. I'd just been excited at all the things I wanted to try.

Self-consciously I imagined his view, me in my short sundress covered with sunflowers. Shoot. Did I shave my legs this morning? *To the corner, to the corner.* Then I'd catch my breath after he'd passed on by.

I swung around the corner and leaned against the cool stone wall, waiting for him to stride past. I closed my eyes and took a gaspingly long inhale and exhale. Opening my eyes I was faced with Evan, sunglasses still hiding his eyes but mouth fighting an amused grin.

"Again. You need help?" he asked.

"Ugh! No. I'm fine. I, uh, just wanted to feel the texture of this wall," I said ridiculously.

"Right."

"Okay. Well, I'm guessing you're the chivalrous twin too." I gestured for him to keep walking straight. "I'm all right, thank you. You can go on your way."

"Oh, I'm headed down this way."

"You *are* following me."

"I'm not."

"What do you call this then? Stalking?"

His jaw flexed, his lips tightening slightly. He opened his mouth, then closed it. Then he took his glasses off, so I had to be subjected to those hazel eyes that were a whirl of spring and fall. He tucked the glasses frames into the V of his shirt. It drew my attention down to the skin at his throat, the very light smattering of hair close to his collarbone.

"Good to see you, Sunflower," he said softly, and then walked on ahead of me, leaving me confused and annoyed and ashamed I was being so rude and childish. And damn, but the man could wear the shit out of a pair of jeans.

I snapped my eyes closed and sank back against the cold wall, letting my bag drop to the ground for a moment. Okay, this was a temporary setback. It wasn't the end of the world if he knew where I lived. Maybe it was better. I'd been planning to ask him to vet my new next-door neighbor after all, and he'd know where I lived then. I was taken off guard, that was all. It *was* nice to see a familiar face. Of course it was. But if our interactions didn't stop, I was never going to get over my stupid infatuation. He literally grew more attractive every time I saw him.

Marianne was coming this afternoon. I was definitely going

to make a plan to go out for a glass of wine with her so I could start broadening my horizons and meet more people.

Gathering my bag, I set off home. As soon as I was inside, I could hear the murmur of a man and woman's voice. I was grateful for the thick door that muffled sound. Marianne must be there already. The entrance was around the side of the building, so I'd have missed her if she'd just arrived.

I unpacked the groceries I'd bought, and then after washing my hands and produce began to lay out the ingredients for a loaded sandwich on a fresh baguette. I might even have a glass of wine with it and indulge myself. I could sit on my front patio since I couldn't eat at the *trattoria* for risk of bumping into Evan on his way back from his appointment. I'd been so focused on his presence and whether he was following me that I hadn't thought to ask what appointment he had.

I was about to cut into the baguette when there was a knock at my door. I counted to three, knowing I was going to have to meet the new neighbor and get it over with.

Peering out the small window, I confirmed Marianne's presence. She was alone. Good. I unbolted the deadlock and opened the door.

"Andrea." Marianne smiled and came inside. "*Bon*, you're home. I want to introduce you to Evan Roark." She gestured just as Evan stepped onto the patio behind her. "He is going to be renting my little unit next door."

"You have got to be kidding me." I growled at Evan over her shoulder.

"Andrea," he said, tilting his head down in acknowledgment. His face was unreadable. No guilt. Nothing. Could it be he seriously did not know I lived here?

"Oh good, you two already know each other, which is *parfait,* because Evan and I were just going to have a quick lunch at the *trattoria.* I was hoping you would join us."

"I've eaten."

Evan frowned. And Marianne glanced behind me where I had not even cut the bread yet.

I sighed. "I mean, I was about to eat."

"Come! It is the thing to do on Sundays, and you don't want to miss it. And you are a local now. Arturo saves the best wine until after the tourists have gone home for the season."

I raised my eyebrows. "Huh. I didn't know people did that."

Evan crowded the door, blocking all the sun. "Come on. It won't hurt. I saw you eyeing that place earlier. I'll buy."

"*I'll* buy," I countered and grabbed my purse, shaking my head. "Fine, let's go. And you can tell me what the hell you're playing at. I know full well you have a condo. Two actually. One in Cannes and one in Nice."

I locked up behind us. Marianne glanced from one of us to the other, but rather than looking concerned, her eyes held a sparkle. A sparkle I'd have to shut down. I gave Evan a slitted-eye look of reproach and he winked back.

"*On y va,*" Marianne said and led the way.

"After you." He swept his arm out.

I traipsed to the restaurant in silence. After a block, Marianne and Evan started chatting again, and I fell back and slunk along behind, focusing on the cobblestones and fuming at the turn of events. Marianne gave him a side-eyed look and giggled at something he said, and my insides twisted. She had a boyfriend, I reminded myself. It was simply that I envied the ability to laugh and joke with Evan.

At the *trattoria*, Marianne introduced us to the owner and found us a coveted round table under the awning on the square where we could see all the goings on. It was crowded, and Evan's knee pressed against mine under the table, the denim rough against my bare skin. "Sorry," I mumbled, trying to move, but there was nowhere to go. I tried to maneuver my chair back slightly and nearly went over backward as a leg caught on a cobblestone.

Evan's hand flew out and grabbed my shoulder, my stomach disappearing with fright. "Whoa there," he said, righting me.

Heat throbbed in my cheeks. "Thanks," I mumbled, my chair settling upright and my skin sliding against his knee again. "Sorry."

"Tight fit," he said with a quirk of his lip.

Marianne was ordering us wine and bread and olives and pretending to be oblivious to the vibe.

"Are you going to tell me why you're here," I hissed.

"I needed a place to stay." He shrugged.

"Care to elaborate."

"Not really."

Marianne finished up with Arturo and turned back to us. "So, how do you two know each other?"

"We used to work together," I said. "On the boat."

She turned to Evan. "Oh, you're a yachtie? I thought you said you were in corporate security."

"I am. But we work for the same boss."

"Worked," I corrected.

"Right." Evan smiled tightly.

"But you were not friends?" Marianne asked. "Forgive me, I am blunt."

"No," I said at the same time as Evan said, "Of course we are."

A look of surprise flickered over his face. Maybe even a bit of hurt? Surely not.

"I'm joking," I said quickly to Marianne with a brittle laugh. "It's just that we haven't seen eye to eye recently. Evan has problems sometimes remembering where his security job begins and ends."

"And Andrea sometimes forgets that I care about her ... safety."

If looks could kill, Evan would be gasping for his last breath. Instead he'd made Marianne go all goo-goo eyed as she looked back and forth between us.

"*Alors*, this is a beautiful coincidence, is it not?" she noted. "Andrea, you told me you were worried about safety, and now look, you have someone who will take care of you, right next door!" She clapped her hands together.

At that moment food and wine showed up and saved Evan's life again. The next little while was spent discussing some of the village characters. Occasionally Marianne would stop talking and wave at someone and other times drop her voice because everyone knew everyone here. "This village has some real nosey old-time characters," she said.

"Oh, I think I met one already. Albert at the *tabac*?" I offered.

"Albert." She hooted. "You didn't buy a coffee from him, did you? Now it will be a war. There is another *tabac*." She pointed across the square. "François will try to make sure you always buy your espresso from him. They have been fighting since they both fell in love with Géraldine. She was the daughter of the lady who ran the old *pension*. Géraldine left many years ago. Now they argue over who is better at boules, and who has the better coffee. It is ridiculous. In fact, you will see them in their nightly boules competition this evening."

"Oh dear. Have I already stumbled into town politics?" I asked.

"What small town doesn't have drama?" Evan added. "We'd better be sure to share our patronage between both of them equally."

What was this *we*?

"I love Albert's coffee," I said. "You take François." That way we could limit interactions.

"And who gets the *trattoria*?" Marianne asked, amused.

"I do," we both answered at the same time.

"We'll draw up a schedule," I added.

"Or," suggested Evan, smugly, clearly enjoying being the better person today. "We could occasionally come here together." He dropped his mouth open and put a hand on each cheek like he was a human emoji of sarcastic surprise.

"You are like a divorcing couple still in love," Marianne said, chuckling. "*Excusez-moi*, I'll be right back. Try not to start a food fight," she added when she saw both Evan and I reach for the last olive.

"Please," he said as she walked away toward the bathrooms. "It's yours."

"No, you have it."

"I guess it will stay on the plate, alone, unable to fulfill its destiny of being enjoyed, due solely to your stubbornness. What is with you today, anyway?" he asked, bringing his wine glass to his lips for a sip.

"Me? I was enjoying Sunday in my new village by myself until you crashed it."

"And here I thought we were friends. I've known you for years. I mean, I love sparring with you, but what's going on right now?"

"I—" He was right. "We *are* friends. I'm being a brat today." And every day recently. *Because I have all these feelings for you that have grown out of control, and I don't know what to do with them apart from to avoid you.* "I'm sorry," I said instead. "Can you just promise me to stay out of my business? If you can do that, then I don't see a problem with you being next door. And part of me is relieved it's someone I know. When I first heard, I was nervous," I admitted. "The timing ..." Understatement.

Evan lowered his voice. "You thought he'd found you."

I looked down, annoyed he knew me so well, and nodded.

"Why won't you let me help you?" he asked, his eyes clear and intense. I looked away from them.

My fingernails bit into my palms beneath the table. "You've done so much already."

"Why does that *matter*?" His voice strained.

I blinked away a sting in my eyes. "Because I've forgotten how to look out for myself. When will I ever learn to trust myself again? To trust my gut? To feel safe on my own. Evan, I've been suffocating. I can't let him steal anymore of my life away." I cleared the tightness in my throat. Dammit. I jutted my chin up. "I'm fine, okay? I just want a life back. One I can call mine. And I need space for that. Space from everything. Even you. I can't breathe."

He sat back, his face going unreadable again, just as Marianne returned.

"I took the liberty of ordering the house specials for us all to share. So, Evan, how long are your parents staying at your place?" Marianne asked him as she sat down.

I snapped to attention. "You have parents?" I asked, aghast.

"What? Did you think I spawned out of the ether fully formed?"

Imagining Evan in a family unit? With a mom and dad? My God, what was he like as a kid? Thoughts swirled. "The swamp, maybe," I joked. "Or forged in the fires of hell." If hell produced sinfully sculpted males with over-protective tendencies. I laughed to show Marianne that we were all jokey jokes here. My cheeks burned.

"My parents," Evan turned his attention back to Marianne, "are ridiculous racing fans. There's a big convention happening in Cannes this month, and I've given them my apartment to stay in."

"What about your apartment in Nice, why aren't you staying there?" I asked.

He turned his attention back to me. "I'm having new floors put in after a huge leak. Very disruptive, and it will take at least a few weeks. Thought I'd try village life for a change."

My phone buzzed on the table and I looked down. Oh. Christian's name popped up. We'd traded numbers at dinner. I hadn't heard from him since and thought maybe my abrupt departure had deterred him. I'd freaked out, yes. But it probably wasn't anything to do with him, I didn't think. I slid my phone off the table but not before Evan saw.

"Are you going to go out with him?" he asked me.

"Who?" Marianne asked, surprised.

I gestured weakly with my phone. "Oh, uh, just this guy from my boss' office."

"Oh good. I think it's important for you to go on some dates while you do all your figuring out your life stuff."

"Are you?" Evan asked again.

I lifted my chin. "Maybe. Didn't we just talk about my life being *my* business?"

"Sure. But as a *friend*, I'm curious."

Marianne popped the last olive into her mouth, like it was popcorn.

"As a friend, maybe I will, maybe I won't."

His eyes narrowed.

Food began to arrive.

By the time we got the check, I was stuffed with *spaghetti alla vongole*, seared duck with seasonal vegetables, and *profiteroles*. We'd avoided any further conversational landmines and talked mostly about how amazing the food was we were sharing as well as other local places to check out. The wine had also been amazing. Too amazing. I could have slid off my chair. I could probably not eat until Monday.

After we paid the check, which we agreed to split three ways in the end, Marianne leaned over to put her wallet away in her purse and then brought out a large iron key and placed it on the table between Evan and me.

We both stared at it like she'd just dropped a scorpion on the table.

"The key to the padlocked door between the units," she explained with a raised eyebrow. She stood. "I must go. Good luck." She blew us kisses and then sashayed away between the tables, waving goodbye to various people.

I half expected Evan to make a grab for the key, but the padlock was on my side of the door anyway. He lifted his palms at first, but then as my hand closed over the key, he covered my hand with his.

The shock of his warm skin startled me. "I have to go too," I said, gritting my teeth and trying to slide my hand out from underneath his.

He squeezed, soft but firm, keeping my hand in place. "Wait. Can we ... please. Let me be here for you. Especially now."

My shoulders sagged. "I can't. I haven't shared my address, and I picked the safest place I could. That has to be enough."

His brows drew close together as he struggled to understand why I'd turn down a friend who was literally trained to keep people safe at a time when I'd made myself so vulnerable. I had a hard time understanding it myself. But I knew if I opened the metaphorical (or physical—thanks, Marianne) door to depending on Evan, I'd never stand on my own two feet. Or get over this stupid crush.

"I'm sorry," I said. "I just can't. Goodbye, Evan."

I slipped my hand out from under his, key tight in my fist, and hurried out of the restaurant.

It was only when I got home that I realized he hadn't seemed surprised to see me when he'd arrived today. And even after ascertaining I lived here, he hadn't volunteered that he would be too. Which meant ... he'd already known. He'd known I lived in this village and had chosen to live here anyway. Whether he'd known I would be next door was debatable, but in a series of noncoincidences, the simplest explanation was usually the right one.

I smacked the connecting door. "Butthead," I fumed, regretting sharing my whereabouts with Meg and Sue. I put the key in a drawer in the kitchen and slammed it shut. What was the point in *asking* if I needed help, if he was just going to insert himself anyway?

Three hours later I had my ear pressed against the thick wood, trying to hear just a tiny hum of sound.

ELEVEN

Evan

I ROLL over in bed and flip my pillow to the cold side. Knowing Andrea's on the other side of the wall and is so upset with me is killing me. Four hours into the dead of night and sleep has yet to claim me. It's a good thing I'm not going in to work tomorrow.

I'd been aware how much me being here in her village would probably aggravate her, but seeing the way she was affected today brought it home. If I'd ever thought she had a thing for me, even a tiny kernel of a thing, today proved I was sorely mistaken. She literally can't stand to be near me.

Perhaps I should have asked Pete to be her security detail. I could have given him a leave of absence to do this, but the truth is I don't trust anyone but myself. For my sanity I need to see with my own eyes that she's fine.

But I underestimated how upset she'd be. In fact, I've

gravely underestimated pretty much everything when it comes to her. Not her courage, of course. You had to have it in spades to have gone through what she has. But I've underestimated her stubborn unwillingness to let me do what I do best. When I begged her to let me help her at lunch, it took everything in me not to scream, *"You're in danger!"* It was like she'd forgotten her husband was a fucking psychopath. I should know, I had to witness his acts of terror in the desert—images that would haunt me for-fucking-forever.

Earlier, I'd strained to hear anything from next door. The walls are damn near a foot of stone and concrete. If she actually needed me, there would probably be zero chance I'd hear, which made moving in next door utterly moot. My only chance is to persuade her to keep the door open between us. A few months ago, I would have said that would be a piece of cake. Today showed me it's probably impossible.

I thump the pillow. *Fuck.*

It's increasingly clear I've approached this all wrong. I'm known for being a bit bullheaded and doing what I think is best for people without ever asking. But if I'd asked Andrea if she wanted to have me around, after today I know the answer would have been no. Earlier when she point blank threw the word "stalking" at me, I had to come to terms with the fact that she wasn't far off. It had definitely hit close.

Jesus. I'm a head case. Is this how it started? A need to protect turning into a full-blown and misguided obsession?

I get up and prowl to the bathroom and splash cold water on my face. It's a tiny room, stone and white tile walls, meant just to be an extra guest space, not for someone to live in. I stare at my reflection in the small mirror. I look tired as hell, but I lean forward and stare into my own eyes, looking for a hint of someone who's lost his goddamn mind. All I see is a thirty-six-year-old man who doesn't know what the hell he's doing here and whose mother has despaired of ever getting grandbabies. I peel my t-shirt off, leaving me in my boxers. Maybe I'll sleep if I'm cooler.

When I go see Pete tomorrow, to check in about our "off the books" project, I might have him order a full and confidential psych eval. Just to be safe. I splash my face again and drink some water. I pace back to the bedroom. At my place when sleep won't come, I can get some work done. Here, I'm enclosed in a stone tomb. My skin itches with the need for fresh air, and my watch is apparently on strike since it's still showing hours until dawn.

Grabbing my phone, I text Xavier. He's on American time and about to try to win Josie back. Focusing on my friend and his love life seems like a good distraction right now.

You good?

X: *What are you doing up so late?*

You know me.

X: *Only when you're stressed. What's up? Did you find out where Andrea is staying?*

I did. Saint Paul de Vence.

X: *And?*

And what? I toss my phone on the bed. Then think better of it, and pick it up, hitting the call button

He answers on the first ring.

"I'm fine, Evan." Xavier's French accent and familiar voice make me smile.

"Let me put my mind at ease, will you? Did you use the car service I organized?"

"Yes. And I asked the driver to be at my disposal for the week."

"Will you—"

"I've already sent her name. Pete is doing the background check since you're taking some time off."

I blow out a breath. "Okay. So, uh, what's it like there? What's the plan?"

"It's hot as Balzac's balls. I don't know how people live with this humidity. And so far my plan is to get Dauphine fed and on American time and buy an engagement ring."

"Holy—" I scrub my hand down my face and swallow. "Yeah." I clear my throat. "Of course you need to. I guess your mother's ring is in trust for Dauphine." Holy shit, he's going to ask Josie to marry him. I knew it was serious.

"*Oui*, I gave that ring to Arriette, I cannot have Josie wear my dead wife's ring, *non*?"

"I agree a thousand times. X, I—I'm so damned happy for you."

"Don't be happy yet. I haven't even seen her and still need to plead my case and beg for forgiveness."

"She's not going to say no to you. You're Xavier Pascale, for God's sake."

"Maybe any other woman. But not her."

"Yeah." I huff out an amused breath as I think of Josie. "Not her." I can tell my friend is nervous. And Xavier doesn't normally do nervous.

We're quiet for a moment.

"Why can't you sleep?" he asks.

I pinch the bridge of my nose. "I'm bored," I lie. "Taking time off work is not my style. Pascale Company is not just a job to me, it's my life. I'm not used to all this spare time and relaxation."

"Tell me about it. Dauphine told me I'm not allowed to work when she is awake." His voice goes muffled as he speaks to his daughter. "It's Evan. No, I'm not working. Dauphine says hello."

I smile. "Tell her hi from me."

"Evan says hi. Where are you calling from?" he asks me.

My lips purse and I suck them between my teeth.

"Evan, tell me you are not where I think you are."

"It's not a big deal."

"Evan."

"X."

He sighs. "I get it, I do."

"What do you get? It's not what you think, okay? I just have a lot invested. It's sunk time cost. I just want to make sure she gets through the divorce. It's a project," I argue. "You know I hate to leave things half done."

"She's a project? You're telling me after how many years of friendship that she's a project and not that you care about her. I hope she doesn't know you think of her that way."

Honestly, I think that's exactly what she thinks but I don't tell X that. "Of course I care." I thank the stars for the thick, thick walls as there's no way she can hear this conversation. "But that's it. Anyway, two things can be true."

"And yet, there you are. What does she think about it?"

Sighing, I go back through all the conversations and interactions Andrea and I've had recently. I try to piece together where her head is at. Today at lunch she said she wanted a life back. Those words sucker punched me. I'd thought she *was* having a life with us, with Pascale Company, with all the crew, on the boat, with *me* even. As a friend, of course. A life that was safe. A life she would never have had otherwise.

A life I'd given to her.

Not that she could ever find that out.

Has she not seen it the same way?

"She's pissed. I messed up, I think. By being here." I clench my jaw. "I don't know how to keep her safe when she doesn't want me to."

"It sounds like you need to respect her wishes."

"X. You know that's easier said than done."

"What's the worst that can happen?"

"I—" I swallow. The words, *she could fucking die* remain unspoken on my tongue.

"You never did tell me the whole story about her and her ex."

"It's not my story to tell."

"*Alors*, but you knew him. What about the story *you* can tell? What's the part that makes you unable to let go?"

I stand and pace to the window. The night is dark as death, not a star to be seen. It must be cloudy and no moon. The window reflects my bare upper body back to me. I clutch the back of my neck with my free hand, habit then making me move away from the window. "I can't get into that," I tell my best friend. "Not tonight. But he's a bad guy, X. Like a really bad guy. And I had Pete do another check into his whereabouts, and he's MIA right now. I think he's coming for her."

Xavier is silent for a moment. "*Alors.* Andrea is like family to me. If it comes to it, you use whatever resources you need."

"I've got it under control," I say, but my shoulders relax with his permission. I've already used Pascale Company resources. But I also have plenty of my own.

"I'm serious," he presses.

"I know. And I thank you. Hey, I know you have Dauphine to get settled. I'll let you go."

"Stay well."

"You too." I hang up. Then text.

I'm sorry. I forgot to ask - When will you see Josie?

X: *I need to get some things in order first. But soon.*

Don't wait too long.

X: *Same to you.*

What's that supposed to mean?

X: *Andrea.*

I start to type back, and then let it go, giving him the last word.

Three dots pop up and then disappear. After a few minutes I know I'm not going to hear from him again and toss my phone on the bed behind me.

At dinner the other night, sitting next to Christian, Andrea said she wants to date again, that she might be ready. I grit my teeth thinking about it. She threw it out there so casually, and as a friend, I should have been happy for her. So why did it feel like she'd skewered me with her dinner fork? I'm guessing this is also what her divorce is about. She's nothing if not honorable. Even though she's still married to an absolute piece of shit, she hasn't wanted to start a new relationship while still being married to him. I respect it even while I hate it. He doesn't deserve her loyalty.

She hasn't so much as *kissed* anyone since the day she arrived at the Pascale estate looking drawn and hunted, lips pale from loss of blood and eyes haunted by loss. She hasn't even had a mild flirtation. I don't think. Except that one night. With me. But that was her drinking too much champagne. There's no way she even remembers how she got so close, her mouth against my neck, and her lips about to tilt up to mine. It took an iron force of will to set her away from me.

I flip over onto my back, staring at the dark ceiling. As far as I know, she hasn't had anyone touch her in years. No one to even write over whatever that asshole did.

An uncomfortable pressure grows under my breastbone. Have I deliberately kept her away from going out or meeting anyone, under the guise of it being "for her protection"?

I sit with the thought, and the heaviness inside me grows.

Oh my God ... I'm beginning to see me the way she must, and it's almost too much to bear.

I've turned into the worst version of myself. I've even gone beyond what's morally right to find a way to be next door to her for fuck's sake. The pressure in my chest increases, like a rock is taking over my insides. I suddenly want to be sick.

No wonder she wants nothing to do with me.

I don't represent freedom from *him*.

I don't represent freedom at all. Haven't for a long time with all my rules and protocols and ... *shit*.

A part of her is telling her I'm just the same. I'm not, but how would she know? At this point, do *I* even know? I mean, I know I'd never hurt her physically. But it was never just about that, was it?

I have control issues. I know I do. If I lose control of a situation, or miss one thing, people are in danger. Not just people, my found family. Xavier is my best friend, but almost a brother to me. All the people we work with, the boat crew, my team at the office, all the staff at the estate. If anything happened to any single one of them due to my carelessness I'd never be able to live with myself. Everything has to be looked into. Double checked. Triple checked. Control everything as much as you can and eliminate the space for chance. Josie, the nanny, and her relationship with Xavier was an unforeseen variable, and during that time, Dauphine ended up in danger. I failed that day. And I wonder if the almost moment with Andrea just days before didn't mess with my head so much I might have seen the danger coming.

Control is how I keep people safe.

But Andrea's husband was also about control.

I sit up and scrub my hand down my face. *Shit.*

Sadly, even if I *wanted* to abandon Andrea and hope for the best and that he's forgotten about her, doubtful, I can't go back to either of my condos. I was telling the truth about that. My parents have taken over my Cannes place for two months, (because I offered it to them this week) and I've finally scheduled the damn flooring to be done in my other place. I did it as cover. And now it can't be undone. There are other places, sure, hotels even, but ...

I picture her today, when I first saw her walk out of the store, her face full of peace and wonder and no responsibility. Standing there in that gorgeous dress covered in yellow flowers, glowing, the bag clearly heavy in her hand as she hefted it onto her shoulder. She was so damn beautiful, like a sunflower who'd finally found the face of the sun, I stopped breathing for a second. Now, I've crushed that momentary peace she found. Me. Just by being here.

I normally loved the way we sparred. It was tension-filled. Energizing even. We're friends, good friends, but I get off on making her react, and it seemed she did too—a spark that was always ready to be kindled. Except recently, it has seemed less like fun and jokes. We've drifted apart, and the spark feels more dangerous, like we could explode the fragile support beam beneath our relationship. And this last week she brought forth an edge to the sparring that was almost like a scared little girl fighting back. I don't like it. And now I realize how much I'm to blame for it with this ill-conceived idea.

But because she's painted a target on herself, I can't leave. I can't leave her knowing he'll probably come for her.

I flop back down on the bed and stare at the heavy wooden door that separates my bedroom from her kitchen.

She needs space?

I'll give it to her. She won't even know I'm here.

She wants to date Christian? Fine.

Not fine, exactly. But …

I briefly entertain a montage of her rejecting him, shutting the door in his face, falling asleep on their dates because he's so dull, or of me punching his smug face in. But no. If she needs to have a date with him, as much as it will annoy me, I'm going to stand back and let it happen.

Who am I to keep her locked away just because I don't want to date her? Not that I don't. Per se. She's objectively gorgeous.

But even if she was free—which she isn't, not yet—and even if she wasn't off-limits—which at this point, she very much is, I can't keep her from finding love again, especially when I'm incapable of or unwilling to provide it myself. And most especially when she can't stand to even be in the same room with me.

But I *am* going to take Pete up on his offer to dig deeper into Christian Fuckface's life and make sure there really are no skeletons. I'm going to double down on finding her ex, so we aren't caught unaware. And somehow, without pissing her off even more, I'm going to have to figure out a way to get her to leave that damned door open.

TWELVE

Of course, a background check will probably reveal that Andrea is actually *safe* with Christian, and they might end up dating long term or God forbid, turn really serious.

Screw that, I think as I sit bolt upright three hours after my restless body finally succumbed to sleep even though my brain clearly never shut off. She can't date that pretty boy. We know nothing about him.

It's just before six a.m. I don't have to look at my watch or phone to tell. My body obviously thinks it's a workday. And it is. Just not my regular in the office kind of day. Pete's been handling the day to day stuff like a legend. As I knew he would.

No. If Andrea needs freedom, she'll get it. But she's damn not getting my blessing to date that dull, womanizing bore, skating by on his looks and delicate bone structure.

The village church bell chimes six times. I get up, tired, but frankly, I've accomplished more on less sleep.

I take a military-grade shower—wet the bod, soap up, rinse

fast—and throw on a pair of jeans and a navy t-shirt. I shave and smack my cheeks with lotion. I finger comb my hair, fasten my watch, and head out to François' *tabac*. What Andrea doesn't know is that François opens at six since he's by the village gate, but Albert gets lazy and only opens his store later.

I'm sure she has a coffee maker at her place, unlike on my side, but I also know she's at least a three-cup-a-day girl. And if I know her well, which I actually do, she'll make one at home and then plan to have maybe one on the way and the last at work. Today is her first day at the foundation in her new role though. She'll be wanting to make a good impression, she may even be in a bit of a rush to get there early. She needs to build a life outside of Pascale Company, and I'm going to do my damnedest to make sure she's successful.

Inside the *tabac*, I greet François, and we make small talk in French about the comings and goings of the villagers, and I let him know I'm a temporary resident for a while. I scan the wall behind him that holds family pictures as we chat, then nod at a framed black and white picture of a man in a military-style jacket standing next to a wooden gate and a low stone wall. "*Votre père?*" I ask, blowing on the top of the coffee he handed me. *Your father?*

"*Oui*, my family has been here for generations. This was my grandfather's business, then my father's, though he … it was during the war and it was difficult."

"He was in The Resistance?" I ask, knowing this area fought hard against Mussolini occupation, what with Nazi's pitting neighbor against neighbor just further north, and they went through what a lot of small towns went through with trust between family and friends being stretched to the breaking point.

As expected, François just waves his hand dismissively, rather than confirming. "Your French is good," he says instead.

"Were *you* ever in the military?" I ask him.

He puffs up. "*Mais oui.* But I was the last generation. My two sons are pacifists. They live up north. One is studying to be a chef, the other works with the capitalists." He says it like it's a dirty word, and I smile to myself.

"I was military too," I offer. "Royal Marines."

His bushy eyebrows shoot up. "Commando?" he asks, clearly knowing his units.

I nod, even though I went beyond Commando to SAS briefly. "Retired now. Private security work."

He whistles, and I can see the time for my request is now or never.

"I'm always looking for people I trust to, uh, keep an eye out for me when I'm trying to keep someone safe." I'm grateful my French is flawless so there's no room for misunderstanding me.

"You have a job here?"

I tilt my head side to side in a kind of "sort of" movement. "A lady friend. She's trying to live a quiet and safe life in your village."

"Our village is very safe." He's almost affronted I'd imply otherwise.

"It is. She has an ex-husband." Or soon to be ex-husband. I pause, letting his mind work through the implication of why a woman would need a Royal Marine level security detail for an ex-husband without actually spelling it out and airing Andrea's business that's not mine to tell. But even so, she'll have my balls for this too if she finds out. And with a village this small, it's only a matter of time before everyone knows. A fact I'm actually counting on.

But in for a penny, in for a pound.

"My sister was married to such a man," François says at last.

I nod once and opening my phone, pull up a picture of Major Angus Robertson. Of course when I met him we were both in the same fire team, and I was a sergeant and he was a warrant officer class 1. He went mercenary-for-hire eight years ago, and if he truly wants to reach Andrea one day, he'll have the strings to do it if he doesn't already.

François takes in the man's pale features and close cropped light hair and pale eyes.

Then I slide a card with my number across the counter. He takes it wordlessly and slips it under his register. "And I'll take another coffee to go," I say. "Double espresso, with cream and an extra dash of hot water." I hand him a silver insulated travel mug with the logo of the yacht on it.

∼

AFTER RUNNING my errand and setting everything up, I head back down to the village gate, waving to François, and exit to the parking lot. The village is only now stirring to life. My helmet is still locked to my bike so I unlock that and the wheel and open the storage box and pull out my leather jacket. The jacket is a layer of protection, not just from the early morning chill, but so my skin doesn't peel off should I come off the bike. I should be wearing better pants too, but after twenty years of riding, I know my risks. I make quick work of putting my helmet on, slinging my leg over the body of the beast and gunning the engine. Then as the first light of the sun makes it over the valley, I take a deep breath of crisp morning air and guide the bike down the curvy mountain roads. Pete's expecting me. We have a lot to discuss.

THIRTEEN

Andrea

DRESSING MODESTLY in a black pencil skirt, blue cotton blouse, and comfortable flats, I checked my hair and makeup for the fifth time and then glanced at the time to make sure I could grab a second coffee from Albert's before I walked to where I parked the car next to the bottom gate.

Thinking back, it had been so long since I'd had those first-day-on-the-job jitters. When I first showed up to work for Xavier Pascale, a job organized through the women's shelter executive director, I had been so broken and tired and just plain relieved to be safe that I don't remember feeling nervous at all. I'd simply felt determined to do whatever they asked of me and to do it better than they'd ever expect so I could stay as long as I needed to. I'd loved working there, starting at Xavier Pascale's estate and then doing a boating course and moving onto the boat. I'd fallen in love with the job and the family, especially little Dauphine who'd just been an almost toddler when I started.

And Evan, with all his security checks and protocols, had made me feel so safe. I needed to remember that.

I stepped out the front door and immediately saw the insulated travel mug with the familiar yacht logo on it and a note held under it.

Coffee for your first day. It's from François' place, sorry. Albert's only opens at 8 (another point for François). Good luck.

Evan.

P.S. You'll forget I'm even next door, promise.

Not bloody likely. Pressing my lips together, I stuffed the note back under the cup and turned and locked my front door. I stepped off the patio and made it three steps before turning back with a growl and taking the coffee. I stuffed the note in my bag and headed in the direction of my car.

It was just coffee for goodness' sake. And it was a really thoughtful gesture. Sweet even. And it had the intended consequence of softening my walls. He'd made sure it was in an insulated cup, and then obviously walked all the way down to the village gate and back before retracing his steps to get to work this morning. And it was coffee. I needed coffee. Even though it was from François and not Albert, I took a tentative sip.

"Mmmm," I hummed aloud. François and Albert were in definite competition. I wondered about the infamous Géraldine they had both fallen in love with. Albert had been an interesting character in my brief meeting with him. I wondered about François.

At the bottom square, I passed the *trattoria* all closed up for the morning, small birds hopping around on the cobblestones looking for crumbs. The fountain was gurgling and the boule pit was quiet and empty. I hadn't come back in the evening to witness the rivalry of two old men. François' *tabac* had a faded red awning that swayed in the crisp breeze, and as I looked, a man came out of the shop with a broom to sweep the stoop. François himself, I guessed.

I started to wave a cheery good morning, but my arm faltered as he stared intently at me. I glanced behind me to see if I was somehow not the target of his scrutiny, but as I looked back at him, he waved enthusiastically with a big grin. I must've mistaken his weird look. Still, I was a bit unnerved and tried a small smile and a good morning as I scurried by.

"My coffee, *c'est bon, non?*" he called, pointing to my travel mug.

I lifted the mug in agreement, silently chastising Evan for sticking me in the middle of the town coffee feud, and kept on moving.

François was portly, where Albert was tall and rangy. But François had a thick head of dark hair, ruddy cheeks, and twinkly eyes. From what I remembered, Albert's gray, thinning hair had been carefully combed back and his eyes were rheumy blue. They both had the look that they'd been handsome in their day. I wondered what each of them had offered Geraldine. Which one of them had been fun and easy going, and who had been passionate and intense? I could probably guess, but I was making it all up in the end. Was it ever possible to have both? Was it impossible to have intensity and passion without obsession and control? Was it possible to have easy and fun and still feel your toes curl?

I wanted to feel it again. That rush. That fizzing inside, like a shaken can of soda ready to pop, joy and happiness flying up my throat.

But the fall ... I didn't want the fall. Not again. I wondered if I'd ever be able to let my guard down with someone without watching for signs. Signs I missed the first time.

I easily found my car in the lot and got behind the wheel, fishing out my sunglasses so I didn't squint against the low morning sun.

In the meantime, I was going to be the best new employee the foundation had ever had. Granted, Lilian had been quick to let me know I would be filling in practically anywhere help was needed, which I'd done as a volunteer anyway. And I wasn't sure how much actual skill that involved. But it was perfect for me for now as I figured out the next part of my life. Obviously I knew how to keep the yacht running smoothly and efficiently, from staff to supplies, but I had no idea how that translated into the world of art.

A short while later, I drove up the elm lined driveway and parked in the small employee lot. Then I pulled my phone out and did the grown up thing.

Thank you for the coffee and the luck.

There was no immediate response, and swallowing my nerves, I stowed the phone and headed inside.

BY DAY four I'd taken so many notes about ideas I had, especially to bring more attention to their oversized Chagall, that I was more convinced than ever I could really get something done here.

"As one of France's first art foundations," Lilian said as she took me down to the lower levels after a quick lunch in the on-site cafe, "started in the sixties, you are aware from previous years that we are as organized as we can be with an archaic paper filing system and years behind in cataloguing this warehouse area full of donated collections."

I nodded in agreement and followed the clip clop of her red high heels that she wore as if they were comfy slippers. She'd promised me a trip into some of their store rooms, and now as a bona fide employee, I was getting to see parts of the building I'd never seen before.

Lilian had always been surprisingly friendly and incredibly knowledgeable, but I'd always kept my distance. I was only working three days a week to start but was excited to get there every day to discover new parts of the foundation. I stifled a yawn, not because I was bored but because I hadn't had my third cup of coffee yet today. True to his word, I hadn't even seen a glimpse of Evan, and while that relieved me on the second day, by day three I was thinking about him far too much. And this morning I'd had the gall to feel disappointed. Which was ridiculous. I missed him being in my business all the time. How stupid was that?

"There is a lot to discover down here," Lilian said, raising her voice slightly over the hum of dehumidifiers and climate control equipment.

I nodded and looked around. There were rows and rows of

crates and shelves. Upstairs, the famous works may be on display but they were also languishing in relative obscurity, only visited by those in the know. The foundation needed to revamp their marketing plan for the works they already knew they had. I hadn't been a marketing student, but even I knew their social media presence could stand to be pumped up.

"Wow," I said as we entered yet another interior room with white stucco walls and recessed lighting dotted like stars on the ceiling and filled with metal shelving units stretching up at least twenty feet. "You probably have hundreds of other masterpieces hidden down here."

"Indeed. Most of the time, if we get a collection donated, we're informed roughly what it consists of. The donor family know for tax or insurance purposes, for example. But every now and again the heirs of an estate might not even know what it is in a collection their loved one bequeathed us, and we just take it. A few years ago, amongst a fairly interesting, but not particularly valuable collection of large pieces, was a small series of Picasso sketches from the artist's early days. It was only Stephen, our warehouse coordinator, who spotted them and had them authenticated. The family had no idea their grandmother had them in her possession."

I couldn't fathom that Picassos could be hidden in plain sight. "Do you ever pass along collections to other museums?" I asked, eyeing what seemed to be a collection of Greek coins and mosaic remnants. "There must be some things here that don't fit with the modernist aesthetic the foundation has."

She nodded. "If we can, we identify foundations and museums that specialize in antiquities and other eras we don't. In the case of any antiquities, we try to make sure it goes to publicly accessible places and not private collections. In some cases, we've even repatriated stolen items."

I raised my eyebrows.

"We're extremely selective about who we share things with—they have to have a similar mission to ours."

"Forgive me," I said. "In all the years I've worked here, I haven't read a mission statement. What is the mission exactly?"

Lilian laughed. "That's the point. There isn't one. We are singularly about art for art's sake. So our mission is simply that. We don't try to influence, or educate, or force ourselves where we don't belong. Education is the byproduct of our existence, of course. And that might be a project you can help with as well. But art should simply," she lifted her shoulders, "be. Without intent. Without purpose. Without judgment."

I smiled, thinking of the massive penis outside in the sculpture garden, and Evan's reaction. No judgment indeed. Miró was probably saying the same thing. "I think I like this non-mission. So much of my experience with art growing up was forced upon me. How does this make you feel? What was the artist's intent? Write a two-thousand-word essay on why the artist chose this medium and these colors and what were they trying to convey ..."

Lilian nodded with a smile as she continued to a set of double doors and scanned another keycard. "I've always thought you would fit here. I'm glad you decided to make it more permanent."

Butterflies swelled in my gut. "Thank you. But I'd be remiss if I didn't confess that by the time I did my art history degree, my passion to pursue a career in the art world was almost extinguished by uninspiring teachers." I grimaced, *and a husband who chipped away at my confidence daily,* but I didn't mention that. "Thank you for giving me a chance to really do this."

She waved me off. "Come, let's see some of the pieces that have just come in for our upcoming exhibit. You might recognize a few. They're from the Pascale Estate."

Surprise had me pausing. In all the years I'd volunteered I'd never mentioned my employer, per Evan's instructions. I'd made sure I just mentioned my art history degree and my experience working and leading teams in luxury yachting, as well as my reasons for seeking the position.

"I saw you chatting with Evan Roark last week," she said. "He mentioned you worked for them. I'm sure you know an endorsement from the Pascale family carries some significant weight. I was surprised you didn't pull that card the moment you started volunteering—it would have been a no brainer to hire you on the spot."

I pasted on a smile, even while the tips of my ears went hot with irritation at Evan. We weren't allowed to say anything, but he could when he felt like it?

And was there nowhere in my life without his fingerprints?

My body. My body had none of his fingerprints.

She hurried on, clearly sensing a vibe from me. "Not that we wouldn't have offered you the position, of course. You know we are in desperate need of help. But if I know Evan," she almost giggled, and a thousand unwelcome thoughts blew through my mind too fast to analyze, "which I do," she went on, confirming the worst of them, "I know he wouldn't have anyone working there who wasn't trustworthy."

"Well, that's great," I said, desperate to say something that belied the green monster inside me demanding to pin her to the white wall and start an interrogation into their romantic history. How had I never known this?

She turned back to the room and began going through the plans for the exhibit and pointing out various pieces. Her chestnut hair was impossibly glossy in a way that I'd always admired and only now really noticed. Her skin flawless. Her calves in those heels ... Ugh. I bet she wore fancy French underwear too. I was desperately trying to focus on what she was saying because I knew it was important, but oh my God, had Evan and Lilian—?

"*Bon*, that concludes the lower-level tour. I'd love to know any ideas you have for us. It's always fantastic to have a fresher perspectives. Otherwise processes get put in place, and we all get too comfortable and never innovate." She watched me expectantly.

"I, uh." I glanced around stalling for time. "You have a lot of not just art, but it seems like texts too. I know you said you pass along things that don't fit, but I'm wondering if you'd ever thought of setting up a reference room for scholars to come and spend time with these texts here. Maybe you can offer universities a membership to send people to study them?" Okay, maybe one half of my brain had actually focused on some of the items she'd mentioned as well as my subconscious taking inventory. "I mean, just as something extra for revenue?" I tacked on.

Lilian's eyebrows were in her hairline. "We, uh, never thought of that. But now that you mention it, one of the original founders owned a printing press and put together some really unique works with artists he knew. We never really knew how to give them their due. How do you display all the pages of a book without pulling it apart? So we let a few scholars come to see them, but you're right, we have a lot of such unique books and manuscripts. Perhaps an 'art library'?" She tapped her chin, eyes sparkling.

I chewed my lip, relieved I'd managed to add something useful on the fly and embarrassed my mind had been so focused on Evan I'd almost missed my chance to actually contribute. That confounded man was determined to live rent free in my brain. I really needed to figure out a way to evict him permanently.

"It's so simple, and so perfect." She pressed her hands together. "I'll give this serious consideration. I'm glad you're here. Let's head back upstairs."

We wound our way back through the lower level to the fire door that closed off the stairwell.

"I hope you don't mind me asking. You and Evan seemed a bit static."

"Static?"

"Like electricity."

I stumbled on the bottom step and then forced a laugh. It echoed up the stairwell and on playback sounded maniacal. I cleared my throat. "Whatever do you mean?"

She tilted her head. "Well, I've known him a long time, and let's just say I notice things about people."

"Because you dated him at one time?" It was out before I could take it back. But I was desperate to know.

"Dated?" It was her turn to laugh. "No. Evan doesn't really date. In the sense he sort of skips straight to dessert. If you know what I mean?"

I swallowed. Did she just admit what I think she did? "I wouldn't know," I forced out, cement flooding my insides.

Her face softened as we hit the landing. "Oh goodness. I'm so sorry. I didn't mean to make you uncomfortable. You're a sweet one, aren't you? Listen, all I'm saying is someone got to his heart a long time ago. So if you end up ..." she trailed off, clearly not sure how to continue.

"Having dessert?" I offered up.

She laughed. "Yeah. My advice? If you end up having dessert, just enjoy it for the pleasure and don't count the calories. There's no point." Her face sobered. "I feel like I just told you Santa wasn't real."

I belatedly schooled my expression from whatever it had been broadcasting without my knowledge. "I'm fine. It's just a surprise to hear. I've never, not once, seen him with anyone." In retrospect that was weird as hell in itself, and I needed to examine it. "And he can do what and who he likes." *Of course he can.* "I don't really care."

The lie was hollow, of course. Obvious to both of us.

We were quiet as we hit the main floor, but then my mouth betrayed me because I was burning for answers. And she'd clearly sampled and I felt sick about it, though I had no right to. "Curious though. The dessert? Is it good?"

She stopped, her mouth twisting in amusement and sympathy but without a trace of judgment. Taking my arm, she leaned in. "Like you wish you'd never even *known* that menu existed."

I closed my eyes, my insides tightening and my shoulders sagging. "I'm sorry I asked. I wish I'd never, ever, known *that* information."

"It was a long time ago. I have no designs on him anymore," Lilian said. Her eyes were sympathetic to my unvoiced jealousy. "And maybe it's good for you to be prepared."

"What do you mean?"

"So, when the time comes, you know what to order." She smiled enigmatically and walked ahead of me.

FOURTEEN

A menu.

A menu?

Lilian's implied comment about Evan's skills in the bedroom continued to ricochet around my head and zip through my belly the rest of the day, and all of today, Friday, which I had off. I suddenly wished so much I was working Fridays, keeping my brain on literally anything else but him.

At least I had an appointment with my lawyer this afternoon to keep my mind occupied. I'd never thought that would be something to look forward to.

I puttered around my perfect little village house and unpacked a few boxes of my belongings I'd had delivered from a storage unit. There were also some books I'd ordered over the last several months I shelved in order of what I wanted to read first. I settled into the comfortable armchair after picking a particularly well-recommended romance and gave up after two pages. It was good, I was simply ...

What did a menu mean, exactly? Maybe it was just lost in

translation ... but she'd been pretty clear. My stomach did a weird loop de loop. I looked up and stared at the door between my unit and Evan's. Was he even in there? I hadn't seen him all week. I got up and wandered to the kitchen, opening my fridge to see what I could make for dinner later. I stared at the contents blankly.

Why was I thinking so much about this? I closed the fridge. What Evan did or didn't do with people who were not me shouldn't be my concern. It was definitely *not* my concern. It would *never* be my concern because that was a line he'd never cross, and I'd never let him even if he wanted to. Not now, anyway. But he'd never wanted to. The man was professional to the extreme. And regardless of the fact we no longer actually worked together, I could never imagine him letting that make a difference. Even though I was no longer under the employ of Pascale Company, Evan had made it clear I was apparently still his job until *he* was done. Ugh. Control freak. Anyway, I had a divorce to worry about.

I slammed a cupboard door closed when I forgot why I'd opened it in the first place.

Pulling out my phone, I texted Meg and Sue. They were still in port and hadn't left for the Alps yet, and I prayed they were free. I needed a distraction and would probably need one even more after my appointment this afternoon. I also texted Marianne just to check in and let her know the house was working out great.

Sue texted back immediately, wanting to come see the village and my little *pied à terre*. Nervous about them potentially bumping into Evan and drawing conclusions, I persuaded them to meet me at *Le Tilleuil*, the small restaurant on the opposite side of the village from the one Evan, Marianne, and I had eaten at last Sunday. I wasn't sure how I'd avoid them wanting to see my place after drinks, but I'd just cross my fingers Evan would continue to stay away like he had all week.

∽

I PARALLEL PARKED my car on a one way street and dug around for a couple of euro coins for the parking meter next to my lawyer's office. A Moped zoomed by with a high whine, and I climbed out into the warm, still air stuffed between five-story high buildings. At the corner, I shielded my eyes from the sun and glanced both ways before crossing to the historic limestone office building ahead of me.

I'd just stepped up onto the opposite pavement when I felt the cold prickle on my scalp that snaked down between my shoulder blades, pinning me in place.

My gut cramped. Knowing I should trust my instincts, I swept my gaze down the street again, not seeing anything untoward. Breathe, I told myself.

I was being watched.

Dragging in another breath, I slowly turned around, unsure what to do. Fear rushed in like an old friend, seizing my insides. Traffic zoomed by, and passersby grumbled at the fact I was standing stock still. I had to act nonchalant, not panicked. But anyone who knew me well, including my soon to be ex, would recognize this for what it was. I pulled out my phone, willing my hands not to shake, and pretended to be cross-referencing a GPS map with where I was. I turned around, making a show out of looking at the street sign and around again.

As I debated whether to head back to my car, the feeling that had my insides seized up suddenly melted away. I blinked and stinging tears rushed to the back of my eyeballs. I shook my head, my insides collapsing into a puddle of idle adrenaline. My limbs felt weak, but I managed to engage them into moving, pushing my chin up, and forged ahead and into the office building.

"Shit. Shit, shit," I muttered to myself as soon I was inside the dim air-conditioned interior. My chest labored as if I'd just run five blocks. I punched the elevator button.

"I think he's found me," were the first words out of my mouth as I sat down opposite my lawyer, Veronica Patel. Her dark, almost black, hair and crimson lipstick screamed "don't mess with me," and were exactly why I'd chosen her.

She leaned forward. "Are you sure? What makes you say that?"

"I think he was watching me when I arrived here. I felt it. Or someone was," I added, doubt creeping into my tone. Now that the feeling had gone, I felt a little silly. "At least I thought so."

"Never discount your instinct. If there's one thing I've learned over the years, it's that women in your situation have a much more finely-tuned fear reaction. You need to listen to it. Did you see anything out of the ordinary?"

"No. Nothing. It was probably nothing."

"Do you think it was nothing?" she pressed.

I shook my head.

"All right then. This will be our last meeting here. I'll text you with other locations when necessary. Did you drive here today?"

I nodded, my heart rate picking up again now that Veronica was taking this so seriously. "I shouldn't have filed. It was stupid. Why did I suddenly feel the need to divorce him? God." The nausea was back full force. "My life was fine. Well, not fine. But it was okay. And—"

"You filed because you cannot live like this anymore. He needs to have no claim on you. We also need to file a restraining order. Do you have someone you can call? A friend who can pick you up? We have a back entrance. You'll have to leave your car parked for now. Maybe you can arrange a friend to come and get it?"

Friends, friends, friends. That was the problem with the low radar life I'd been living. My friends were a small bunch. I trusted them all, but who could I ask to randomly go out of their way to come and collect my abandoned car without explanation? I knew Evan was the prime choice, he'd know exactly what to do, but I'd categorically told him to butt out of my business. There was no way I could tell him this, he'd be all over me like a rash, criticizing my security and suffocating me with his irresistible smell and controlling tendencies. I closed my eyes. That didn't sound all that bad right now, but I refused to succumb and give him an "I told you so."

Chef had just left to visit his parents in Lausanne. I'd never ask our boat captain, Paco. He was too aloof, and besides we didn't have that kind of relationship. Rod, our deckhand would ask too many questions. Other crew weren't really in my circle of trust. And Meg and Sue were too new to my circle.

"I think you aren't used to asking for help, are you?" Veronica said. "I see a battle with your pride going on. But ask yourself if you'd rather you or your pride be injured."

I huffed out a breath. "Neither, preferably." I picked up my phone and texted Meg and Sue.

Hey, since you're both coming up to the village tonight, any chance one of you can drive my car up there? I left it down in Nice today. Long story. Pretty please! I'll tell you where to pick up the keys.

Meg responded instantaneously. *Of course. I've got you. Text the address. Xx*

My shoulders sagged with released tension. "Meg will pick up my car later. Should I take a taxi?"

"I'll get you a car and driver on the firm's account." Veronica nodded, satisfied. "No one will see you leave here. In the meantime, let's get to why I called you in. I've spoken to the judge who's willing to rule on a no contest divorce based on the circumstances: the fact that you are waving your rights to any marital assets in question, and that there has been no contact between both parties for almost a decade. This should work. Angus will have a chance to respond obviously. But if he doesn't respond within a few weeks, or with sufficient reason not to grant you the divorce, then the judge will sign the decree, and you'll be free."

"And we don't have to go into the past?" I affirmed. That had been my biggest fear that we'd end up in a trial, and I'd be forced to relive everything that happened, or worse, people wouldn't believe me. I had hardly any documentation of what had been my reality. The only evidence was I'd escaped with the help of a women's shelter that technically didn't exist and couldn't corroborate my story and risk exposing themselves. That and the scar on my ribs and X-rays that showed a lot more.

"No. No reliving the past," she confirmed.

A sob broke past my lips. "Shit. Sorry."

Veronica passed a box of tissues within her reach.

"Th-thank you. I'm sorry, I didn't realize tears were so close to the surface."

"You had a shock just now and were rightly fearful. Now you've heard good news. This is all normal emotional processing. Crying is good. You're going to be okay."

I sniffled a laugh, embarrassed. "Did you ever consider being a therapist before being a lawyer?"

"Honestly? Yes. But in this field of law, I get to do both." She smiled.

I returned it, but her promise I was going to be okay pinged about the room not landing. She couldn't promise me that. No one could. No one who knew Angus would ever promise me that either.

FIFTEEN

I waited to meet Meg and Sue in the evening sun at a restaurant in Saint Paul clear on the other side of town from the *trattoria*, so I didn't bump into Evan. I'd also chosen this location because I needed to talk about him, and I didn't want to have this conversation at home in case the walls were not quite as thick as I'd thought. On a whim I called Josie and briefly filled her in on what had transpired in the conversation between Lilian and me about Evan. I decided not to bring up my weird episode with maybe, maybe not, being followed this afternoon.

"Like a sexual menu?" Josie asked, her voice clear across the line from America.

"I don't know," I wailed in a half whisper.

"Start at the beginning."

I'd called Josie because I needed real girl talk in a way I couldn't have with Meg and Sue since they'd be working with Evan next year. When she first answered, I'd waited the requisite amount of time for her to tell me Xavier was there so I didn't blow the surprise, but when she didn't mention him, I realized maybe she hadn't seen him yet. What was taking him so long, I had no idea. "It kind of became clear Evan and Lilian may have been together before and—"

"Wait, hold up. Your boss at the gallery and Evan?" Josie demanded. "When?"

I grimaced as the little jealousy monster leapt onto my shoulder, trying to get my attention. "I don't know."

"How do you feel about that?"

"Fine. Of course. It's fine. Why wouldn't it be?"

Josie was quiet.

"Okay, I don't know how I feel about it," I admitted.

"But not great, I'm assuming."

I ran a finger around the base of my water glass, catching the condensation. "I—I don't feel like analyzing it, to be honest."

"Okay. So, go on."

"So, *then*—I couldn't help myself—I asked her if it was good." I cringed, my cheeks heating with mortification.

"Wow, Andrea. Bold. Didn't know you had it in you."

"Ha, me neither. And that's when she said it was like a menu you wish you didn't know existed. Or something like that."

Jose squeaked. "Holy shit. I didn't think Evan had sexual adventure in him. Or maybe it just never occurred to me."

"Of course it didn't. You were caught up in a haze of sexual tension with my boss." I laughed. "What's the latest with that, anyway?" I asked, hedging to buy myself a second out of the hot seat.

She sighed. "Ugh. It's too complicated to discuss. I have to move on. I know I do. But it's so damn hard. Enough about that though. Let's get back to the menu."

I covered my eyes with my free hand and wished I could tell her Xavier was on the way to win her back. "I honestly don't know what to make of Lilian's comment. And now I can't stop thinking about it. Why did she have to tell me that?"

"Duh. You asked her." Josie was amused.

Lowering my voice, I added, "I've had this stupid, stupid, crush on him ever since you put the dumb idea in my head."

"Hey, I saw what I saw. And you've had that crush longer than a few months. Maybe I had heart-eyes due to my own condition, but the chemistry was hard to miss. And it wasn't new."

"Well, he's never given any indication to me I'm more than an annoying job to him."

"Yet," she paused, "he's moved in next door to you."

"His explanation is plausible. Sort of. Plumbing. Floors. Parents. Blah blah." It wasn't, and we both knew it.

"Andrea. I love you, girl, and I know you've been out of the game for a while. But I'm telling you, him being next door is no coincidence. Of all the tiny French villages in all of Southern France. You know I'm telling the truth. That man wants in your pants."

"But don't you think that's also slightly stalkerish?"

"Do you find him threatening?"

"To my sanity? Yes."

"Physically."

In so many ways I found him physically threatening. What if he touched me and I froze, like I had the night with Christian? Evan was so warm and fiery, and I was cold and frigid. And especially after what I'd heard from Lilian, I was probably far too uptight. He'd probably scoff at me and walk out the door.

But that was too much to share, so I told Josie what she was expecting to hear. "That too." I laughed. It was brittle.

"Not *that* kind of physical. I mean do you think he could do you harm physically?"

I inhaled. "Never. No. Of course not. He'd never." My pulse quickened.

"Look, let's say I'm wrong about him being attracted to you—if I know Evan, and true I probably don't know him as well as you—he's been looking out for you for a long time. Now you've suddenly resigned and up and moved, and he probably doesn't know how to stop looking out for you. And, I'm just saying, but that's a lot of effort to go to for someone you don't deeply care about."

I pressed my lips together. "We're ... friends?" I offered feebly. What Josie was saying made sense. There was caring, and then there was ... caring.

"Why don't you just talk to him?" she asked, her tone gentling. "Find out what he's thinking?"

"I have. Kind of."

"You have? And?"

"And ... actually I didn't really ask him what *he* was thinking. I told him to leave me alone. I—I just, I'm enjoying feeling independent. At least I was until I freaked out a little in town today. But that was probably nothing. I haven't felt this free in so long. I don't want him knowing my every move. And I don't want to be a job to him." I glanced around to make sure I was still not being overheard. "Also, how do I get over the feelings when he's right next-freaking-door? I thought I wouldn't have to see him anymore."

"Maybe you don't get over them."

"What?" I squeaked. "You're no help at all."

She laughed and then sobered. "I'm saying this as someone who is currently living with a bunch of regrets. And I'm saying this to you, someone who knows how precious time is. You want to date again, right?"

I nodded, though she couldn't see me. I did *want* to date again. Technically. I'd seen enough movies and read enough books to know that real love on my terms might be possible. But what if it was all made up? And what if I ... *couldn't.*

"And you're nervous about taking those first intimate steps again." It was like she was in my head.

"I am," I whispered. I'd confided in Josie when she'd been here this last summer just how long it had been since I'd been with anyone. It was a long, long time.

"You trust Evan. And he's right there, looking out for you. And he's apparently in possession of the secret specials menu. And you like him. Why don't you ask him to be that for you?"

My insides dropped away. "Be what, exactly?"

"To be your new first. Your practice round before you date for real. A dating coach. Your bodyguard with benefits. I don't know—call it what you want. But who wouldn't want to make sure their first foray into dating life was ... satisfying?"

I opened and closed my mouth. The walls of the little village suddenly felt really close. The evening sun too hot. My fingers were tight around my phone and losing feeling. I couldn't tell her I'd sort of tried to cross the line with him the night she and I went out clubbing, and that he'd made it clear he was *not* open to that. But that was then. Maybe if I pled my case? God, no. If he said no again ...

"You there?" Josie asked.

Since I couldn't feel my body, it was debatable. Was this what disassociation felt like? I took a deep breath and tried to pull my stomach back to my body. I wiggled my fingers not holding the phone and toes in my cute flat strappy sandals.

"Yeah. I'm here."

"I didn't mean to shock you. But after what little you shared with me about your ex and how long it's been, if you're really determined to get out there and date again, you're going to need to start slow and with someone you trust."

I pressed my lips together.

"Right?" Josie encouraged.

"Hmm."

"It doesn't hurt that he's hot as hell and cares about your well-being, or that he's apparently good in bed."

My gaze, which had been unfocused on the edge of the wall of a stone building in my line of sight, suddenly sharpened as Meg and Sue rounded the corner and came into sharp relief.

And right behind them, dressed in a tight black t-shirt and made-for-him dark jeans, Evan.

"Shit. I have to go. He's here," I whispered. "I love you. And you're crazy. And I can't believe you just said all that. And I'm going to call you tomorrow and berate you. But right now I have to hang up. Gah! Bye!"

Josie laughed down the other end. "Tell him I said hi."

I mashed the end button and plastered a smile on my face toward Meg and Sue, deliberately ignoring Evan.

"Look who we found!" crowed Meg, indicating behind her. "Obviously we had to drag him along. It's Friday night and he has no plans."

Standing, I gave the girls each a hug. I nodded at Evan. "Hi."

"No hug for me?" His lip curled up on the left, and he stepped toward me.

I blinked, chagrined. There was no way I couldn't. "Of course," I managed overly loud and pressed in.

His arm slid around my waist and pulled me tight against him for a split second that was over before I could appreciate the hard lines of his body he'd just imprinted on me. Screw Josie. My body was all messed up now and firing off weird uncomfortable signals. Heat crested up my neck to my cheeks and then raced back down to the core of my belly. Evan never hugged me.

My throat was lodged closed, and I somehow managed to step back around the table and sink into my seat without landing on my ass.

Sue was staring at me expectantly. Meg quizzically. I shook my head as I belatedly realized one of them had asked something, "Sorry, what?"

"I said have you ordered any drinks yet?"

"Oh. No. No. Just water."

I glanced over at Evan, who'd sat down opposite me and was now wearing a shit-eating grin, his hazel eyes sparkling green in the evening glow. "What?" I grumbled. Did he know where my head was? Impossible. There was no way I could do what Josie suggested. I snapped my gaze away from him as his lips broke into a blinding smile. I was about to internally combust into a puff of smoke just sitting here. I had to pull it together. Had to.

"Let's get a bottle of rosé," Meg suggested as the waiter

showed up. She looked up at him. "Do you have that Post Malone Rosé?"

"*Mademoiselle?*" The waiter, nonplussed, frowned and looked helplessly around the table.

Evan was still staring at me when I glanced back at him, but he answered the waiter. "It's called *Maison Neuf*. Maison Nine," he clarified to the waiter, his eyes never leaving me. "Post Malone bought a vineyard."

"So, who were you chatting with?" Meg asked me, breaking the odd stare off.

"Oh, uh, Josie. You didn't meet her. She was Dauphine's nanny over the summer."

"The American, right?" asked Sue.

I nodded.

"Jeez, of all the boats I've been on, I've never found a boss worth shtupping and ruining my career for." Sue laughed.

"Hey." Meg glared at her.

"Not that I would. Jeez. I'm a professional. I was just joking." Sue glanced at Meg and then Evan. "Honest."

The waiter arrived with the bottle and tension eased.

He let Evan taste the wine.

I couldn't drag my eyes away as I watched him swirl, inhale, and taste. Not in an obnoxious way, but simply to know it wasn't corked. I could almost sense the cool liquid slipping down his throat, his Adam's apple punching out and informing the journey. His skin was smooth and stubbled. If he didn't shave, his beard would reach almost to his neck. I liked beards, but I liked Evan's jaw and neck more. And his collar bones. I liked those too.

A foot nudged me under the table, and Evan spoke, snapping my eyes back up to his.

My cheeks burned. Caught.

"So, how is she?" he asked.

The waiter had poured each of us a glass of wine. I'd totally missed it. Luckily Meg and Sue were having some kind of stare off and hadn't seen me staring at Evan.

"Fine," I said. "She says hi to you."

"You say anything?"

I narrowed my eyes at him. "What?" Oh, he meant that Xavier had gone to get Josie back. "No. Obviously. Though I don't know what's taking so long."

"He wants to do it right, I'd guess."

Meg and Sue glanced between us. "Who are we talking about?"

"He loves her. She loves him," I answered Evan with a quick apologetic glance at Sue for ignoring her question. "What is there to get right?"

"I think you of all people know things are rarely that simple," Evan responded cryptically.

"Well, they should be," I said, only realizing how those words related to me after they'd left my mouth. Ugh. I really regretted calling Josie.

"Hear, hear," Meg said, raising her glass. "Don't know who you are talking about. But if two people like each other, they should just go for it. Life's too short." She winked at me, and I narrowed my eyes at her, which made her laugh.

Sue huffed but raised her glass. They clinked, and I reluctantly raised my glass and tried to avoid Evan's gaze as we all clinked and took a sip.

I'd thought tonight would be a good distraction, but it was going to be the longest evening in history with Evan sitting across from me with those ridiculous muscles and smirky mouth. Not to mention the weird vibe with Meg and Sue. I gulped down another larger sip, avoiding Evan's probing gaze.

"Oh, before I forget. Here are your keys." Meg fished them out of her purse and dangled them in my direction. "For your abandoned car. You better spill that story, girlfriend. You have a boozy lunch today or something?"

Shit. Not in front of Evan. I grabbed the keys. "Thank you." Evan didn't miss the exchange, or my reaction, and I sensed his immediate shift into control freak. "Damn," I deflected, pointedly looking at my glass. "Post Malone knows how to do it. I think we better order another bottle."

SIXTEEN

"What the hell was that?" Evan growled as soon as Meg and Sue excused themselves to go to the ladies room. "You abandoned your car today? What happened? Are you okay? Why didn't you call me?" He'd spent the last forty minutes trying to catch my eye during our conversations. By some miracle, Meg had dropped the question as I kept her engaged with question after question regarding everything about her life when she didn't have her mouth full of baguette or appetizers. I'd even agreed to shots, which I'd downed happily and Evan had declined.

"That was black belt level conversational avoidance," he added, telling me I'd been utterly transparent. "I think I know more about her upbringing than my own."

"I'm surprised," I snapped back. "You usually know whether someone picked their nose in middle school with the kind of background you pull."

Evan sat back, apparently stung.

I blew out a breath. "Sorry. Truly. I'm just tense."

"*Are* you sorry though or is that how you really see me? Do you think I want to know shit for my own sick curiosity?"

"No. No, I know you don't." I paused. " I don't know. Wait, do you?"

He shook his head with a huff. "Unbelievable. There's damn sure a lot I wish I didn't know." He paused. "And a whole lot of shit I wish I did. Like why you're so tense for example. I can see something is bothering you. And I'm praying it's not the simple act of *me* sitting here."

My gaze found his, and the browns and greens swirled like autumn leaves. He was hurt, and he was letting me see it. He never let me see it. My chest caved in response. "Evan—"

He inhaled at the sound in my tone.

I let my wineglass go and squeezed the bridge of my nose with my finger and thumb.

After today, I knew I needed him. I needed him and I didn't want to. I was going to have to tell him everything and ask for help and hope he didn't see my ridiculous attraction to him. Or worse, try to act on it only for my insecurities to smack him down and ruin every ounce of friendship we might be able to salvage when all this was said and done. I took a deep breath. "I—I think I was followed today." Exhaling at the relief of giving voice and giving in, I fluttered my eyes open to see he'd leaned forward. Outwardly casually, his elbow on the table, every muscle group on his body was instantly vibrating with tension as he slowly and nonchalantly glanced toward every part of the restaurant and village he could see. "When?" he asked, his voice low.

"I went to see my lawyer today. After I parked, I walked

toward the building and I ... I just felt it. It was probably nothing—"

"It wasn't nothing."

I gave a tired laugh. "Yeah, my lawyer said the same thing. How everyone expects my instincts to be working when I've been so led astray before is laughable."

"How did you get back?"

"My lawyer ordered a car. They have a back exit. Meg went and picked up my keys."

Evan gave a quick glance to see Meg and Sue were on their way back. He leaned forward. "Look at me," he whispered.

I dragged my gaze to his and was enveloped in his concern and his strength, and suddenly I didn't know why I'd been batting him down. I wanted to stay here in this look. It was safe here. I swallowed heavily, my insides melting away.

"You and I are talking tonight," he rumbled, words coming quickly in the mere seconds we had left alone. His tone brooked no argument. "When we leave here, you are going to show them around your place and then say good night, and then," he paused, "then you are going to unlock that door between us."

My throat closed, and my chest heaved. I didn't think he meant that to sound so fucking sexy, or imply so much, but my underwear melted off in that very second.

I blinked, embarrassed, knowing my cheeks were probably giving me away and somehow managed a nod before plastering a smile on my face for Meg and Sue. "That was some bathroom gossip. You guys were gone forever!" I chirped. Inside, my pulse was pounding, and I tried to steady my breathing that had somehow forgotten the rhythm of keeping me alive. It was exactly the kind of high-handedness I'd said I hated. And yet ...

"Yeah, well," said Sue. "We were placing bets on you two hooking up."

"Sue!" Meg snapped.

Sue giggled and hiccupped. "Oops. I guess that wine went straight to my head."

I couldn't look at Evan. I couldn't. "Don't be ridiculous," I said loud and weird. "I'm not his type."

"Huh." Evan's voice was amused. "And out of interest, what would be my type?"

I shrugged, looking anywhere but at him as my mind scrambled. It latched onto Lilian. "Tall, statuesque, dark-haired art curators who can skewer people with a stiletto or a well-timed look."

"That's oddly specific," mused Sue, and I glared at her.

"And sounds oddly jealous," added Evan. "You been talking about me at work, Sunflower?"

"What? Don't be ridiculous."

"Aw, he even has a pet name for you," Meg cooed.

"He doesn't—he's never. Never mind. This is stupid." I tossed my napkin down, ready to leave them to it. I couldn't do this tonight. It was good natured teasing, and I knew there was no malicious intent, but it was too close to the bone. Or I was too raw.

Sensing my fight or flight gathering for the latter, Evan jumped in. "Ah, let it go, ladies. Andrea's had a bit of a day. Anyway, she's probably right. I do have a thing for brunettes and stilettos." He laughed and poured more wine into our glasses.

Meg covered hers and indicated to Sue. "No thanks. I'm driving this fool back to port."

I knew he was taking the heat off me, but there was truth to his statement and the taste was bitter. I practically lived in flat boat shoes for four to six months out of the year. Right now I was in flat sandals. Smiling wide to hide the sting, I clinked glasses with Sue. "Lush," I chided brightly.

Then the four of us chatted about plans for the winter and latest shows to binge now that we had time. Before I knew it, I was sucking down water to sober up and we paid the check.

"Come on, I want to see your place." Sue hiccupped.

"Nope, no way, babe," Meg said. "We are going straight to the car and going home. We gotta get you into bed. You can see Andrea's place another time."

Relief swept through me. The secret of Evan being next door was hidden a bit longer. "Yes, let's do it another day. It's late."

We all walked back through the village. Well, Evan, Meg, and I walked. Sue leaned heavily on Meg. I said goodbye at the corner before my street and promised another get-together.

"Wait here a sec or walk slowly" Evan told Meg and Sue. "I'll walk you to your car. Let me just make sure Andrea gets into her place."

"I'm fine," I argued.

Evan gave me a look, so I turned and walked down the street and around the bend to my little house. The wine had made me fuzzy, and I fumbled the front door keys. Evan's warm hand closed over mine and gently took them. He unlocked the door and slipped in ahead of me. "Wait a minute," he said, leaving me with his spice and cedar scent as he melted into the darkness.

I felt for the light switch along the rough stucco wall.

Finally reaching it, I flipped on the lights just as he materialized down the stairs from my bedroom.

"You're all clear," he said.

"You can see in the dark," I mumbled. I was really tired, and I'd definitely had too much wine. And Evan had just been in my bedroom. "Like a cat."

"All right, Sunflower. You're drooping. You need to go to bed."

I touched my finger to my hairline in a salute. "Aye, aye, Captain."

He stopped in front of me and took my hand away from my forehead before leaning in and replacing my fingers with his lips. It was over before I could process it.

He'd just had his mouth on my skin.

Then he was past me.

But he turned back and my breath caught. "For the record," he whispered, "I've seen you in stilettos, and it fucking killed me. Lock up." And then he was gone, the front door closed between us.

I turned back and sank against it, heart pounding, head light. My chest rose and fell in rapid breaths as his words replayed in my head, my body lit up like he'd just struck a match.

What had he just said? What did that mean?

That had been clear, right? Unless I misheard or misread. Was he saying he might be attracted to me? Now? After all this time?

Ahead of me, the thick wood door between the units screamed at me. He'd told me to unlock it, and my mind had immediately gone sexual. But I'd had a lot of wine. There was no way I had the guts to do anything with Evan, not after the last time. But what if I wasn't misreading anything?

If I opened that door, was I inviting him into my bed? How did I know what *he* would read into? I needed him close. I knew that. I trusted no one else to look out for me. I trusted no one else, period. That tiny gesture of quickly casing my place before I entered and not making a big deal of it, now made my eyes prick. I couldn't mess up that trust. But if he and I ... I swallowed heavily, my limbs weakening ... if he touched me and I freaked out, or if something went really wrong between us, would he still be there looking out for me? He didn't do relationships, just hookups. I didn't know what I was capable of handling.

The door beckoned again. Just knowing he was staying next door for sure would bring me comfort. It would be enough. Then I could close the door back up before he got back, and he would have to understand my boundaries.

Checking the time, I figured I had mere minutes until he was back from walking Meg and Sue down to Sue's car. I locked my front door behind me and hurried to the kitchen drawer, yanking out the iron key and telling myself I simply wanted to see for myself he was really living next door.

SEVENTEEN

Evan

WALKING BACK into the village from the lower parking area, I detour toward François' *tabac*. It's closed obviously, but I know he lives upstairs. As I cross the cobblestones and approach the small red door to the right of the shop front, I smell the sweet scent and see the glow of a small cigarillo. "*Il est tard,*" I say as I make out his form sitting in the doorway on the stone steps. It's late.

"He was here," François says to me in French. "He didn't stay long, just a few minutes, but he was here."

There was a second at dinner where I hoped the gut feeling Andrea had in town was simply Pete watching her. But I've already checked with him, and now I'm glad I've listened to my own instincts. So Angus had obviously watched the car and followed Meg up here. He may not have seen Andrea yet. He may have concluded it was Meg's car that Andrea borrowed, and so he was temporarily off her trail. But that wouldn't last long.

I had to hand it to Andrea's lawyer, and Andrea. She must have done her best to act cool. No wonder she's so on edge tonight. I admire—no, I fucking adore—her independent streak. She's no damsel. But dammit if I wish she would just let me take care of her for once in her goddamn life.

Today could have ended differently.

The reckoning is coming.

I just have to make sure to intercept the son of a bitch first. And find out how Pete missed it.

Angus may not have stayed long. But he'll be back. "That's a problem."

"*Oui.*" François crinkles his brown eyes, and they disappear under his bushy eyebrows. "What do you want me to do?"

"Just this. For now. He'll be back." I ask for François' phone and program in my number, not trusting he's done that already. "Text me the moment you see him anywhere. Even if it looks innocent. And especially if you see them together. Even if it looks fine, it isn't."

"*Je comprends.*" He nods his understanding. Then he fumbles about in the breast pocket of his beige lightweight evening coat after putting his phone away. "Cigarillo?" he offers after a moment, and I realize I haven't moved yet.

I know she's back there waiting for me, and I asked her to unlock her door tonight, and, fuck, I'd been blatant with that comment about her in stilettos. I need to get myself together. Her life is in danger, and I've almost gotten myself completely distracted from her situation by *her*. That moment earlier at the table when I'd commanded her to leave the door open for me tonight, and I watched her eyes dilate and her skin flush—I hadn't realized what I was implying until I saw her reaction.

I scrape a hand down my face.

I haven't spontaneously gotten as hard as fast since my fifth form French teacher forgot a button on her blouse and leaned over to help me with my conjugations. I'd gotten a close-up view down her perfect cleavage and her stunningly smooth skin. Madame Robin. Damn that was a crush and a half. Memories. But nothing compared to the raging situation that happened in that moment at dinner tonight. I'd turned Andrea on. I now have first-hand knowledge, and I can't fucking get it out of my head. But worse was the sudden fear that flooded her eyes as soon as she felt it. Angus is lucky he isn't still here.

François gestures again to the cigarillos in his hand. He must wonder what I want, standing here like a fool.

"No. Thank you." I wave his offer away. "That shit will kill you," I add in French, causing him to let out a wheezing, guttural laugh.

I chuckle too.

He wipes his eyes after a few seconds.

"You win tonight?" I ask, nodding toward the square and the *boules* pit.

"I win every night."

I smirk. "Of course you do."

I bid him goodnight and trudge up the steep cobbled incline. The village is quiet and peaceful. A few stray cats dart in and out of shadows. The peace is an illusion, now that I know Angus will be here soon. Somehow I need to persuade Andrea to go somewhere with me. I know she has this job with Lilian now, but the days are numbered for how safe a location that will be too.

I don't know what the end goal is to get her safe. If Angus doesn't stop, how far I'll go to stop *him* is a question Pete posed to me just yesterday. I didn't answer. I couldn't. And today I can categorically say, there is no limit. The idea of that piece of shit going anywhere near her again is untenable. But I'm no judge and jury, and I've never taken anyone's life that wasn't under direct orders from the Crown.

And now my entire existence is being narrowed down to this one choice, that may not even *be* a choice, and I don't want to be a murderer.

~

I CLOSE my front door behind me and immediately know she's been in here. My eyes go straight to the door locked tight between our units. Before turning on the lights, I close my eyes and breathe in, trying to pull out the gentle notes of vanilla and a light floral—like a batch of fresh baked cookies left on a blanket after a lazy picnic in a sunny field of wildflowers. And under that something deeper, more womanly. I've never considered myself a smell person, and she wears it so subtly most people might not notice. But I've been cataloguing her scent for almost a decade, and now I'm so attuned to it, I crave it. I can tell in seconds when she's been in a cabin on the boat before me. And I know now she came in here. Did she want to wait for me or was she just curious?

I asked her to leave the door open and she didn't. I'm disappointed, but I get it. She's not sure what I meant by it. I need to convince her she's safe with me and keep my damn hands to myself. No more kisses on the forehead and weird suggestive comments. I don't know what came over me tonight. I need to let her know about Angus, but that means coming clean about having eyes on her. She'll be mad. But I need her to know. Pete was supposed to have been watching the law office, and he apologized profusely over text that he missed Angus today. He's sending two guys up tonight, one for each gate access to the village. I have to hand it to Andrea, she picked a great place to defend.

I pull out my phone and text her:

You okay? I'm back.

Three dots pop up and disappear. Then pop up again.

Andrea: *I'm fine. Good night.*

I sigh and text her back.

I'm aware the door is closed and locked. I know you have good reason for that. Can you come down and open it so we can talk face to face for a few minutes?

Andrea: *I don't think that's a good idea.*

I mash my lips together in frustration. My stupid comments tonight have muddied everything.

I know you don't. And that's my fault. Please. I need to apologize and explain in person.

Andrea: *You really don't.*

After I'm done talking you can close the door again. I promise. I walk to the door in question and lean my head against it, staring at my phone.

Andrea: *If you're going to take back the things you said tonight, don't.*

My stomach hollows.

Andrea: *Maybe you didn't mean them. It was just the moment.*

Andrea: *But for a second, I remembered what it was like to feel stuff like that again. I felt beautiful and desired and not in a way that I knew would lead to pain. And I'd like to keep that. Just for tonight. Tomorrow we can move on.*

Holy fuck. My breath comes out shallow, and my groin tightens. I don't know how to play this. She's never been this open with me. It's probably the wine and the feeling of safety behind a screen. But knowing I made her feel that and she likes it is making my chest tight and my stomach drop.

I spin around and put my back to the door and slide down to the floor.

Sunflower, I text. Then I don't know what else to say, so I hit send.

Andrea: *Don't.*
Please open the door.
Andrea: *I can't.*

I blow out a breath and lean my head against the thick wood.

You can keep those words forever, Sunflower. I meant them. But I know they scare you. I'm sorry for that only. You are safe with me, I promise. I'm here for you. Right now, I'm here to keep you safe. If you feel safer with this door closed I'll honor it. And I'd never see you opening it as an invitation to anything more than letting me keep my promise.

There's no response.

I text again. *And I know that it kills you to ask for help. That's why I'm doing it without you asking. Because I WANT TO. You know it's no coincidence I'm next door. I crossed a line.*

And I'm sorry for that too. You know I'm not good at not being in control. But I'm trying. I expect you to keep telling me if I cross any more lines.

After a while, when there's no response, I realize she might have fallen asleep. Maybe she'll see my words tomorrow. She's safe here tonight. But tomorrow I'll come clean about Angus being in the village and help her figure out what to do and where to go. And if she doesn't want me with her, then so be it. I pull myself up off the floor and head to the bathroom to take care of business and brush my teeth. I grab a quick shower and wrap a towel around my waist before exiting the bathroom and—

"Shit!" I jerk in surprise at the silhouette in the open doorway. Her golden hair is down, her t-shirt only reaches her thighs, her legs carve a glorious shape in the near darkness. She's shaking, and I'm immediately right in front of her. "You okay? What happened?" I want to pull her into my arms, but I'm all skin. She steps back immediately anyway, and I inwardly curse.

I can see her eyes drinking in every available inch of my damp skin, and I grit my teeth, not wanting to call her out and embarrass her, but shit, I can feel it in every cell of my body. That hunger. "You okay?" I croak. I grow lightheaded as my blood rushes south. I clear my throat, one hand coming to the knot of my towel to keep it from being dislodged by the growing situation. "Baby, what's wrong? Please answer."

Her eyes snap to mine and she shakes her head. "Did you just call me, baby?"

My throat is thick. "Yeah. Sorry." My other hand comes to the back of my neck. "That was ... it just came out. Sorry."

She starts to laugh and all the coiled tension snaps and dissipates, leaving me disoriented. "Holy shit," she says. "I—can you go put on a shirt or something? Or," she shakes her head as if to clear it, "never mind. I'm going to go to bed. After today," her smile fades, "the scare. I'm too tired and buzzed to talk. Not even sure what we were supposed to talk about. And everything feels weird tonight. But I just thought maybe the door would be better open. Not to go through." She glares. "Just open. So when you asked, and I said I can't, like I literally couldn't, because I dropped the key earlier and it slid under the fridge. And now I've just done a freaking workout to get it, and, ugh, I think there were mouse droppings. Gross. And anyway, door's open now. Happy?"

Goddamn, but she's adorable. I burst out laughing.

I should tell her now about her ex, I think. But she's flushed and amused and kind of adorably drunk. And right now she feels safe. She should get one night's full sleep in her sweet little village house before I break the news to her. The door is open now, so I'll hear anything that threatens her. Tomorrow, I need to figure out how to get her away from here without freaking her out.

"Just open," I agree.

"Great," she says.

"Great."

She backs up and starts to slip around the corner of the stone stairs. Her feet are bare, and I bet the stone makes them cold. I wonder if she'd be the type to sneak her icy toes between my calves to warm them up in bed. I wonder if I'd like it.

"Hey," she says. "Thank you."

"For what?" I ask.

"I'd never have felt safe having all those drinks tonight without you there. You're a good friend."

Friends. Jesus Christ.

She disappears around the corner. "Night, Evan."

I let go of my towel and clutch the door frame until my knuckles are white. The towel eventually falls, and I just stand there, still ragingly hard, with nothing but darkness as my witness, and just fucking own it.

I want her. And I'm terrified that when all this is said and done, I'm going to lose her.

EIGHTEEN

Andrea

AN EARLY MORNING sunbeam skewered my wine migraine into the inside of my skull. I'd forgotten to close the blinds Marianne had warned me about. I groaned and rolled over, pulling my pillow over my head.

Next to me, my phone buzzed. I made a small peek-a-boo space and cracked open one eye to fumble for the device. Meg and Sue were bad influences. But Evan had been there. Warm, fuzzy, and vaguely concerning tendrils wound through me as I tried to catch snippets of talking to him. There was something …

My phone buzzed again in my hand. I gingerly pulled the pillow off my head and scowled at the screen out of one eye. I mistyped my code twice. Of course my phone pretended not to recognize me, judgmental little jerk.

There were two texts from Marianne, my landlady. The time read seven-thirty in the morning on a Saturday. Thinking something must be wrong, I blinked and tried to sit up, my head almost falling off my shoulders. I wasn't used to drinking so much, and I definitely hadn't had nearly enough water yesterday. With that in mind, I braced on an elbow and fumbled for my water bottle on my bedside table, putting my phone down. Taking several long guzzling gulps, I blinked and sat up finally, taking several deep breaths.

Sunflower.

Suddenly everything came back to me. Evan ordering me to keep the door open, him kissing my forehead. Oh my God. I bring my hand up to it. He kissed my forehead. He'd never done that in all the time I'd known him. And then he had said another thing I couldn't remember, but that had my chest burning and butterflies launching in my belly. And I'd texted him. Oh no. I grabbed for my phone, bypassed the texts from Marianne, and read my exchange with Evan, heart pounding.

What had I said? My eyes scanned my words.

God. I'd totally laid myself bare, pathetically grateful of his few drops of attention he'd paid me that had obviously been done to make me feel better and fluff up my ego. I groaned in mortification. And he'd responded that he would never see me opening the door as an invitation. Of course he wouldn't.

And I'd been ridiculously jumpy from my visit to the lawyer and getting that weird vibe, which had probably been a total false alarm, and I'd overreacted by asking Meg to drive my car home. Honestly, I had really embarrassed myself yesterday.

My heart sank as I relived the forehead kiss. It was obviously his way of making sure we stayed in the friend zone. Why kiss me on the forehead when my lips were right freaking there? Unless I'd totally misread everything, which I clearly had. His mixed messages always left me so off-kilter, no wonder I was always so snappy with him.

I allowed myself a minute more of self-flagellation and then erased the text chain so I didn't have to relive Evan's kind and pitying words. God. I was so pathetic. It could have been worse though. I could have actually told him how attracted to him I was. Thank God I hadn't gone that far. An image of his bare chest, water droplets beading on his skin seared the backs of my eyelids as I closed my eyes. He'd just gotten out of the shower. Jesus. He was so fit. I'd probably looked like I was in heat when I saw him. He still hadn't acted on it.

I opened my eyes again. How on earth would I face him today?

Marianne. Landlady. Probably an emergency. Focus.

I clicked on Marianne's text.

Marianne: *New friend! You say you want to go hiking. The weather is parfait! Cyril and I go to the Verdon Gorge to hike and camp out tonight. It will be fun! We have extra tent and sleeping bag. Just bring water, snacks, and a change of clothes. And good shoes for walking. Yes?*

Marianne: *some others may join us. We will take care of food and drinks. We will pick you up in one hour! You must not say no!*

My body had never felt less like hiking or camping, but the idea of disappearing and not having to face Evan today was too much of a divine miracle to pass up.

I texted back. *Thank you for inviting me! See you in an hour. I'll meet you at the village gate?*

Marianne: *Wahoo! Yes, meet at the bottom gate.*

Smiling and proud of myself for having plans, I gingerly

pulled myself out of bed. Now I just had to close that door downstairs so Evan didn't see me before I could get out of the village.

～

DOWNSTAIRS, only that open door was now evidence of my encounter with Evan. I tiptoed over and peered in. His bed was made and the bathroom door was open. He wasn't here. I sighed with relief and closed our mutual door, reaching for the key in the lock, only to find it missing. I vaguely remembered losing the key under the fridge last night, but where would I have put it after I found it? Had I found it?

Fine, it could stay unlocked. As long as it was closed.

After breakfast and coffee, I hurriedly put some snacks and a couple of water bottles in a backpack. I threw in a flashlight, my travel toiletries kit, and bug spray. I'd dressed in yoga pants, a t-shirt and sunscreen. My shoes weren't marketed for hiking, but they were sturdy running shoes and would work perfectly. I tied a hoodie around my waist in case it got cooler this evening and then sunglasses on my head and locked up and headed to Albert's for a coffee.

Only Albert's was closed with a sign on the door that he was taking a month off. My shoulders sagged, and my eyes prickled. Poor Albert deserved a holiday, and I was being a hungover, self-pitying fool. Of course now it meant I had to share a coffee shop with Evan. I huffed.

Squaring my shoulders, I trudged down the sloped cobblestone streets toward the bottom gate. François' coffee shop was more convenient for today, anyway, I assured myself. The air was fresh and cool, the sky cloudless and wildly blue. It was going to be a scorcher for autumn, and probably too hot to hike, but I would push on rather than spend a weekend with Evan and that door unlocked between us, having to pretend I hadn't just let him see my weird and lonely, desperate self.

∼

COFFEE IN HAND, I stopped dead outside the village gates as I saw Marianne, and I was assuming, her boyfriend, Cyril. But I didn't even have a chance to get a look at her boyfriend because Evan was standing there chatting with them dressed in green combat trousers and a fitted white t-shirt and a military-issue backpack. *No.*

No.

He handed Marianne and Cyril a small cooler bag that was at his feet, and his pack, which had a tent bag and rolled up sleeping bag attached, and they were chatting and laughing.

Nope. No. No way. I'd text Marianne and cancel as soon as I slipped back out of sight.

And then Marianne waved at me. "Andrea!" she called, a big smile on her face. "Come and meet Cyril and his cousin, Frédéric."

Frédéric? There was someone else in the tiny car, who was climbing out. Everyone turned toward me, and I stood stock still, coffee in hand.

I was guessing Frédéric was my plus one, and maybe Evan was just lending them some gear. That had to be it. Frédéric was wearing a sleeveless tank, rolled up jean shorts, and had a strange little mustache to go with his small round orange tinted glasses.

Putting one foot in front of the other, I approached. "Good morning." I held my hand out to Cyril, who I noted had shoulder length hair and the same little mustache as his cousin but for some reason could pull it off. "Nice to meet you."

He shook my hand. "*Enchanté*. This is my cousin." He motioned to the smaller man next to him, and I dutifully shook his hand too. He had a sweet face and friendly smile, and I was zero percent attracted to him.

"Nice to meet you," I repeated. "Morning, Marianne. Thank you for the invite."

"Morning, Sunflower," Evan said from beside me, his eyes hidden behind those dark aviator sunglasses he always favored.

"You lending us some gear?" I asked, flipping my own shades down over my eyes to hide from him.

"*Au contraire*. I'm coming with you."

Marianne clapped her hands together. "Yes, *fantastique*. Now it's good because you can ride with Evan on his bike, and we have room for everything in the car."

"His what now?"

"Ahh, *c'est magnifique*," Cyril crooned from beside a gleaming mass of death and shiny metal.

"Um. I don't think so." This was Evan's? "I'll just drive my own car."

"*Non, Non*," said Marianne. "The parking at the trail is very difficult. We must hurry anyway. This is better."

Cyril gesticulated and garbled something in French to Marianne that sounded like he'd ride with Evan, to which Marianne elbowed him and muttered with irritation and an eye roll and gestured to their car. "Come. *On y va.*" Then she winked at me as they climbed into the tiny Peugeot.

This day was shaping up to be the worst day for a hangover in history.

"Were you going to tell me you arranged a damned double date today?" Evan growled from next to me.

"I didn't—what?" I spun to face him. "What in the hell are you doing here anyway?"

"What does it look like? Apparently I'm going on a hike and then camping out."

"Well, enjoy it, because I'm not going." I spun around. Then I spun back. "Were you invited, or did you volunteer?"

His jaw ticked, and his nostrils flared slightly. He reached up and slid his shades partway down the bridge of his nose, skewering me with those swirling hazel eyes. "What do *you* think? Goddamn it, but you're difficult."

"Has this only just occurred to you?" I folded my arms. "Why? Is the question."

"I thought we covered this last night. Because I want to be there for you. Even if you won't ask me."

I had no idea when we'd discussed that. "Fine. But that doesn't include you inviting yourself out on my dates."

"That," he pointed at the departing Peugeot as it sped down the bend, "was not a date."

"You literally just accused me of it being one. Argh!" I yelled, then cringed with a curse as my head reacted.

"You're not hydrated enough for a hike."

"Good thing I'm not going then," I snapped back.

He turned around and opened a pack on the bike where I now noticed a second helmet rested. He held out a fruit and electrolyte drink in a plastic bottle that was damp with condensation from being kept cool. "Here."

My mouth watered.

"Just take it, you stubborn girl. Taking it is not giving in."

"It is."

"To what?"

"Do you always talk in riddles?" I complained.

"I do when I'm being fed mixed messages."

I huffed out a shocked breath. "What? That's not—I didn't—If anyone is—"

"It's fine. Shit." He also sighed. "You know I didn't mean that the way it sounded. You're feeling vulnerable after confessing how I made you feel last night."

"How I—"

"You want to avoid me, Sunflower. I get it. But just get over it, okay. Stop being so fucking stubborn. Drink up."

My mouth dropped open, and I closed it again with effort. He was right and I knew it, and I hated it. I hated that he knew exactly why I was acting the way I was. I didn't like feeling this vulnerable. I avoided this feeling whenever possible. I was embarrassed at this one-sided thing, and I was being ridiculous. And deep down inside me, I also truly *loved* he knew exactly how I was feeling. And that he was still here. And I'd never admit it, but I kind of loved that he'd developed a nickname for me.

"We're going hiking and camping today," he stated as I guzzled the drink down like I'd been in the desert for days. "It's a beautiful day. It would be a shame to waste it," he went on. "And if you don't want to say a word to me. That's fine too. But we're going."

"But I'm supposed to travel there with you on that?" I pointed at his monster of a bike after capping off the now empty bottle of juice. "Shouldn't you be heading up a motorcycle club with questionable income sources on that thing? Seems a bit wasted on a clean cut, plain white tee, straitlaced, law-abiding citizen who enjoys hiking on the weekends."

His jaw ticked for a moment before he burst out into a chuckle. That was one thing I'd always loved about Evan—a smile was always quick to the surface. He was generally a happy guy. And sure, things got serious in his job once in a while, and he took it seriously, but he was also one of the only people who could make my ex-boss, Xavier, laugh. Apart from Xavier's daughter, Dauphine. And until Josie came along of course.

"Straitlaced?" He laughed harder.

I tossed the plastic bottle into the recycling section of a nearby bin and then folded my arms.

"Come on, Sunflower. Get on." He held out the spare helmet. "I won't bite."

I took the offered protection.

"Not hard anyway." He winked.

NINETEEN

"Stop that," I grumbled at his wink, taking the helmet from him.

"Stop what?"

I hesitated to say flirting because ... was it? Or was it Evan just being Evan as always. "Calling me Sunflower," I said, tucking stray wisps of hair into the helmet and then fumbling with the chin strap. "Since when have you had a bike, anyway?"

"Here." He tucked his shades into his neckline and brushed my fingers out the way as he stepped close and tilted my chin up. I held my breath and stared straight ahead at his neck stubble. Damn, but he smelled good on this autumn morning. He'd showered and used that woody scented gel I'd snooped and sniffed at last night. "I've ridden practically my whole life. I keep it very separate from work. I don't get much chance to ride anymore. Bought this beauty three years ago."

My stomach was tying itself in knots at the thought of having to mold myself around his body and hang on to him while that beast of a bike throbbed between our legs.

"Why are you suddenly calling me Sunflower all the time?" I asked to get my mind off what was coming.

"It's not sudden." The strap clicked into place, and he stepped back. "You've always been Sunflower since I saw you for the first time. But it wouldn't have been very appropriate in the workplace. And now we don't work together anymore."

I frowned, his explanation not making sense. "People have nicknames for each other all the time at work. What's inappropriate about it? As long as it's not insulting. Wait. Is it?"

He smiled and clipped his helmet on and slung a leg over his bike, the fabric of his tactical pants stretching across his muscled legs. The movement kicked up the dust from the pebbled lot over his hiking boots. I could see the outline of his back muscles and shoulder blades through the white t-shirt as his arms stretched forward to the handles. "No, it's not insulting," he said. "I'll explain another time. You ever ridden a bike before?"

I shook my head.

"Good. Get on."

"Why good?" I hesitated and tried to work out how to get on without touching him too much.

"You're going to have to touch me, Sunflower." He caught my eyes, and I was thankful for my sunglasses.

I swallowed, put a hand on his shoulder, and swung my leg over and sat, my butt immediately sliding down on the leather to connect with his body. Jesus. "Sorry." I tried to scoot back, pushing against his back.

His palm landed on my knee, stilling me. It burned through my yoga pants. "It's okay," he said, his voice sounding rough.

"Stay there. In fact, you're going to have to hold on to me really tight. Slip your arms around my waist."

"Where do I put my feet," I practically squeaked because I was trying not to hyperventilate. I swear my insides had rearranged. My heart was somewhere blocking off my oxygen, but I could feel my pulse pounding heavy and hot somewhere so low in my belly it had basically moved to between my legs. My stomach was nowhere to be found.

He showed me where to put my feet and then pulled my arms around his middle, crushing me against his back. I held hands with myself rather than feel his washboard stomach, though I was dying to. I could smell his skin close up now, notes of cedar and sunshine—and God love his responsible streak, sunscreen—through his shirt. It made me want to bite through the fabric so I could lick his skin and taste him for myself. I'd become depraved.

He took a breath and shook his head.

"What?" I asked from over his shoulder.

"Nothing. Just hang on." He turned the engine on and revved the throttle, cancelling out any ability for us to talk anymore. The growl and rumble of the engine vibrated up through my body. As he eased from stationary and rode off the hill, I found myself pressing against him harder, my palms now flattening out against his hard abdomen, feeling the steady pound of his heart, and my knees hugging him for dear life.

I closed my eyes and accepted every delicious sensation, even while my adrenaline at being on such a dangerous contraption heightened everything a thousand-fold. Heat pooled, hot and damp and urgent. It almost took my breath away. Note to self, never accept a motorcycle ride from someone you had an uncontrollable crush on. This was probably going to go down as the most painfully erotic thing that had ever happened to me, and I tried to remember if I'd packed a change of underwear in my rush this morning.

I hadn't been this close to another male body in a decade, and I loved it. I never wanted to let go. In fact, I wanted more. So much more.

And it occurred to me this was the best way to get me past my nerves of being close to someone's body—have it be about something totally different than expected and have me be the one hanging on and not being held. I didn't have any idea if Evan even realized the gift he was giving me, but he couldn't have done this better if he'd planned it on purpose.

We wound down the mountain, the wind whipping over our skin, and before long we were on the highway. The feeling of danger ebbed and sheer exhilaration seeped in. My smile broke free, and then I was laughing in sheer joy. Tears came then briefly, pent up tension seeking release.

Catching myself and slowing my breathing, I forced my eyes open to take in the countryside. The fields and hills were sunbaked from late summer, the air whooshing past was mostly clean, and the faint scent of cut grasses and harvested yields ticked my senses. It felt like too soon when the bike slowed, and we took an exit with large brown signage for *Les Gorges du Verdon*. We began winding up and down country lanes. I wasn't sure how much longer we had to go, but I never wanted this ride to end. I didn't want to let go.

I hugged closer as we took a hairpin bend. My hand was splayed across his chest and there was no reason for it to be except I wanted it there. Beneath my hands, his lungs took a large—and it felt like—unsteady breath.

I was reveling in the feel of his body so close, like some kind of perv. I was taking advantage, and I knew it. The physiological release I needed was not going to come any time soon. In fact, it had settled into an honest-to-God ache. I tilted my pelvis forward slightly before I was even aware I'd done it. Oops. Okay, that might have been a bit much. The exhilaration of the ride had almost made me drunk with lack of inhibition. I quickly pretended I was shifting and stretching my back. I cringed and closed my eyes.

My hands sought out each other so I could go back to holding myself around him without touching his front. God, hopefully we could pretend none of that ever happened. He probably never even noticed.

The bike slowed, and I opened my eyes to see us approaching a dirt road between a stand of cypress trees and volcanic rock. There was no parking lot I could see, just a small clearing off to the side of the road. Evan stopped the bike, kicking the stand down.

I put my foot down as the engine came to a stop. The silence was deafening after the growl of the engine. "Why are we stopping?"

"Get off," Evan growled, and I scrambled at his tone, my legs almost giving out on me. But no sooner were we both on solid ground than he picked me up round the waist and dumped me sideways on my ass back on the seat of his bike.

I gasped.

His helmet was off in seconds, and he stepped between my legs. Then he unstrapped mine and slipped it off my head, tossing it on the ground behind me. He was so close, but his hands fisted at his sides, not touching me. His eyes were on fire. "Jesus Christ, Sunflower. You are going to give me a Goddamned heart attack rubbing on me like that."

Oh shit. "I'm sorry," I blurted, embarrassment crawling through me.

He'd noticed.

Oh my God. I wanted the ground to swallow me up. "I'm so sorry."

His eyes grew stormy. "Don't apologize for touching me."

"Even if you obviously didn't want me to? I'm not a damn charity case, Evan. I have some issues. I'm dealing with them. Or at least I will. But I'm sorry, okay? Please, for God's sake, don't let me cop a pity feel because you feel bad for me." My cheeks burned with mortification, nausea filling my gut, my eyes pooling with tears. Damn hangover. It wasn't like I could afford to lose the hydration.

"Shit. Look at me." His tone gentled.

"I was out of line. Predatory. I'm sorry. It won't happen again. Just accept my apology. Please."

"Fuck no."

"No?"

"I should be the one apologizing. I made sure you had to ride with me even though I knew what it would cost you."

"What it cost me?" I blinked in confusion. "My pride, you mean? Yeah. I left that somewhere back on the third exit of the first roundabout. Or maybe last night sometime," I added with a pained laugh.

"I don't have a lot myself right now."

"Pride? Why do you say that?"

"Because I'm close to begging you to let me kiss you, even though I know I'm taking advantage of the situation right now, and if you had your head on straight, you'd never look at me the way you are."

I'd forgotten how to breathe, my chest practically caved in. I tried to process his words.

Kiss.

He wanted to kiss me.

"I—why wouldn't—wait, how am I looking at you?"

He stared at me, his brow furrowed. His breathing was jagged. "I can't—" He swallowed, the sound heavy. His gaze fell to my lips, then he blinked and stepped back.

No! Wait! Come back!

We were both breathing like we'd run here, not ridden. And frankly I didn't even know how I got here. "Evan." My hand darted out and twisted in his t-shirt and pulled him forward so our bodies collided.

Evan groaned. "Fuck it," he barked and then his mouth was on mine, his hands fisting in my hair.

Oh my God. His mouth.

A guttural moan erupted from the depths of his body as I surrendered to his kiss. The sound he made was answered in my own body as heat raced down my skin, flooded my veins, and pooled hot and aching between my legs.

So, this was what kissing Evan Roark was like. It was like being caught in a summer storm on a hot day, dangerously electric, the heat reaching a fever point and breaking the sky right open. It broke *me* right open. His rough hands cradled my face. His lips molded over mine, searching, tasting—his tongue, hot, sliding into my mouth, tasting, drinking. His tongue. I was desperate for it. I opened under him, parched and whimpering, dragging him closer, needing more of that hot slide. And giving him mine.

He angled my jaw with one hand, taking more, his other arm now banded around my lower back, pressing me against him, and I wrapped my legs around his waist—they were useless for anything else anyway. My hands came up to his hair, raking my fingers through those soft brown locks anything but gently. I was ravenous. I was a storm of want. I didn't want to breathe if it meant breaking my mouth from his, from the feeling of his tongue stroking mine, his mouth moving like it was making love to my entire body. I could drink from his well forever. I would drown under the hot summer rain of his kiss.

Then he slowed and pulled back.

I tried to follow, craving more before I fluttered my eyes open, blinking and dazed.

His eyes were closed, chest heaving, brow furrowed, not looking at me. He gently peeled my hands and legs from around him, and I was grateful to still be sitting on the bike though I'd forgotten it even existed. "Evan?" I croaked. My hand pressed against my lips like I could keep the kiss.

"Don't," he said, finally opening his eyes and looking at me, the green and brown a dark swirl. "I need a minute. That shouldn't have happened." He stepped fully away, raking his hands down his face and breathing out into them. "Fuck," he exploded and peeled his eyes off me. He bent over and then stood and turned away from me, hands on his head and face tilted upward.

I cringed at his outburst. God, I hadn't kissed a man in

almost a decade, and Evan was acting like he'd just dropped his cell phone in the toilet. Or worse.

"Wow," I muttered sarcastically to hide my hurt at his reaction.

He swung around and opened his mouth to speak.

A high-pitched honk sounded as a small Peugeot flew by us, kicking up dust and screeched to a halt and reversed. It was Marianne, Cyril, and Frédéric. We must have passed them on the highway.

They climbed out, apologizing and bickering. Apparently Cyril had been in charge of filling up the car, and he'd forgotten so they'd had to stop for gas.

We both turned to face the group we'd seen less than an hour ago. But the world had changed forever.

TWENTY

I attempted to talk and follow conversations, but all I could think about was that Evan had kissed me. And not in a poor-woman-needs-to-get-some kind of way, but in a I-have-to-taste-her-right-now kind of way. And *holy shit,* I wasn't sure I'd ever been on the receiving end of a kiss like that. Scratch that. I hadn't. Period.

And now I had to hike for half a day and try to keep my mind off it, and I could barely put one foot in front of the other. I pressed my palm to my belly to tell my insides to calm the hell down. I was uncomfortably damp between my legs, my heart hammering, and I felt like I had a neon sign on my head telling the whole world I'd just had the shit kissed out of me. None of the others seemed to notice my entire universe had shifted to narrow its entire focus on the feel of Evan's mouth on mine.

I suddenly wished fervently I hadn't deleted his texts this morning so I could reread and analyze them. Did he actually mean the things he'd said last night? And what had he even said again? Were there clues I missed that this was coming? And what did he mean just before he kissed me when he said if my head was on straight I wouldn't look at him like that? But then every time I thought of his reaction right afterward, I also died a little inside.

The parking lot was less than fifty yards from where we'd stopped, so after we parked both vehicles, backpacks were reassigned from where they'd traveled in the car and supplies divvied up. Evan strapped the extra sleeping bag Marianne was lending me to *his* pack since mine was just a day pack, And Cyril took the extra tent, so I took some of his water to even up the load even though he assured everyone he would be fine.

Evan had a pair of hiking sticks that looked like ski poles and handed me one. Everyone else had two. He tried to catch my eye, but I refused to look at him. He needed a minute? I needed a goddamn lifetime to get over what had just happened.

All I could manage in my current state was to take instructions and start walking. After a mile I found myself staring at the back of Evan whenever I had a chance. He walked ahead of me, and what a view that was anyway, though he glanced over his shoulder every few minutes, looking past me and scanning the surroundings. Security conscious Evan was back. He hung back when he saw another hiking party gaining on us. He waited until they passed and from then on he was behind me, bringing up the rear of our group. We were slow, and I could tell he was only operating at about twenty-five percent of what he was probably capable of.

After a while, as the pine needle strewn ground became more and more rocky and rooty, I had to watch where my feet were going. Frédéric kept pace with me and tried chatting in French before it was clear hiking wasn't really his thing. Sweat poured off him, and his breathing started giving off a high-pitched whine. When we paused for a water break, he pulled out a pack of cigarettes and I shared a brief what-the-hell-is-he-thinking, he's-already-about-to-die look with Evan, to which his look silently replied, "And you were going to double date this guy?" I chuckled silently, relieved Evan and I were at least on "not speaking, speaking" terms, like we were on the boat sometimes with particularly difficult situations like a drunk guest or worse. We might be able to salvage something of our friendship.

Marianne saw the cigarette and started cursing and grabbed it out of Frédéric's mouth, putting it out on a tree and yelling about forest fires. At that realization, we all seemed to get a bit serious. It *was* very dry out here, and forest fires were common. Evan made sure the sparks were out with some water from his canteen.

After about two hours, the scream in my thighs and calves had leveled out to a pained howl, and we crested a ridge. I gasped at the view ahead as the limestone cliffs gave way, plunging steeply down to a gorge where a bright turquoise river snaked along the bottom.

The five of us stood in awe.

"Wow," I managed.

"I know," Evan said, stepping up next to me. "You see pictures, and you don't believe a river can be that color."

"Are you going to tell me what makes it that color, or are you going to let me believe it's magic?" I asked him, not taking my eyes off the incredible sight. Far below us, a couple of red and yellow kayaks rounded a bend in the water.

"What would you prefer?" Evan asked.

"The magic," I said. "Obviously." There was a bit of a

breeze up here due to the open exposure, and it danced over my skin, cooling the sweat.

"Yeah, me too." He paused. "But sometimes you just know too many facts."

I scoffed internally. Trust him to ruin a good moment. Again. Farther down the river, a two-person kayak had pulled into a cove and a couple were in the water, extremely close. Not that we could see anything from this distance. I dragged my eyes away though, a pang going through me at the sight.

Beside me, Evan's gaze darted to Marianne as if to judge how far away she was from earshot, and he took a slight breath as if he was about to say something.

"How much farther until the campsite?" I asked, heading off any kind of further apology he might have been about to give. I really didn't want to think about the fact I'd just had the best kiss of my life, and Evan was filled with regrets and wanting to take it all back. Talk about mixed messages.

"Listen—"

"The temperature is really kicking up," I went on. "This breeze feels really good."

Marianne wandered over, leaving Cyril and Frédéric chatting about what sounded like *futbol* scores. Frédéric wasn't even looking at the view. Why on earth did they bring him hiking? Unless it really was a double date. I needed to sit Marianne down and talk about my type.

"Hi," I greeted her. "Frédéric doing all right?"

She rolled her eyes. "It was Cyril's idea to bring him." She eyed Evan. "I would have said no if I knew the hunky bodyguard was coming," she added, confirming Evan's assessment.

I refused to look at him, a) because he'd been right and b)

because Marianne was assuming we were a thing, or about to be, and to say it was complicated, was an understatement. I sensed Evan turn away to the view as if he wasn't listening, but I knew him too well. "*Alors*," Marianne continued. "You need to go do the pee pee, yes? I was going to wait until we are down to the river, but," she mimed, crossing her legs and doing a pee pee dance.

That juice and coffee I'd had earlier had also worked their way through me so I nodded, and we scurried off the trail, leaving the men at the ridge. My last view over my shoulder was of Frédéric dropping his denim shorts, baring a bright white ass and aiming off the cliff and Cyril following suit.

Marianne had toilet paper and a small bag for trash. After we did our business, standing guard and holding out paper for each other, we both used hand sanitizer on our hands and then slipped our packs back on.

"*Alors*, the bodyguard ..." Marianne said.

"Ugh," I complained. "I don't know."

"But you two are to set the forest on fire. It's crazy. What is the problem?"

"I'm trying to figure that out."

"Maybe he thinks it will be too much. You know men get scared when they realize a woman is for the rest of their life." She tightened her straps and clipped her water bottle back to her waist pack.

"Ha." I squeaked. "I don't think that's it. I know from another of his women that he does not do commitment. Only sex."

"Hmm. Is this a problem for you?"

"I would say no. But I don't know. I think I told you I

haven't been with anyone in a very long time." I shared the bare bones of an estranged husband and a divorce. I had no idea how any emotional fallout of having sex with Evan would affect me. I'd known him for ten years. What if after we crossed that line, assuming I wouldn't freeze up into a frigid corpse and we could actually do it, he reacted badly again? Rejected me immediately. I wouldn't be able to bear the hit to my ego if his reaction to us kissing was anything to go by. We'd lose our friendship completely. As much as his overbearing tendencies rubbed me wrong, it was also one of the things I loved most about him. He took care of everyone around him. As he'd said just over a week ago, we used to be friends. Good friends. Things had gotten strange between us lately, but I never wanted to lose that friendship.

"Ah, I see. That is a lot of pressure for a man. To be the first after so long."

"Not really." I thought of my earlier experience on the bike, and I shook my head with a chuckle. "Considering it would be the easiest orgasm he'll probably ever give."

Marianne cackled so loud a huge pheasant-sized bird went flapping out of a nearby bush, making us both shriek in fright and then bust out laughing.

I was laughing so hard, I had to lean against a nearby trunk.

By the time the men burst through the trees, led by Evan, panic etched over his features, we were both wiping tears from our faces.

∼

WE CONTINUED up the ridge trail past the ruins of a premedieval church built against the cliffs and blending into its surroundings. There were the remnants of cloistered arches running farther up the hill.

"Old monastery, I think," Evan offered from behind me. He'd fumed for the first few minutes after ascertaining Marianne and I hadn't been in any danger. Which honestly had made Marianne and me laugh even more.

"It's the perfect place," I agreed with his assessment, pausing to admire the history. "Beautiful and silent."

"And fucking freezing in winter," he added.

Frédéric passed us, mumbling something in French, and now we were the last two of our group on the trail. In fact, there were so many trails around the huge canyon national park we hadn't passed or been passed by more than about twenty people all day.

I smiled. "I'd hate that. I don't like to be cold. But with enough blankets, books, wine, and a roaring fire, I'd cope." I looked around. "In fact, I miss England sometimes. Especially up north. I never thought I would. How green it is, you know?" I hadn't let myself think of England in years. I hadn't missed it in the beginning, lulled and seduced first by just being away from Angus and then by the unique beauty of Provence and the Mediterranean. But I really did miss England.

"I have a place like this there, up north," said Evan, his voice quiet. "Well, not like this. But it's beautiful and rocky. And covered with heather in the summer and emerald green and gray all winter."

I turned to him. "You have a place in Northern England. Why didn't I know this?"

He pushed his sunglasses up into his hair. "No one knows. Not even my family."

"Well, I do now."

"Yes. You do, now." He looked back out over the gorge, then back at me. "If you need to get away. Ever. It's yours. It's safe there."

"Okay, James Bond with his secret Skyfall getaway."

"I mean it." His eyes pierced me, serious, his lips not returning my smile.

"Okay." I kicked at the rocky ground with the tip of my hiking stick. "You're being weird. But, thank you?"

"Look, I have to tell you something," he said.

"If it's how you regret kissing me, I'm not interested." I took a breath and squared off. "That was the best damned kiss of my life, and I don't need you ruining it after the fact."

Evan stared at me. His mouth went slack for a second before closing. His jaw tightened like he was fighting saying something. Good.

"There, I said it." I raised my chin. "It's fine if it wasn't that same for you. But it's *my* memory now. Leave it alone." I turned and stalked down the trail, not hearing him follow right away. I'd humiliated myself enough in the last eighteen hours, what was a couple more times? Besides, I was telling the truth.

He just had to deal with it.

Then I heard him right behind me before his fingers grazed down my arm. "Stop."

Shrugging him off, I kept walking, picking up the pace as we began our descent down the rocky path. My knees jarred, and I stumbled and righted myself with the hiking stick.

"It *was* ... Slow down before you fall. Shit, Sunflower. Just let me get out what I need to, okay? It's not to do with the kiss. Not directly. But on the subject of that, it *was* that for me too."

I stopped and spun around.

He slammed to a halt. "Okay?" he asked. "Are you happy? Slow down before you get hurt."

"It was?"

His eyes were dark and broody. I never knew if I preferred broody or happy Evan.

"Fuck, yes," he whispered.

There was a resounding thump in my gut. "Then, why did you leap away from me the second you came up for air?"

"Because first of all, I knew the others were about to arrive."

The rest of the human race hadn't even existed for me at that point in time, but hats off to him for being able to think of literally anything. "Fair," I offered when it was anything but. "Go on."

"Also, that was some stratospheric level of heat only going one way, with me taking you right there on my bike on the side of the road."

My stomach hollowed out, and there went my damn panties again. "Anything else?" I croaked.

He bit his lip, his brow furrowing. "But the most important reason I stopped is because I've been lying to you."

TWENTY-ONE

Evan

I QUICKLY GLANCE down the steep mountain trail to make sure Andrea and I are still alone.

"Lying to me about what?" she asks, but I can see her glow over me admitting our kiss was life altering isn't fading despite my admission. That's about to change.

"Less lying, more not telling you something. A lot of things. Lying by omission." I glance down the path again. I also don't want to get too far behind the others, but this talk needs to happen while we're in as private a place as we could possibly be. "You were right about me following you. *Stalking.* Whatever."

"I know that, Evan. You all but admitted via text that you were in Saint Paul next door to me, on purpose. I should be mad, and yes you crossed a line with that, but I feel safer with you. It pains me to admit it, but I *want* you close. I thought I didn't. But I do. You win, okay?"

"It's not about winning or losing. You never asked me how I knew where you even were."

"I assume Meg or Sue gave me up."

I blow out a breath. "They did, but I already knew where to look. I've been tracking your cell phone locations."

She folds her arms and narrows her eyes. "I know. Creepy as shit. But you literally kept telling me to my face to keep my locations on."

I wince. "But I tracked your movements even after you turned them off."

"Oh." She frowns. "How?"

"I have some technology. Pascale Company does. The point is, I have someone else watching out for you too. Pete from the firm. And some others," I admit carefully.

Her mouth opens and closes, and she seems to pull into herself, her glow dimming. "Pete?" she asks, and I can see how rattled she is now. "I've met him. He's watching me? How long? Was that who—"

"Not watching *you*. He was supposed to be watching the law office."

"Wait, how do you know where my lawyer is?"

"Are you even listening to me? I've been tracking you. Your cell phone. One *I* issued you. This is exactly what you accused me of. And I'm sorry. I didn't want to, but I had to when you refused to let me do it the normal way. Which is high-handed at best and completely out of line."

She's finally glaring at me now, feeling her privacy violated. Rightfully.

But I push on. I need her to really understand the bigger picture. "Anyway, I don't know what happened, but Pete wasn't there yesterday at the law office. He should have been, or *someone* should have been. The bottom line is, *I* should have been. But no, what you felt, that wasn't Pete watching you." I fist my hands at my sides to keep from reaching for her.

"Maybe I did imagine it then," she says.

"No. You didn't." I pause, hating being the one to deliver this news. "It was Angus. He saw you. I think he saw you."

At the sound of her ex's name, she flinches and her breath puffs out in shock.

I keep on. "Then he must have followed Meg up to the village because François at the *tabac* confirmed he walked into the village last night. He didn't stay long," I quickly add. "In fact, he left pretty much immediately. I assume he thought it was a dead end."

She goes almost translucent with shock. Shit. I reach out just as she sways, but she throws my hand off like it burns. "Don't touch me. Oh my God." She catches herself on a tree trunk.

"Sit down, maybe." I quickly take my pack off to get an energy bar or something. She's really pale, and I don't need her passing out. I find a bar and hold it out. "Here. Eat this. You've had a shock. You need the sugar."

"Stop! Just stop it! I'm not a child. What the hell are you telling me, Evan? And François at the *tabac* is in on this? And I, oh my God," her voice fades out, "we sat out at that restaurant." Her eyes turn accusingly and she raises her voice. "So much for your damned security. You let me sit out there? And he could have been in the village? And you keep asking me to let you help me, keep me safe. Blah, blah, fucking blah."

"I didn't know then. You only told me you'd thought you'd been watched when we were already sitting there. At that point, I hoped to hell it was Pete. You don't fucking tell me anything, or want me knowing where you are, but then you're mad at me that I didn't know? Jesus."

"How do you even know what his name is? What he looks like? I don't understand. I can smell pizza. Can you smell pizza? I'm losing my damned mind."

"I know his name. Of course, I do. I've been keeping you off his radar for almost ten years. I just didn't know you were going to suddenly tell him exactly where to fucking find you," I all but shout, chest heaving. "And yes, I smell pizza too."

"He's in France? He was in my village. Why didn't you tell me?" She pokes at my shoulder with force.

"I am literally telling you right now."

"You could have told me last night."

"Over text? Because you wouldn't open the damned door?"

"Yes!" she yells. "No," she amends. "I don't know."

Both of us glare at each other as Marianne comes up the hill, gasping for breath, the two guys in tow, clearly drawn by the commotion.

I've run out of time for any more truth bombs.

"*Alors*, would you two just fuck already?" Marianne stops, leaning over to catch her breath. "I thought there was a real problem."

"There is a real problem," Andrea says, pushing past me toward Marianne, and jerks a thumb over her shoulder toward me. "It's him."

"We have another problem too," says Frédéric. "*La tente est cassée.*"

Andrea stops. "The tent is broken? Which one?"

"The one I was carrying for you," confirms Frédéric. "But it's okay. My tent is big. You can share it."

"The fuck she will." I grunt, walking past all of them. I hadn't realized we were so close to the campsite, and I see no one's got their packs on anymore. And somehow someone is actually cooking pizza somewhere. My stomach growls. I could murder a pizza I'm so hungry. Hangry. Sexually frustrated. Whatever. "I'm going to fix the tent."

"There's a missing tentpole," says Marianne as I pass. "Good luck."

I stop and turn to her. "What happened to it?"

"I don't remember." She shrugs but looks utterly unapologetic, which sends my suspicions flying.

"What do you mean, you don't remember what happened to the other tent pole?" I press, looking her straight in the eye.

"I'm sorry. But I do not. But she can share. Like Frédéric said." She smiles and begins to walk down to the campsite.

I follow. "She can share with you though, right? In your tent?" I say as soon as we are partly away from earshot.

"*Non.* Cyril is too horny, especially with all the sexual tension flying around today." She winks.

I let her walk ahead.

"Anyway," she calls over her shoulder. "We are all going swimming now to cool off. We can decide later whether she will share with you or Frédéric."

"I don't have a swimsuit," says Andrea, passing me by without looking at me. "I'll just watch."

"I'm sure I have a spare one thrown in the bottom of my bag. I always do." Marianne loops her arms through Andrea's as she catches up.

"Okay, but I don't do bikinis," says Andrea.

"With your body? But you must. You can change in my tent."

Their voices fade as they pull ahead.

I turn around and glare at Cyril and Frédéric. "Are you all in on this stupid broken tent thing?" I ask in French.

Cyril holds his hands up. "I am never in on anything with Marianne. She tells me next to nothing. I'm just along for the ride." He waggles his eyebrows. "It's a good ride."

Frédéric shrugs. "I am happy to share with Andrea. Are you two even dating? Do you mind if I—"

Cyril barks out a laugh and says some French equivalent of "read the room" at the same time as I give Frédéric a look that chokes the words dead in his mouth.

∼

THE CAMPSITE IS on a series of steppes that were probably used for agriculture and irrigation at some point in the distant past. Over the years trees and shrubs have taken over most of them, apart from an area kept clear to allow several flat areas to pitch tents. By my count there are three other tents of people who've gotten here before us dotted amongst the trees. As with most of the camping sites here, there's a steward, a full-time person to "run" the campsite who tends to the common areas and also sells cold drinks and supplies. We've lucked out, or Marianne is a genius, because this campsite is run by a lady who's built a stone pizza oven in the middle of nowhere and makes honest-to-God made-to-order pizzas. Hence the smell.

There's a common area and fire ring in a larger clearing below with wooden benches and picnic tables, followed by a short walk down rocky steps to the river. I've seen some areas of the river that have sandy sides allowing a small beach when the water isn't high from recent rain. In contrast, this area is a natural swimming hole surrounded by rocks on three sides—deep and clear aquamarine and slightly pooled off from the main flow. The only way in is to leap or climb down from the rocks, and the only way out is to pull oneself up on a rope left dangling for the purpose.

I don't know what's taking the girls so long, but the temperature has climbed to sweltering highs for fall, and the river is calling my name. It's too early and hot to sit around a campfire or even eat a piping hot pizza. Another energy bar and a refilled water bottle have reset me for now. But my mind won't stop. I fucked up big time today, and I don't know how to move past this.

I've kept myself busy by setting up my tent in the trees a level or two above everyone else and away from Marianne and Frédéric's tents that are closer to the campfire. Especially if Marianne and Cyril are planning to get busy later as Marianne suggested. Tents are *not* soundproof, and no one needs to hear that. And it will be awkward as shit with Andrea lying next to me all night as it is. I'm utterly screwed. What the hell with the missing tent pole scenario? I know Marianne is to blame but have no way to prove it.

There's a family of four already seated at one of the picnic tables and waiting for their pizzas. The young kids are sleepy and sun-kissed, their hair wet, and clearly they've spent the afternoon in the water. I nod my head in greeting as I make my way to the river, dressed in my swim shorts, and check my waterproof watch. Five. It's going to be a long damn night.

Cyril and Frédéric spot me and call out, both heading down to the water to join me. Cyril wears appropriate thigh length swim shorts and is surprisingly, actually pretty stacked. He told me earlier he works as a bag handler at Nice airport, so it kind of makes sense. As I expected though, based on nothing but a hunch, Frédéric sports a forest green banana hammock and unruly chest hair. I bite back a smile.

I glance up to Marianne's tent by habit, wanting to catch Andrea's eye so we can have one of our silent conversations about Frédéric. And not that I'm looking, but he's surprisingly hung. I'm sure the swimwear is akin to him spreading his feathers like a peacock since this started out with him thinking he was on a double date weekend. Suddenly I'm glad Andrea isn't down here. Not that she'd be affected by the size of his junk, I don't think. Then again I have no idea what's going on with her lately. Apart from the one time she'd drunk too much champagne with Josie at the nightclub and she didn't know what she was doing, she has never, and I mean *never,* given me vibes that she wanted anything more with me beyond friendship, so the last twenty-four hours is really fucking with my head. And the way she was on the bike? It was a miracle I got here without running off the road.

She was just horny, I tell myself. Really horny. And I was the nearest recipient. That has to be it. There's no way after the way she's been avoiding me lately that this is anything but that I was in the right place at the right time. Or wrong time, in my case.

I grab the back of my neck and squeeze. This is all so messed up.

Luckily for Frédéric and my mood, he's carrying a six pack of beer cans and pops three off the plastic necking, handing one each to Cyril and me.

"Cold beer," I praise. "How did you manage that?"

Cyril nods up to the lady of the campsite busying herself at the pizza oven with a large metal paddle. "Marianne always chooses this place because the madame keeps it stocked and civilized—wine, beer, pizza. It's the best kept secret of the gorge."

"It really is."

"She lives up here by herself year-round. Tough as freaking nails. Hard to talk to obviously but makes the best pizza you'll ever eat." Cyril then leaps off the edge into the clear turquoise water, holding his beer high. He comes up with a grin and a quick snap of his head to shake off the water from his shaggy chin length hair. I see the depth of the water is about chest high. "Cheers," I tell him and pull the ring of my beer, taking a long quenching sip.

Then I almost choke on it when Andrea and Marianne materialize.

Jesus Christ.

Next to me Frédéric gives a low whistle. "*Mec,*" he says. "That woman is looking for some balls for her necklace. I'm kind of glad mine are safe."

What the hell has Marianne persuaded Andrea to wear?

TWENTY-TWO

Marianne's spare swimsuit is a tiny fire engine red bikini that barely covers Andrea's assets. Her curves are on full display. I immediately sit my ass down on the rock since my swim shorts won't be able to hide my reaction. Not after what happened earlier today. Apparently I haven't quite doused that fire.

I take another sip of beer, grateful for the millionth time I invested in the darkest sunglasses known to man so I can perv the shit out of her body. Just for a moment, obviously, before I pull myself together. Fuck me. I'm finished. I've been avoiding looking at her like this for years. But now I've blown up every boundary I ever had with that kiss.

I can tell immediately she's uncomfortable but fighting it. She bobs her chin up and squares her shoulders. Marianne whispers something to her and squeezes her arm, and Andrea gives a small smile. Her eyes skim over me. She keeps herself slightly angled as they approach, laughing at something else Marianne says. Marianne's suit is blue and not exactly cut any more generously, but I only have eyes for the woman next to her. I've never seen her in a bikini, she always wears a one piece, and even then it's rare she ever swims when I'm around. I'm going to have to do my best to pretend I'm used to seeing her this way.

They come to the edge where Cyril whistles at Marianne and cajoles her to come join him in the water. Andrea turns to me. "Hi," she says. "You coming in?"

"Are we speaking to each other?" I ask because I was expecting her to still give me the cold shoulder after what I admitted to earlier and our argument.

Putting a hand on her waist, she cocks a hip to the side. One eyebrow raises in challenge. "I guess we don't have to." She bites her lip nervously. "But I'd really like to know if you like this swimsuit."

So much for pretending I hadn't noticed if she's going to make me address it outright. My ribs tighten as I realize she's nervous as shit but playing confident. I suddenly feel so proud of her, which is really not my place.

Frédéric takes a running jump, making the other two squeal and yell as he hits the water. It's just Andrea and me left.

I decide she needs the truth. I can give her at least this, if nothing else. I take off my glasses so she can see my eyes and drag my eyes slowly up her body. I make sure to lewdly pause at the little triangle between her legs, her soft belly, then again at her barely covered breasts. I lick my lips and watch goose bumps ripple across her arms before finally bringing my gaze up to meet hers.

Her mouth is parted, her eyes dangerously dark. Unfortunately my perusal also affected *me*, but I fall back on my ability to school my expression and tone. "Is that what you're calling it?" I ask.

She swallows, even more nervous now. "Well? I'm assuming you like it?"

"Yes," I admit. I'm already in hell, so one more ounce of truth won't make it worse. "I can't get up right now because there are children present who would be scarred for life. Does that answer your question?"

"I guess it does." She smiles, and it's brilliantly wide and guileless.

Then she takes her hand from her waist and turns toward the water, and something snaps in my chest. The sharp winded sound I make draws her eyes back to me.

She has an old and angry jagged scar on her side from just below her ribs to the top of her hip bone.

"He did that." I manage in a hoarse whisper.

"Yes. He did."

My mouth is dried out when I try to swallow. I tighten my grip on the beer can to stop my hand shaking and hear the sharp crack of crushed metal. I'm sick with rage. I want to kill that fucker. I want to watch him die. The violence of the thoughts shock me. It's going to be a real fucking problem. I'm going to have to tell Pete, and I'll definitely tell Xavier in case I end up needing a really good lawyer. "Sunflower." I choke. "Can you talk about it?"

"I'll tell you. I will. Just not now. Evan?" Her eyes are glowing, and she blinks away a sheen. "Thank you."

"What the hell for?"

"For making me feel desirable just then." She says it like it's an alien concept. "But more than that," she goes on before I can formulate a reaction. "Luckily, thanks to you, I'm forewarned. I was shocked before when you told me everything. You violated the privacy I asked you for. But I know you only crossed the line into my privacy because you care. And it turns out you were right to be so concerned. That shock was nothing compared to knowing he saw me last night. To be honest, I think on some level I knew he would come, and I definitely knew I was being careless. And I'm guessing you did too. I pretended he wouldn't come because I wished so hard it wasn't true. That he'd moved on. *I* just want to move on and for that chapter of my life to be over. I've waited so long for it, and I'm scared it will *never* be over. I'm scared, and I took it out on you." Her gaze dropped. "I always do," she added quietly.

She could take anything out on me always. One day she'd realize that. Her bravery in admitting all that to me and also coming out here in that bikini and showing herself to me, to the world, after hiding the evidence of her pain for so many years, takes my fucking breath away.

"Tomorrow I have to face the reality of him," she continues. "But for tonight, I'm safe out here in this beautiful corner of the universe. And I'm safe with you. Right?"

I stand up. We're only steps apart, but I don't touch her. I can't. Not now. It's better when she's in charge of that anyway. And after how vulnerable she's just made herself, I don't want to show pity either.

But more than that, I realize how far in over my head I am. I'm no white knight. She has a battle to fight herself, and I'm just the sentry. I'm guarding the walls and that's it. And today I took my eye off the ball. I failed at that one simple job. Because today, while I had my tongue down her throat, Angus could have walked right down that road, and I'd have never seen him coming.

Yes, she is safe with me. *Now*.

But today she fucking wasn't.

She needs someone she can depend on, not someone taking advantage of her newfound bravery. I told myself I wouldn't ever cross a line with her, and yet that is exactly what I did by kissing her. Jesus, I want to punch my own face in.

I wait until she looks me in the eyes before I speak. "You're so brave and so fucking beautiful. You know that, right?"

Her lips curve.

"And you will get through anything. You've already proved you can. Come on." I step to the edge, hold out my hand, and she doesn't hesitate to take it. "Jump."

TWENTY-THREE

Andrea

EVAN TOLD ME TO JUMP. And I did. We spent the next couple of hours in and out of the water. The five of us laughed and relaxed. Beers were drunk, wine consumed, and pizzas ordered and inhaled. It had been years since I hung out with a group of friends and just existed for stupid conversation and companionship. And before today, and apart from Evan, I didn't even know these people. It felt good. It felt like my world was slowly expanding.

We talked and laughed, and I realized how long it has been since I allowed myself to really relax. As much as I could, obviously, in a barely-there-bikini that not only Frédéric caught himself gawking at but the dad of the nearby family. Awkward. I kept checking to make sure my pertinent bits were covered. They were, but it didn't seem to help.

It was also really obvious Evan was *not* looking. After that weirdly graphic perusal he'd given me earlier it was surprising and deflating, and I couldn't help chalking it up to the fact something had changed after he saw my scar.

With all that to worry about, I stayed covered in the water as much as possible until I was pruning and starting to shiver. I'd be thankful to change and get into a sleeping bag.

The sun was long tired of lightening the sky above us, and we would have to leave the river too soon. There were a couple of lanterns at the water's edge, but when night came it got really dark.

Frédéric and Cyril tried to one up each other on funniest workplace stories. Frédéric's were hilarious since he worked in his family's mechanics business and considered himself quite the Don Juan of his neighborhood, pissing off a few husbands.

But it was when Cyril, who worked in baggage handling at Nice Airport, told a story about a bag of sex toys that exploded as they threw the bag onto the conveyor belt, that we all laughed until we were crying. The dildos and vibrators, and other things he was at a loss to describe, went round and round and round, and Cyril had to try to pick them all up, jogging alongside the moving belt out in the baggage claim hall because his boss wouldn't shut off the machine.

Apparently at the first turn an old granny stepped forward and picked one out like she was selecting conveyor belt sushi. The whole hall of people stood shocked, holding their collective breath to see what she would do. She stuffed it in her purse and hotfooted it out of the airport without even picking up her own suitcase. Apparently after that it was pandemonium, people were scavenging and arguing, and others were shielding their children's eyes. It made the nightly news.

"You brought one home for me too, remember?" Marianne reminded him.

He leaned over and they shared a really long and sloppy kiss. "I do, baby. I do," he crooned.

I looked anywhere but at anyone else. Evan cleared his throat.

"Did you bring it?" I heard Cyril ask Marianne.

My mouth dropped open.

"Christ," Evan said. "No, thanks. Not listening to this."

Frédéric hauled himself out of the water. "Time to dry off and leave these two here, I guess." He looked over at me, hands on his hips, one foot up on a rock so his tiny wet and clingy swim trunks displayed his full asset. The small lanterns on the rocks were his spotlight.

"Put that away, Frédéric," I chided and tried to keep a straight face and not look directly at it.

"*Voulez vous coucher avec moi ce soir?*" he sang to me, but I could tell he was baiting Evan.

Evan whacked the water with an arm and sent a wave spraying over the Frenchman's legs.

"*D'accord, d'accord!*" He laughed. Okay, okay. "Let me know if you change your mind. The French do it better, *tu sais*." He toweled himself off and wandered toward his tent.

Actually, I wouldn't know if the French did it better.

I leveled a look at Evan. "What if I *wanted* to share with Frédéric tonight?"

"Do you?" Evan shot back in an amused tone.

"Why is that funny? What if I did?"

"He's not for you."

"Reeaaaally?" I drew out the word. "And what makes you say that?"

"I know you. And ... no. He's not your type."

"What is my type?" I challenged and raised an eyebrow. Everything between us was back in an instant.

"Let's get out," he grumbled. "We don't need a porno soundtrack for this conversation."

The temperature for Marianne and Cyril was rising even as the night temperature plummeted.

I scrambled to the rope in full agreement. "Can you get out first?"

"Why?"

"So that you're not staring at my ass, obviously," I said.

He smirked. "It's a bit hard to avoid at least looking at something with that excuse for a bathing suit on, but I'll do my best. Anyway, you are mostly just a silhouette at this point so you can relax." He climbed out, easily hauling his weight up onto the rocks, his muscles bunching and water rivulets catching the low lantern light as they streamed down his skin.

Gah. He was so dang hot. Had he always been this attractive or was my libido working overtime to make him hotter every day? I'd always been drawn to Evan in a way, but he'd never, *never,* made it seem like we might be more than platonic. I'd never felt more than platonic, not at first. But at some point that had started to change. And when Josie came to nanny for Dauphine, she made me look at everything differently. And now I was wondering if there'd always been chemistry, but I'd been so shut down, I'd never even felt it. Because there was no way today had come out of nowhere.

Of course, now I knew he kissed like a god. A god whose

sole purpose was to fry the brains of damsels in distress while they loved every second if it. No matter how hard I tried, I couldn't keep the way he'd kissed me out of my head. It was like a blinking neon sign on an endless scroll. Evan kissed me. Evan kissed me. Evan! Evan, who'd always been there, a solid rock, a friend, a pain in the ass at times. Evan with his cyborg expressionless face who'd never, ever given me any kind of flirtatious sign he might be into me. Evan. Who'd been my beacon. My sign that men could be strong and *also* protect, not destroy. Evan. Evan had kissed me like he was starving for me.

Lilian had warned me he didn't do serious relationships. And considering I'd never seen him date anyone in all the time I'd known him, he was obviously discreet and not a long-term guy. That shouldn't have bothered me, but it sort of did. Maybe that made him a bit of a player, but the only game he'd played with me was avoidance all afternoon. He'd been friendly. But that was it. There were no lingering looks or accidental touches. And slowly I was starting to think I'd imagined this morning. Or at least the intensity of it.

My toes found the little crevice foot holds and I pulled up on the rope. Evan reached down a hand and I grabbed at it with my free one. "Thanks," I said as he hauled me up. "It got chilly all of a sudden."

"Did you bring a towel?" he asked.

I shook my head and crossed my arms over my chest, shivering. My nipples were like bullets. "Considering I didn't bring a swimsuit, and I had a severe wine headache, it's a wonder I put shoes on my feet this morning."

He picked up his sunglasses and towel where he'd laid them while we swam and handed me the towel.

"W-what about you?" My teeth chattered, and I stared longingly at the campfire.

We started toward Marianne's tent, nodding at the husband and wife of the family from earlier and a couple of others who were enjoying the flaming warmth. "I'll be fine. I don't get cold easily. We can share. Let's go get your stuff so you can dry and get changed. I already have your sleeping bag."

A gasp and a giggle came from the water behind us. I rolled my eyes and quickly grabbed my bag from outside Marianne and Cyril's tent.

Up and through the trees, which took a second to gingerly get to on bare feet, we got to Evan's tent. I bent down to look inside, giving him a full view of the ass he said he didn't want to look at. He'd laid out our sleeping bags side by side and my insides deflated a little when I saw they were top to tail rather than lined up head next to head. He was really serious about this distance he'd started this afternoon.

I climbed in and zipped the tent closed behind me while he went to brush his teeth and use the bathroom. Luckily the steward lady also had great facilities—a toilet and sink. A hot shower would have been nice, but still this was a better tent-camping experience than I imagined a lot of them were.

Evan's clothes were piled neatly on his sleeping bag. He was a neat freak even camping.

I untied and peeled off the wet bikini, shivering in the cool air, and quickly dried off as best I could before putting on fresh underwear, leggings, and a long sleeve jersey shirt. Then I pulled my hoodie on, thankful I'd tied it around my waist this morning. I was still chilly. The sleeping bag would have to keep me warm. I stared at the bags now, crammed side-by-side into the small tent. How did we get here, Evan and I, and only one tent? All these romance books I'd read with the oops-there's-only-one-bed-at-the-last-available-room-at-the-only-hotel-in-town tropes, and the irony of the situation hit me full force. I stifled a pained laugh.

"What's so funny?"

I inhaled in surprise at the sound of his voice right outside. "You're back quick."

"I came back for the towel if you're done. Well?" His voice sounded amused.

"You wouldn't get it."

"Try me?"

And admit I was picturing us in a romance novel with a perfectly happy ending? Which kind of shocked me. "Nope. That's okay." I unzipped enough of the tent to hold the towel out. My crush on Evan, as intense as it was, hadn't extended into fantasizing about having an actual relationship one day. I hadn't allowed myself to think of *any* future relationships at all. I needed to get through this divorce first and be just me for a while. Me who wanted to try dating and living a normal life like other single women my age. And maybe have sex again? Good sex like I always read about but never experienced. Josie seemed to think Evan was the perfect candidate for something like that. Lilian had confirmed it wouldn't be disappointing. And if what he'd made me feel with that kiss this morning was indication ...

I picked up his t-shirt, taking a moment to hold it to my nose and inhale the heck out of it. Damn but that man smelled good. How he could smell more like a fresh river in a pine forest than the actual place we were in was beyond me.

In none of those only-one-bed books had the hero kissed the

shit out of the heroine and then stuck their feet in her face for the night. Nope. At worst they took the floor or couch, if there was one, until she took pity on him. Well, there was no floor. We were on it. I quickly spun one of the sleeping bags so they were both lined up head to head. Even better, now the zippers faced each other. He could argue with me about it later. And with any luck he wouldn't notice until we were both settling in.

TWENTY-FOUR

"Hey," I whispered up into the darkness of the tent.

Evan groaned. "Go to sleep."

"I can't just go to sleep on demand." I turned my head in his direction. "Can you?"

"Yes, I can. Surely that hike and swim tired you out?"

"Maybe I'm overtired."

"That's not a real thing."

I'd managed to persuade Evan that us lying in tandem, rather than top to tail, was better for us to have whispered conversation no one would hear before we fell asleep. "It is for me. Tell me about your parents," I said.

He gave a long suffering sigh that made me smile. "What do you want to know?" he asked.

"What are they like?"

"That's broad."

I waited.

"Well, my dad was kind of in the same business I am. He

worked for Xavier's parents for a while when I was a teenager before we moved back to England. That's how I met Xavier."

"I actually knew that. How about your mum?"

"She was a teacher."

"Of?"

"English and French lit."

"Here or in England?"

"Both."

This was like pulling teeth. "Is she nice?"

"She's amazing."

"How did a bodyguard and a teacher meet?"

"Are you sure you're not tired?" he grumbled.

"Nope." I smiled. Evan didn't realize the favor he was doing me. We were sharing a tent after all, and I could simply practice being close with someone else tonight. Maybe it didn't have to be sexual. At that thought, my mind rebelled, immediately calculating the distance and layers between us. About eight inches, two sleeping bags and two t-shirts. What I wouldn't give to feel my bare skin pressed against someone else. Just for a few moments. I swallowed hard.

He'd made it obvious earlier he was trying to backtrack everything that had happened this morning even though he had admitted the kiss was the same for him as it was for me, and I'd never taken him for a liar. His reasons for backing off this evening were his own, and I was determined not to take them personally.

But maybe he could ... do me a favor? If I found the right way to ask him. But for now I tried to keep him engaged in conversation. "So, how did they meet?"

"Through a mutual friend."

"That's it? That's the story?"

I heard and felt rather than saw him roll in my direction. "It's not the story. The story is that my mother ..." He paused. "My mother, my incredibly strong and intelligent and beautiful mother, was trapped in an abusive relationship."

I held my breath, not even blinking. I hadn't known this.

"My father helped her leave it. It wasn't romantic for them. Not at first. She had a young son, and her abuser kept her financially and emotionally captive, so my father found a way to help her. In the end they fell in love."

He delivered the words quickly and detached, like CliffsNotes. There obviously was so much more. But the parallels to our situation clearly made him want to get through it unemotionally. Apart from that one thing. "The young son?" I asked.

"Me," he confirmed quietly. "And before you ask, my father is my father. I don't know, nor do I want to know anyone else. My father raised me. My father taught me everything but especially about how a man can be strong without hurting the people around him."

I turned my head toward him, wishing I could see his face. "I'd say he did a really good job."

"Now can we go to sleep?"

"What about your mother? What did she teach you?"

He was quiet for a long time. I thought he'd fallen asleep, but then he spoke. "Everything, is the short answer. But specifically that the shame a woman, or any victim, feels in an abusive relationship is always placed *upon* them by the abuser. The abuser counts on that shame and humiliation and embarrassment to keep their victim from asking for help. It keeps the abuser in control."

I didn't feel them coming, but suddenly tears were streaking down my temples, and I was so thankful he couldn't see. I swallowed the ball lodged in my throat and hoped it would leave my voice steady. "I feel so much shame," I whispered, my voice wobbling slightly. "How did I let it happen? I should have known. I should have seen it earlier."

"You couldn't have."

I squeezed my eyes shut to get myself under control so I could talk. "You never want to believe these things, even when they start happening to you. They are so small at first. Tiny. He was so charming when we met that it completely disarmed me, blinded me. And maybe it wasn't charming, not in hindsight. What I saw as confidence was arrogance."

"Tell me about how you met him. Why him?"

"The first night we met was at an officer's barracks party. I'd been invited along by this girl I worked with. To cheer me up. She had someone she wanted to introduce me to. It had been a bad year with my mum getting sick. And that week, I was so down. I never did meet the guy I was supposed to, but there was this other guy there. I'd noticed him that evening, of course. He was handsome and also newly single as my friend quickly found out through her friends. We were all in a group, and someone new came up and joined us and was being introduced to everyone. And the new person, out of the blue, looked between Angus and me, we weren't even standing next to each other, mind you—hadn't even spoken yet—and this person asked, 'Are you two together?' I just laughed, super uncomfortable, but Angus immediately said, 'Not yet.' And stared straight at me. And honestly, it stunned me. That confidence was so attractive. I'd never had someone claim me like that. Be so sure. Then he spent the evening talking to me, asking me everything about my family, making me feel as if I were the only girl in the room and showing sympathy in the right places. I really felt like I'd met someone special. If only I'd known."

"Again. You couldn't have." He swallowed loudly, and I felt like he was about to say something else. But he didn't.

Other memories began to flit to the surface. "There were so many clues," I whispered. "But the one I remember the most was a story he told me early on in our marriage. My mother had blessed our marriage before she died. Begged me to stay married and not give in so easily to divorce. She always felt like she and my father could have worked it out despite the fact he happily went on to marry and have another family with his mistress. I don't even know where my dad lives anymore. But I digress. Anyway, I was predisposed to just sweep problems under the rug, you know?"

"What was the story he told you?"

"He told me a story about when he was little. About how a kid in his kindergarten class had teased him about the new tricycle he'd gotten for his birthday because it had glitter bits on it. At the party at Angus' house, which the whole class had been invited to, that kid had, Angus thought deliberately, poured his cup of glue from the craft table all over the wheels and gears. It had gotten all gummed up and never worked right again.

"And Angus' dad had refused to fix it. Maybe he blamed Angus. They had a tough relationship anyway. Angus was devastated and angry. He never forgot what this kid had done, and years later when he was a young teen, he got his revenge. Angus tracked the kid down and found out he lived in the housing estate on the other side of town. Poor as a church mouse. But Angus watched their neighborhood for weeks and weeks and finally identified the local bully, the head of the local thug group, who incidentally had a bike he rode around on. Angus waited and then one night slashed the tires and ripped off the chain. There'd been no good leather on the seat so he'd settled for burning holes in the plastic with his dad's lighter.

I grimaced in remembrance. "Angus was so proud of this story. He came back early the next morning before school, right when the vandalism was discovered. He walked right up to the thug, who was impotent with rage over the state of his bike, and calmly told him he'd seen it all happen. Then he named that poor kid from his kindergarten class who probably had zero recollection of *ever* crossing Angus' path."

There was dead silence. "Jesus," Evan finally breathed.

I remembered how that story had chilled me to the marrow of my bones. The moment I'd questioned everything I knew about my new husband. And I *still* hadn't paid attention to my gut. I didn't leave then. I should have left him then. But it was an old story, I'd told myself. He hadn't hurt *me*. Yet.

"What happened to the kid?" Evan asked in a strangled voice.

"I don't know. I imagine he probably ended up in hospital, if he was lucky."

"That's a big if."

I'd barely escaped my marriage with my *own* life. For not the first time since I'd made the decision to get divorced, I questioned how stupid the decision actually was.

"Angus never forgets." Evan voiced the same conclusion I already knew.

"I was *his*, Evan. Just like his bike. And by running away, I humiliated him. I should have known he's been waiting all this time for me to show myself." Tears sprang to my eyes, then burned down my cheeks, sliding cold into my hairline. This time I couldn't hide the shake in my voice. "I should have known. I should have known now. I should have known then and left sooner. Then—" I choke off what I'd been about to tell him.

"Shhh," Evan soothed, and his rough finger pads found my neck in the darkness, stealing my thoughts, and then found their way up my chin and to my cheeks where he brushed away my tears.

I reminded myself to breathe. God, the feeling of him touching me. It made me cry more.

"Shhh. It's okay," he said, his words a balm in the darkness, his breath stirring the fine hairs around my ears as he shifted closer. "I'm going to keep saying it. You couldn't have known. It's *not your fault*. His need to hurt, is not your fault. His need to intimidate is not your fault." Evan's hand cupped my jaw. "His need to dominate is not your fault. His need to scare you *now*, after nine years, is *not your fault*."

"It is though. *This* is. You being here, having to watch out for me because I was stupid enough to put myself in danger again."

"I'm here because I want to be."

"Evan."

"Sunflower," he whispered, and his thumb brushed over my lips once. "Tell me about the scar."

TWENTY-FIVE

It was so pitch dark in the tent, I wouldn't be able to see my own hand if it were an inch from my face. Darkness felt like the safest place to talk. I'd promised Evan I'd tell him about the scar, so now was as good a time as any.

I took a breath. "I was pregnant. I was so careful not to be. I didn't want to bring a child into his world, not when I knew I had to leave. But in the end my birth control failed me. I'd already made plans to leave. I'd met this woman. Well, I saw a flyer in the women's bathroom of a coffee shop I always went to, and one day I called the number. I was terrified, but I knew I had to do it. God bless these women who help other women get free." I reached up to wipe my eyes of the remains of my tears, and he took my hand, holding it tight, holding it between us. I drew strength from his firm hold. "Anyway, I was terrified he'd find out I was pregnant. And I didn't know what to do. I knew I could find the courage to leave him, especially with help. But if I had his child, it would be so much harder. I would always have something of his, something that belonged to him, and I knew he'd never let me go. So I went to a clinic and scheduled an abortion." I paused, waiting to hear Evan's reaction, but his breathing was steady and his thumb stroked my hand softly, gently, encouragingly. I went on. "The day it was done, I felt so much sadness but also profound relief. I thought there might be a chance for me to have a family one day, but there was no way I could have one in that situation."

"You don't have to explain yourself to me. It's okay."

"Is it?"

"I'd never judge you for a decision you had to make for your own well-being."

"People think women in my situation who make a choice like I did are negligent or uncaring. But they don't know what it's like when you can't breathe in your own skin in case it sounds wrong and sparks a fight. I was exhausted. I had nothing left for myself *except* a will to live. Certainly nothing left for another human. I didn't see getting pregnant as a sign I should stay with him, I saw it as a final test of my strength to save my own life."

His hand squeezed mine.

"He found out though. I don't know how. I think he'd followed me. Oh my God, but he was wild with rage. I thought I would die that night. I was weak from the procedure, I couldn't fight him off. He took a kitchen knife and told me that if I could so easily cut a child of his from my body I didn't deserve to even have a uterus. That night the woman who was going to help me leave came to my door. That's all I remember, because I woke up in hospital, having almost died, and then I came to France. The network had organized new identity documents and found me a position with Pascale Company as long as I was prepared to train. I was, I did. I would have done anything not to go back. I never saw Angus again after that night. I don't really remember that he stabbed me, only that he did. I should have pressed charges. He should be in jail, but the thought of ever facing him again and having to explain to everyone how I'd stayed married to him so long was more than I could bear. Hiding seemed easier."

Evan was quiet as I finished. "I knew you had been through a lot when you got here," he said after a bit. "I'm so fucking sorry that happened to you."

"Now you know." I gave a brittle laugh. "And now you know why I haven't dated or gotten close to someone in all this time. Even if I trusted myself not to pick the wrong person again, the thought of having to explain that scar has been too much. Too humiliating. But now I find that I haven't been touched in so long I've made myself terrified of it."

"I know."

"You know?" My body tensed.

"I'm not blind. I've had friends from the service, those with PTSD, that suffered a bit similarly. Not saying that's what's happening. But, I see you flinch sometimes when someone gets too close. Not always, not girlfriends. But I saw it with Christian. I see it with men. Even that night you went out with Josie to the nightclub, you looked like you were walking a tightrope on a dare on that dance floor."

I stiffened as he mentioned that night. I'd never thought of my nerves around touch as being the result of trauma. Rather just how long it had been since I'd had intimate human contact. But it made sense. Maybe it was a touch of both.

"I see it with me," he added.

I turned my face toward his in the blackness. "But I refuse to let Angus win this one." Today Evan had given me the gift of touching him, of pressing my body against his. And liking it. It seemed remiss not to mention it. "Today I got to be close to you. Closer than I've been to anyone in a really long time. Thank you for that. It felt monumental. I know whatever happened between us today was unexpected, and I know you wish it didn't," I said by way of answering him. "But I'm glad it did."

"It's not that I wish it didn't."

"Is it just that it complicates things? Like are you worried we might not be able to stay friends?"

"No." I could almost hear the struggle in his silence. "But it is complicated, yes."

I thought of Lilian saying she thought Evan had given his heart away a long time ago. "Why are you single?" I asked. "You are slightly stalkery and controlling, but for good reason, I guess. But you said all the right things during my horrific story. You care about everyone around you. You're funny and smart. Gainfully employed. You have the body of a god, and you kiss like one too." I finished and it was dead silence. Damn this truth-inducing darkness. "And I want to zip this sleeping bag over my head and never come out again. I can't believe I said all that."

He was still quiet.

"Are you even awake? Did you freaking fall asleep while I said all that?" I sat up on my elbows.

I heard the soft sound of him shaking in silent laughter. "Yes, I'm awake. I was just making sure my recorder was working. Can you repeat all that please?"

I slapped in the direction of his sleeping bag and hit a hard fabric-covered shoulder. I hoped. "Oaf," I complained and lay back down. Now in the intimacy of the darkness and after what we'd shared so far I began to feel bolder. "I wanted to ask you something. Lilian ..."

He gave a grunt. "Are you *sure* you're not getting sleepy yet?" There was a rustling sound and a long sigh. And I imagined him flipping onto his back. "What about her?"

"When did you ... *you* know?"

"Can't even say it?"

I huffed. "Sleep with her."

"I wouldn't call it sleeping."

"That's what she said," I grumbled.

"Are you jealous, Sunflower?"

I threw that questionably flirty tone back to him. "Would you like me to be jealous?"

"Hmm," he hummed. "It was a long time ago. And it was never serious. You have no need to be jealous."

"I'm *not* jealous. I never said I was jealous."

"Okay."

I lightly slapped his form again. "I'm not," I insisted. *I was.*

"But to answer your earlier question about my single status ... I haven't dated seriously because if I put someone first, which I would, otherwise I wouldn't date them, then by definition I don't put my job first. My profession requires, at its most basic level, keeping people alive. It's hard to reconcile those two priorities. Impossible, actually."

I turned my head to stare at where I thought his head must be. That was a pretty good reason. "What about just sex?"

"I have that. When I need it."

"Like with Lilian."

"Are you sure you're not jealous?" he teased.

"Of Lilian? No." I gave him a small lie before my truth. "But of people having sex, yes. I miss it. So much. The touching, specifically. The feel of another person's hands on my skin for the express purpose of giving pleasure." They should put people in pitch dark rooms for interrogations. What was it that allowed me to whisper so freely all my deepest secrets and desires? "But I'm not sure I've ever really experienced that. The pure pleasure part. I mean, I know I can touch *myself*, but it's not the same. Besides, the only time I've ever orgasmed is by my own hand."

There was a faint choking sound, like he'd been in the middle of swallowing and inhaling at the same time.

"Did I shock you? Did you not think I'm the type to get myself off if I need to?" I felt the low throb between my legs waking up. "Because I do need to."

"Jesus, Sunflower. You're killing me."

I smiled into the darkness. "Am I?"

When he deliberately bantered with me, it got difficult to know what he really wanted. I decided to go all in.

"Well, I'll shock you a little more then. Today, on your bike ... the things you made me feel ... God, Evan. I was so close, just from being pressed against you, the vibrations from the bike, the feel of your body under my hands."

"Stop." He let out a strangled groan.

I slipped my hands back into my sleeping bag and down my body and into my leggings. "I can't," I said. Now that I'd made this decision, it was like a switch had flipped. All my edgy arousal from earlier that hadn't been satisfied swelled back into my bloodstream, swirling beneath my skin and gathering low, demanding to be dealt with. "You don't have to touch me. But I really need ... something." I gasped as my fingers slipped between my legs. "As a ... friend ... I'm sure you won't mind if I—"

"Are you touching yourself?" he asked, his tone breathy. Incredulous.

I nodded, forgetting he couldn't see me.

"Tell me."

"Yes."

"What are you doing?" he growled.

"I'm t-touching myself. Between my legs. I wish it was you."

Evan moaned, a sound that felt like utter defeat. "Fuck."

The sound of it spiked my arousal. But I knew he probably still wouldn't allow himself to touch me. Not unless I really asked. But I wanted to be sure when I did, there'd be no hesitation. "It feels okay. Good. But not like today," I admitted truthfully. My finger moved in tight circles, but it was mediocre at best. "Maybe, you could, I don't know. Talk me through it?"

"Sunflower," he warned.

"I mean I know you don't want to touch me ..."

"I do. Fuck. I do."

I still didn't ask. "But you won't. What would you do if you *were* touching me? What should I do to make it feel better?"

He moved closer, his breath stirring in my ear. "Slip your free hand under your shirt, baby."

The sound of that endearment on his tongue speared through my stomach, causing it to clench. And just like that, with that simple word, and he might as well have been in my sleeping bag with me. I did as he asked, his whispers against the skin of my ear sending goose bumps flashing down my body. I arched up as my hand reached my breasts.

"Are you bare? Are your nipples aching to be touched?"

They were now. Damn. I'd had no idea Evan was a dirty talker and would go all in with me.

"Answer me," he demanded.

"Yes."

"Touch them. Stroke them. Pinch those tight buds between your fingers."

Oh my God. "C-can't believe I called you straitlaced before." I did as he asked and gasped even though I was already panting.

He gave a low chuckle that set my nerves on fire. That soul deep ache he'd ignited in me was back. Wetness flooded under the fingers between my legs. My fingers slipped lower, harder. Never mind Evan being a practice round. The key to my pleasure might just be Evan. I'd felt urgent arousal early in my dating years and certainly in the beginning with Angus. But never like this. And he wasn't even touching me. It was just his voice in my ear. His steady presence. The fact that I knew how safe I was right here with him. That I could tempt him to the depth of the most animalistic part of his soul, and he still wouldn't take from me unless I offered it to him. I could bare the deepest parts of my own desires, and he wouldn't touch them unless I wanted him to. It made me want to tear myself open and offer him everything.

"Tell me what your other fingers are feeling?" he asked.

"Slick." I gasped. "Wet."

He let out a soft moan in my ear. "Christ."

I widened my legs as much as I could in the sleeping bag. "I wish I wasn't wearing clothes."

"But you are," he whispered. "You'll just have to make do. Keep pinching your nipples. Are you rubbing your clit?"

"Yes." I bit my lip. My heart was pounding.

"Does it feel good?"

"It's not enough," I admitted on a moan. "I'm aching, Evan."

I felt him turn and press the front of his body into the ground as if to find some relief of his own. But he didn't touch himself. *I'd know.* And for some reason I loved that. I loved that he was denying himself for me.

His lips stayed near my ear. He inhaled. "You smell too good. I wish I could inhale every part of you. Do you ever put your fingers inside yourself?"

"Yes."

"Do it now. Maybe that will help," he added as if he was a kindly doctor just helping me out. For some reason the way he said it made me even hotter. Not that I'd ever had a doctor-patient fantasy, but God, I'd play that out with Evan in a heartbeat.

I slid a finger lower and dipped it inside of me. I was so wet, it slid inside easily, making my body arch. "It's not enough." I tried to rub myself at the same time with my thumb. It was torture being so close to the edge, being so close to *him*, and not being able to reach either. "It's not enough," I sobbed quietly.

"Two then."

"Mmm," I hummed as I followed his orders. "It's a little tight, but I'm really wet so—"

His breath elevated into pants. "Jesus. I've never been so hard in my life. Fuck, I wish I could taste you. Touch you. Be inside you. You. Are. Killing. Me."

His words were a physical pleasure rushing through my veins.

The way he was denying himself, keeping himself so still, was such a damn turn on, I could hardly stand it. But I didn't want this to end. When it ended, he'd go back to duty-filled, I-can't-allow-myself-to-get-distracted-from-my-job, Evan. But I was so close, I might not be able to drag this out any longer. Before I could think about it, I slipped my hand out from between my legs and up and out of the sleeping bag. I knew exactly where his mouth was whispering naughty suggestions in my ear, and I pressed my soaked fingertips against his lips. "Taste me then," I whispered.

There was a millisecond of shocked silence before he devoured my fingers, sucking them into his hot mouth like he was starving. A desperate sound wrenched from his chest.

I cried out, I couldn't help it. Holy shit. And suddenly I was quaking, an orgasm rolling through my empty body. I was coming hard, the only contact between us my fingers in his mouth. I arched and ached, empty and quivering. It was the best and worst thing I'd ever felt. "No," I gasped, shocked my body could do that and devastated too. "Not yet." I'd wanted his hands on me. I was aching for his touch on my skin. And now I wouldn't get it. He would do what he always did and go cold on me.

I pulled my fingers from his mouth and folded in on myself, curling away into a small ball. I was going to cry again, and I didn't want him knowing.

Why was I so fucking broken? My body shuddered again as my legs squeezed together. The sound of our heaving breaths filled the tent.

"Sunflower." The word broke off in his mouth. "I'm s—"

"You did nothing wrong," I snapped. "Don't apologize. Not again."

He was quiet for a long time, and I was grateful. The chances of sleep after what just happened were practically zero. Eventually our breathing slowed.

He shifted. "I know you didn't ask specifically, but I'll tell you anyway," he said in a low voice, "why today freaked me out. Why it's not I wish that kiss didn't happen. It's because if I'm looking at you, Sunflower, then I can't see what's *coming at you*. I can't watch your back when you're all I can see. When all my focus is on how fucking good it feels to kiss you and feel you against me. And now ..." there was the sound of a hard swallow. "Now I know what you taste like. What you sound like. I can't. It's too much of a distraction. I explained before why I don't date. I can't be both your lover and your protector."

"I never asked you to be my protector," I said stupidly, even though I was grateful he was. And now his cold rejection to my drunken make out attempt all those months ago made sense through this lens. He'd always been "on duty."

"But it's what I chose. And it's what you need from me right now. And when this is all done, and you are free of him, you won't think of me at all. And I'm okay with that."

God, that hurt.

"I want *life* for you, Sunflower," he continued. "You have so much of it to live. You need to be free to do that."

"Why do you call me that?"

There was a long pause. Then the shape of his sleeping bag molded around mine. Not holding me, but as comforting and as non-threatening as it could be. "It's my favorite flower. It's made up of thousands of tiny flowers. A thousand small and beautiful things that make up its whole. You have so much life in you. You always have. It gets brighter every day. I can't wait to watch you following the sun."

I did really cry then, huge fat tears. How could he say and do such beautiful things? I had a horrible feeling this crush I was indulging, wasn't a crush at all. This raging need to be free and to find love again wasn't just because it was time. It was everything all at once.

It was him.

I wanted him.

I loved *him*. And I think I had for a really long while.

TWENTY-SIX

Evan

I COME AWAKE EARLY AFTER ONLY four hours' sleep. I hear birds chattering and the pitch-black darkness of the tent has turned into dark gray. My arm is draped over Andrea, and she's let me hold her. Sure, she's sleeping, but it feels like a win. I don't push my luck and carefully lift away. She shifts a bit but goes back to deep and even breathing.

Last night comes crashing back to me, my morning wood finally having a solid reason to exist—the sounds she made, the way she followed my instructions, the taste of her soaked fingers. And fuck. I think she came when I sucked her fingers. *Christ.* I almost groan aloud. I should go cool off in the river.

It was the hottest night of my life, and no one took off any clothes. But I'm left with that raw vulnerability where I desperately want to rewind time. To do something different. But I don't know what.

After what transpired I'm sure she'll feel vulnerable too when she wakes up. She won't want to look me in the eye. Every time I see her breaking holes in her walls, she builds them back just as fast. I sigh, staring into the early morning grayness. Then the rest of what she shared last night, the story of her and Angus, guts me. I swallow hard, more determined than ever never to let last night happen again.

Today I'll need to make a plan for her. Or help *her* make a plan, I amend, catching myself. And also work out how to build up some distance to protect myself, and keep my promise, without hurting her feelings.

Sitting up, I reach for my phone to check in with Pete.

Any surprises last night? I type.

Sneaky Pete: *Nick and Gabe clock out at six. Nothing so far.*

Are you sure it was him?

Unless my guy in the village was wrong. It was an old picture.

Or he's waiting until the guys leave?

Something feels off.

Sneaky Pete: *I agree. I might take a run up there.*

I'll be back in the village in four hours, give or take. Meet you there.

I GLANCE over at Andrea's sleeping form. She's safe here. She has a ride back with Marianne. It will be a squeeze in the car but doable. Especially if I take my sleeping bag and backpack with me. I send a quick text to Marianne, apologize for leaving them with an extra tent to take, and tell her to leave it with Andrea and I'll get it later. Then I carefully remove myself, my sleeping bag, and my pack from the tent, and slowly zip it back up. Andrea mumbles but doesn't wake. I know she'll feel shitty I left without word, but what better way to bring back some distance between us.

After lacing up my hiking boots and a quick visit to the facilities, I begin the long hike back in the invigorating cold of the morning to where we parked our vehicles. Since it's just me, and mostly downhill, it will take me a third of the time. I need to get back to the village and see things for myself and meet with Pete.

The whole time, my mind tumbles through everything that's happened between Andrea and me. No matter how much I try to shut my spinning thoughts up and focus on Angus, and what his next move might be, I'm too distracted. And this is exactly what I've been trying to avoid.

I pause to watch the sunrise at the cliff edge overlooking the gorge where we'd stopped briefly yesterday. Mist that will burn off later has poured over the river like smoke. The glow of a new day bathes the cliffs in terra-cotta, and I wish Andrea could witness it with me.

I'm torn. I knew she had issues being intimate with someone. I was honest last night when I told her I'd noticed, but I hadn't realized just how much she was struggling. It makes me feel even shittier about how I shut her down so coldly a few months ago. Not that she probably remembers. She didn't invite me to touch her, not once, even when she was saying and doing everything that in a normal situation would have been all the invitation anyone needed.

In a normal situation ...

I don't know how I got through it. The need to touch her

and to be the one to bring her that pleasure almost did me in. But for some reason I knew holding back was the only way she would trust me and keep going. If I'd done something and touched her and she'd frozen, or I'd made her scared, there would be no way to take it back.

I'm torn because I so badly want it to be *me* that she crosses that intimate bridge with but know I can't be. For one thing, I can barely keep my mind on track as it is. And then there's my history with Angus.

I pick up my pace into a jog, reveling in the burn.

After she opened up to me about Angus, the last thing I wanted to follow it up with was "Oh, by the way, I know." That's something I made a decision about a long time ago. Not to tell her. Telling her now would destroy the basis of our trust. I'd almost told her everything yesterday, but we'd been cut short by Marianne. And last night in the tent ... just hadn't been the right time. In the cool light of the morning, I realize that was probably for the best.

There's still so much I want to understand—about her, about her relationship with Angus, about what she wants for her future. I'm not fool enough to try to be in it, but I will do anything I can to try to get her where she wants to go. And to do that she has to still trust me.

When I get to the lot, I'm breathing heavily, knees shaky and thighs burning from the repeated impact of the steep downhill jog. An old shrapnel injury from my time in the service bleats at me, finally sick of the two-day abuse. But it's finally worked to keep my mind from going over and over what the hell I'm doing with her. I feel clear now—there'll never be a repeat of this weekend—no more lines will be crossed—and maybe one day when she's moved on and built a new life, I'll tell her. And by then it won't matter.

My bike is where I stowed it, slightly out of sight beneath a gnarly olive tree.

I take a second to drink water and catch my breath and inhale in the crisp morning air. Then I strap my helmet on and wheel the bike out to the edge of the narrow blacktop country road. There's not a thing except low stone walls, fields, and forest in either direction. The sight of rolling bucolic fields glistening with morning dew, wisps of mist and sparkling morning sun makes everything seem like it's going to be all right.

∽

I'M BACK in the village parking lot well before midmorning. I exchange my helmet for a ball cap and sunglasses. Not much of a disguise, but it might give me a minute if Angus is around and watching. I'm assuming I'm out of context, so hopefully it works. But not if he sees me with Pete.

I check in with François, get a coffee, and find Pete at a small bistro table across the square. I almost don't recognize him in that ridiculous straw Panama hat, but I sure wouldn't miss him. He's reading a two-day old copy of *The Sun*.

"That shit will rot your brain," I mumble as I pass him and sit at another table like we're strangers.

"I know," he responds from behind the page. "But I keep hoping one day I'll open it and there'll be a topless babe on page three."

I roll my eyes behind my glasses. "Sure."

"Fine. You know I only buy it for the racing results."

"Which are easier found online."

"The horoscopes then."

"Same."

I hide my laugh behind a sip of coffee. He's only been looking at the paper to give himself cover for sitting and watching the lower gate. And I know he doesn't gamble.

"By the way, you stink," he says.

"Thank you. I ran down a mountain then rode straight here. Anything?" I ask.

"Nope. Doesn't make sense. You'd think he'd have circled back here already with it being the best lead he has."

"I think the law office is the best lead he has. And Meg. We might have to put someone on Meg. We don't need any innocent casualties."

Pete nods and out of the corner of my eye, I see him pull out his phone and text someone. "I already put Joe on it. Where is she anyway?" he asks, and I know he's referring to Andrea.

"We went on a hiking and camping weekend in the Verdon Gorge. She's with people. She'll be back this afternoon."

"How was it?" he asks.

I take a sip of coffee. "Our landlady who organized the trip is a matchmaking busybody. And Andrea and I had to share a tent," I tell him and inwardly brace myself. I'm so thankful we are not facing each other right now.

In my periphery, he cocks his head to the side and puts his phone to his ear like he's talking into it. "Reaaally? *Had* to share? Afraid of sleeping outside these days?" he asks. "Civilian life is making you soft."

I don't answer but crumple up my small white napkin.

"Only one sleeping bag too?"

"Fuck off," I growl quietly.

Pete laughs, then sobers. He pushes back his chair. "Let's go check out her place then. I saw no signs of forced entry on yours or hers."

I wait a minute, finish my coffee and get up. We go separate ways, and he's waiting at the top of Andrea's road, pretending to be a lost tourist when I round the corner along the town wall to the door of my unit.

Inside, my place looks exactly as I left it. Pete joins me inside but doesn't speak until I've opened the separating door and checked Andrea's place too. Andrea will be annoyed when she realizes I've taken the key so she couldn't lock the door again. No wonder I drive her so crazy.

"This is not right," I say. "We need to find him and get on the offensive."

"And then what?" Pete asks. "Seriously though. What's your plan?"

"I don't have one. I don't have one to deal with Angus, and I don't have one for her." Except not to cross any more lines.

"You need a plan for both, and soon."

"Fuck. I know."

"Can I get personal?" he asks.

We always warned each other if shit was about to get personal. Pete is the only person aside from Xavier I can trust. And Xavier has his own stuff to deal with right now. It still doesn't mean I want to discuss Andrea. "If you have to."

"Still not sure why you haven't thrown your hat in the ring."

"There's no ring."

"You're in denial. Christian already threw his hat in."

"It doesn't matter if there's a ring. I can't be a contender. I can't pursue her and protect her at the same time. Plus, she doesn't know I know him. It's not fair to her to keep that lie."

"Maybe you *should* tell her."

"What?"

"Tell her everything."

"No. After almost ten years, what? I'm going to say oh by the way, I know your ex? Especially after—" I press my lips together.

Pete's shrewd gaze pins me. "After?"

"I think I might have accidentally given her a clue about my soft spot for her. I need to walk it back but not hurt her feelings."

He chuckles. "I doubt it was soft. But you admit it finally at least."

"Hardy har har. You know what I mean. Fuck, Pete—" I blow out a breath and drag my hand down my face. "I kissed her. I shouldn't have. Then last night was ... I'm so screwed."

"You slept with her?"

"No. God, no."

"How is just kissing her screwing up? I'm still not seeing the problem. Unless she didn't want it?"

"She did." I think of her in the tent last night. "It was more than a kiss, really. I mean not actually. Jesus, I don't know what I'm saying. I screwed up. And I can't take that back. Part of me doesn't want to. Besides I don't think *she* even knows what she wants. How can she?"

"Actually I think that assessment is more accurately applied to you, my friend. She sounds like she finally knows exactly what she wants. That's why she's filed for divorce."

"Then it's not me she probably even wants. I just happened

to be there. I need you to watch out for her, Pete. I feel like I'm going to miss something because I can't keep my head on straight."

He doesn't know that she tried to kiss me when she was drunk, and it fucked with my head so badly for days that Dauphine had ended up in danger. I would never forgive myself for that.

All my clear thoughts I thought I'd settled on this morning are now all blended together into a jumbled mess. I have to admit my resolve to resist her if we end up in an intimate moment again will probably wear really thin, no matter what my conscience says. If Andrea wants sex, I'm right here, under the same roof, my mind objecting but my body ready and willing. "It's complicated."

"For the record I'm beginning to think you could complicate a ham sandwich. I honestly don't know why you can't just date her."

I lean against the wall and Pete sits on the end of my bed. I fold my arms across my chest. "You know people like us can't date the same way other people do. You know what happened with you and Millie."

"Goddamn, I hate it when you bring her up." He leans forward and rests his elbows on his spread knees. "But Evan. It was different with Millie. Life was different. I wasn't working this cushy mostly desk work security job for a privately held corporation. I have you to thank for that. But I'm telling you, you can delegate. You have me, you have a whole team you've trained. Look at you taking a month off right now, and you haven't even asked me for a security report. She is your only focus. And that's fine. We're all fine. Pascale Company is fine.

You aren't going on those questionably financed missions anymore, not knowing if you're coming home or who you're working for. I have you to thank for getting *me* out of it. It's too late for me with Millie. But you're dividing up your life like we're still doing that kind of work. You can date, Evan. You can even admit you're in love with her and have been for years."

Sweat beads at my hairline, and I swallow. "I'm not." I refuse to say it out loud and make it real. Everything inside me rebels.

I've definitely been denying how deep and wide what I feel for her is. There were times I thought I'd put her up on a pedestal for convenience—a way to give myself a reason why I never really dated or got close to anyone else. But there's nothing convenient about this. She's all the things I've always known she was, and more. And last night, the way she trusted me like she did, when I was keeping so much from her, almost broke my fucking heart.

He gets up and places a hand on my arm. "It's okay to admit it to yourself, you know I'm right." His blue eyes normally miss nothing, but even he can be wrong sometimes. "Even if you never do anything about it," he adds.

"Fine. I'm attracted to her. She's beautiful. I care about her, and I want her free of that son of a bitch once and for all."

"So that she can go off and date other people?"

"Yes," I say, though it's harder coming out of my mouth now than it sounded in my head earlier.

His eyes narrow and he steps back. "So, if you saw her with someone else, saw someone holding her, kissing her, knowing he'd get to go home with her and take her to bed, it would be okay? Someone else to undress her and make love to her?

Someone else to get all her sighs, and laughs, and tears, and touches? Someone else to get all her trust? To get her future?"

Jealousy rips through me. "Stop it," I grind out.

"Well, I know what the fuck that feels like, and it ain't good."

"I'm sorry that happened to you, Pete. But you and I are not the same." I turn and walk to the door, my fists curled tight. "This situation is not the same. And if she's with someone who is better for her, who can make her happy, someone who hasn't lied to her for nine and half years straight, then I want her happy." I swallow. "I want her safe. And I want her happy. And I want her free to make that choice without worrying about how *I* feel." And that was it really, wasn't it? Deep down I wonder if she was right at lunch that day telling me she needs space and freedom to understand who she is. I've made her so dependent on me she might think she wants me, but she's had no example of a healthy relationship. And I sure as shit haven't given her one. She doesn't want *me*. She just wants *someone*.

"And so, I rest my case," he says. "You're in love with her."

I glance back to see him cross his arms over his barrel chest.

"At least let her know how you feel so she can decide for herself," he says.

I try to think of something, anything, to deny what he's saying. But all I can think about is how much I fucking know he's right. I'm in love with her. But it still doesn't mean shit. "And you know from experience that doesn't mean we end up together. Especially with how much I've kept from her. And it also means I can't tell anymore whether anything I do is for her good or mine. Am I keeping her safe or keeping her with me? All these years I've fashioned a life for her, discouraged her from going out and putting herself in danger. What if I was doing that so she didn't meet anyone else? What kind of a person does that make me? It makes me no better than him."

"She *was* in danger. She still *is*."

"And that's all I should be focused on right now. Until she's free of him. And then I have to let her go."

"Tell her how you feel, Evan."

"Never in a million years," I say.

"Then you're a fucking fool."

TWENTY-SEVEN

Andrea

IN THE COLD light of day—and it was cold and very bright in the gorge—what Evan said last night made sense. When I was free of my past, maybe I wouldn't think of him at all. Maybe I was full of endorphins and thinking I loved him, but in truth, I was like a baby fawn in the arena of relationships. A baby fawn who'd already lost everything to an evil hunter. So why I thought I could trust myself *now*, just because I'd been awash in sex hormones, was beyond me. Also, *also*, I was 'of the age'. My biological clock was obviously trying to get some action in before last call, making me hyper horny. It made sense. Poor Evan was just the nearest person. And I was still shocked that I'd literally orgasmed with nothing but his mouth sucking my fingers. That was the universe calling my bluff after I'd told Marianne that it would be the easiest orgasm he'd ever given.

Waking up alone in the tent and realizing he'd left was all

the cold water I needed for whatever sentimentality I'd been harboring though. This was what he did. He might be attracted to me. But he didn't want to be.

I couldn't deny, and I bet he couldn't either, it had been hot as hell. Even now, busy rolling up the sleeping bag and working with Frédéric to break down the tent, warmth rushed through me in remembrance. The sound of his voice in my ear, demanding, coaxing, setting everything in me on fire. We might not have a future, but I was more determined than ever to ask him to be my first time—to be the one to touch me after so long. It could be no strings attached, just like Lilian said Evan preferred it.

We had pizzas for breakfast with egg, ham and spinach and cups of piping hot coffee.

Marianne pulled me aside on the hike down. "*Alors? Que s'est-il passé?*"

"Nothing happened," I answered her question in English. "I tried. It didn't go very far."

She frowned. "That man is too, how do you say? *Honorable.*"

I smiled. "I agree." I couldn't explain to her how he hadn't even touched me and how much that meant to me while at the same time I'd wanted him to thoroughly debauch me and erase every memory of every touch on my body except his.

We chatted on and off as we ascended back to the lip of the gorge before heading down the steep mountain trail that would lead to the parking lot. My body hurt from yesterday's hike, and my glutes screamed on every step. I actually loved it. I wasn't sure when I'd last used those muscles so strenuously, though walking up and down the streets in my little village had certainly helped. "I think I'm into this hiking thing," I said, using the opportunity to practice my French.

"You have truly never been before?"

"No." I shook my head. "I'm not crazy about sleeping in a tent, but one night wasn't too bad."

Frédéric turned his head from ahead of us. He'd been grunting with pain all morning. "You would enjoy the tent with me," he rasped on a wheeze.

"Are you even alive?" Marianne quipped in French.

He swore at her, and Cyril chuckled.

The rest of the trip down was done in silence as we all conserved our energy.

At the car Cyril opened the trunk and stopped dead, shaking his head.

"*Quoi?*" Frédéric joined him and looked inside. Then they both looked at Marianne who looked sheepishly at me.

"What?" I asked. "Did one of you stuff a body in there?"

Cyril pulled out the missing tent pole. "No, but maybe you want to put Marianne's body in here?"

"Cyril!" Marianne whisper hissed.

My mouth opened and closed. And then I turned to Marianne and held up my hand.

She flinched and chewed her lip. "What is this? You want to hit me?"

"No." I laughed. "Put your hand up."

She tentatively lifted her palm.

"I'm giving you five," I said and smacked it. "Evan looked like he wanted to murder you last night. It's really good to know I have a friend who's willing to risk her life to try to get me laid. Thank you."

She grinned.

"*Les femmes.*" Frédéric rolled his eyes and Cyril shook his head.

"But I failed. This time," she added.

"It was a good try," I said. "Don't forget you also gave me the key." Though I couldn't quite remember where I'd put it Friday night.

I took my pack off and dug for my phone, switching it back on now we were off the mountain.

"You unlock the door, yes?"

I nodded. "It's unlocked. I think tonight, I might go through it."

She jumped. "Yes!" She took her pack off and handed it to Cyril who stuffed it in the trunk. "Why wait until tonight?" she sang as she jumped into the passenger seat.

I climbed in the back behind her. Frédéric had to put his pack, tent, and sleeping bag between us on the back seat as it was a bit of a squeeze now.

My phone finally eked out a bar of service as we pulled out onto the road, and then it started going nuts with missed calls, voicemails, and text messages. The last text message was from my lawyer.

Veronica Patel: *Call me as soon as you get this! It's urgent.*

"Oh my God," I mumbled as my heart raced and cold sweat prickled down my body.

Evan. I needed Evan. But I needed to speak to Veronica too. I dialed Veronica's cell phone number and nothing happened for long seconds before an impotent beeping sounded. I yanked the phone from me ear. No service again. "Does anyone have service?" I gasped, my voice panicky. "How long until we have a signal?"

"What is the matter? Are you okay?" Marianne turned around in her seat. "Cyril, stop the car!" she ordered, taking one look at me. "Andrea will be sick."

"No," I yelped. "Keep driving. I need service. Shit."

"*Qu'est-ce qu'il se passe?*" Cyril shrieked. He swerved trying to turn around to look at me.

"Drive!" Marianne reprimanded him. "And calm down."

"*Je ne sais pas,*" Frédéric responded to Cyril's question, also peering at me. "What is it?"

"Andrea, what is wrong?" Marianne asked, concerned but handling it better than Cyril.

Cyril had floored the gas. He swerved around a car, earning another earful from Marianne.

I couldn't breathe. Shit. "C-call Evan," I told Marianne with great effort. "My lawyer said it's urgent. I need to call my lawyer." My phone had two bars of service. I pressed the buttons with shaky fingers and tried Veronica again.

"She is freaked out!" I heard Marianne talking. "Yes, something about her lawyer. Yes. Okay. What is going on? She is hysterical."

Was I?

Veronica didn't answer. Her voicemail picked up.

I pulled my legs up and wrapped my arms around them, resting my head on my knees with my eyes closed. I was as small as I could get, and I simply breathed and listened to the grumble of the engine and one side of Marianne's conversation. "Okay," Marianne said. "*D'accord.* Yes. We will see you there."

Breathe in. Breathe out. Breathe in. Breathe out.

Just because Veronica was calling me didn't mean anything bad. It could be good news. On a Sunday? It wasn't good news.

But it might be.

It wasn't.

My phone buzzed.

Safety Patrol: *Sunflower. You are fine. You are safe right now. I'm in the village and he is NOT here. I've had it watched the whole time we were away. You're okay. He doesn't know where you are.*

But for how long?

There was a pause and dots disappeared and reappeared. The phone buzzed, and I looked down, reading the words and feeling them crawl into my chest.

Safety Patrol: *I'll die before I let anything happen to you.*

Tears streamed down my cheeks.

"*Merde,*" Frédéric mumbled, seeing me start crying. "I dodged a bullet with this one," he added in French.

Marianne reached into the back with a rolled up magazine and slapped him over the head. It was so absurd and such a perfect reaction to the situation by Frédéric that my tears turned into hysterical laughter.

"*Tu vois!*" Frédéric said to Marianne in his defense as he watched me in bewildered confusion. "I think she might be crazy."

The phone rang in my hand. *Safety Patrol.* I wanted to see his name not the stupid moniker I'd programmed into my phone. I'd be changing it as soon as possible. It felt so trite and spoiled now that I would have made fun of the way he took care of everyone. Especially me.

"Hey," I managed, answering.

"Thank fuck you have service," Evan barked. "I've been trying to get through." He was quiet a moment, and then his voice dropped. "Did you get my text?"

"I got your text."

"Okay." He blew out a breath. "I mean it."

I swallowed. "I know," I whispered.

We were both quiet so long he'd probably hung up. There was so much in the silence. Too much. An admission neither of us was ready for. Certainly not him.

Cyril zoomed along the highway.

Marianne's hand came back and took my free one, squeezing hard. I squeezed back.

Evan took an audible breath. "Did you try Veronica? Do you know what she wanted so urgently?"

I didn't even try with how he knew her name. I didn't even care anymore. "She didn't answer."

"I'm sending someone to her house and her office to make sure she's okay."

Shit. "Oh God." I hadn't thought of that. My tears streamed faster, my nose burning. Trying to swallow so I could talk or thank him felt monumental. I nodded but he couldn't see me, though he could probably hear my crying.

He let me cry. I should have been trying to call Veronica again, but I couldn't let go of this connection. I couldn't stop drinking in the strength he provided even when he wasn't with me. Fuck Angus for still having this control over my emotions.

Marianne found a travel pack of tissues and handed them to me. Eventually my tears eased, and I wiped my nose.

"You still there?" I asked.

"Always," Evan said. "Have a look and see if she sent you any more texts when she couldn't reach you."

"O-okay. Don't hang up," I added.

"Never."

I took the phone from my ear and opened the messages. There was only the one message I'd already seen asking her to call me. I went to voicemails and saw two from her.

"I have two voicemails."

"Did they transcribe?"

"No. And I don't want to hang up."

"Wait until you get here. How far away are you?"

I squinted out the window at the land streaming by. "No idea. Hold on." I took the phone away from my ear again and went to my settings.

I flipped Location Permissions back on.

There was a long pause when I brought the phone back to my ear and then, "Sunflower," he croaked. "Thank you. Marianne is bringing you to me. Just come straight to me."

"Y-yes."

∼

CYRIL PULLED Marianne's car around to the top gate, the opposite end of town to the square and the parking lot we'd left from yesterday. There wasn't a lot of space for cars, which presumably meant less chance of one of them being Angus. I wasn't sure I was safe in my village anymore, but if Evan said I was, I'd trust him.

As we neared, I saw Evan in jeans and a white t-shirt resting against the stone wall, one foot propped up. His eyes were covered with sunglasses, and he had a ballcap pulled low. One arm was crossed over his chest, the other held the phone to his ear. He looked nonchalant and sexy as hell. My heart pounded so hard at the sight of him, I felt it might come out of my ribs.

I felt rather than saw his eyes on us. "You're safe to get out, there's no sign of him." Then he pulled the phone from his ear and pushed off the wall toward us.

"Phew," cooed Marianne. "I don't know what is going on, but if I had that man to protect me, I would not be afraid of anything."

Cyril grumbled something in French under his breath as he threw the car into park. Then he got out and went to the trunk and pulled my pack out.

I said goodbye and thanked Marianne and Frédéric, who grunted. "I'll call you and let you know I'm okay," I told Marianne. "I'm sorry about what happened in the car."

She squeezed my hand. "It's okay."

"Thank you." I took my bag from Cyril.

Then I set my eyes on Evan and walked to meet him halfway. I wanted to collapse into his arms. But as I approached I wasn't sure he'd know what I needed, he was so used to not touching me. Until he stopped, and after a brief hesitation, opened his arms.

With a helpless sob of relief, I fell against Evan's body and pressed hard against his chest. My bag dropped to my feet, and I wrapped my arms around his waist.

TWENTY-EIGHT

Evan closed up around me—his body, his arms, his strength enveloping me. One hand cradled my head, his face bent down to bury in my hair. It was the single best thing I'd ever felt.

We stood like that for long moments until he shifted and inhaled. "Sunflower," he whispered. "Let's go."

He eased back and took my bag and my hand, and we hurried into town. We passed *Le Tilleuil* restaurant where we'd sat with Meg and Sue, then up and down the cobbled streets until we were at his door. I blinked in the dim interior after the brightness of outside. He closed and locked his door behind us. Then he pulled the curtain across the small window, turned on a lamp, and laid his sunglasses on the bedside table.

His neatly made double bed loomed, and so did his side of our separating door. The room smelled of his recent shower, the woodsy scent of him at its peak for being warm and damp.

I suddenly felt awkward and out of place, and God knew what I looked like having hiked down a mountain and then crying my eyes out. I brought a hand up to my hair.

"You look beautiful." He took his ball cap off, tossing it on his bed, and rubbed a hand through his own damp hair, mussing it up.

He took a breath and started toward the separating door. It opened easily. "I checked your place earlier. It's fine. We should listen to the voicemails. Let's sit in there." He waved toward my living area.

"Right." I started forward and darted past him. "Can I offer you a drink or anything?"

"I'm fine. Come on. Let's do this." He entered behind me and immediately hit the light switch in the kitchen and then drew the curtains across both windows in the living area. "Safe side." He shrugged.

"I'm scared, Evan."

"I know."

"What if he's hurt Veronica? Or threatened her? How will I live with myself? What if he comes here?"

Evan walked up to me and took my wrists from where I'd brought both hands up to my face. He gently drew them down. His beautiful hazel eyes grounded me. "He won't. You can do this. Let's just listen, okay? It might be nothing."

I nodded and pulled my phone out of the pocket of my bag. "Have you heard from Pete?" I asked.

"Not yet."

I blew out a puff of air. "Okay."

I opened the voicemails where we stood and went to the first one Veronica had sent so we could listen in order and hit play.

"Andrea, it's Veronica Patel. Sorry to bother you on a

Sunday, but I need you to call me urgently." The message ended.

"Damn," I said. That had told us nothing.

"Go on."

I pressed play on the next message, which was her most recent.

"Hi, it's Veronica again. Please call me. Um, does Angus have a brother? I need to know." My eyes flew to Evan's, and I nodded to his unspoken question. But Angus and his brother were estranged as far as I remembered. "I've been contacted by someone claiming to be his brother," Veronica went on. "He says he has information about Angus. He says he's been looking for you. Don't panic, okay? But I think you should come in and meet with me tomorrow. I have an opening at ten. Can you make that? Shoot me a text and let me know. I have to run out for a family commitment now and won't be back until late. Okay, bye."

I frowned and called her back just in case I could catch her. It went to voicemail again.

"Do you know his brother?" Evan asked.

I shook my head. "Not really. He was at our wedding. But then we never really saw him after that. Angus said he moved away or something. The family wasn't close. Kind of like mine, I guess."

"Well, she didn't sound panicked. I'm going to reach out to Pete and let him know what Veronica said and see what else he can find out. Okay?"

"You're *asking* me?"

"I'm asking you. I'll be honest though, if you said no, it

would be really fucking hard and the chances are, I'd do it anyway. I have a real problem with—"

"Boundaries? Control?"

He clutched the back of his neck. "Yeah," he admitted, eyes on mine. "When it comes to you. Yeah."

My throat tightened.

"And I'm sorry about that," he said.

"Don't be. I trust you. Completely."

His gaze dropped, and he turned away. "You hungry? It's already three. What's your grocery situation? I can make you something while you shower. If you want." He walked around to the other side of the kitchen table.

"I guess," I said, confused at the topic change, and watched him open and close everything in the kitchen, familiarizing himself. "Last time I saw Veronica and I thought I was being watched, she said we shouldn't meet at her office anymore. Why would she ask me to come in tomorrow at ten, then?"

Evan straightened from looking in the fridge and pulled his lower lip between his teeth.

"I don't know what to do," I added.

"There's nothing *to* do." He turned to me and placed eggs on the counter. "We have guys watching both entrances to town. You picked the perfect place, by the way. You're safe here until you need to go into the city to meet with your lawyer tomorrow. And I'll come with you. If you want."

"I'd like you to. Don't you, um, have work or something?"

"I've taken some time off."

I blinked. "From Pascale Company? You took time off? When? Why?"

"It doesn't matter. Do you want an omelet? I can have it ready when you get back downstairs."

My gaze darted to the stairs and back. The need to shower and see what on earth I looked like felt urgent, but I was scared to go up alone. Also the vibe between Evan and me had shifted—there was a new intimacy between us that it seemed neither of us knew what to do with. Everything suddenly felt awkward.

"Do you want me to come up there with you?" he asked.

"I'm sorry. Yes. I'm jumpy."

He came around the kitchen table. "It's fine. I'll go up first."

"Okay."

He headed for the stairs but stopped in front of me. "I hated how scared you sounded today."

"I hated being scared," I whispered, tilting my face up to meet his gaze. "I'm tired of being scared. Thank you for being here for me. I'm not used to needing anyone, or asking for help."

He lifted a hand and tucked a stray strand of hair behind my ear. "I'm here as long as you need me." His gaze, a kaleidoscope of greens and browns, roamed my face.

I reached for his wrist before his hand lowered and cupped his hand to my face, pressing into it. I closed my eyes at the feel of his callused palm on my skin.

"Sunflower," he said roughly before he slipped his hand away.

I blinked.

"Come on," he said. "I'll check out upstairs for you, then you can shower and I'll make you some food."

He rounded the corner of the stone wall and jogged up the narrow stairs, ducking at the low ceiling. I appreciated the back view of him for a second before following. His presence was both comforting and disconcerting, familiar and bizarre. And as I got to the top step and saw him in my bedroom, overwhelming.

"Bathroom's clear," he said and closed the linen window curtains, casting my room into a hazy shade. "I'll be downstairs. Anything you don't want in your omelet?"

"I'll eat whatever you make. Thank you."

He brushed past, barely looking me in the eyes. It was so unlike the Evan I knew.

The Evan I knew was devil-may-care, twinkle in his eyes, quick with a joke or a jab to raise my hackles. A tease to make me engage. Today he was none of those things. Today had rattled him as much as it had me.

I quickly gathered clean clothes—a fresh pair of leggings and a t-shirt. Then I thought of underwear and rummaged in my drawer for some actual matching and pretty underwear, finally settling on a black lacy set I'd bought last summer on a whim.

I wished I knew what I was dealing with. It was an utter curve ball to suddenly think of Angus' brother. What was his name? Neil? I barely remembered him apart from the fact Angus had told me he'd moved out when Angus was only fourteen.

Turning the shower on, I spun the dial as hot as it would go and undressed. I shot a quick text to Veronica and let her know I'd be there at ten. I needed to put Angus out of my head until tomorrow, until I could meet with Veronica. And the funny thing was, now that I knew Veronica was probably all right, and that Angus hadn't been here, I actually *could* get it out of my head. When I was with Evan, there was no room to think about Angus—my husband's power over me waned.

Part of me revolted at the thought it took another man to gain the sense of peace I craved. But I realized that all the peace I'd had over the years had been precisely *because* Evan had been there. He'd given me that. He was still giving me that. And he'd never asked anything in return except that I let him know where I was at all times. And I had taken that away from him too.

I let the scalding water slough all the tension from my body from the roots of my hair to my toes. I scrubbed my scalp and my skin, imagining I was peeling the layer of fear off that I'd experienced today. It had been blind panic. I'd had smaller panic attacks from time to time, most recently at my lawyer's office, and also a few weeks ago when I'd worried about who was moving in next door, but today's had erupted so violently it had shaken me to the core. Eventually I turned the shower off and got out. I moisturized my body and combed my wet hair. I'd caught the sun on our hike, and my skin glowed, shiny and flushed. I towel-dried and combed my hair back, securing it in a low, lose bun. I pulled on my pretty underwear, refusing to let myself contemplate why. Then I dressed and added fuzzy socks before padding downstairs.

"Mmm, it smells good," I said.

"It's ready." Evan, the dishtowel over his shoulder, was plating the two halves of a huge, fluffy omelet on two plates. He'd garnished the edge of each plate with sliced tomato. His chestnut hair had dried, mostly straight, the odd curl swinging up around the shell of his ear and at his nape. He normally wore his hair very short, but every now and again toward the end of the summer he let it grow a bit, and I enjoyed spotting the few natural waves and cowlicks that sprang up. He had a small line between his eyebrows as he concentrated on his task. "When you've finished staring, what would you like to drink?"

I smiled sheepishly. "White wine?" I reached into a drawer for napkins and placemats. "That smells and looks so good."

"Hope it tastes good too. You have wine. I'll stick with water."

"Music?" I asked and when he nodded, I started a Giant Rooks playlist and poured a glass of wine from the fridge. I laid placemats and napkins on the scarred wooden farm table so we sat opposite each other, and Evan set down the plates and grabbed utensils. We took our places, me on the bench side and him on a chair, and then I looked up and met his gaze.

"*Bon appetit,*" he said.

"Thank you. You too." I dug in. "Mmm." The warm herby flavor was comforting and delicious.

I picked up my wine glass. "Cheers." We clinked glasses and drank.

"Pete texted. There's no sign of anything wrong at Veronica's home or office. She's probably fine and at a family event, like she said. He'll let us know when he gets eyes on her. And nothing and no one is coming into the village tonight."

"Having you here, and the fact you have people watching the village, it's amazing but ... perplexing."

"How so?"

"Well. Who's paying them for one?" I took a bite of omelet.

"You don't need to worry about that."

"You clearly don't know me *that* well then." I let out a small uncomfortable laugh.

He chewed and swallowed. "*I'm* paying them."

"You are? Do they work for Pascale Company?"

"Some of them do."

"I'll pay you back."

"You won't."

I scowled. "When did you take time off from Pascale Company?"

He cocked his head and looked at me expectantly.

I swallowed hard and reached for my wine when he still didn't volunteer. "I'm guessing when I resigned?" I winced and took a sip.

"Correct."

"I don't understand." I shook my head, guilt bubbling up.

"Don't you?"

I stared at him. "I didn't ask you to do that."

"I chose to."

I pushed my omelet across my plate and managed another two bites. It was surprisingly filling. I chewed and swallowed. "So, you care about me as more than one of Xavier's employees?" I ate my tomato, trying to act as confident as possible.

"We've been friends a long time. Of course I care about you as more than an employee. How can you even question that?"

I took a sip of wine and looked him dead in the eyes. "But it's more than that even. Right?"

He stilled and set his fork down.

Taking a deep breath, I set my fork down too. "And just so you know, I care about you as more than a friend too."

"No, you don't. It's just that I'm here, and you're going through a lot. It's easy to get confused." He looked away.

"I thought so too, at first." I took another huge gulp of wine, and then set my glass down. "But no. It's you."

"Sunflower. Stop." He leaned back, rubbed his palms along his thighs. "Don't say anything else that you can't take back."

"I won't want to take it back."

"You will. Believe me."

"I *believe* I just mentioned you don't know me as well as you think you do. And you definitely don't know what I'm thinking."

"You need to eat."

"I need *you*."

His breathing hitched as his tension coiled. "You don't know what you're asking."

"Yeah. Actually, I do. I want it to be you, Evan. I want you to be the one who touches me. And I don't know what you're into—Lilian seemed to imply your tastes ran a bit exotic—but if that's why you're holding back with me. Don't."

"Lilian doesn't know what the fuck she's talking about. And I wish you'd stop bringing her up. She was nothing to me."

"Am *I* nothing to you?"

His swallow sounded like he hadn't had a drink for days. "Fuck, Sunflower. You know you're not." His shoulders lowered like he'd given in to the admission.

"I want you," I whispered. "I want to lose my mind with you. I want you to help me get out of my head and forget what's going on—to forget what's happened to me. I want to remember what it's like to crave touch, not shy away from it. And you've already given that to me. I crave your touch. Last night I needed it so bad, and I didn't ask. Well, I need it now. I'm asking now. I need you."

Evan's eyes hadn't left mine as his breathing shallowed and accelerated, and his eyes darkened. His chest heaved. "Please,

Sunflower. I told you already I can't be both your lover and your protector. It's a rule I live by."

"You said we were safe here for now. Did you lie?"

"No. I didn't lie." He squeezed his eyes closed, and his jaw ticked. I imagined that under the table his fists were drawn tight, if the bunching of his shoulders and arms were anything to go by.

"You said you'd be here as long as I needed you. Well, I need you." My heart thumped loudly with nerves, almost jumping up my throat. "This is the way I need you. And this time I want your hands on me. I want *your* fingers inside me."

We stared at each other, breathing in and out heavily.

And I saw the exact moment he caved. The shift in him. His hazel eyes morphed into deep forest green, the pupils almost blacking them out.

My insides practically disappeared.

"Go on," he croaked. "What else?"

I was burning up from the inside out. Dampness pooled between my legs.

"Go on," he demanded again. "You get to be in charge here. What else do you want?"

"Are you going to give me what I want?" My words were jagged as I struggled to control my air. "O-or is this just a hypothetical wish list?"

"I'm going to give you everything you ask for," he said and arousal spiked, hot and sharp, through my insides. "But I need to know what and how you want it. What you're comfortable with."

"I—I want you to touch my nipples and between my legs."

"And my mouth, baby? Do you want my mouth there too?"

Oh my God. I froze for a split second in shock and then nodded, panting.

Evan reached over and slowly moved my plate and glass of wine to the other end of the table. Then he did the same with his, his gaze not leaving mine. He leaned forward on the newly cleared-off table, food forgotten. "Take your shirt off."

TWENTY-NINE

I complied so quickly to Evan's command to take my shirt off the neckline caught on my ear and then pulled my low bun free. I dropped the shirt on the floor. Thank the stars I'd put on the sexy black push up bra after my shower. His eyes raked hungrily over me, and seeing the way he stared at my chest made my belly flip over.

"And your leggings."

I couldn't believe he was going through with this. I wanted to congratulate myself, but there was no time. Heart pounding, stomach tense, I lifted my ass on the bench and shimmied the leggings down, hidden from view by the table, and took them and my socks off over my ankles. Then I lifted the clothing high to show him and tossed them on my discarded shirt.

"Come over to my side."

I don't know what made me bold enough, but instead of climbing out from the bench and walking around to where he sat on his kitchen chair, I stood and put a knee on the table and then leaned forward and climbed onto the table and crawled over to him.

"Jesus." His jaw was slack, his chest heaving. He sat back.

I bit my lip.

His eyes were trying to take in every part of me at once. My scar, my breasts, my face. "Goddamn, you're beautiful." He raked a hand down his face. "You're going to destroy me, aren't you?" he asked then, looking up into my eyes.

"I hope not." I smiled nervously, and then shifted my weight and set my butt down on the table and swung a leg to each side of him. I leaned back on my arms and spread my knees, my feet swinging. His hands gripped the table either side of my thighs and his eyes traveled down my torso and zeroed in between my legs. His nostrils flared as he inhaled. His gaze was like a magnet, making me want to lift my hips toward him. I congratulated myself again for taking a chance and putting on the sexy underwear, and thankful I always scheduled regular waxes.

My breathing grew erratic. "Are you just going to stare?"

"It's your show, remember?"

"Please," I begged. My courage only ran so far.

"Please what, baby?" He glanced up, only for a split second, but enough for me to see the twinkle in his eyes I loved so much, and my courage rushed back.

"Touch me."

His hand landed hot on my thigh and skated over my skin. "Here?"

"Yes. And ... between my legs."

He pulled his bottom lip between his teeth and then looked up at me as one finger trailed up my thigh to my hip and then my belly button. He dragged his fingertips back and forth to my waist and lingered on the edge of my scar, making my belly tense, before beginning a downward journey. At the line of my panties, he hesitated.

"More. Lower." My stomach quivered, and my head dropped back as the next touch ghosted over my clit through the fabric and down to my center. "Again," I gasped.

He repeated the action, and I pressed closer, needing more pressure. I was getting so wet, he must have been able to feel it.

"Harder?" he asked, his voice was strained.

I nodded. "Yes. Please. More. Harder. Again."

He swore and complied. "Baby, you're soaked. Can I feel your skin?"

I nodded.

He slipped my panties to the side. "Fuck," he said softly and groaned.

And I gasped as his fingers connected with my slick flesh. "E-Evan."

His fingers pressed against my clit and moved in circles. Over and over until I was quivering and aching. His fingers slipped a bit lower in my wet heat at every pass.

"Inside," I cried out. I needed to push my feet against something to lift my hips more. As I had the thought, his other hand dragged my hips to the edge of the table and threw my leg over his shoulder.

My eyes flew open and I saw his face, cheeks flushed with arousal, mouth sightly parted as his finger sank inside me. "Oh God." I reached out and clutched his hair.

His eyes found mine for a spit second and I nodded. Prickles raced over my skin.

And then his hot mouth was on my center, his tongue flattened against me, swiping up in long licks.

"Oh, God, oh God, oh God," I chanted. "Feels so good." More words came from my mouth, but I was incoherent with need and desire.

Inside me, his finger stroked in and out, my hips seeking more at each retreat. "More," I begged. "I need—I don't know what I need."

He stopped and withdrew. "It should have been me last night." And I blinked as I watched him suck two of his fingers into his mouth and then lower them back to my entrance. He slid them both inside me.

I gasped and cried out, my body bucking. "Oh God, yes."

His mouth returned, his tongue licking and pressing.

My arms holding me up collapsed down to my elbows. "Evan," I moaned.

His fingers plundered me, his tongue pressed harder, and faster, and I begged and pleaded and bucked and then his lips closed over my clit and sucked hard, his fingers inside curling and pressing upward.

I went rigid as the orgasm slammed into me, a scream climbing up my throat and then I shattered, the room and my world and my body dissolving from existence.

"Holy shit," I whimpered. I came to with him standing and gathering me up in his arms and holding me as I sat at the edge of the table still quaking.

Enveloped in his arms, I clung to his hard shoulders, my face pressed against his chest as he stood at the table, his heart pounding. "That was ..." there were no words. I'd never experienced that before. Sure, I knew people did that, but Angus never did.

My hands roamed Evan's back and under his t-shirt, his muscles quivering as I touched his warm skin. I sat back and pulled his shirt up to take it off.

His hand stopped me. "Sunflower."

"It's still my show." I glanced down to see the hard line of his straining erection against his jeans.

"Oh really." His eyebrow raised.

"Really. And you look uncomfortable."

"I'm fine."

"*I'm* not fine. Not yet." I reached for his jeans button and pulled it open and lowered the zipper. "Take your t-shirt off," I begged.

We locked eyes, and I silently challenged him as he fought me. "We're doing this," I said softly, eventually. "And not just once."

He closed his eyes on a long blink and met my gaze again. "Once would never be enough. Not for me."

"Not for me either. Besides, I need lots of practice." I smiled but a shadow crossed over his features. It was so fast, I almost missed it. "I have lots of time to make up for."

He reached behind his head and pulled his t-shirt off.

I took a second to admire the shirtless god in front of me, his jeans hanging low and open, and moaned. "How do you stay so in shape?" God, but he looked good. All bulk and muscle and promises. My eyes went south. And he was so hard, the tip of him poked at the top of his dark gray boxer briefs, a dark circle of moisture spread around it.

"I work out. Obviously." He smirked and his eyes dragged

down my body, making my stomach clench. He licked his lips. "How do *you* stay so curvy and delicious?"

"Croissants for breakfast. Obviously." I gave a quick eye roll, and dug my teeth into my lower lip to keep from smiling at the unexpected compliment.

His head tipped back exposing the smooth skin of his throat, and a laugh broke free, cascading over my skin. The sight of him in that moment, made my chest seize. I'd never felt safer or more beautiful or more attracted to another human in my life. I wanted to crawl into him. Or have him crawl into me. On that note ... the mood shifted and tension blazed. I raised my hand.

He held his body still as I reached out and ran fingers down his hard stomach, the muscles twitching under my touch, his breathing getting shallower and faster. Then I pulled the top of his boxers down to reveal the head of him. With a single finger, I swiped the small bead of moisture at the tip and sucked it into my mouth.

Evan's chest caved and a deep sound wracked him. "Jesus. Fuck. Sunflower."

"Kiss me, Evan."

He dove forward, his hands gripping my face and his parted lips meeting mine. His tongue slipped straight into my mouth, and his body slammed against me, cock hard against my belly.

His mouth devoured me, hands gripping my head, angling me for better access. He tasted of the essence of me and just ... him. I met him kiss for kiss, stroke for stroke. My hands raked over his body, trying to get him closer and touch more skin. I *loved* his hands holding me.

Finally his touch slipped from my face into my hair and then down my back, making me shudder. The feel of him holding me and touching me was so exquisite, prickles raced over my skin.

He pulled back. "Okay?"

I nodded. "So okay. Your hands on me. Amazing." I couldn't speak in complete sentences.

"You feel so good," he whispered, and his fingers came over my shoulder down to my lace covered breast. "So soft."

I arched into his touch and covered his hand with my own, squeezing, giving him permission. He dipped his fingers under the lace and pulled the cup down.

"Yes." I nodded, exhaling shakily. "Do what you asked me to do in the tent."

His throat bobbed and his hand closed over my breast, his thumb and forefinger squeezing together, catching my nipple. I felt it like a line straight to my core. Then he dipped this head and took it into his mouth.

I cried out. I was a sunbeam glowing and burning with pleasure radiating through every cell. Using the space between us, I slipped my hands into his jeans to cup him, squeezing along his hard length and loving the strangled sound he made while his mouth was full and he couldn't speak.

He sucked me harder, almost to the point of pain. "Yes." I loved it. He switched to the other breast, yanking my bra down and then fumbling behind me for the clasp. He paused.

"Take it off. Please," I begged. "And you need to stop hesitating. I want this. I want everything." I grabbed his face and kissed him deeply and pulled back and stared in his eyes. "I want all of you, you control freak. It's killing you to hold back, so stop doing it."

"I don't want to hurt you, or trigger something, or scare you."

God. This man. "You." I kissed his lips. "Won't. It's *you*. I trust you completely. It would be impossible."

He pressed his forehead to mine. "God, Sunflower, I—" His heavy swallow seemed painful as his eyes closed into a grimace.

"You what?"

He didn't answer but just kissed me slowly, softly, gently. His tongue stroked, his hands cradled. His mouth moved to my ear, my hairline, my forehead, then my lips again and down my throat. His lips were sublime, his hands, as they roamed my back and gripped my hips, heavenly. "I can't resist you anymore," he whispered as his tongue swirled over my skin, and my fingers threaded through his soft brown hair.

"Good. Same boat." I laughed. "Just give in."

"I am. I have."

I tucked my thumbs into the fabric at his hips and pushed his jeans and boxers down. Then I lifted a foot and used my leverage sitting on the table to shove the jeans down to the floor. His hard length bobbed free and I ached at the sight, wanting him inside me so badly. He reached down and helped push his jeans off, toeing off his socks. And then he was naked. He was so damn beautiful.

He returned the favor, curling his fingers into the elastic and lace at my hips, and I lifted up for him to drag my underwear down my legs.

"I'll never be able to eat at this table again," I joked.

"Really?" Evan teased. "Coz I just did. You, in fact. And I'll do it again anytime."

I laughed and pushed at his shoulder. "Heathen."

"Stating facts. Shall we go upstairs?"

I reached out and took his cock in my hand, causing a hiss to escape his mouth. "No. No time. I'm so ready to have you in me." I kissed him, then lifted my heels to the edge of the table, my glutes protesting from the hike.

He looked down letting out a hiss as his gaze zeroed in between my legs. I guided him to where I was spread and so ready for him, "Sunflower." His voice broke. "What are you doing to me?" He kissed my lips and my nose and then his hand took over from mine and he slipped the head of his erection up and down, spreading through my wetness. "You on the pill?"

I nodded. "Shot. Please." My head fell back and my eyes closed on a sigh as I anticipated him pressing into me.

"Watch me, Sunflower," he said. "I need your eyes on me. I need you with me. I want you to see who's bringing you this pleasure. I need you to know it's me."

I blinked, barely capable of speech since my pulse pounded in my throat and the arousal was wound so tight around me, I could barely breathe. His tone sounded so vulnerable it made my heart ache. "*You* are. Evan." The head of him notched in, and I whimpered at the exquisite feel of him.

He was wider than his two fingers and it had been so long. So long. I didn't even want to think about the last time.

"Relax, baby. Look at me."

My eyes flew to his, surprised he could tell I'd tensed.

"It's me, Sunflower."

I nodded, biting my lips together and tears suddenly springing to my eyes. "Just do it."

"We should go to a bed. Or we can wait until you're ready."

"No." I grabbed his waist and pressed myself further onto his length. "Here. Now. *Erase* him."

I felt the exact moment something inside him snapped. All that control and restraint he'd exhibited last night, and maybe for years—the thought was fleeting and gone before I could analyze it—collapsed. He wrapped an arm around my waist, gripped my nape, and covered my mouth with his.

Then he thrust into me.

"Fuck!" he roared.

THIRTY

Evan

THE FEEL of Andrea in my arms, the way she shudders with pleasure under a simple touch of my hand on her skin, her soft body wrapping around me, her eyes full of trust and pleasure and emotion undoes me. The cry of surrender she lets out as I thrust inside her. The feel of her tight, wet heat around me breaks every vestige of restraint I have left.

I need more. I need her. I can't believe I've held out for as long as I have. I withdraw and slam back inside, seating myself as deep as I can go. I grunt. "God."

She cries out again, clutching me closer, her fingers digging in, but I can't feel any pain. I need to hold her closer and still have leverage. I ... can't ... get ... enough. Also, I'm bare. I never do this. Never. But ... it's her. It's raw, every nerve ending firing, my skin feeling like it's stretched so tight on my body I might split in two. I've never experienced anything like this.

My hands roam her entire body, wanting to imprint my touch on every inch of her skin. She leans back on the table as I slide in and drag out, and I revel in every inch of sensation. My eyes devour the sight in front of me. Her glowing skin, soft curves, her gorgeous tits, taught nipples, and the scar that brought her to me.

She matches me stroke for stroke, her ankles locking behind me. I'm so fucking close, but there is no way I'm letting this end so soon just as I got to this place.

I slow and gather her up. She protests as I lift her, but then groans as it makes the angle of our joining deeper for a moment.

She squeezes her arms around my neck, her breasts flattening to my chest, her breath in my ear. "You feel so good," she whispers, her body wrapping around me like a monkey. I stagger over to the couch and sink down, disconnecting us briefly.

"Your show, remember?" I remind her.

She smiles and straddles me, lifting onto her knees. The living area is a lowlight haze from the last afternoon sun, and the soft kitchen light makes her body glow. Faint freckles are visible across the bridge of her nose. Her blue eyes have tiny bronze specs in their depths.

"You're beautiful." My tongue feels thick in my mouth. Her hair is damp and curling sightly, her skin dewy and sun-kissed from our weekend. I'm so fucking in love with her, I don't know how she doesn't see it in every sweep of my gaze, in every touch of my fingertips. I don't know how I've denied it as long as I have. I may as well be screaming it. It's going to kill me when she's free of him and starts to live her life again and leaves me behind. But I want that for her more than I want her for myself.

I'll take whatever she'll give me now and be grateful for it for the rest of my life. When she begged me for this, I'd had the urge to ask her if she could handle it. Now I realize I should have been asking myself that question.

I hold myself steady in one hand, the other hand cupping her jaw, my thumb running over her lips. I don't know if she sees the emotions pouring out of my eyes right now, I'm powerless to try hiding behind the mask I always wear around her.

She positions herself and then we lock eyes and she sinks down, taking me all the way to the base.

"Fuck," I swear quietly, overcome. The tightness and heat of her takes my breath away. Especially when she stills at the bottom, and her eyes blink slowly like she's trying to keep them open against the onslaught of sensation. I know the feeling.

"I want to stay like this forever," she whispers and leans forward, her head bowed. "I want to feel like this forever. I didn't know," she adds faintly. "I didn't know it could feel like this."

My throat closes as I kiss her forehead, the top of her head, and pull her in close.

She doesn't know what she's saying, I tell myself, even as my stupid chest cracks a little inside. We're making love. And she doesn't know what she's feeling. She's never known a way to tell the difference. But I do now.

Out of the speaker she connected to a playlist earlier, Dermot Kelley is singing his song "Power over Me," and I realize this moment was utterly inevitable. I'm destroyed. There's no coming back from this. I'm going to have to go all in, lay my cards on the table, tell her everything, and be willing to deal with the fall out. I need to tell her. I know I do. But the words won't come.

Instead I let my hands roam, bringing me back to the physical. I force the sudden emotion and guilt away and focus on the feel of her skin and the way her body reacts as I run my hands down her sides and over her hips and butt. Her cheeks are tight and smooth under my palms. Her breathing hitches, and my cock jerks inside her, demanding attention.

She sits back, and her hips ripple back and forth.

"Ride me, baby," I whisper. "Take what you need."

Her eyebrows pull together. "What about you?"

My hands roam up her belly and cover her breasts. "I have everything I need right here. And trust me, it won't take much. I'm trying my best to hold back here." The sensations are gathering in intensity. Urgency. I force the tide back.

She bites her lower lip and lifts and lowers, and I can't help but immediately grip her hips by instinct. I force myself to let her keep the pace. She moves up and down slowly, like she's never really done it like this before, and I push the thought away. By the time we're done I want nothing left of that son of a bitch to be anywhere near her mind or mine. "That's it, Sunflower." The pressure is building, and sweat beads over my skin.

Her head falls back and her rhythm gets smoother, faster, making me grit my teeth. "God, Evan."

My hands roam. I caress her belly, I pinch her nipples, I hold her shoulders and rake her scalp, I dance my fingers down her spine, and massage her ass. Goose bumps ripple out across her skin when I do that, so I do it more, vowing that if I'm ever lucky enough to have her in my life and bed permanently, I'll dedicate myself to learning every erogenous zone on her body.

Eventually she's panting, and I can't keep the tension from flooding and gathering in my lower spine and groin. And my heart. My fucking heart. It's splayed open and pumping on the outside of my skin. What have I done?

I grab her hip and the thumb of my other hand presses hard where we join, trying to find that spot that gives her the most pleasure.

"Yes," she gasps and leans back, giving me better access.

Her blue eyes are liquid and drowning me. "Please, Evan, just move me like you need it."

A groan rips out of me, and I grip hard and jerk her roughly down to meet my thrust. Pleasure radiates in a deep pulse, and I do it again and again.

She cries out, and then replaces my circling thumb with her own fingers, circling madly. "Please," she says again.

Now I have two hands to grip her, and I take her permission. My fingers dig into her hip bones as I move roughly to meet her, pistoning up and out of control. The need too strong. The crest is barreling toward me, and I can't stop. I'm hurtling toward the edge, the grip of pleasure tight and crawling down my spine.

"Oh God," I grunt.

"Evan, yes. Don't stop."

"I ... can't." I fucking can't stop. I never want to. But the pleasure is almost pain. And the fear is just as potent. I've stood right in the path of destruction, and it's going to take me out. The regret of what I'm doing slams down like a flimsy break wall, but it's too late.

She cries out my name and her body jerks.

The tsunami crashes through me, tearing my body in half.

~

HER FINGERS DANCE over my chest. We're in her bed where she dragged us after she tore my soul out downstairs. I want nothing more than to go through the door to my side and get some distance and perspective and try to rake the pieces of myself back together. But I don't. I can't. Now I'm in her bed and breathing her in, and my chest aches.

"Sometimes I feel like I've known you forever," she says dreamily, head on my shoulder. "Like you're home for me. Does that sound crazy?"

She can't see my face as I flinch at her words. I clear my throat. "You've known me a long time."

"But I felt it when I first got here. You seemed so familiar somehow."

I swallow heavily and try to relax. "Hmmm." I hum.

"And today, when I saw the messages from Veronica. You were the first person I needed. And I realized you've always been my lighthouse."

My jaw clenches under her words and how they batter at me.

She lifts her head and swivels, resting her chin on me when I don't respond.

My fingers run up and down her upper arm.

"You okay? You're awfully quiet."

"Yeah."

She lifts up on an elbow. "Am I misreading this? Do you—"

She swallows hard. "Do you want to go?" She sets her mouth in a determined line, trying to look brave. "It's fine if that's the case. I know that's what you do. I know it's just sex. We don't have to do this cuddling stuff."

I internally cringe at her calling it just sex, but I knew what I was getting into. I lean up and take her mouth in a thorough kiss. "No. It's not that." And I need to examine what else she just said. That this is what I do.

She relaxes slightly. "Is it because I made you break your rule?"

"What?"

"The," she drops her voice to mimic mine, "I-can't-be-a-lover-*and*-a-protector thing. That's what you told me last night."

"It's still a real thing. And yes, that is on my mind. If I knew where Angus was, I'd feel better. I'm handing over a lot of mental trust that the guys have us covered. That Pete has us covered. And they better. I trained them after all. But feeling as though we're sitting ducks just waiting for him won't leave me alone. And I just lost myself in you. What did *he* do for the last few hours or so?"

"Wow. I think you think of him more than I do," she jokes, but I can tell my words rattle her.

She sighs and rolls onto her back. "Just knowing he's out there is bad enough. But out there and looking for me is … it's unbearable. Thank you for taking my mind off it for a few hours. I feel unreachable when I'm with you. Like I'm in another universe."

I roll over to face her. I can tell she wants to say something else.

"The bottom line is," she says eventually, turning to look at me, "I don't know if I'll ever truly be free of the fear. Will Angus even grant me the divorce? And if he does, or is forced to by a judge, will he leave me alone to build a new life? Or will he bide his time and come after me?" She blinks and presses her lips together. "And what does he expect from me? For me to go, 'Oh I'm sorry, my bad, yes, let's try that all again.' No. No, what he'll do is hurt me. Just like he did that boy he knew growing up."

I'm struck speechless with horror that she always comes back to that story.

Eventually I reach for her hand. "And this new life you want, tell me about it? What do you want?"

She sighs, deep and wide, and glances at me gratefully. "Safety. A sense of peace. I've grown to love the water, but I'd be happy to be landlocked for a while. A place I can wake up with the sun and be warm in summer and cold and cozy in winter. I miss snow and rain. Is that bizarre?"

I can't help thinking of the little secret cottage I bought in England I'd told her about. For some reason I suddenly know without a doubt I'd bought it with her in mind. I swallow.

"I want to laugh," she goes on and I force myself to focus. "A lot. And not worry so much. Maybe I want a goat, actually."

"What? A goat?"

"A fainting goat," she says, and I chuckle.

"You'd panic that it had died every day."

"Maybe. Maybe just a regular little goat then. I'd dress it in pajamas. You can't not smile around a goat in pajamas." She shifts to face me and folds her hands under her cheek. "I want a kitchen where the smell of home cooked meals permeates through the house. Even if I'm not the one cooking," she adds with a smirk. "I don't know if I can really cook. Like elaborate, delicious things. I guess I'd like to know if I enjoy it too. Cooking amazing meals for someone else, not just me. If it's just me, I make a sandwich or eat a couple of olives." She laughs, then sobers. "And kids. I guess I would like to cook for kids."

I cough to dislodge the ball in my throat. "Yours?" I manage.

"I think so," she whispers. "If I can. I don't know if I can still have kids."

"Human ones, not goat ones?" I ask deadpan to break the difficult subject that just reared up. Fuck Angus.

She laughs, deep and throaty.

My groin tightens. "And art?" I change the subject. "Is that something you enjoy."

"I enjoy it, sure. I even used to paint. I lost that somewhere along the way. But working in an art gallery? I don't know. It's early days in this new roll at the *fondation*, and let's not forget I'm working with one of your ex-girlfriends."

I growl. "She wasn't a girlfriend."

"What was she?"

"A woman I slept with."

"I lied last night." She looks me in the eye. "I was jealous. I *am* jealous."

"You have no need to be."

"Really? She made you sound quite adventurous. Maybe *I'd* like to sample a little more of the menu..." She licks her lips, and my cock goes from half-mast to hard. "Unless that was all false marketing," she sasses, trying to save her pride.

"What did she say exactly?" I ask.

"She made it sound like you were in possession of the secret specials menu," she says, her tone grumpy, making me smile.

I lean closer and slide my hand around her waist. The ridges of her scar under my fingertips shock me again as I learn her body. It's a reminder to be careful. "I seem to remember you being very pleased with what's on offer." I run my hand up her torso and dance my fingertips around her tightening nipple.

Her breath catches, her back arching.

"You were, in fact," I roll the tight bud, "pleased ... twice."

"I was. Another helping of the regular menu would be just great. And don't stop touching me. Please." The last word stutters out of her mouth.

I chuckle and roll on top of her. Her legs open immediately, cradling my hips. We both groan at the sensation. "Is this okay?" I whisper, and she nods. "It's not some crazy kink I'm into if that's what you're thinking. I just think I can tell what a women likes ... whether she wants it fast ... or slow. Or where she wants it," I add with a slow roll of my hips, drawing a soft moan from her. "How she wants it."

Her lips part and her cheeks flush. Her blue eyes get darker and less focused. "Don't talk about other women. Not when you're doing that."

"But you make me second guess everything," I admit. "Like I've lost the map and taken a road I don't know."

Her gaze softens at the vulnerability I've let into my tone. "I'd say you were doing just fine," she whispers. She presses her hips up, and my cock slips against the hot liquid between her legs. *Fuck.* "I think you must have an inbuilt compass." She lets out an amused gasp. "It seems to know the way."

I grin. "What else did you discuss with her that I should know about?" I brush a blonde strand of hair that's curled along her cheek.

She hesitates, the glow in her eyes dimming a bit. "That there's no point of thinking about more than sex with you because you gave your heart away a long time ago." She breaks our eye lock, staring at my throat.

I'm surprised at Lilian's observation, so it takes me a second to respond. And when the words really sink in, I go still.

"That's true, Sunflower," I finally admit to her, even though I know she'll misunderstand. "I did."

THIRTY-ONE

Andrea

AS SOON AS I woke up alone in my bed, I thought I'd imagined everything. But then Evan came up the stairs freshly showered. He held a steaming cup of coffee, and his face creased into a smile as we locked eyes. But his look was more guarded than I was expecting, his smile tight. "Hey, Sunflower. Glad you're awake. It's eight."

He sat on the edge of the bed, setting the cup down on the side table.

I curled onto my side in his direction, and he brushed the hair from my forehead. "You okay this morning?"

"Yeah." I nodded and smiled sleepily. "You?"

"Not so much, actually. I need to talk to you about something."

I sat up on an elbow. "From the tone in your voice, I think I better have coffee first." I reached for the cup with an uncomfortable laugh. I really hated the way he always pulled back after we got close. I'd thought after last night maybe that would have changed.

He stood. "Why don't you have your coffee and get dressed, and I'll meet you downstairs?"

My stomach sank. I was guessing this was the let-her-down-easy-the-morning-after talk. "Right. Okay." I must have seemed overly eager, inexperienced, and clingy. And for someone like Evan that was probably a trifecta of red flags. All three of those things were true though, so what could I do?

He disappeared, and I forced myself up and took three large sips of coffee while inside my stomach rebelled. Yesterday afternoon and evening had been amazing, earth moving, and I had zero regrets. But it was clear Evan did. I shouldn't be surprised. I kind of knew I was luring him out of his comfort zone. But at some point he was a big boy, and if he hadn't wanted to sleep with me he could have said no.

By the time I'd showered, dressed in leggings, booties, and a drapey sweater, I was feeling irritable and hard done by. All the delicious orgasm-induced endorphins I'd enjoyed last night had drained away. And I still had to see Veronica and potentially face Angus. The last thing I needed was to feel rejected and vulnerable before going into that meeting. Which meant I should never have put myself in the situation of sleeping with Evan. I only had myself to blame. It wasn't like I didn't *know* Evan was emotionally unavailable. I lightly curled my hair and added a light touch of makeup.

I was annoyed and jumpy from nerves when I got downstairs.

There was a plate of fresh croissants, jam and butter on the table where my ass had been sitting bare last night while he rocked my world. I paused at the visuals and then shook my head.

Evan was perched on the edge of my couch, another place in my house where he'd blown my mind, but he was bent forward, shoulders tense through his gray t-shirt, and texting madly. He looked up as he registered me in the room.

"Hi," I offered.

He indicated the table and rose. "You should eat."

"Should I?" I bristled. Actually, I was starving and fresh croissants with jam and butter were my literal favorite, which of course he knew as we'd shared many breakfasts together along with the crew of Xavier's boat over the years.

He pressed his lips together.

My stomach rumbled, making me roll my eyes. "Fine. I'll eat." I sat down. "Is this buttering me up for the delivery of bad news?" I asked, grabbing a croissant and tearing off a piece, showering my plate in pastry flakes. "It's what you always do. I step over the line, you shut me down cold. I guess I should be thankful you're predictable."

"What are you talking about?"

"In the nightclub in Saint-Tropez. I ... thought we had a moment. I went to kiss you. You acted like I'd spat on you."

"You'd had a shit ton of champagne. You had no idea what you were doing. And you're mad I didn't take *advantage* of you?" He shook his head.

"I knew exactly what I was doing." I frowned. "Sort of. Anyway, then after our kiss yesterday, you practically wanted to climb out of your own skin. And now I guess this morning, well, we need to talk." I make air quotes. "So talk."

He moved to sit opposite me, an eyebrow raised.

"Actually, can you sit at the end?" I indicated the chair at the head of the table. "I don't need to be remembering you going down on me last night while you try to explain it was just a hookup. And it's fine, honestly, I know I came on strong. I just really needed to get laid. I figured your reputation made you perfect for the job." I took a bite of my croissant and moaned fully aware I was lying to him about what it meant to me. "Good God. Are these local?"

"Are you done?" he asked and sat at the end of the table.

"No, I'm eating the whole basket. I hope you already had your fill."

His face had gone through a gamut of emotions. "That's not what I meant."

I missed when I got cyborg Evan because then I didn't have to think about his reaction to what I was saying—because he didn't have one. Normally it was like emoting to a stone wall. There was zero reaction and zero consequence. Not so this morning. In fact, not so last night. Now that I was thinking about it, maybe not even for the last two weeks. What was happening?

He was staring at me. He looked tense, aroused, amused, annoyed, and regretful.

I slapped the croissant down. "Okay, out with it."

He opened his mouth. Then closed it again, seeming to think better of whatever he'd been about to say. "I never realized how *not* a morning person you are. Do you need your second cup?"

"Evan," I warned.

He blew out a breath and pinched his plump bottom lip

with his thumb and forefinger. "That was a lot to unpack. It wasn't *just* a hookup. Obviously."

"How so?" I asked casually.

He scowled. "Because it wasn't. It was you and me. And it was ... amazing."

"Massive understatement." I smiled, part of me unwinding. "An amazing hookup."

A sad smile ghosted across his tense features. "But—"

"There it is." I looked away from him and picked up the croissant again. No "letting me down gently" was going to ruin a perfectly good buttery, flaky croissant. I slathered more butter and jam onto the remaining piece, justifying the calories with the amount I'd burned through from hiking and sex.

"But," he repeated, "it can't happen again. It can't be a ... a thing."

"You mean, I didn't reform the emotionally unavailable bachelor with my magic hoo ha?" I covered my distress and rejection under the joking response.

"Your magic—? What?"

"It's a thing in romance novels. Confirmed bachelor, manslut, sleeps with everyone and never settles down until ... *her*."

"Her?"

"The one with the pussy to end all pussies. Keep up. The one who he thinks he's just having sex with but suddenly can't live without."

"Are we still asleep? Am I dreaming this conversation? Also, manslut?"

"Look, it's fine. I'm just another girl to sample your ... menu. Honestly, it's fine. I'm fine."

"I feel like this is a trap. Am I supposed to assure you that you're not just another girl and that I think your pussy is magical? Because yeah, it felt pretty magical."

I snorted out a laugh.

"But it's complicating things. I told you already that I've made your safety a priority, which means I'm not sleeping with you again. It's why I've been trying, and recently failing, not to cross the line with you. Last night was ... another really brutal lapse in judgment for me. I'm not proud of it. And I'm not comfortable with you staying here anymore, not after he could see you in town this morning and follow you. I want you to pack an overnight bag and after the meeting with Veronica, I want you staying at my place in Cannes. It's a secure building. It's alarmed and has twenty-four hour security and cameras."

I wanted to smile at his admission that he'd been trying to resist crossing lines with me for a lot longer than I might be aware, but my hackles were up with his high-handedness after just basically ending us before we were even a thing. Did I even want us to be a thing? Beyond really mind-blowing sex? "Are we back to you telling me what to do? I'm not one of your guys to boss around. Why don't you just *ask*?" I grumbled. "Now I just want to throw the bread basket at you."

He sighed. "I'm sorry. It's a habit. But if it means that much to you ... please will you allow *me* the courtesy of allowing *you* to stay in *my* apartment where I *know* you'll be safer." His sarcastic tone and the roll of his eyes made me smile.

"Fine. When you put it like that." I smirked, then sobered. "Okay. And thank you. That's very thoughtful." I picked up another croissant as promised. "Wait. I have questions. Aren't your parents staying there?"

"They happen to be there, yes."

I dropped the croissant on my plate. "You want me to meet your parents? I think we might be moving too fast," I joked. "For a hookup, anyway."

He was fighting a smile.

"Okay," I said. "How many bedrooms?"

"Two."

"So, you really could have stayed at your place instead of moving in next door to me."

"I feel like we've already covered this. I'm a stalker and a control freak. Blah, blah, blah."

"Do your parents stay in your room or the guest room?"

"The guest room. Obviously."

"Not obviously. So you want me to stay in *your* room? In *your* bed?"

He mashed his lips together. "Yes."

"In your sheets?" God, I could wrap myself in his scent.

He pinched the bridge of his nose.

"Will you be in there too?" I asked when he didn't answer.

"And shack up with a girl under the same roof as my mum?" He dropped his jaw in mock horror. "God, no."

Obviously he was joking. "Where will *you* be?"

"Here, probably." He wasn't joking. He was going to palm me off for someone else to look after. I scowled.

"Can I go through your shit?" I asked.

"I don't have any shit."

"That remains to be seen."

"I also need you to tell Lilian that you need a few days off."

"No way. I'll go nuts."

"Andrea."

"Evan."

"I'll think about it," I conceded. "I was off today anyway. And I'm looking forward to meeting the people who raised you." I had one more bite of the second croissant before realizing I was full and laid it down. I sucked my oily and flake-crusted fingers into my mouth one by one.

His gaze missed none of it, his jaw tight, his eyes dark.

What I wasn't looking forward to was missing out on more sex with him. Clearly he wasn't happy about it either. It was criminal that I was finally getting some, and now he was going to withhold it. There were still things I wanted, no needed, to try.

"How long until we have to leave?" I asked, getting up to clean my breakfast. Nerves about my upcoming meeting with Veronica swam into my belly again, the rush of delicious feelings that had kept me distracted last night abating.

He pinched his lower lip between his fingers. "Ten minutes."

I moved toward him. "Push your chair away from the table." This also might be my last chance to do anything with Evan.

"What are you doing?" he asked but did it anyway.

I grabbed a pillow off the couch and dropped it on the floor between his legs and knelt down.

His jaw went slack.

"We have to see if maybe I have a magic mouth, since my hoo ha didn't work on you."

"Get up, please. We aren't doing this."

I ran my hands up his thighs, enjoying the rough denim feel of his jeans. His fists clenched the arms of the chair. "But the thing is," I went on, "I'll be too scared to do this with anyone else. And you're about to lock me away in a tower with your parents, so I may never get the chance to try."

His throat bobbed and his cheeks flushed. "Wow," he managed, his voice thick. "I think you might be manipulating me."

"Do you hate it?"

"Yes."

I walked my fingers up to the button of his jeans. "Do you want me to stop?"

"Yes."

I pulled my hand away, a brick dropping in my stomach. Humiliation flooded through me. A guy turning down a blow job? I wasn't clueless—that was as personal a rejection as you could get. "I'm sorry." I pushed back to get to my feet, my face burning. "You were serious."

"Wait." He reached out to stop me, dropping his hand at the last minute. His voice was gritty. "Why?"

"Why what?" I leaned back on my haunches, looking up at him.

His gaze was deep and dark and confused. "*Why* do you want to do that?"

"Is it something you don't like?"

"Fuck. No. I—of course I do. It's just ..."

"You don't want *me* to do it?"

"The idea of my cock in *your* mouth is fucking heaven. I promise you. But I just told you we couldn't, shouldn't do anything else. And it feels like it's like a bucket list item for you or something. Or you're trying to prove something. And I want to punch myself in the face for turning down a blow job for *any* reason. But Sunflower, if you're doing it because you feel like you need to, if you think I'll *like* you more or something, or change my mind about putting your safety first, then please stop. I ... *like* you enough already. And I'm not breaking my rule again."

"Stupid rule." My gaze dropped. So much for distracting myself with a blow job to keep from getting so nervous about this meeting. Though that wasn't fair to Evan. But there was also another reason, something maybe he would understand, and I steeled my nerves to speak. "Maybe I *am* trying to prove something. I'm sorry. Not to you. To myself."

"What?" he asked gently, lifting my chin with two fingers.

I'd hoped never to have to admit it. "Because I know you won't force me. Or gag me. Because I want to do it. I want to bring someone pleasure that I *choose* to give and wasn't forced to."

Evan's face crumpled. "He forced you?"

"In so many different ways. But particularly like this. It was some kind of power trip thing. And I may not ever get another chance on my terms. And the next time, like if I'm with someone in the future—"

"Shut up." He hauled me up, his mouth covering mine and swallowing my words. He kissed me breathless, and I crawled onto his lap. His arms wrapped around me, holding me gently, but so close, his lips moving over mine.

Slowly his kisses gentled rather than moving us in the direction I wanted to go.

"Let's go meet with Veronica," he said, breathing heavily, and rested his forehead against mine.

EVAN FOLDED himself into my tiny car, the ridiculous spectacle of it keeping me from wallowing in my nerves about the meeting ahead of me.

"Wait for me at the elevator," he said as he dropped me at the back entrance to the building of the law office that I'd left from previously so he could park, and I scurried inside.

It was five excruciatingly long minutes until Evan joined me. When his frame shadowed the entrance to the vestibule of the back entrance, my insides unclenched.

He walked straight to me and took my face in his hands, placing a kiss on my forehead. "You good?" God. How did he do that? Just calm me down like throwing me a rope in the middle of a wild sea?

I clutched his forearms and nodded. "Thank you for coming with me."

Veronica met us as soon as we got off the elevator. "Oh good. You're here."

"This is Evan." I indicated the strong, calming presence next to me. "He's—"

"Security," he said and held out his hand.

"He's accompanying me," I explained. "Your messages freaked me out yesterday," I hurried on. "Is everything okay? You said we shouldn't meet here anymore."

She glanced over her shoulder, then showed us into a side conference room with a Formica table and plastic chairs next to the receptionist desk—not her very dignified office. She closed the door. "I think you better take a seat."

My skin turned icy. "O-okay. For the record, I'm now really freaked out again."

She squeezed my shoulder and sat down next to me. "There's a man in my office claiming to be Angus' brother."

Evan immediately stood.

My mouth opened and closed. "Right now? Like here?"

She nodded. "Yes. I was going to meet with you first to discuss his call, but he just showed up a few minutes ago. He says his name is Neil. Have you ever met Angus' brother?"

"Once at our wedding."

Veronica laid a hand over mine. "Well, he just told me Angus is ... dead."

THIRTY-TWO

Dizziness swamped me at Veronica's words. "What?" It was a good thing I was sitting as my legs had disappeared. Angus, dead? How? The small conference room was suddenly freezing.

"This is a lot, I know." Her hand laid on my arm, anchoring me to reality.

Evan folded his arms. "First things first. We need to make sure this man is who he says he is. It could be Angus using his brother's identity as a way to make contact. It's extremely easy to buy counterfeit documents when you know the right people."

"Oh my God," I whispered.

Veronica handed me a United Kingdom passport. "I checked his picture, but you better look at it."

I stared at the booklet and tried to make it come into focus.

"Andrea. You good?" Evan asked.

I blinked and focused on the document. "It looks legit."

"The picture inside," Veronica pressed. "The picture matches the guy in my office, kind of, it's a bit dated obviously."

Flicking to the picture I saw a gaunt blonde man with a

slightly squat nose like a fighter and piercing eyes. He was familiar and so similar to the man I'd married. But it wasn't Angus. "They look alike, but that's not Angus."

"*You* can tell, but can I?" Veronica asked. "That's the question. I'm sorry, I should have thought of him using his brother's passport." Veronica was only going off of an old service photo she'd found online for his file because when I'd left Angus, I'd arrived with nothing, not even my cell phone. Especially not my cell phone.

Evan held out his hand and I gave him the document. Adrenaline throbbed through my veins, my foot bouncing with nerves.

"I think the best way for you to corroborate his identity is to see him in person," Veronica went on while Evan examined the document. "But if it *is* Angus, and he's gone to this much trouble to get close to you—"

"It seems genuine," Evan said. "But yeah, I agree. He could have gone to the trouble. I'll go first."

"I need to see him." I stood up, making for the door and yanking the handle. "Now."

"Wait!" Evan darted around the table. "Shit."

My insides were liquid. I couldn't wait. Adrenaline was pumping so hard it had replaced my blood. I was high with it. I was angry. I was terrified. And I wanted to meet it all head on. I was so fucking *angry* about having my life wiped out, so tired of being fearful. I barely registered that Evan was trying to stop me.

Veronica's office door was ten feet away and in milliseconds I was crashing through it,

A man leapt to his feet in surprise, his face then creasing

into disgust. "So, it's true."

"Neil." The relief it wasn't Angus nearly floored me. Adrenalin ebbed, leaving me weak with shock.

"You abandoned my brother for ten years, not knowing what happened to his *wife*," he spat. "Not able to move on, leaving him in hell, searching for you. And then you have the audacity to file for divorce? Well, it's too fucking late. He's dead. Are you happy?"

"W-what? Are you sure?" I couldn't focus on the other stuff he'd said beyond the fact this was Neil, not Angus. And Angus ... gone. "He's dead?"

"Please," Veronica said, hurrying in. "Please sit down. Both of you."

I'd never seen Veronica anything but cool and calm, but she looked as rattled as I did.

"And you, I guess," she gestured behind me.

I turned to see Evan standing just inside the office with us, his whole body vibrating with tension, his eyes glued to Neil.

"Belinda," she called to the receptionist. "Please bring another chair in here for—"

"Evan Roark." He stepped forward, neatly slipping himself between Neil and me, and held out his hand to Neil. "Personal security for Lucy Robertson."

I spun to face him. My mouth dropped open. *What the hell?* He peeled his eyes off Neil and looked at me, his eyes trying to convey apology and a thousand other things. There was no time right now, but I'd get to the bottom of that in a minute too.

"Evan Roark?" Neil frowned. "How do I know that name?"

"You don't," Evan snapped.

"Can we please address the issue here?" Veronica's

commanding voice jolted me. I sank down into a chair in front of her desk, my mind racing. Neil took the far chair, and Evan sat between us on the plastic chair Belinda had just brought in. "I'm sorry for your loss," Veronica addressed Neil. "Do you have proof of your brother's passing."

My heart pounded. And next to me, Evan moved his chair closer.

Neil opened a backpack at his feet and pulled out a folder that he handed to Veronica. "But her request for a divorce negates that, right? She's not entitled to his estate if she was divorcing him."

Veronica looked up at him from the open folder in front of her. "The divorce is not final because your brother could not be reached."

"Because he was dead!"

"They were not divorced before he died," Veronica explained patiently.

Angus was *dead*.

"She abandoned him." Neil's head whipped toward me. "You absolute bitch," he spat. "You destroy his life, and now you get to take what's left? I'm fighting you for it. You don't deserve a fucking penny."

Evan was out of his seat, looming over Neil. "Don't you dare fucking speak to her like that. Your piece of shit brother almost fucking killed her."

I was ice cold, and my vision grew blue around the edges. My whole body was shaking, convulsing even. I couldn't stop it. Loud whooshing in my ears drowned out the voices until someone yelled, "She's going to pass out."

I was falling sideways. Strong hands grabbed me. "Sunflower. Shit."

∼

THE SOUNDS CAME BACK FIRST. Veronica calmly explaining the reason for my divorce request. "She requested a no contest proceeding because she didn't want him coming for her, rather than citing years of abuse."

Evan's voice. "Sunflower," he said softly. I was on a hard surface. God, I was on the floor.

"That's absolute bull shite," Neil said, but I could tell the wind had gone out of his anger.

I blinked slowly. Gorgeous pools of green and brown filled with concern stared down at me. Evan's eyes widened with relief immediately. "God, you scared the shit out of me, baby. You okay?"

I shifted with a wince, feeling bruised on my hip.

"You went down pretty fast, thank God you were already sitting."

Angus. A surge of emotions rushed into being—grief, inexplicably, being one of them—and burned my ears and eyes, though I fought it. And relief. Oh my God. "Is it true? Is he dead?" I whispered. The image of Evan blurred as my eyes filled.

"I'm going to have it verified. But yeah. It seems like it. Can you sit up?" He fastened his opposite hand to mine and hooked his spare arm around my back, helping me up.

As I came upright, I locked eyes with Neil. He didn't seem as angry and affronted as when I'd first seen him. He stood and offered a hand and I accepted, letting both of them help me back to the chair.

"Here." The receptionist came in and handed me a glass of water, which I took gratefully.

"I'm sorry," I mumbled, embarrassed. "I guess I had a shock."

Everyone was quiet as we regrouped.

Veronica glanced through all the documents Neil had handed to her. She passed me a death certificate, and I stared at it, unblinking for a few moments, utterly numb to it. I handed it to Evan.

"Neil." I angled my chair slightly and looked over at him. "I'm sorry for your loss."

"Thank you." He nodded.

"I know he was your brother. But I didn't abandon him. I escaped. And it's true, I barely escaped with my life."

He bowed up, mouth moving like a fish. "Ms. Patel tried to tell me some bullshit story about him being violent toward you," he said eventually. "But Angus? My baby brother? I find it really hard to believe. I was always protecting him before I left home. He wasn't the type. Maybe the service did something to him."

"Protecting him from whom?" asked Evan, disbelief etched in every chord of his voice.

"So, who are you again?" Neil scowled at Evan.

God, Neil looked so like Angus when he did that, I felt an ice cold trickle between my shoulder blades and shook it off.

"Listen." I put my hand up. "I think ... do you think Neil and I could chat in private?" I asked the other two.

"I don't think that's a good idea," said Evan.

"I concur," added Veronica.

"Please?" I asked and swallowed my nerves. I needed to do this.

"Apologize first," Evan growled at Neil.

Neil cleared his throat, and I realized Evan was staring him down. "I'm sorry I shouted at her," Neil said to Evan, and it almost made me smile at how Evan had made Neil back down with just a look, but there was no room for amusement right now. "To her," Evan said.

Neil's gaze shifted to me. "I'm sorry I shouted at you."

"You better not touch her, either," Evan said.

"Evan, I'm fine now," I assured him. "Thank you." I reached for his hand and squeezed it briefly.

Veronica stood. "You both stay here. Mr. Roark and I will be outside."

It took Evan an eternity to leave the room, and I could literally feel his disagreement with my choice in every molecule of air.

After they left, it seemed neither Neil nor I knew how to start.

Neil was even thinner than I remembered. And he'd aged. His hair was thinning, and his eyes were shadowed.

"He was sick," Neil started eventually. "He had an aggressive cancer. Colon. He didn't tell me until he only had months to live and even then he refused treatment. I moved into your house you'd shared with him."

My mouth was dry so I took another sip of the water Belinda had given me, but it was like drinking sand for all the good it did. I set it down.

"For years he devoted his life to looking for you. Said you left him for another man. Is that him, that guy?"

"What? No. I never left Angus for anyone."

"I don't understand."

"That makes two of us. Neil ... your brother ... he was an abuser." I blew out a breath. It had taken me a long time to even be able say those words. "He hurt me."

"I saw you at your wedding. I can't reconcile that vision. You two were so happy. And I know him. Knew him."

"We were happy in the beginning. I was swept off my feet, and it was a wonderful thing happening at a really bad time with my mum dying. It started so small, it was hard to notice. At first it was just teasing." I didn't know how to summarize years of insidious, escalating behavior, but I forced myself to keep talking. "At first he'd simply say stuff like I was 'porking up a bit,' or I had a 'hard time making friends,' didn't I? Or I 'hadn't finished my degree because it was a bit much for me,' wasn't it?" I let myself remember how when I doubted myself, or had a particularly hard test, he'd say that maybe it was the wrong thing for me. Or that I should try something easier. When I'd get upset he wasn't encouraging. He would tell me he was just trying to support me, and I was acting ungrateful. And worse, deep down I wondered if he was right about me not being cut out for finishing my degree. In retrospect, he hated me gaining independence and making friends at school who he didn't know. I swallowed and fisted my hands on my lap, forcing myself to continue. "The teasing turned meaner over time. Making me feel dumb or stupid for not remembering something or misspeaking became the norm. I guess at some point, it was bullying and shaming and ..."

I picked the water back up for something to focus on, but my hands had started shaking again. I squeezed the burn in my eyes away. It was so hard to talk about. To admit. That was the thing about abuse—the shame. The shame that you let someone say those things to you. Do those things to you. That you didn't think more of yourself to stop it. You can't understand how you got to where you are. You explain it away and convince yourself that either they don't really mean it, or you deserve it. Either, equally horrifying.

And I'd had no one close to me to see the signs. To question anything.

"I find this so hard to believe. He adored you. Never shut up about you."

I untied my hair and felt my scalp behind my ear for the small bald strip that was flat after so many years. "This is from where I fell against the kitchen counter after he tripped me as I was carrying our dishes in from a barbecue we were having in our backyard. There were twenty people at our home, and none of them saw what he did. That was my first trip to the hospital."

"A mistake, surely," Neil rasped. "He didn't mean to. It must have been an accident."

Neil's words sliced into my chest with pain, but I tried to keep talking, to stay calm. "That's what he said, yes, when he apologized afterward when we got home from getting stitches. His apology was that he was just messing around, and if I hadn't been so clumsy I'd have probably not fallen. By the time I went to bed that night, I was convinced if only I'd looked down, I actually could have prevented it, that it was my fault after all."

He shook his head vehemently. "I'm sorry, but this is too

much. He's dead now. You can let sleeping dogs lie. This was my brother."

I squeezed my eyes closed and blew out a breath. Then I curled my fingers around the hem of my sweater and gathered it up at my side and lifted.

"What are you—?"

"This is from a knife wound. This was the last time he attacked me."

Neil stared in shock and then dragged his eyes away and sat forward. He cupped his hands and blew a breath into them. His eyes grew wet. "Oh, God. Angus, what did you do?"

I started crying silently, tears streaming down my cheeks. It felt as though a weight had been lifted, but it didn't feel good either.

"But it makes no sense," he whispered, his tone lost. "He adored you."

"Did he? Or did I just belong to him?" I wiped my face and tried to pull myself together. I'd shed enough tears over my abuser.

"I—"

"Look, Neil. You don't have to believe me. It doesn't matter anymore, does it?" I modulated my tone with great effort. "There are a million wounds I *can't* show you. Physical and mental. They're inside me. Only I know they're there. He took my life away from me. He sliced me down to the shadow of the girl I once was and then forced me into a situation where my only option was escape or die. It's taken me years to heal and years to realize it was his fault and not mine. Years to remember I'm not dumb, I'm actually pretty smart. Years to even contemplate another relationship. I haven't been able to live with my own *name* in case he came looking. He took the very best years of my life." I thought of Evan. "Maybe even my chance to have a healthy relationship or a family one day. To be honest, I didn't know until I walked in here, but I was disappointed to see *you* and not him because I'm finally ready to fight back. And he's not even here. My rage at what he took from me has nowhere to go. And it's lucky he's already dead, Neil, because ... if he was sitting where you are right now, I think I would kill him." My voice grew thready under the force of the thought. My throat and chest were so tight with relief and impotent rage and grief it was hard to breath.

"You don't mean that."

"I don't know," I stated, honestly. "That's how I feel right now."

Neil sat back and rocked his head up to stare at the ceiling. "I nursed him, you know? At the end. I moved in and nursed him. Don't people usually have a deathbed confession. Wouldn't he have told me what he did?"

"Do you really think he would? Half the time he did stuff he'd convince me I'd misunderstood, misread, misinterpreted, or done something to warrant whatever it was. And I think ... that's what *he* believed too. I don't think he examined what he was doing." I tried to stay strong, but I hated that I was defending myself still. My voice wobbled. "I don't think he felt he had anything to confess."

Neil's eyes went to my side, now hidden under my sweater again. "But how do you stab someone and not understand that's wrong?"

I pressed my lips together because it didn't warrant an answer. It wasn't that I thought Neil didn't believe me. And the truth was, I never saw Angus again after that, so I don't know whether he ever took responsibility for it or realized how wrong he was in everything.

"How long ago did he pass?" I asked instead.

He pressed fingers tips to his closed eyelids. "It's been about two weeks. It was your birthday the day he passed. He had it circled on the calendar on his fridge."

My birthday. Lucy's birthday anyway. The day I'd woken up and realized how tired I was of hiding. Some coincidence. And to think about all the fear I'd experienced since even then. But it had also brought Evan right to my doorstep. Literally. Life was so weird. "Did you follow me?" I managed.

"Yeah. I—I found Veronica's address on the divorce paperwork. He never saw it, by the way. I saw you down here last week and was trying to figure out where you live so I could come and ... God. I'm sorry. I wouldn't have hurt you. You know that, right? I just—"

"You were angry and grieving."

"Yes. I'm sorry. I wanted to confront you. Demand answers. I'm glad I waited and saw you here." He shook his head like he still didn't understand anything.

I didn't know what else to say. There was some healing in telling Angus' brother and speaking about Angus out loud to the closest person to him I could. But all I'd done was tarnish his memory of his brother after he'd died.

"I suppose you want your house back," Neil said, more as a statement than a question.

Exhaling, I rubbed my eyes and wiped damp hands down my thighs. I would never live there again. I couldn't. But that wasn't a decision I could make right now. "I don't know."

"And his pension. I guess you get that too."

I glance at Neil. "Again, I don't know."

"He had some money our parents left us. And a bunch of savings bonds." He trailed off, looking utterly desolate.

My heart went out to him. His brother had been a monster, but Neil hadn't known that. Angus was his little brother and now he was dead. And from what he'd just said, so were their parents. I'd never gotten super close to them since they'd lived about a five hours' drive away. But the loneliness shrouding Neil now was palpable and kind of heartbreaking. And I'd just made that worse.

"Are you—did you ever get married?" I asked.

"Divorced. Been five years now."

"Kids?"

"Nah. Too much bother." He shook his head and rubbed the back of his hand over his eyes. He inhaled deeply, and then his face creased up and he doubled over with a sob. "Angus, you little shite." He leaned forward, shoulders shaking. He'd been bottling up his grief, redirecting it into anger at me, and now he had nothing to do but face it. The sound of his sobs was gutting.

I reached over to Veronica's desk and snagged the same box of tissues she'd offered me just days ago and held them next to Neil. I rubbed his back awkwardly as he cried. "It's going to be okay," I soothed, wondering how I got to this place where I was comforting Angus' brother.

He accepted several tissues, wiped his eyes, and blew his nose loudly.

I did the same.

"God, this is ... I'm so sorry," he said. "Our upbringing wasn't easy. My dad was harsh. It's no excuse. I don't know if the way my dad was with us had anything to do with it. Doesn't matter now, does it? And I know it's not the same. But you're owed an apology and he can't give one. So I'll give one for him. I'm sorry. I know, wherever he is now, he's sorry too. I'm sure of it."

I wiped my eyes. It wasn't the same. And it wasn't true. And we probably both knew that. But I accepted the apology anyway because what else could I do? "Thank you," I whispered.

He looked past me to the door, and the slim glass panel that showed Evan leaning against the wall glowering and probably confused about me comforting Angus.

"Oh, now I know where I remember that bloke from," Neil said. "He was in the service with my brother. Grew up in our same town. So what's he doing here with you, then?"

THIRTY-THREE

I stood out on the pavement at the front of the building, blinking in the sunshine.

The world had changed. Again. Angus was dead. I could hardly wrap my mind around it. And apparently Evan and Angus knew each other? I shook my head.

Veronica had knocked on the door of the office and poked her head in, and I hadn't had a chance to ask Neil what he was talking about regarding knowing Evan, or to ask Evan anything. Veronica had asked Evan to wait outside while I debriefed with her and Neil.

I hadn't even answered Neil's question of why Evan was there with us because I didn't know how to. Veronica listed the assets Neil mentioned and referred me to an estate lawyer to handle my case from there out. I wasn't sure what I'd do, but I knew I'd have to deal with being left an inheritance eventually. But not now. I couldn't fathom spending Angus' money. I had more than enough savings, and sometimes you had to let things go so they held no power over you anymore. Trying to go back to, or sell, or even see the house I'd left so long ago would probably mess with all the healing I'd done over the years. Sometimes it was good to face trauma, and sometimes it was best to cut the line with the bloody hook on the end of it and let it sink to the bottom of the sea. Had a feeling this was one of those times. But I'd deal with what to do another day.

Evan pulled my tiny Lego car up in front of me, looking like a giant, and leaned over as he came to a stop to pop my door open.

Neil and I had exchanged phone numbers, and I was now clutching a folder of legal documents standing in the sunshine outside the law office. I was in a trance and barely processing everything. The breeze was cool and fresh, the sky a vibrant fall blue. The Gingko trees that lined the street had turned a brilliant yellow gold, and the breeze blew leaves down to swirl around my feet.

There'd been no panicked back entrance exit from the law office today.

No hiding.

I could be Lucy Robertson again. If I wanted to be.

"Sunflower, you getting in?"

Rousing myself, I started forward and climbed in, facing forward.

"You okay?" Evan asked.

I blinked slowly.

A car honked right behind us, annoyed with us blocking a lane.

"All right, all right," Evan muttered and threw the car into first gear. We zoomed through the streets and out to the roundabout that led to the highway, swinging west.

"Where are we going?"

"I thought I'd stick with the original plan and take you to my place."

"Why?"

"I figured you were going to have some questions." He glanced over at me. "Do you want me to take you back to the village right now?"

I shook my head, my shock wearing off. "No. I still want to meet your parents. Questions about what?" I played dumb.

"I heard what Neil said before Veronica went back in the room. He was loud."

"And you think we should talk about that with your parents? Maybe you should pull over and talk about it right now?"

"Later."

"And me? How did you know my real name?"

He looked over at me quickly, mouth straightening, still driving at the one-twenty kilometer highway speed limit. "I know the background of every single person who works for Pascale Company. Of course I would know."

I drew my eyebrows together.

"Let's just wait until we get there," he added, clearly knowing I didn't believe that explanation for a second. "And if you want to go back to your place tonight, you have your car. You can go wherever and whenever you want."

"I can, can't I?" I gulped. Then let out a laugh. "Oh my God. I can go anywhere I want."

I rolled down the window, the wind whipping my hair across my face, and leaned out. "I'm free!" I yelled into the universe.

I reached over and turned the radio on and scrolled the playlist on my phone. Oh my God, what did one play to commemorate this feeling?

"Please, for the love, don't put on Gloria Gaynor," Evan groaned.

"Please." I rolled my eyes with a smile. "This is a moment for Destiny's Child." I pressed play on "Survivor."

Evan shook his head and rolled down his own window, resting his elbow on it. The wind swirled around his hair. I turned the knob on the volume to max, the base making the car vibrate. I sang along to every word. I'd played it enough times over the years when I needed a pick-me-up. It was almost obsolete for my current situation though, I was so beyond surviving.

I was free.

I was free.

I was free.

I queued up "Firework" by Katie Perry, followed by P!nk "U + Ur Hand," and then for a touch of classic, Aretha Franklin's "Respect."

The exit for Cannes appeared in the distance as I lost my cool.

I sang, and I threw my arms up, and I laughed. At one point I cried during "Firework." My soul was bigger than my body. I could make the sun shine, I could make the moon rise. I could fly if I wanted. As we approached the outskirts of the city, I looked over at Evan, eyes on the road, his brown hair curling deliciously over his collar. His lush mouth was turned up slightly in amusement. My heart grew and grew until I found it hard to breathe. I suddenly realized Evan had no reason to stay near me anymore, and the thought of it rushed in, almost crushing my chest.

I looked down and scrolled to find P!nk and picked "Please Don't Leave Me." I'd always loved the song, but now, the words. God.

I let the song play loud, the words paining me. I didn't know where he and I went from here. He'd told me he couldn't sleep with me while he was playing protector, but that no longer applied. But maybe that had just been an excuse to let me down gently. He was attracted to me sure. But that didn't equal anything deeper than that.

I didn't even know what I was going to do or where I was going to go. Just the thought of my tiny little village house suddenly felt confining. Claustrophobic. I was lost. And Evan sitting silently next to me like the lighthouse he always was hit me with the force of a truck coming at me sideways.

He was going to let me go. I knew it as surely as I knew I'd never find another man like him. Never find anyone as perfect for me, as caring, as protective. As beautiful. As willing to put the safety of people around him before his own wants. Evan had always had my back even before I'd known I needed him.

He turned the song down toward the end as he pulled up to a modern metal gate set in a long white stucco wall. I leaned out the window and looked up, seeing a modern steel, white concrete, and glass building soaring above us.

"Wow," I said. "I never knew you liked such modern places, must be weird staying in that little stone room of yours."

"I like both. But yeah, that place felt like a tomb. Your side of the door is better."

"Obviously, coz *I'm* there."

He leaned out and typed a code in a discreet keypad. The metal gate slid silently open. "I'm glad we're here," he said. "I almost grew ovaries."

"Heathen." I rolled my eyes.

He pulled into a guest parking space, and we got out. It was only after we were buzzed into the cool lobby with a trickling water fountain and soft soothing colors I realized we'd left my bag in the car. He really thought I wouldn't be staying.

He greeted the burly security guard who called him, "Mr. Roark, Sir."

We stepped into the elevator and there were no buttons. "Um."

"He's sending us to my floor. He programs it from his terminal. It's better security than a key fob someone could steal."

"You're fancy, Evan. I had no idea."

He gave a tight smile that didn't reach his eyes. "I've done all right."

The elevator whooshed up silently and smoothly. There were no buttons, but the lights above the door indicated we were slowing on the tenth floor. "How many floors?" I asked suspiciously. The buildings here had a height limit so there couldn't be too many.

"Ten," he muttered.

I whistled. "The penthouse, Mr. Roark? *Sir*."

His eyes flashed at me. "Don't give me dirty thoughts right before I see my mother, if you don't mind."

I cracked up, even as my belly buzzed. *Oh my God*. He didn't have to protect me anymore. That meant he could stick his tongue down my throat or any other thing in me and not worry about his stupid rule. *If* I could convince him we were worth a shot.

He gave into a grin at my laugh, but a sad flash entered his eyes.

The doors slid open into a lobby of pale Scandinavian wood floors, high white walls, and reflected light from a lot of windows beyond the archway ahead of us.

"Mum," he called.

"Oh, so it opens right into your place? Wow."

"Curious. Where did you think I lived?"

"I didn't. I just thought you phased in and out of existence and right into my business usually."

"Funny. I guess they're out," he added, referring to his parents. "They should be back soon. My mom is excited to feed us."

"How long will they be gone? Do we have time to fool around?"

He spun to face me.

"Don't look so horrified. Your stupid rule doesn't apply anymore."

"It wasn't stupid."

"It still no longer applies." I bit my lip and looked around the elegantly furnished space. It was masculine and beachy but a little impersonal. I assumed a decorator helped him. A cozy blanket on the couch along with a paperback cracked and upside down to keep a place in the story were the only signs a human lived here. At least his mother was a reader. "Can we make out on the couch?" I grinned at him.

He blew out a breath and glanced away from me.

"Oh," I said. "So, it *was* a stupid rule because it was actually just an excuse."

"That's not it."

"Really?"

"You just got some huge news. You don't need me ... distracting you anymore."

"Distracting me?"

"That's what you said yesterday when you begged me to break my rule. That you needed me to help you forget. That that's how you needed me. Your exact words. To keep your mind off him. That's even what you said this morning."

"And I don't seem to remember spending too much time persuading you," I snapped. "Or that having sex with me was a terrible experience for you."

"It wasn't." He grabbed the back of his neck, sounding exasperated. "I told you it wasn't. But you don't need me. You just wanted *someone*. I was there. Lucky me. And I get it. It's okay."

"Excuse me?"

"Maybe you don't even know what you want yet. But you don't need me in your business anymore while you work it out. I can get back to work, and you can sort out the rest of your life. Isn't that what you wanted when you resigned and rented that place, got a new job and told me you needed space, even from me, to figure shit out? You don't need me for that," he added, his tone gentling. "I only ignored that boundary because I thought Angus was a threat. Well, he isn't. He wasn't. You could have been getting on with this new life weeks ago. What happened between us was a ... mistake. It only happened because we were working off missing intel about Angus. And we were in each other's space. And the stakes felt really high. And that does crazy stuff to people. Now you can have all the space you need."

I was breathing tightly. Everything he was saying was true, not the mistake part, but ... my chest hurt.

"I know it probably feels scary to be alone after the shock of this morning. But you're going to be okay. And you're not alone, not really. You have friends. Me, the girls, the crew. We're your family even if you don't work with us anymore."

"Stop being so damned condescending."

"I'm sorry."

"Is it so easy to let me go?" I asked in a whisper, blinking back tears, because I was still a masochist, no matter how many girl power songs I'd just listened to. Jesus. This hurt. I mean, I knew I was kind of naive and sheltered by virtue of my circumstance and probably not the usual type Evan went for. I mean, just look at Lilian. In fact, look at *this* place. I sought out storybook villages, and he sought out a sophisticated, if soulless, box. He was calm, strong, and unflappable, and I'd been an anxiety-ridden, hysterical, and frigid damsel. I felt frumpy, and silly, and really, really, dumb. To think I'd gotten on my knees for him this morning, only for him to reject me. He must have been embarrassed at how ridiculous I was. My stomach cramped with nausea.

"Yoo-hoo!" a female voice called, and a pretty woman with chestnut hair the same color as Evan's and cut into a bob, appeared in the archway from the entry hall.

"You must be Andrea," she said, her lined face creasing into a big smile.

"You can call her Lucy, Mum. It's okay."

I stared at the woman, rooted to the spot as flashes and images came screeching up from the past.

"Evan thought you might recognize me," she said.

THIRTY-FOUR

"How?" I asked the dark-haired woman in Evan's apartment, even while goose bumps erupted over my skin. "Wait. I do recognize you."

"It was a long time ago. I've changed my hair since then. Shorter. So have you! I'm Abigail. Abby. I'm Evan's mother."

Her hazel eyes hadn't changed though. The ones so similar to Evan's. "I wasn't sure you were real," I whispered. "I have memories from that night. I was in a hospital, and someone was sitting by my bed telling me I should pretend not to know my own name. You were the lady who I reached out to on the flyer."

The entire ordeal came pouring back to me. I'd thought of it plenty over the years, but something about seeing this woman's face was prying loose the boards I'd nailed over everything. Someone had come and handed me a new passport and a plane ticket, and I'd just followed the instructions I was given.

It was her. "It was you." A sob left me. I started forward.

"There, there. It's all right." She came forward to meet me

and pulled me into a warm hug. "Come on. Let's sit. Evan, love, put the kettle on, would you? There's a dear."

I allowed her to lead me down to the couch as I rubbed at my face. "What a day. I'm sorry."

"It's fine, dear. You've had a shock. Evan texted me and told me about your husband, Angus. May his soul stay put."

A watery smile broke through. "Yes. May his soul stay put."

Her arm folded around my back, and she sat next to me, holding me close. It felt so good. So comforting. If I had any tears left, I'd be crying them all.

"Are you feeling all right?" she asked.

I nodded, but I couldn't stop staring at her. She was so pretty. An angel. She'd been my angel. "I've had too many shocks today. Maybe I'll become immune. That would be a good thing."

"You just need a cup of tea and some food. Then you'll be right as rain."

"That's how Evan knows my real name? Through you."

"Actually, I know you through Evan. He was the one who came to me and asked for my help all those years ago."

I swallowed and frowned. "What?"

"I'd built a network by then with Sam's help. That's my husband. Evan and Pete were helping with new identities and paperwork. And when he came and told me about you, we began to put flyers up in all the women's bathrooms near where you lived and the places you went to. Evan wanted to just go get you, and as time went on, he begged me to reach out to you, but I persuaded him it had to be your choice."

The man in question came in then with a tray holding two cups, a teapot, and a plate of chocolate Digestives.

"You have a teapot?" I said stupidly, wondering how cyborg, muscley, lives-in-a-sterile-box, Evan owned a teapot. Unless it was his mother's.

"Of course he does, dear. Though I bet it only ever gets used when *I'm* here."

He held up a hand with an indulgent look for his mother. "Guilty."

"Who *are* you?" I asked, staring at him. He was human. So human. And I loved it. I loved him. And he'd just dumped me.

God, what a perfect disaster.

Presumably sensing the mood shift, his mom leaned in. "How much do you remember from that time?"

I thought back to when I'd first seen the flyer. It was the morning after a particularly rough night. The bad nights all melded together in my memory now. I'd jumped at the chance to leave the house to go pick up some dry cleaning and gone into my favorite coffee shop to have some alone time before I went home, and I'd seen the flyer in the bathroom. I saved the number into my phone. It took me three weeks to build up the nerve to call and when I did and a lady had answered, I hadn't known what to say, I'd been dead quiet. I was about to hang up when she spoke.

"You said," I took a breath, "You said, 'Whatever you tell me, I'll believe you. And I'll believe *in* you. And I'll help you.'" I blinked up at Abigail.

She squeezed my hand.

"But I didn't call again for weeks." I glanced at Evan. He was pinching his bottom lip, his brow furrowed, his soft brown hair floppy and unruly.

"It's true," he said. "I was out of my mind with worry."

"But then fate kind of forced our hand a bit," Abby said, pulling my attention back to her.

She looked up at her son, and he sank into the armchair across from me and rubbed his hands on his jeans. "Yeah. I—it was dumb luck," he said. "There were rumors he was ... hurting you. I didn't know for sure, but I hired someone to look into it." He swallowed. "Into you. Yeah, apparently I've always had an issue crossing lines where you're concerned. When I suspected the rumors were true is when I asked Mum to put up the flyers in that area. And I found out about the clinic appointment. Something about the way he came home early that day really bothered me, and I called Mum and begged her to just go to your house."

"Good thing I did. Though I should have called the police, not gone there myself. The statistics do show that a woman is in the most danger the moment she tries to leave."

My insides clenched. "Did he hurt you?" I asked Abby.

"No. Actually, I think he shocked himself with what had just happened with you. I said I was a friend and would call him from the hospital. Then we left. Evan met us at the hospital."

"I—I don't remember that. I'm so sorry." This was horrific. These people were involved in and witnessed the most horrible day of my life, and I hadn't known it. It felt humiliating. And shameful. And as much as I was also grateful, I felt lied to. I'd shared my story with Evan this weekend in the tent, and he'd let me as if he didn't know. It felt like a terrible betrayal. But right now I had to focus on the good stuff.

Abby grabbed my hand. "No. No apologies. None of it was your fault."

"Abby." I squeezed her hand. "Thank you so much for

helping me. Thank you," I repeated. "I don't think I ever got a chance to say that. You saved my life."

"With Evan's help."

I nodded. "I'd like to speak with Evan alone."

"I thought you might. This was a lot. Evan, why don't you take her to your room. It's more private. I'll see you both in the kitchen. Salad and cold cuts. I'm not cooking because I figured we'd have lots to talk about, and I didn't want to be scrambling or worrying about things getting cold. Also Sam is in the kitchen, he'd really like to meet Lucy when you're ready."

Lucy. That *was* my name, yet it felt so foreign. "I, uh, I think I'll stick with Andrea. If that's fine. I'm used to it. And all my documents ..." I trailed off as my gaze landed on Evan. Documents Evan had provided. Of course he freaking knew my real name. Always had. He'd probably shown up at the foundation on my birthday *because* it was my birthday.

Evan stood and turned back to the entrance hall, and I followed. There were two other openings opposite each other. I followed him through to one opening that was a short bedroom hallway. The other side must have been to the guest room. He held open a door and I passed him, entering a large bedroom suite with a king-sized upholstered bed made up with white linens. By the floor to ceiling windows there was a couch and two chairs. Honestly, it looked like a hotel room. There was nothing of Evan in here. But then again, I wouldn't know what Evan's style was even when he was right in front of me. Not anymore. He felt like a damn stranger today.

"I'm sorry," he started after he closed his door. "I didn't mean for it to be such a shock."

"Which part?" I asked, feeling weirdly numb.

"Mum, obviously. I was going to tell you about her before we left for Veronica's office, but with everything that happened this morning, I didn't know how to start. It seemed too much to add to everything."

"Some warning would have been nice."

"I suppose there's never a good time."

"I ... can't believe that's really her."

He walked to the seating area, silhouetting himself against the bright outside sky. "I should have told you from the beginning. Honestly, I thought you knew or remembered or something. But it was a long time until I realized you didn't. You didn't look at me with recognition. Or with anything really. And then time passed and I couldn't bring it up. You were starting to recover, and the last thing I wanted to do was be a reminder." He scrubbed his hand through his hair. "And you made me second guess everything. Like I'd lost a map I didn't know I needed and taken a road I didn't know—" He stopped and closed his eyes before giving his head a shake. "Sunflower ..." He gave a humorless laugh, but it was short lived. "You were wearing a gray t-shirt with a sunflower on it when you got home from the clinic that day."

The memory blasted me and stole my breath. "I remember that shirt."

"I know you're probably upset."

"You lied to me."

"I know."

"You had ample opportunities to tell me when I was confiding in you, just this weekend."

"I know." He squeezed his eyes closed again.

"You looked so shocked to see my scar. Was that a lie too?"

His throat bobbed heavily. "I *was* shocked. I hadn't seen the result of what had happened to you. You were in the hospital and then almost fully healed by the time we crossed paths again here in France."

"This all makes me feel like a fool. It makes me question everything about the entire time I've known you." I heaved a breath, temporarily at a loss for words.

He didn't answer.

"Tell me about you and Pete," I said eventually.

He leaned back against the glass and stuffed his fingers in the front pockets of his jeans. "Pete and I set up new identities and passports if needed, not all do, for the women who reach out to my mother's network. It's all anonymous. And obviously it's high risk. Our contacts for paperwork aren't the most scrupulous, as you can imagine. We have some high net worth private donors—"

"Xavier?"

Evan nodded. "And others. Anyway, in most cases we put together a small starter fund and send them on their way. There are also other organizations we partner with that help people get back on their feet with jobs and training. They usually help people who have escaped being trafficked, but they work with us too."

"That's ... that's really incredible." It was stunning really. I'd worked with him for years and had no idea. "Why didn't you ... send me on? Why did I stay where *you* were?"

He'd tucked one hand under an arm and the other one wiped down his face. "I—I thought he'd come for you. I knew he wouldn't let you go. I thought the yacht was the safest option for you. I didn't know how to keep you safe unless I could make sure of it myself."

"Are you always so worried about the women you're helping?"

"Of course. I mean, I wouldn't be doing this otherwise. We break a thousand laws to move people across borders."

"But you kept me at Pascale Company? Had you ever asked Xavier to employ anyone else?"

"That's the real question, isn't it?"

I approached and took a seat on one of the chairs, waiting. "Well?"

"No. You were the only one. It was ... different." He gave me a look, then turned to the view out the window I hadn't even looked at. I'd bet it was amazing—the city of Cannes and the bay beyond.

"Different because you knew Angus in the service? Neil said that's how he knew you."

"Partly." He took a deep breath. "You asked earlier if you were easy to let go. The answer is ... no. Not at all. It wasn't easy then, and it sure as shit isn't easy now. Not now that—shit." He squeezed his eyes shut. "It doesn't matter. Just—Here goes. First things first. Remember you told me that story. The one that shocked you. The one that made you rethink the man you were married to?"

"The one about the kid and the bike?"

"Yeah, that one."

"What about it?"

"That was me."

"What, sorry?"

"That story was about me," Evan said in a pained tone.

"He destroyed your bike?"

"No. He pointed the finger, and I got the shit beaten out of me. I was the kid he'd apparently held a vendetta against for all those years. But I truly had no idea why. Not until you told me that story. I didn't even know him then. He got the wrong guy, obviously. If there ever even *was* a guy, or he just liked fucking people up and somehow I crossed his radar."

My heart, I swear, it stopped in my chest. "Wh—what?"

"I was the poor kid in your story. The skinny, shy kid who was just trying to stay in the shadows and not become a target, trying to be a good quiet son to my mum who was trying to make ends meet after being married to a narcissistic sociopath, so I didn't cause her more stress. Who somehow crossed the radar of Angus Robertson and had no understanding of how I got there."

"Evan," I breathed, my heart cracking open.

"I was fourteen. My growth spurt hadn't started. I got the absolute shit kicked out of me."

I let out a small, pained howl.

He looked up. "Fuck, baby. Don't cry anymore. Please. Not over *me*." He came toward me. "I wasn't trying to make this about me. I swear. I just, I wanted to come clean."

I shook my head and held my hand up to stop him from coming closer. "No." I would break down if he held me right now.

Especially now with my roller coaster of emotions, I didn't trust myself not to humiliate myself again by begging him to give us a shot when he'd just clearly dumped me moments before his mother showed up. And also, this was a lot to process. Part of me wanted to crawl into his lap, or frankly, have him crawl into mine after the story I knew. The image of Evan as a frightened little boy, so different to who he was now, was doing me in.

He dropped his arms, looking lost.

"Go on," I managed after inhaling a deep shuddering breath and trying to keep my emotions in check. "How did you end up bumping into Angus again?"

"My mum was seeing Sam at the time," he went on, "but resisted marrying him even though I was all for it. I just wanted a dad, a real one, and I adored him, but she found it hard to trust again. Obviously. When Sam came to the hospital to see me after what happened, I told him I wanted to be strong like him, so no one could ever hurt me again. He told me he could help me be strong physically but that it would come with a great responsibility never to inflict on anyone else the kind of pain Angus had inflicted. I swore to him right then that if he'd be my dad, I'd follow his exact footsteps."

My heart pounded with a deep ache. "That's—"

"Unrealistic? I know."

"Heartbreaking."

"And of course, Sam told me that his love was unconditional and he already wanted to be my dad, no matter what."

I sniffed and blinked back more tears.

"Anyway, Sam had been a Royal Marine, and so, of course, that's what I wanted to do too. There were pros and cons. I mean, you had to learn to kill, right? And I did." He swallowed, heavily. "But the other side of it was amazing. A sense of honor. A mission. A team. Guys you could depend on. Guys who had your back. And the physical side was a game changer at a time I finally had my growth spurt." He smiled ruefully. "But the day I realized Angus was in my regiment. God. It was a gut punch. But I was stronger then. He didn't mess with me. I'm not even sure if he put two and two together since I went by Sam's last name."

I frowned in confusion.

He sighed. "And also I was bigger. Taller. In fact, Pete and I made it *our* mission to keep him on the straight and narrow. I was a fucking hawk on his shoulder. Though I wasn't there when Angus met you."

"The party at the barracks."

"Yeah. I ..." he rubbed his face. "You said you were supposed to meet someone, but instead you met Angus? It was supposed to be *me* you were introduced to that night. I think. My buddy said his girl was bringing a friend. It can't be that much of a coincidence. But I've never been able to get it out of my head."

My mouth opened and closed. "What?"

"I was late arriving. Then, well, I guess I was too late. Fuck. Maybe part of me did wonder if he knew it was me. Maybe he stepped in on purpose. I don't know. But, fuck, I could have warned you about him or something. I felt, *I feel*, responsible."

"You shouldn't."

He let out a humorless laugh.

"I'm serious, Evan. Have you been hanging on to a sense of *responsibility* all this time?" Because the idea that I'd been this huge obligation to him all these years settled into my gut like a bag of harbor rocks. I'd accused him before of pitying me, and now, given all that had transpired between us over the last few weeks, me coming on so strong, him trying to back off all the time, I was starting to realize I'd been an absolute fool. No wonder he'd been trying to break it off gently for days, even though I kept pressuring him. He pitied me and didn't want to hurt me.

I held my stomach. "I feel sick," I mumbled.

"You need to eat."

"No. I need to get the hell out of here."

"What?"

"This is a lot to process. And I've always been aware you knew of my circumstances, but I didn't know you *knew* knew. Or that you knew *him*. God, you must have been shaking your head all this time that I could be so clueless and stupid to marry someone like Angus."

"I've *never* thought that! It wasn't your fault."

"But it was really. I mean clearly he didn't *become* something awful. He'd always been awful. And I was too dumb to see it."

"You aren't dumb."

"Well. That remains to be seen, doesn't it? Angus had me believing I was. Maybe he wasn't wrong after all. I clearly have really fucking bad taste in choosing men."

"Thanks."

"I don't mean you. Not really."

"Why? Because I was just a means to an end?"

I stood. "This is too painful for me. I can't process everything that happened today and also that I was a pity fuck for you."

"Sunflower. Goddammit, I—"

"No. I get it. I'd love to see your mother again sometime to thank her properly. Maybe even help somehow. But you and me ..." I swallowed. "You said it yourself, you only crossed the boundaries with me because you thought Angus was a threat. Well, he's not. So thank you, I guess, the sex was great."

He grabbed his hair in both fists. "I only crossed your *privacy* boundaries because of Angus." He moved closer, his eyes bottomless. I wanted to fall into them. "The personal ones, the intimate ones, that was because I—" He stopped abruptly, and everything in his expression shuttered away.

"What?"

He stepped back and dropped his hands to his sides. "You're right. You should go. You have a lot to process. You're free. I'm so happy for you." His hand fished into his jeans pocket and pulled out my car keys. "Here." He dropped them into my palm. "Good luck, Sunflower."

I gasped out a breath like it had been punched out of my chest. Ouch.

Then I closed my fist over the keys and ran out before he could see me break.

THIRTY-FIVE

Evan

WATCHING Andrea walk out the door of my apartment and not chase her is the hardest thing I've ever done. I can't stand her thinking I fucked her out of pity, but I know it's for the best. It's cleaner this way. She's mad at me. She's had a whole heap of stuff dumped on her today, and the very last thing she needs is my fucking *feelings* complicating shit.

Besides, when she moves on she'll do it without having to feel guilty about hurting me. She doesn't need to worry about anyone else but herself right now.

"Knock, knock," my dad says quietly from the doorway. "Your mother said I should come and check on you. We heard Lucy leaving."

"Her name is Andrea."

He eases into the room. "Andrea," he says with a nod.

"Did you know that *I* chose her new name? Andrea means

strong and brave. Mom always said it was important for a name to mean something, like a quiet wish for the soul's journey." I blink. My chest is aching, a hollow emptiness inside it that feels like a vacuum of nothingness about to crush my ribs inwards. It will pass, I tell myself. Please God, it has to. This is too painful.

"So, you kept her close to you all this time?"

"I shouldn't have," I whisper, my voice failing. "I should have allowed her the freedom to make her own choices and go her own way. I should have let her go sooner."

"But you were worried about her."

"Yes."

"And you love her."

I swallow audibly. "Yeah," I croak. "Which is what makes this all so unforgivable. She's not processing what I did yet. But she will. She'll realize I built a safety net around her that meant she lived in constant fear of leaving it. That I ... trapped her into depending on me."

"Evan." My dad starts forward. "That's not—"

"It was subconscious, on my part, I realize that. But that doesn't make it better. I never wanted her to leave, Dad. That really makes me no better than Angus."

"Stop! That's not true. And you know it."

I bury my face in my hands.

My dad's quiet presence settles at my side. "Evan, the way you acted was understandable given what you knew of Angus. No one can blame you for being extra cautious and keeping an eye on her."

I looked at my dad. His strong frame, his salt and pepper hair, and his kind brown eyes. Sam Roark had always been a bulwark, a port in the storm. He was quiet and patient and strong and kind. Not like me. I was controlling, and impatient, demanding and apparently dishonest.

Sam Roark would never have done what I did. He would never have kept the truth hidden. He was always honest, even if the truth was hard to hear. It meant you always knew where you stood. "I wish I could have been more like you were with mom."

"You are *you*, Evan. And who you are is an intelligent, principled, strong person who will never let anything bad happen to the people around him."

"But what I did *is* bad."

"That's a difference of perspective. I bet you wanted to tell her you knew Angus, that you knew what he was doing, and you had something to do with giving her a lifeline. And then perhaps time got in the way, and before you knew it, it was too hard. Like it would shatter the delicate balance of what you had with her."

I stare at him.

"In a different way, I did the same to Abby. I went to Xavier's mother, Madame, and I begged her to employ Abby to tutor Xavier. I told her everything about your mother's situation. I promised I would pay Madame back, and I did. I persuaded her to pay Abby into a separate bank account her husband didn't know about. She gave Abby some story about how all women need their own funds their husbands don't know about, making her feel like it was okay, like they shared a secret together. But it was my secret. I was trying to create some financial independence for her so she could leave. And look, your mom is an incredible teacher. Kids respond to her. She's really good at teaching. But you can imagine how she felt when she found out. Like she hadn't earned it. Like she wasn't good enough. Like I'd pitied her or she was some charity case." He shook his head. "That was the worst time in my life. I'd meddled. If I'd just told her up front—"

"She wouldn't have accepted your help."

He purses his lips.

"You know it's true."

"Yes. I do. And that was a hard truth for her to hear."

I sit back.

"But she did hear it. In the end. Still kept me at arm's length for years until—"

"Until Angus orchestrated for the shit to be kicked out of me, and I lay in hospital and begged for you to be my dad and for you to marry her."

He chuckles. "Yeah. I guess I'll always be grateful to Angus Robertson for causing a family crisis that allowed me to marry the love of my life."

"I hope there's a liberal lacing of sarcasm in that statement."

"Yes and no, son. I hate to be cliché, but sometimes we all need a kick in the pants. And when we wait too long, the universe delivers it for us. Your mum filled me in a bit about what's been going on. The fact that Andrea filed for divorce and quit working with you, causing you to run to her side is pretty standard fare for when something is 'meant to be.' Throw in the fact Angus had passed and wasn't a real threat at the point. Well, that's just beautiful. The universe works in mysterious ways."

"Dad. I never knew you to be such a romantic. I appreciate the sentiment but this is different."

"How so?"

"You were patient with Mom. And you never embodied the

traits that she would associate with ..." I can't even call him *my father* because he wasn't. He isn't. "Him. It's different with me. Angus was a controlling, possessive asshole. And I think there's a lot of how I am that probably reminds her of him. I made her tell me everywhere she was going. I tracked her locations on her phone. And when she switched them off a few weeks ago ... I found her anyway. And it would have been one thing if Angus were a real threat, but he was already fucking dead at that point. I just didn't look into it enough—maybe I avoided it. I was so fucking ecstatic that she needed me, that she was pulling down her walls, that she suddenly looked at me in a way she never had. I tried to resist. But in the end, I took advantage."

Visions of Andrea begging for my touch assault me—her opening up to me, trusting me—and the way I just took. And took. And took. "Fuck, Dad. I really did take advantage. You have no idea."

There's a soft knock at the door.

We both look up to see my mum.

She's aged in the last ten years, but in the most wonderful way. I only notice it after long periods apart. She's smaller, and softer, and a tiny bit rounder, and she's still so beautiful. I'm so grateful Sam is there to love her and take care of her. And she him.

"Come and eat, boys. I should have gotten something a bit more substantive, but either way, big thoughts need big baguettes."

My dad stands. "You know, every time you say that it sounds vaguely sexual."

"Ha. Well, you should be so lucky. I'm just talking about calories."

I have no appetite, but I follow my dad out as he tails my

mum, and they have a moment where he winks at her and kisses her temple. She blushes before he gently places a hand at her lower back. I watch as her body language leans in as soon as he does it, as if she wants more.

They're my parents so I avert my gaze, but it still sends a pang through me.

∼

AT THE TABLE, Mum makes sure we all have food before she levels her gaze on me. "She needs space."

"I know, Mum. Trust me. I know." I push the salad across the plate and spear a piece of ham.

"But don't let her have space too long before you tell her how you feel." She shares a quick look with my dad.

Sam gives her a little nod.

"It's a risk," she says. "I know that. But she needs to know your heart. Otherwise it's no better than how you kept everything else from her."

God. "Mum." I hadn't thought of it like that.

"She needs to have all the facts, Evan. And it might take her a while to come back to you." She sets her fork down. "She might never come back to you."

My breathing falters as my chest seizes.

"But," she goes on. "That's the risk."

"If you love her," Sam adds.

I look down at my plate, unseeing. "I do," I whisper.

"What are her plans? Do you know?"

"To date again. Maybe have kids." I toss my napkin back on

the table. "Go back to England. I don't know. Nothing that includes me."

"Why not?"

"Because my work is here. I've built my life here. Who knows where she'll go. And she needs to figure that out without me breathing down her neck. She deserves to go explore the world and find out who she is and where she wants to be and what she wants to be."

"Why do you think that can't include you?"

"Because, I have to let her go. I have to *not know* where she is at every hour of every day. It's the only gift I can give her to show her I'm not the person she thinks I am. That I'm not a control freak and a stalker."

"I think that's more to prove it to yourself than to her," Sam suggests.

"Maybe. But either way." I fold my arms across my chest, tucking my palms under my biceps. It feels comforting, like I can control the damage the chaos inside my chest is causing. All I want to do is leave the table and go ride my motorcycle. Or run. Or ... fuck, I don't know. Actually, I do know, I'd like to fuck. But only her.

"How do you think she feels about you?" my mum asks gently.

"I think ... I think she hasn't had feelings in a long time. And I think some of what we shared probably tricked her into thinking she had feelings for me."

"You don't think they're real."

I shake my head. "No. I don't."

"Why?" she asks.

"How can they be?"

"Why shouldn't they be? Just because the last few weeks have been intense doesn't mean her feelings aren't genuine, or that they weren't there for a long time before. Yours were."

"No," I argue. "She never gave me any indication there was anything else there. Not before and definitely not the last couple of days." Not before that silly drunken moment in the nightclub anyway. In fact, she reiterated repeatedly that she needed me as a distraction and a first step before being with other people. God, even this morning with that attempted blowjob, mentioning being with someone else someday. I fist my hand under the table as pain knifes through me. Goddammit.

"Did you give *her* any indication of yours?"

"We worked together," I explained patiently, getting annoyed. "That would have made it awkward, and it might have made her feel uncomfortable working together."

"Exactly."

"Mum."

"Evan," she parrots.

I exhale angrily. "It was a fuck ton of sexual chemistry, okay? And we had an amazing time. And anyone could have gotten their feelings confused."

"Are *you* confused about what's sexual chemistry and what's more," she challenges me.

"No," I all but shout, my frustration and pain feeling all consuming. "But—"

"Then at least give her the courtesy of assuming she's mature enough to know the difference too," Mum snaps.

I stand up from the table. "Thank you for lunch. I have to get back to work. I've been gone far too long." I love my mum to bits, but sometimes I want to strangle her.

I grab my plate and take it into the kitchen. Then I change into a suit and call a cab back to Pascale Company.

I have to get back to work. And *not* check Andrea's location on my terminal. Then I have to make a plan to get my stuff from my room at the village house and pick up my bike. It's time to cut the cord and let go of her. I'm not sure I know how to do it. But I'm going to try.

Because if there's one thing I need to prove to myself and to her, it's that I'm not a stalker or a control freak, and that I *can* let go.

THIRTY-SIX

Andrea

I BARELY REMEMBERED the drive away from Cannes. And I didn't know where I was going. Everything seemed overwhelming. At some point I became aware I needed to eat. And I needed to go to the little village house. A borrowed home. Not *my* home. I had no home.

God, I'd needed to figure that out too. Did I need to hide away in a little village when I had no one to hide from?

At some point over the last few days, my emerging ideas about where I might go and the life I might live one day began to include a tall, strong, beautiful, brown haired and hazel-eyed guardian at my side.

When Evan had asked me just the night before to tell him about the life I wanted, and I let my imagination run, he'd been present in every vision I'd voiced. I wanted to go back to England one day, with *him*. I wanted to putter around a little home I'd created, with *him*—a house full of love and family, that included *him*. There might even be kids there, that I'd chosen to have or adopted with *him*. I wanted to find a career I loved and come home every day, to *him*.

It wasn't someone. It was him. And home wasn't a place. It wasn't a rented house in a storybook village, it wasn't on the boat, it wasn't my old house I'd shared with Angus. Home was Evan. It had been for years. Painful emptiness sliced sharply through me.

My phone beeped with a low battery warning. Even the damned phone made me think of him. Passing a local *Carrefour supermarché*, I suddenly turned in and parked. Inside, I bought a new cell phone. I debated whether to get a new number and start fresh, but in the end, I asked them to port my old number into my new phone so people didn't lose my contact. God knew, I felt alone enough as it was.

I plugged the new phone into the USB for handsfree and pulled up the GPS to map my way back to Saint Paul de Vence. The phone rang as soon as I left the parking lot.

"Hello?"

"Andrea! It's Josie!"

I burst into a smile, my heart warming, before my throat closed up. "Josie. So good to hear from you," I managed, my voice wobbly. "Thank goodness I didn't change my number."

"Are you okay?" she asked immediately.

I blinked and swallowed hard. "Ugh. Kind of. Great and not great. It's just really good to hear your voice. How are *you*?"

"No, you first. What's wrong?"

"How do I even begin? I thought I was being followed by my husband, though now it turns out he's dead, and in the meantime I threw myself at Evan. We had incredible sex before he politely disentangled himself from me and told me to be on my way. And now I'm completely lost and have no idea what to do with the rest of my life."

Josie had punctuated my rant with a gasp, and a squeal, and a long moaned, "Noooo."

"Well, what about you?" I volleyed back as I took the exit onto the motorway.

"Stop. We'll get to me in a minute. So your ex is dead. My God. How did you find out? And are you okay?"

"I'm fine. Totally fine. Relieved, actually. Emotional a bit because I have a lot of unresolved shit I want to get off my chest, and now I'll never get the chance. And I found out through his brother. Which is a whole other thing I have to deal with. But the last few weeks Evan has been on me like a shadow because we thought Angus was here and following me, but it turned out to be nothing. Which just makes the whole thing feel pretty stupid." I flicked on my blinker and entered the passing lane. "It's like that scene from *Almost Famous* when there's all that turbulence, and they think the plane is going down. Everyone is yelling and admitting shit they would have kept buried for a hundred years because they think they're going to die. And all of a sudden, a few minutes later, the plane levels out and the lights flick back on, and they're left feeling ridiculous with all this shit out there that they can't take back. That's how I feel."

"Maybe Evan feels like that too?"

"What, that he admitted a bunch of stuff he wouldn't normally? Because he didn't admit anything. It was sex. Amazing sex. But just sex."

"Maybe not with words, but that he acted on something he

probably never would have. Something that was there all along but he was keeping buried. Like a very massive attraction."

"I think that's more what I did, not him."

"And is it just sexual attraction on your part, do you think?"

I blew out a breath. "No. I mean there's that, sure. But God, I realized this weekend my feelings run so much deeper. I called him my lighthouse, and I think that's what he's always been for me. Just quietly, solidly, *there* for me. And I think ... I think I fell all the way in love, if I wasn't there already." I pursed my lips and exhaled, feeling vulnerable for admitting it out loud when there was no future in it. "And obviously that sounds ridiculous."

"Well, Xavier told me, and he made me swear to keep it to myself, unless I *had* to share it, and I think this warrants it, Xavier said he thinks Evan has been in love with you for years."

My foot slipped off the gas. "Ha, ha." My voice pitched high. I gripped the wheel and indicated to get back into the slow lane. This was a slow lane conversation.

"I'm serious."

"Maybe you misunderstood him," I said, breathing shallowly. "I don't need to be getting my hopes up. I feel shitty enough already. I'd rather just deal with the rejection now than drag it out." My insides grew mushy and my head light. I peered ahead for an exit. This might be a pull-over-before-you-get-yourself-killed kind of conversation.

"Xavier told me that yesterday. Seriously, when I told Xavier I'd spoken to you and jokily suggested you use Evan for practice. Xavier said, and I quote, 'She'll break his heart if that's all she wants from him.'"

A weird squeaking sound came out of my throat as I tried to swallow and talk and breathe all at once. I needed to pull over.

"I wanted to call you immediately," Josie went on. "But it was super late your time, so I figured I'd try you first thing this morning, coz God knows, that's not a texting piece of info. So here I am. Xavier thinks Evan is in love with you. On God."

"That's not true," I whispered. "Have ... to ... pull over."

"Oh shit, are you driving? Yes, pull over."

Swerving to the exit, I nearly wrecked. My hands didn't know how to steer anymore apparently. Or they were too sweaty to hold the wheel. A loud honking came from the car behind that screeched past as I got out of their way. My heart pounded. At the top of the exit ramp there was a freaking roundabout because that was what I was capable of right now. I managed to take the first exit onto a small country road, and a hundred yards down there was a dirt pull in off to the side next to a low stone wall.

I rolled to a stop. "Holy shit. Give a girl some warning." I dropped my head back on the headrest.

"I'm so sorry. Are you okay?"

"Yes, I found a place to stop." I turned off the car and scrubbed my hands down my face.

"Okay, well. I don't think Xavier would say that unless it was based on something real."

I mentally rewound the last two weeks and tried to put that lens on it. Me saying I needed him, and Evan saying I didn't know what I was asking of him. I tried to remember the texts we'd had that night when I'd had too much *rosé*. Something about what he'd said niggled at me. Why the hell had I deleted them? I thought back to our first kiss, and then the night in the tent. *I can't watch your back when all I can see is you.* But that didn't mean anything more than reiterating that stupid rule of his.

"What's happening inside your head?" Josie asked.

"I'm trying to look back to see if there was anything that I maybe didn't clock, or didn't understand, that might be different within this new context. And honestly, I can't. It was just sex for him. I'm sure of it. Great sex. I mean sure, he cares about me as a friend too, but ..." I frowned. "And he had this stupid rule that he kept citing that he couldn't be both my lover and my protector. That sleeping with me would compromise his ability to look out for me or something."

"Hmm." Josie sighed.

"No. It wasn't like *that*."

"Wasn't it? Why would it compromise his ability unless he knows he gets so lost in you he has to keep you at arm's length."

"That sounds like love brain talking. Oh my God!" Everything Josie said came hurtling into focus. "You said you spoke to Xavier yesterday! Well? Did he confess he's in love with you?"

"He's here in Charleston. But I'm guessing you knew that already." There was a smile in her voice.

"I did! Tell me, tell me, tell me!" I squealed and she laughed.

"Okay. Well, big news first, we're engaged."

I screamed. Loud. "Holy shit! Yes!" I pumped the air.

"It's a good thing you pulled over." Josie was giggling.

"No kidding. Girl, how can you keep that from me for the whole first part of us talking? You need *to lead with that!* Oh my God, I'm so happy for you." Aaaand I was crying again. Tears of joy this time. I sniff and rummage in the glove box for a tissue. "How did he, when did he, tell me everything."

And she did. For twenty minutes, Josie shared the most gorgeous story of Xavier coming with Dauphine to Charleston to win her back, and my heart was gooey by the end of it. "I'm so happy for you," I whispered, overcome.

It had been so hard for Xavier to admit how he felt and to trust in love again. Especially after his first wife dying. I was overjoyed he'd finally found a way to happiness. "It's hard for men like Xavier and Evan to admit to what's in their hearts and make themselves so vulnerable," Josie said. "Especially if they've been hurt before. It's hard for anyone, I guess."

"That's something Lilian said too. That someone had gotten to Evan's heart a long time ago. I asked him about what she said the other night. And he admitted it—"

I broke off, the vision swamping me. Evan's warm weight on my body, the feel of his skin, the depth of his eyes as he pressed my hands into the pillow either side of my head. *"... you gave your heart away a long time ago."* I'd said. *"That's true, Sunflower. I did."* And then he'd made love to me, so gently, his lips barely leaving mine as his body brought me to pleasure—showing me without words what he maybe didn't want to admit. *"That's true, Sunflower. I did."*

"Oh my God," I said, my heart pounding.

Unless I was a naive idiot. Which, given everything was a possibility. I explained to Josie what had crossed my mind. "I mean he could also have been reaffirming the fact that we were only having sex. Like, yep, I gave my heart away a long time ago, so let me shut you up with kisses and my penis."

Josie sighed. "I don't want to get your hopes up if it's not true. But why would Xavier say that if it wasn't based in some kind of truth?"

"If Evan really felt that way why hasn't he told me? After all this time? Probably because it's not true."

"Or," Josie drawled. "Or, he doesn't believe you feel the same way."

"Or *wouldn't* believe me if I told him I did. There's no way for me to know." I sighed. "And if he's not telling me out of some misguided sense of what he thinks is best for me right now, I swear, I'll smother him in his sleep."

Josie laughed.

"All right." I leaned my head back on the headrest and glanced at the rearview mirror noticing a car turning in to my little country lane. They were probably lost based on their slowness. "I guess I should get back on the motorway. Someone is going to report me as an abandoned vehicle soon. Before you go, tell Xavier congratulations. And also Dauphine. Tell her congratulations on gaining a wonderful *belle-mère*," I added, using the French word for stepmother.

"I will. Drive safe. What will you do now?"

"I'll go back to my little *Beauty and the Beast* village." I sighed with a wry chuckle. "I started off thinking of Evan as Gaston, but he very quickly became the beast."

"Cute," said Josie. "And then?"

"And then I guess I'll go back to work tomorrow and start figuring out if working in a gallery is what I want to do." I had a feeling it wasn't. I had a feeling I actually might want to go into social work and see about helping in Evan's mom's organization. I had some savings for a diploma at least. Xavier had paid generously. "Anyway, when are you and Xavier coming back?"

"Probably not for a while. We're going to put Dauphine in a school here for a bit and see how she likes it. I still have my new job and I'm loving it. I definitely don't want to quit so soon. Not without another plan. We're planning on staying here at least six months to see how it goes. Xavier will fly back and forth, so I'm having Tabitha find us another nanny."

"Babe, you're marrying a billionaire. You know you don't have to work, right?"

"I would go out of my mind. You know I would."

"Yeah, I hear you. I would too." I laughed. Maybe. "And a wedding?"

"I'm making him wait until the spring. I'll keep you posted."

"You'd better. I'm so happy for you, Josie." My phone beeped with an incoming call and a quick glance told me it was Neil, my brother in law. Ex-brother-in-law? Whatever.

"Thanks, Andrea. I'll be crossing fingers that you and Evan sort your stuff out."

"You might be crossing them a long while, but thanks."

We said goodbye for real this time, and I pressed end on the phone, feeling a thousand times better, even if I was still reeling from the events of the day.

I had messages from both Meg and Sue. I opened them up.

Meg: *Hey! I heard the news about your ex. Wow. Do you want company this evening?*

Sue: *Meg and I thinking of popping up to see you.*

I wrote back. *That would be great! You guys are the best. I have wine. Then we'll pop over to the* trattoria *if it's open. If not, I'll make pasta.*

There was some idle chatter in the group chat, but otherwise my new phone was silent. I debated whether to call Neil back. But decided to see if he left a message first. It had been a rough day, talking to him again might be more emotion than I could handle.

Breathing deeply, I turned the car back on. My voicemail beeped with a message. I hit play as I put the car into drive.

Neil's voice filled the car. "I'm so sorry. I didn't know. I tried to stop him. I'm so, so sorry, Lucy. If I'd known, I never would have gone along with—"

I was thrown forward so violently, my forehead almost cracked the steering wheel but the airbag blew up in my face and everything faded.

THIRTY-SEVEN

Evan

"I'M COMING. I'll be at the office in thirty max," I say to Pete as he calls for the second time in two minutes while I'm getting in a cab that finally showed up.

"Where the hell are you?" barks Pete. "The motherfucker was lying. He was lying."

"What? Who?" The panic in Pete's voice shoots ice through my veins.

"The brother. Angus is not dead."

My insides fucking drop twelve stories. "Tell me this is a sick joke." The cab starts moving and my instinct is to jump out and take my own transport, but we're already moving and I don't have my bike.

"*Monsieur, vite, s'il vous plaît,*" I beg the cab driver.

"The papers are legit, but something didn't sit right," Pete is saying. "The medical examiner's name rang a bell. When he said the name, I remembered it. Another soldier turned mercenary. Kept his medical license, apparently.

"Our man Gavin was already in town watching the law office last night, so I asked him to swing by and follow the brother after your meeting. Caught him down the street frantically dialing and begging someone *quote unquote* not to go through with it. Then the brother called Andrea. It took a few minutes of listening for Gavin to figure out what was going on. Neil called her Lucy, but Gavin just confirmed it was definitely Andrea's number. Gavin's bringing him in. I tried to call her. No answer."

Panic and terror are white hot and crowding my vision and crushing my chest. "Fuck, fuck. Fuck." The world whizzes by far too slowly outside the window of the taxi that I am now powerlessly trapped in. Sweat beads, prickling my temples. I failed. So spectacularly. I snap at the driver to speed up again and haul a hundred euros out of my wallet and push it over his shoulder.

"What do you want me to do?" Pete asks in my ear.

"Fuck. Where is she? Did you track her phone? Jesus. Fuck. She better have her location permissions on. We ..." my fist clenches and I pound the side of it on the door.

The driver swerves and yells at me.

"*Désolé*," I apologize. "*Désolé*," I repeat, and put the hand up to show I'm truly sorry, before raking it through my hair and clutching the back of my neck. I need to stay calm. I've always been able to stay calm. Breathe.

"What were you about to say?" Pete asks. "We, what?"

My throat feels like sandpaper over the words. "We didn't end well this morning. For all I know, she threw her phone out the fucking window." I look at my watch. At least the driver has sped up. Probably to get me out of his cab faster.

"Well, I'll kick your ass for that later," Pete says. "But I'm pulling up her cell phone tower pings now to check. She left your apartment approximately one hundred minutes ago. She drove straight on the A8. Looks like she missed the exit for Saint Paul de Vence, so she was either distracted... "

"Or he was already on her," I voiced my fear.

"Wait. She pinged near the Carrefour City in Les Vallieres for around twenty minutes," Pete continues, and my hope increases that we're overreacting.

"Carrefour." I breathe out. She's just shopping. "Picking up supplies for the village house. She had little there for breakfast this morning." Fuck. Breakfast feels like a lifetime ago. "And then?"

"And then the phone goes offline," he says.

"Offline? What do you mean? Did it die?"

"Hang on. Damn. No. Looks like the SIM was deactivated. The carrier changed. Maybe she bought a new phone."

"Shit!" I yell, earning me another terse look from the driver. I mime drive faster with my hand. He bursts into several expletives in French.

Grabbing another one hundred euros, I shove it over his shoulder and he shuts up and presses his foot down.

She was shopping. She's likely headed home. I just need to get hold of her to warn her.

Pete speaks to someone in the background. "And I'm having someone keep trying it."

"Good. Yes. Have them call Marianne too, her landlady. Number is listed in Andrea's file."

"Will do. Maybe she's heading to the village, as you say." When Pete tries to go best-case scenario with me, I know he's worried as shit.

There are cell towers all over the fucking place. We don't tell anyone that we have that backdoor into the cell companies—and it's hardly new technology—but you can usually triangulate a number to within twenty meters. And then even if the number changes, as long as it's our device and the phone has power, we're good. Not as accurate, but effective when all else failed. I'd used it on Andrea before, and it was how I'd found Dauphine when she'd been taken by Xavier's degenerate brother-in-law. Back then, I'd told the police it was a lucky tip I'd remembered from a prior conversation with the suspect. But if she's changed phones and turned her Pascale-issued one off. Well, we're now dependent on her keeping her new number and phone active.

While I wait not so patiently for Pete to break the law, I direct my very nervous taxi driver to the office entrance so I can get into our situation room with Pete.

The cab pulls up with a screech, and I leap out of the car without a goodbye, leaving the driver yelling out the window at me.

∼

"THAT WAS FAST," Pete says as I skid into the room, slowing from a sprint up the stairs because the elevator was too fucking slow. Of all days to wear a damn suit.

"Find her?" I bark, loosening my tie and top two collar buttons.

He looks down at the map and presses a finger to the screen. "After Carrefour, we switched on the tracker in the Pascale phone, but it's powered down."

"Shit."

"Her number on her new phone still tracked for a bit though. She returned to the highway. It pinged on Avenue des Alpes. I think she left that road at the next exit and then there's no movement."

"She still there do you think?"

"It's not pinging at all. There or anywhere else."

Dread thuds through me, making me feel like I weigh ten tonnes.

"We need eyes in the sky," I croak. "And where's Neil?"

Pete points behind me, and I turn.

Dressed the same as this morning, his face pure torture and contrition, he's sitting with his hands, raised palm forward, tied with zip ties in front of him. "I'm sorry," he says. "I'm sorry!" his voice rises as I stride toward him, my arm pulling back, black rage clouding my vision. I vaguely register the flurry of activity behind me and then *I'm* grabbed in a choke hold, my fist frozen in midair as Pete grips it hard.

"Get the fuck off me!" I buck and drop, and in seconds Pete's on his back on the floor.

It snaps me out of my fugue state. "Shit. Sorry."

"We need him right now," Pete wheezes. "Cool it."

I'm panting hard from my sprint up the stairs and my anger, and I take a second to register the truth of Pete's words. I can barely find sense over the panic that's bound itself around me. Reaching down, I help Pete to his feet, both of us breathing hard. I pin my eyes on Neil, even as Pete claps my back. "Does he have her?" I ask Neil.

"I don't know." Neil's eyes drop. "Yes. I think so."

"And what's the plan?"

He shakes his head, and I feint a menacing step toward him as he shrinks backward. "I don't know, I promise. I'll tell you what I know. He's in my rental car. He was following her and he wouldn't tell me what he planned. Just that I'd understand. But I don't! I'm sorry. I didn't know he had ... hurt her before. I thought—"

"Is he even sick? Does he have cancer?"

"Yes. Yes. He's frail. He's ..." Neil shook his head. "I don't know what he's doing. He ..."

"What?" I growl.

"He has nothing left except her."

"What does that mean?"

"It means ... he doesn't have much time left. They gave him five months. It's been eight. He's weak. I think he wants her to go with him."

"Go with him?"

Neil gulps and his hands are shaking. His eyes fill. "I ... think ..."

Pete's hand digs into my shoulder. "He means to kill her and then himself. To kill them both somehow."

Neil nods at Pete's guess and squeezes his eyes closed. A tear streaks down his cheek.

My body is ice. And I'm not even in it. I'm somewhere disassociating and I can't seem to get my body to respond to commands.

Suddenly, Pete is in front of me. In my face. "Listen to me.

Andrea is strong. She will fight him. You heard Neil, Angus is frail. *You have to believe in her.* But in the meantime, we need to get in the sky. Xavier's pilot is not on duty. So I'm flying." He grabs my face. "You will *not*, under any circumstances, do any James Bond shit. Am I clear? No jumping out in mid-air or hanging from the skids. You are of no use to Andrea dead. Do you hear me?"

I nod. My heart rate is slowing, and panic and fear are morphing into purpose. I will get her back.

Pete turns to one of his men, Gavin, the one who picked up Neil in town. He's been standing quietly behind our captive. "Don't let this piece of shit out of your sight. If he needs to pee, you watch. He needs to shit—"

"Got it, Boss."

"Get anything else you can out of him that could help. Where's Angus been, what has he read about, talked about? Anything that could give us a clue to where and how."

Gavin nods. "Yes, sir."

Then he gets two other analysts from outside the room. Briefs them quickly, sets them up in front of my station and the underlit table, and pulls up satellite imagery. We don't have a current live sat feed, but they can warn us of terrain or find a landing spot if we need one.

I take a deep breath and look down at Neil. "And you. You better think really fucking hard. It's too late to save your brother. He's already dead, according to British authorities, so wherever we find him, he's not coming back," I promise. "Do you understand?" I let that sink in. "But you? If Andrea gets out of this unharmed, you still have a life if you want one, despite how fucking stupid you are to let your brother do this."

A few seconds pass and then Neil nods, tears covering his face now.

"We're moving," says Pete, and I follow him to the exit stairwell and continue up two at a time to the roof of the building.

~

"SATELLITE IMAGES PUT her last number signal near green space. It's rural. There aren't many houses around." Pete's voice is tinny but clear in my ear through the headphones.

We both sit with that for a second, neither of us voicing the obvious worst-case scenario. That she's already dead. And all I can replay in my brain is almost telling her how I felt, but instead letting her walk out the door. What the fuck is wrong with me? The vibrations of the helicopter pound through my body, and below us the world dips away as we ascend. I hold my hand to my heart. Would I know she was no longer in the world? Would my soul feel it?

Pete breaks the silence. "Maybe she got a flat. Maybe he hasn't caught up to her yet."

"Maybe," I agree, but my stomach is cramping with how badly I've fucked up. And I'll never forgive myself if something has happened to her.

The conversation with Neil this morning in the lawyer's office whips through my brain as I frantically search for a hint I should have picked up. But honestly, he looked absolutely sick when Andrea told him about his brother being an abuser. The plan was obviously already in place, even if he did believe her.

"We need plates for Neil's rental," I say.

"Already on it. There." Pete points ahead and I follow the

road and the exit, and a small roundabout, making out a tiny car parked up against a low stone farm wall.

My heart rate hitches at the sight. "It's hers. Set her down."

Andrea's car has a smashed back bumper. The driver's side door is hanging open, and the airbag deployed. My hope drains and my lungs feel like they have no air.

Pete sets down on the other side of the road and I already have the door open and am jumping to the ground before the skids touch.

I race under the down blast of the blades, squinting against the churned up dust. At the car, I stop. Blood is drying on the deflated white nylon.

My throat closes and my ears roar. "Shit!" I yell and grab my hair in my fists.

"Hit her from behind. She was probably stunned. Could just be a hit-and-run." Pete's trying to reason with me through the wireless headset I forgot to take off.

"He's taken her."

"If she's been hurt in a hit and run, though, maybe she'd have gotten herself out of the car and is lying nearby." Pete is trying to best case me again and give me tasks.

I call her name and round the car, walk up and down the road and peer over the low stone walls. I jog a quick widening circle around the car in the fields, vaulting over stone walls when necessary. The nearest building is a dilapidated barn with a caved in roof. She's not here.

Then I stop dead as I see a cracked smart phone glinting a few meters ahead of me in the grass. Obviously thrown as far as possible from the vehicle. I reach and pick it up. Not Pascale-issued. My heart sinks. I power it on—there's no security feature set up yet—and call my number from it.

Sunflower pops up across my screen and the sight of it almost doubles me over. I press end and press my fists to my eyes. I can't fucking breathe. I try and count and take long slow inhales, calling on my crisis training. Usually, I can compartmentalize. And this is why getting involved with her was such a fucking bad idea. I can't shut it off. The terror, the panic that she's hurt or worse. I need to get calm to have a hope in hell of finding her.

Pete continues talking in my headset but the roaring in my ears makes it hard to follow. "Can you check?" he asks.

"What? Can you repeat that?"

"Check her car for the Pascale-issued phone. We turned on the tracker remember? There's a chance she may still have it. If she has it, maybe she'll power it on. Would be good to know to watch for it." I appreciate Pete calmly keeping me from losing my mind by issuing instructions.

Jogging back to her car, I rip at the airbag, pulling out a multi-tool knife I always keep in my pocket with my wallet. I get the deflated nylon hazard out of the car and spot the keys still in the ignition. Looking around, I see nothing else.

There's no purse. I turn and check the tiny storage space behind the seats seeing nothing. "Nothing. Not her purse, either. I did a perimeter. All I found was the new phone he'd tossed. I could have missed the other one."

"Okay, so he had her bring her stuff. That's promising. He wants to keep her alive for now, perhaps traveling somewhere?"

"Or he's just covering his tracks so it doesn't look so suspicious. An abandoned purse in an abandoned car screams abduction."

"Okay. Get back here. We've got French police running the rental plates."

I crouch-run back to the bird, and haul myself in. Dust covers my dark suit and I rip at the loose tie around my neck to remove it as we rise above the earth.

Both of us are silent as we slowly follow the main road, guessing blind that he may have gone this way. Every second seems wasted.

"I can't lose her."

"I know," Pete responds, and only then I realize I spoke out loud. "I know," he repeats.

THIRTY-EIGHT

Andrea

I WAS LYING down in a moving vehicle, a realization that was suddenly eclipsed by the blast of blinding pain in the front of my head and face. *Ow, holy shit.* I scrambled to remember where I was and what I'd been doing. My nose and my forehead throbbed with painful pressure. I tried two things at once, to open my eyes and touch my face. I couldn't do either. My elbow bumped a surface right above me and I immediately knew I was in the trunk of a moving car. Fear, cold and ruthless, bolted through me. My mouth opened immediately to call out, but instinct made the sound die in my throat. There was no good or rational explanation for me to be in this situation, and drawing attention to myself was probably a mistake until I knew more. I pushed my tongue out and licked my lips, tasting the copper of dried blood. I wasn't gagged, so that was something. I wiggled my fingers and moved my wrists and ankles. Or tied up.

The memory slid into place of sitting in my little rental car and something hitting me from behind. I must've face planted into the steering wheel or the airbag exploded in my face. Airbag injuries were no joke, but where was I? If a car hit me by accident, I should be in an ambulance or the hospital right now.

The car I was in had gone around several bends and what had felt like a roundabout since I'd been awake and now it was definitely going uphill. I didn't know how long we'd been driving or in what direction.

I tried to open my eyes again, noting the smell of gasoline, hot engine, and musty fabric. My eyes opened into little slits. There was barely any light, and the air felt close and confined. I was lying on my side, curled up, and I cataloged the rest of my body to see if anything else hurt. Cramped and uncomfortable, my body was curled in on itself, and if there was any other pain, the pain in my face eclipsed it. Unfolding my arms, I used my fingertips to feel around. Industrial carpeting or lining like a car might have in the footballs or in the trunk. Panic flared again when I noted how restricted my movements were like this. I had to stay calm, but my breathing got fast as my pulse pounded at an increasing rate, my breath shallow. I'd been on a rural road, a woman alone. That was situational safety 101 utterly failed. I had to stay calm. We had been given training by the Pascal security team—and Evan in particular—that if we were ever taken or kidnapped to stay calm, and to look for weaknesses, and escape routes. And definitely not to let the panic crowd out rational thinking.

Evan. A silent sob burst out of my mouth, my eyes flooding. The idea of never seeing him again was worse than thinking of what I was going through. And he'd blame himself. Forever. I owed it not just to myself, but to him, to get myself out of this. I had to think and think fast before we got to wherever we were going.

The memories of the rest of the day and why I'd been sitting in my car alone in the first place rushed in. The sweet, beautiful way Evan had taken care of me after the hideous meeting with Angus' brother Neil. And the pain of leaving him. I'd been talking to Josie, though I couldn't remember what about.

Suddenly, Neil's voicemail came back to me loud and blaring. *"I'm so sorry. I tried to stop him...if I'd known..."*

Oh. My. God.

It couldn't be. But my gut told me what my head didn't want to listen to.

Nausea rolled inside of me not just from the motion but at the fear I was trying to keep at bay. What kind of man had Angus become in the ten years since I'd known him? And was he at all ravaged by cancer? Or had that been a liberally laced lie to get me to let my guard down? I'd believed Neil. Trusted that he'd been telling the truth. He'd cried for God's sake. And he'd believed *me*. Or so I'd thought. Betrayal and anger oozed through me, crowding out the fear and shock.

My mouth was dry, and getting dryer as the miles flew by beneath my body. I wracked my brain for a strategy. First things first. I needed to see what else was in here with me, in case there was anything I could use as a weapon. It was definitely a sedan shaped car based on the shape of the space I was in. The lumps below me biting into my body were probably the spare tire well, and would house the jack and the crowbar. A weapon, for sure. But no careful maneuvering and feeling about found me the place where I could lift anything to check. And even if I could,

I'd never be able to get my body out of the way. I could barely move, and couldn't roll to my other side.

A lot of newer models of cars had emergency pull cords, in case of anybody being trapped in the trunk, which—come to think of it—was a freaking terrible indictment on humanity. Trailing my fingers around the perimeter I could reach yielded nothing. Luckily, I'd never been supremely claustrophobic, but even so the dark, close, quarters felt so coffin-like it was hard to keep my fear and panic at bay. The throbbing pain in my forehead and nose, along with my anger, actually helped keep me focused. I carefully rotated and moved around, aware that I didn't want to alert Angus, or whoever was driving the car, to my consciousness.

I tried to think back to where I'd put my phone or if I'd been on it when the car hit me. If so, there was pretty much every chance I had dropped it. Or more likely, whoever had me had relieved me of any means of communication.

I still had my boots on, but I felt what could be a bag next to my foot. It might contain something I could use. Carefully, I used the soles of my booted feet to grab the bag and then to push it up toward my lower back by bending at my knees and arching my back. It took forever, and I was sweating and gasping for breath by the time I could reach my hands behind me to grapple for it. Canvas. It was mine! My purse. I gasped in relief and hope. My fingers closed over the fabric and as soon as I had a good grip, I dragged it over me, squeezing it between my body and the roof of the tight space I was in. Cradling my bounty to my abdomen, I took a couple of slow, deep breaths. Then I felt around for the opening and stuck my hand in. It was a fool's search. There was no way Angus had left me with anything that could help me. There'd be nothing to find except my wallet, a pack of tissues, my earphones, and a bunch of receipts I hadn't gone through yet. And then all of a sudden, my fingers closed over what felt like my phone. It couldn't be. There was no way he would have let me keep a phone. Unless ... he'd ditched one he saw and didn't know I had another. It could be my new one and I could call someone.

Heart pounding, I pulled it out and swiped the screen with my thumb on the same hand. When nothing happened, I powered it on. My heart, soaring in elation, quickly nosedived as I realized it was my old phone. Of course I was, and there was no signal because I'd deactivated the sim to keep my old number. I wouldn't be able to call anyone.

All my barely held in check emotions I'd been fighting came flooding through. I hunched forward, curling into an even smaller ball, and tried to smother a howling sound of anguish. I had done everything I could to stop Evan from being in my life for weeks and now I would probably pay the ultimate price for it. If *he* couldn't find me, then no one could.

Then the car lurched as it left rough ground and began traversing a very uneven road surface. It felt like we'd been steadily rising in altitude the last few miles, but now it was intense. I tried to get my shit together, breathing deeply and wiping my eyes, then blowing my nose with a tissue from my purse. I had to save myself. It was the only way. I depressed the power button on the side of the phone five times, trying to remember an old women's safety post I'd read about, and hoping it actually worked when there was no network or sim. Highly doubtful, but worth a try. Then I stuffed the phone into the waistband of my leggings and strategized.

∼

THE CATCH CLICKED and bright light streamed in so I couldn't open my eyes right away.

"Angus?" I asked, holding my hands up to shield my face from the brightness.

"Can you get out by yourself?" His voice, though familiar, was raspy and different.

"Uh ..." I shifted, and pushed up on stiff arms, surprised he hadn't hauled me out himself. He'd obviously had no problem getting me in here. Getting onto hands and knees, I blinked and then looked over. I was shocked by what I saw. A gaunt old man stared back at me. Once larger than life, dark-haired and barrel-chested, now there was a frail, sparrow-boned man with the color leached out of him. His hair was limp and grey, his skin the color of cement-dust. The whites of his eyes were yellow. Pity was my overwhelming first reaction.

"Don't look at me like that. Just get out of the fucking car."

I sat up fully. "I thought you were dead."

"You seem really broken up about it," he leered.

I was so confused by his plan. Surreptitiously taking in my surroundings—wooded—and his appearance—weak—as I sat and picked up my purse, I wondered how he'd gotten me in the car. I wasn't light, that was for sure. His arms, poking out from the sleeves of a beige t-shirt that did nothing for his complexion, were bony and covered in bruises. Blood pooled in patches beneath the surface. He was dying. I wasn't sure how long he had left, but it wasn't long.

"You can leave that. You won't need it." He nodded to my purse.

I swallowed hard and took the strap off me and laid it down. I swung a leg over the edge and climbed out onto stiff legs, making sure my long sweater didn't ride up.

"Where are we?" I asked.

"Somewhere I won't be disturbed while I have a reunion. With. My. *Wife*."

I shuddered—a full body shudder—and glanced around. The altitude felt high, the air thin and cool. It reminded me of the hike I'd taken with Evan and Marianne, what seemed like eons ago rather than days. We were so isolated here. There was clearly no point in screaming. I tried to keep my voice steady as I asked, "What are you doing, Angus?"

"Taking back what's mine. You *are* mine. Or did you forget?"

His hand came around from where it had been concealed behind dirty jeans. I saw the blade immediately glinting in the sunlight.

"Have you been down here in France with that prick laughing at me all this time? Huh?" His voice rose. "Did he get to fuck that pretty cunt of yours?" he snarled. His free hand darted forward suddenly and grabbed me over my leggings between my legs. I jerked back from his painful, surprisingly strong fingers, tears stinging my eyes.

"Please don't," I cried.

He stepped forward, and I pressed back against the car, heart thudding and mouth dry. "Pl... please let me go," I whispered, my voice failing as old terror rushed forward and crowded out everything. Immediately, I was back in the kitchen, him advancing on me, helpless and immobile with terror, unable to move, shaking uncontrollably, knowing he wouldn't stop this time.

"I think you've had enough time away from me, don't you?" The tip of the blade made contact at the base of my throat and stung as he slowly scraped it down towards the valley of my breasts, tearing the sweater as he went. I sobbed a terror-filled breath. "You're looking good. Healthy. I bet he thinks he won. But he didn't win. He doesn't get to win. *You* don't get to win. *I* get to win. *I* get to keep you." He smiled. His breath was sickly sweet and rotting as he closed in on me, his teeth yellowed like his eyes.

My whole body was frozen, trembling, my limbs leaden, and I was trapped inside. The image of him blurred as my eyes filled, and then the tickle on one cheek as the saline spilled over seemed to snap me out of it. No. I shook my head, or tried. No. This wasn't who I was anymore. No. *No.* I was strong. I had survived him.

"No!" I yelled, hands coming up suddenly in a violent shove. He hadn't seen it coming, and he stumbled backward, his featherlight frame a surprise under the vehemence of my push. He teetered and then went backward.

I wasted no time. "You sick fuck!" I yelled, as I turned and ran into the trees. Fuck these trendy little boots I'd thought looked so good. I tripped and caught myself and forged ahead, gasping for breath from exertion and fright, and running as best I could.

Behind me, Angus's voice carried. "You bitch. How far do you even think you're going to get?"

I tried to pick up the pace, branches scratching my face, legs and ass burning as the ground inclined steeper and steeper ahead of me. Behind me, I heard him gasping and determined. I chanced a look and saw him, his gaunt face feral. He looked otherworldly. A corpse risen from the dead. A nightmare.

There wasn't enough foliage for me to hide, so I kept going up, hoping he'd fall back in his weakened state. Slowly, too slowly, our gap widened, but there was still nowhere to go. The air grew icier and windier. There must be a clearing ahead. A thumping sound that I thought was my pounding heart suddenly grew louder. I scrabbled and clawed my way up a small rocky hill. I heaved myself up, flinging my weight forward onto my belly to climb the next waist high rock, branches in my face and clawing at my hair.

Suddenly, the world fell away in front of me. I screamed and caught myself from sliding forward with momentum. My hands loosened bare rocks below me, which went plummeting into the canyon, hitting the sides and exploding. That could have been me. Gasping for breath and shaking, I righted myself, pushing back from the edge and looked around for a tree or another rock to hide behind. The wind whipped my hair around my face, obscuring my vision. The foliage was plentiful, but thin. There was no way. Hearing him so close now, I knew if he made it up here, it would be a dead end. For both of us. In more ways than one.

Frantically searching around me to conceal myself somehow before Angus saw me, I inched along the edge carefully, climbing over tree trunks, roots, and rocks. If I could get far enough along, maybe I could double back down the mountain before he realized. But I was making no progress. It was too difficult and slow going. My eyes kept being drawn to the gorge below, the turquoise river visible now but so far away at this height, it looked like a piece of string. My heart pounded, and my stomach swam drunkenly in a sea of adrenaline and vertigo. My legs were weak. The pounding, a deep throb, grew louder, echoing all around the canyon. It wasn't my heart, it was something else.

My attention was snatched away by movement to my right and suddenly a black beast of a helicopter rounded the curve of the canyon into my line of sight, coming toward me. I froze. Angus had been military. Did he have someone helping him?

Seconds stretched as I debated what to do, stay still or draw attention to myself. It was coming for me. The beast grew closer and closer. The blast, adding to the wind, dislodged loose leaves and branches and pebbles. I shielded my eyes. I had to take the chance and wave for help.

Then the machine was side long and a figure crouched at the open door frantically shouting. My God, like a miracle, it was Evan!

He was shouting and pointing, but I couldn't hear anything. Then suddenly, I realized he was warning me. I turned just as Angus' face appeared, feral eyes fixed on me. A hand outstretched. The flash of the knife in the sun. I screamed and dodged, losing my footing. I hung tightly to a branch with one hand as the world gave way below me. And then a blur that arrested into slow motion as Angus kept coming for me and missed as my body swung sideways. He couldn't catch his feet, and horror and resignation flew across his face. With my free hand, I reached for him by instinct, to save him. But my hand grabbed at his t-shirt without success and suddenly he was airborne—a frail feather on the wind as gravity and wind pulled him windmilling downward. Then he was face up and his hollow eyes never left me as his body plunged downward.

I screamed in horror and turned my face away as I clawed back to safety. My feet found rock, but I couldn't let go of the tree, hugging the trunk and too terrified to move.

THIRTY-NINE

The helicopter went up and over me. Behind me the sound of it grew louder as it hovered above the tree-line. I angled my head and squinted, trying to see despite the wind. The sight of a suit-clad Evan clambering out of the craft and then hanging on this skids felt like I was watching a movie. Nothing was real. I was in a dream. A nightmare.

I barely reacted to the fact that Evan had somehow made it to where he leaped off the skids, disappearing into the trees and out of sight. The helicopter banked and flew sideways and still I stood clinging to a trunk, trembling, and too afraid and stunned to move. The gorge yawned below me. I had to move. Evan could have hurt himself. But I couldn't move. I was catatonic.

And then he was there, suit dirty and ripped, hair all over the place, gentle hazel eyes etched in terror and relief as he reached me. His mouth was moving.

"Andrea?" His voice finally broke through.

I stared at him. I loved him. God, I loved him. I hadn't

thought I would see him again. His image blurred as my eyes filled again.

"Andrea, baby. Sunflower? Can you hear me?"

Blinking, I managed a nod.

"Okay. Can you let go? I've got you."

I shook my head.

"I've got you. I promise. Just let me pull you away from the edge. You can fall into me. My feet are stabilized. I'll catch you. I promise."

I forced my arms to loosen as I realized his hands had found my waist. He gently pulled me toward him and away from the edge. I closed my eyes and let go of the tree, shrieking as my body fell onto him. And then he had me, arms wrapped tight, his breath in my hair, his hands holding me, caressing me, pressing me against his chest.

"Fuck. I thought I lost you. I'm sorry. I'm so sorry."

"Not your fault."

"One hundred percent my fault. I fucked up. I'm so sorry. I should have known."

"A-angus ..."

"Shh, baby. I know. He's gone."

I sobbed in relief at the confirmation and horror at what had happened. Nausea tidal waved through me.

"Oh God, I'm going to be sick." I pushed back and Evan helped me turn, just in time for me to wretch bile and water from my empty stomach to splash on the rooty and rocky ground. Evan's hand soothed my back, one hand pulling my hair and smoothing it back. My head and face pounded in pain from my airbag injury, made worse by the force of trying to vomit.

A few minutes later, the nausea slowly passed. "Ugh. I don't have water." And God knew what I looked like: bruised face, dried blood and vomit.

"We'll get you some."

I staggered upright. "Was I dreaming or did you jump out of a damn helicopter into the trees? You could have died!"

"I jumped. Pete is pissed. He made me swear I wouldn't do any 'James Bond' shit. But you were in shock and about to go over the edge yourself. I didn't really have a choice." He cradled my face and tucked my hair behind my ear. "Plus, he had a knife. Did he cut you?"

I shook my head.

"You look like shit, Sunflower. And in so much pain."

"Yep."

"But you're alive and that's the most beautiful thing in the world. You're ... I—"

He swallowed. Emotions burned in his eyes, and I waited for him to add something. Moments stretched, and the silence grew uncomfortable. I willed him to give me *anything* that would allow me the confidence to admit how I felt about him. But there was nothing.

Of *course*, he jumped out of a helicopter to save someone. That was what Evan did. It wasn't because he was suddenly going to tell me he loved me. "How did you find me?" I asked, dropping my gaze.

"You turned your Pascale-issued phone back on. Thank Christ. It has a geo-location tracker, remember? I'm so pissed you got a new phone. We almost couldn't find you. Especially as the nearest cell tower outside this park is too fucking far away. We took a chance and flew through the canyon. I was beside myself. I knew you were down there, but there was no way I could pinpoint where." He scrubbed a hand down his face, blowing out a breath. "Then I guess you got to the top, and the signal pinged twenty kilometers that way." He pointed across the canyon behind me.

I touched my waist and ran my hands around until I found the bulge of the phone I had stuck into my legs and retrieved it. I stared at it, then handed it to Evan and he tucked it into the breast pocket of his suit jacket. The shoulder of one jacket sleeve was ripped open, and he was covered in dirt, sap, and pine needles. I blinked at him. He was my very own hero. And even through my current fog of gutting emotions, he was so damn hot I could hardly stand it. If I hadn't just vomited, I'd be tempted to kiss him.

"It was dumb luck," he continued. "We flew to the midpoint between the two. It was the national park. As soon as I saw the canyon was the midpoint, I just knew. I spotted movement on the ridge right away."

I shuddered involuntarily. It was the cold and shock, well and truly setting in. And the memory of almost going over the edge and then Angus... God.

"Let's get you out of here," Evan said, and gently drew me to his side to steady me. The two of us slowly inched down the hillside, him in office dress shoes and me in my little low-heeled booties. My feet were now also on the long list of things on my body that hurt.

At the clearing sat the car Angus brought me in. I gave a shudder. "He locked me in the trunk."

Evan flinched. "Christ, I'm so fucking sorry. Let's hope he left the keys in it." He let go of me to head to the driver's door.

The image of Angus' body plummeting into the gorge hit me again and again, and I inhaled sharply with a cringe. "What about Angus?" I murmured. My hands were cut and bleeding too, and beginning to sting. It was hard to keep up with all the pain points in my body.

Evan to the passenger side to open the door. "Keys are here. Hop in."

As soon as we were in the grey sedan and buckled up, Evan turned to me. "Angus is already dead. That's just a body in a canyon that not even a hiker will find. Especially when no one reports him missing. Wolves will have gotten him by morning."

"Wolves?"

"Yeah. Wolves."

"No one mentioned wolves while we were camping!"

"Well, they keep to themselves. They're elusive and opportunistic, but they definitely will not pass up a ..." he trailed off. He didn't want to acknowledge the grisly death any more than I did.

"And Neil?"

Evan turned the car on and punched up the heat to combat my shivering, then turned to me. His eyes swirled with conflict and determination. "I told Neil Angus wasn't coming back. No matter what happened today."

"Evan."

"I know, Sunflower. But if it was you or him ..."

"I know. I'm glad you didn't have to ..."

"Me too. But I'm sorry you had to go through that."

I drew my knees up and wrapped my arms around them. "I —I just want to go home." The village house didn't feel like home yet, but it was all I had.

"The village?" he asked.

"Y—yes." I didn't want to be alone, but Evan would have a lot of things to take care of. He'd risked enough for me already. Besides, our conversation from this morning still stung. "Maybe call the girls and ask them to stay with me. They were going to come up and visit, anyway. I—I don't want to be alone." I glanced at him.

His hands were tight on the steering wheel, his jaw locked. We bumped down the barely visible track down the hill. "Yeah. Sure. I'll call them."

"I'm sorry," I said.

He glanced at me, then back at what passed for a road. "What for?"

"Well, thank you, but also I'm sorry ... for always having to rescue me. I should have said that this morning. I've been your job for almost a decade. I'm sorry."

"And I told you this morning I didn't do it out of obligation."

"You *say* that. But given the circumstances of how I'm even here in France, how could it not be? And then I almost got myself hurt by him again. Well, now that he's well and truly gone, it's over, okay? You are released from your duty. You don't have to worry about me anymore."

"And that's what you want?" He glanced at me again, eyes flat, jaw hard.

What I wanted was for Evan to be in love with me the way I was with him. I wouldn't settle for anything less than that. Ever. I was so glad we'd had the time together that we had because I would never meet his equal. And it was going to be a long time until I ever gave myself sexually or emotionally to someone like that again. If ever. No one would ever compare, and I'd never trust anyone but Evan.

"Y—yes. I no longer want to be someone you have to worry about all the time. I'm grateful you were here today. God knows what I would have done."

"You would have dodged him. He would have still fallen. You would have gotten down off the ridge, found this car and driven home. Because you are strong and you can handle anything. You don't need me, Sunflower, never have. That's clear."

"Does that upset you?"

"No. I'm fucking proud of you."

A wave of exhaustion overtook me suddenly. I wanted to sleep, but we were emerging off the mountain and onto a dirt road along some fields.

Evan thumbed his phone. "Pete. Do you copy?" Then he nodded. "Yeah. We have to ditch the car, though. Sending you coordinates now."

He pulled over. "What's going on?" I asked. I was slurring as exhaustion and spent shock well and truly did me in.

"French police have run plates. It's too late to call it off. We'll come up with a story for Neil that it was stolen, but I don't think you and I had better be driving it. Especially with what we currently look like. Too many questions. You'd have to tell them everything that happened. It's your call obviously, but I think it's best to let sleeping dogs lie. He was already dead, according to paperwork."

"I can't think straight. But yes, I trust your judgment. I think that's what I'd prefer."

"Okay. I'll get *your* car picked up and back to the rental company to switch it out. You were insured, right?"

"Full coverage."

"Good. Should be easy then. Also, you need to get checked out. You could have a concussion. I'll call the girls to meet you at a clinic." His jaw ticked. "They can get you home."

"Oh. Okay. Thank you." It was what I had asked for, but I felt dejected anyway.

He opened his mouth and closed it. Then pinched the bridge of his nose, before letting out a deep sigh. "And here," he said eventually, and reached into his jacket pocket. He handed me the Pascale-issued phone. "I know you're no longer using it, and I know you don't want me bothering you anymore. But if you ever need help, ever—and I hope to God, you never need to use it—just switch it on, okay? It'll pop up in our list of monitored devices for the family."

I stared at it. He hoped I never summoned him.

He sighed. "Just take it."

I did.

The sound of the helicopter approaching ended any further discussion. I was numb.

FORTY

"I think I'm going to go out with Christian," I told Meg and Sue seven weeks later.

They were due to leave for the Alps and their winter ski season the next day. We were having farewell drinks down in Saint-Tropez at one of Meg and Sue's favorite little bistro bars after a day at the market. The port was so pretty in the early winter. They'd begun to hang holiday lights, and on market days they ran red carpets down all the cobblestone streets. The smell of roasting chestnuts and candied almonds pervaded everywhere.

Summer tourists had gone home and the few places that stayed open usually had blankets folded over each chair and roaring fires. Heat lamps had just been outlawed because of global warming and rising energy prices, but it didn't stop people still getting together and enjoying outside spaces when they could. We all just huddled closer together.

Sue's mouth dropped open. "But I thought you and Evan

were going to be a thing. What is *taking* so long?" she added with a whine.

Meg's mouth twisted. "I hate to be that friend," she said to me. "But that wouldn't be fair to Christian."

"I know," I admitted. "But the truth is, Evan is probably never going to happen. I told Christian I've just come out of a relationship and we'll just stay friends. But I do need to start getting out there again. Trusting men again. It's a 'friend date'."

"No such thing," said Meg.

Christian had been texting every now and again, and we'd had the odd phone call. He'd turned out to be a really caring and sensitive person, and even apologized for coming on so strong in the beginning, and a genuine friendship had formed, though thus far I'd evaded any invitation to meet for drinks or dinner.

"Is Evan coming tonight?" Sue asked.

"No idea," said Meg. "The others are."

I shrugged as my belly cramped with nerves that he actually might show. "I don't know either."

"God, I can't believe this place is closing after so many years. Next year will just not be the same," Meg moaned, and they began discussing the demise of their favorite hangout.

Evan had avoided all group get-togethers. He was practically dead in the group chat. I kept meaning to run by Pascale Company and drop off my old phone, but I was torn between terrified I might run into him, desperate to run into him, and loath to give away my last reason to go there.

He had come to the village one day while I was at the gallery and cleared out his bedroom at the village house. I only knew because the key had miraculously shown up on my kitchen table. I'd opened the adjoining door to see if his stuff was still there, and it was a gut punch to find he'd already vacated. The room was still and empty, the bedding neatly stripped and stacked, and dust motes floated in the fading daylight from the small window. I'd slammed the door back up and locked it, gasping for breath. I hated the emptiness on the other side of that door. The shadow of the emptiness cast itself over my side too. It gave me the chills to be there some nights, knowing this dark empty place existed right next door. It felt haunted. Haunted by his absence. Him moving his things had made my new home just a house. Which was ridiculous because we'd hardly spent any time coexisting on both sides of that door. Not in the grand scheme of things. But I *felt* the loss keenly, like I'd been awfully careless with something special.

Some nights I'd play all the songs that made me think of him and really wallow. I'd just found out my husband died, which came with so many complicated emotions, but it was Evan I was grieving.

Honestly, it was the hit I never saw coming. Like I was lost at sea and someone snuffed out the lighthouse beam, leaving me shivering and on the verge of drowning. Lighthouse lamps weren't ever supposed to go out.

Days went by and I finally began to fill them with work, friends, signing up for an online degree in social work through a British university, and dealing with an estate attorney. I eventually bought a few knickknacks for my rental to make it feel more like home, including a tiny oil painting of the *Saint-Jean-Cap-Ferrat* lighthouse at a gallery in the village because it made me think of Evan when I saw it.

I met up with Marianne a few times for a day hike, just the

two of us. I had to face my fear at the gorge. She and Cyril were rocky, she said. Day by day, I began to feel stronger and more balanced. I shared my patronage between François and Albert, who was finally back from his long vacation, without the other knowing. Exploring every corner of the village, I'd found a little bookstore down a narrow alley and read every single English language title they had before asking the lady who owned it to order more so I could keep supporting her shop.

Arturo at the Trattoria greeted me with an operatic blast from *La Traviata* whenever I showed up and often comped my glass of wine if I ordered one. I didn't mind eating there alone because he was always so entertaining. Though he kept warning me he was going to introduce me to his cousin if I stayed single long. I hadn't met his cousin, but it sounded ominous. The guy was in "sanitation" in Naples, which immediately made me think he was in the mafia. Though perhaps that was from all the books I'd been devouring. I told Arturo I wasn't exactly single, it was just ... complicated.

"There you girls are!" Rod's voice boomed, and I snapped out of my thoughts.

"Sorry we're late," said Chef as they both strolled up to the bistro in the port. "I refused to let Rod come with the animal he'd grown on his face."

I glanced at Rod to see he indeed had a beard, but it was all nicely trimmed close to his face.

"It was keeping me warm," he grumbled as we all hugged. "It was my winter pelt."

"Well, I think it looks really good," Meg said with a strange look on her face as we rearranged the seating, and she sat down next to him.

Rod split into a wide grin. "Really?"

"Evan coming?" Sue asked.

"Beats me," said Chef and sat down. "I need a bloody coffee, it's fucking freezing."

"They'll have a spot for us inside soon," Sue assured him. "Anyway, we have a few more people coming to join us."

"Wait, you have more friends than just us?" Rod sassed.

The night went on. We moved inside at some point. More friends of Meg and Sue's showed up. They'd been working in the area almost as long as I had, but of course they'd lived a different life—more open, more out there.

I'd kept such a low profile for so many years, I found it difficult to break the habit. Even this evening, I'd slipped out of frame when the photos started being taken, feigning getting some more peanuts, needing some air outside, going to the bathroom. And maybe it wasn't so much the picture taking, but that I'd developed a kind of social anxiety. And I *missed* Evan. My energy had revolved around him. It was so clear now that he wasn't around how much a part of everything he'd been for me.

After a while it was obvious Evan wouldn't be coming tonight, and at some point knowing that, I found it hard to muster the ability to keep smiling and laughing. I wanted to go home and climb into my pajamas and get back to my current read. I was obsessed with romance novels at the moment because they were full of women who self-actualized and ended up with perfect-for-them partners and had a guaranteed happy ending. Part of me wished I'd started reading them early in my marriage. Maybe I would have seen the problems in my relationship sooner. There was nothing better than reading about women finding themselves, owning their sexuality, leaving men who didn't serve them, and learning to live life on their own terms. I drew strength from every character on the pages.

I offered to accompany Chef outside when he nipped out for a cigarette, a nasty habit he'd recently picked back up. I put my coat on and grabbed my bag so I could make an exit from there. I'd text Meg and Sue a goodbye so as not to spoil their vibe. It was chilly, and I stamped my feet and blew into my hands as Chef lit up. The quiet night outside the small restaurant bar was a relief—the faint lapping of water and creaking of boats, a balm after the raucous indoor scene.

"I miss when we could smoke in bars," Chef grumbled, blowing out his first inhalation away from me.

"Ha. I don't. Why did you pick it up again, if you don't mind me asking?"

He squinted and hesitated, taking another drag. "Recently the urge to start drinking again has been really strong. It's a dark path I keep staring down, and I ..."

I laid my hand on his coat sleeve as he trailed off. "It's all right."

"No, this is good to talk. Rod and I hang out so much, and we talk, but he's young, you know? And he's always drinking. It's never been a problem for me. But recently it's been really tempting to just say, 'Fuck it.'" He pursed his lips and ran his free hand through his dark hair that was slowly graying at the temples.

"Go on," I urged gently.

"I kind of looked at my life, and I realized I thought I'd be further along by now. I thought I'd have found someone by now, maybe making plans for a new place of my own. It was sort of crushing to realize how far away or maybe even unattainable that all is. Like, what am I even trying so hard for all the time?" He slipped the cigarette back between his lips. Chef had lost his marriage and his restaurant to his alcoholism and addiction years ago. It had been a long road to recovery. Xavier had given him a job and a promise that when he was ready, he'd fund him in a new venture.

"There is no timeline for this sort of thing," I said. "You should be really proud of the life you have built over the last eight years. *We're* proud of you, not that it's our place—the work was all yours. And you're like the glue in our crew. We love who you are." I squeezed his sleeve again before dropping my hand. "I'm sorry you've been feeling this way. I'm glad you shared it."

Chef was always relentlessly optimistic, always posting inspirational quotes in the group chat. It was a surprise to hear he wasn't feeling it these days.

"There are good days and bad days. Mostly good. It's hard off-season because that's when I really look at my life and feel the disappointment that I'm not further along. But I *am* proud of myself. And I never want to be in that place again. And I don't *think* I'll ever slip, but I guess nothing is a guarantee. Every day is a new promise to myself." He stared at the cigarette. "It really is a disgusting habit, isn't it?"

I shrugged.

He stubbed it out, half smoked, on the stone wall of the building. "So, what about you and Evan?"

I mashed my lips together and hugged my coat tighter. "I can't speak for him, but I'm doing fine. I've started an online degree in social work. So far so good."

"That's great news, but I meant you two together."

I sighed. "I knew what you meant," I admitted, my chest tightening. "I don't know honestly. I thought he might have feelings for me and maybe come to his senses now that I'm a free woman, but I think I was wrong."

"There is no way Evan doesn't have feelings for you. You have been the North Node on his compass every day of every summer, every *year*, since I've been on that boat."

I blinked away a burn in my eyes. "He's been mine too," I said.

"Then why are you waiting for *him* to come to his senses? Maybe he just needs to know that even though you're free to do whatever you want, he's still the one for you."

"That's a huge assumption. And I don't know if I can stand for him to brush me off again."

"Sue said you were thinking of going out with Christian."

"Yeah."

"Please don't. I know Evan and I aren't best friends, but I see enough. I think if you went down that path you might actually lose him."

My throat tightened.

"I can only speak from my perspective, but if I put myself in Evan's shoes, and the woman I've wanted for years is suddenly free and chooses someone else over me, no matter how casual, I don't think I'd ever recover."

My chest grew tight and my belly flipped. "Why does everyone think he's wanted me for years? He's never said anything. Never shown that. And when I gave him the chance to, he made it seem like it was … like it was …" Him giving in to my request for a distraction. A pity fuck. God, I hated that term.

"It was what?" Chef prompted.

"Never mind." In my weakest moments, I kept coming back to what Xavier had told Josie and the things I had replayed from our times together. But the evidence was so flimsy, and I was so terrified it was wrong or wishful thinking. If it was true, Evan wouldn't have been able to stay away. I mean, his need to find out where I was at any given time had been a compulsion I didn't think he'd be able to break so easily. Not if I was more than a job, or an obligation. I guess I was wrong. Not that I'd made it easy, changing phones. If he did try to see where I was, he wouldn't be able to. But he knew where I worked. And he knew where I lived. Everyone said they "thought" he had feelings for me. No one knew first hand. How was I supposed to just infer. Was I just supposed to trust he was out there waiting for me to come to him? And what about all that stuff he'd said the last day about me not having enough experience to know what I wanted? It wasn't about that. I'd been lost at sea, and that wasn't the same thing as not knowing what you wanted. And ...

"Shit," I said.

"What?"

"I guess even if the beam goes out, I still have to trust the lighthouse is there."

"Ummm ..." Chef's eyebrows went in opposite directions as he tried to make sense of me.

"I mean, it's not a search light. It's a beacon," I said

"What?"

"I can't just give up."

"Are we still talking about Evan," Chef asked. "Maybe *you* should lay off the drinks, love."

"Sorry, I'm leaning in heavy to the clichés, but—" A bubble

rose in my chest as my spirits lifted off the ground. "Chef, do you think you could help me? I may have a plan."

It was less of a plan and more of a last ditch effort. If I laid all my cards on the table now and Evan didn't pick them up, I'd have to begin my emotional recovery all over again. But then at least I'd know I tried.

FORTY-ONE

Evan

I DRUM my fingers on my desk, the reports blurring in front of me. I came into the office before five this morning, unable to sleep a second more. Not going to the crew get-together last night was difficult as hell. Time crawled even more slowly than for the last eternity since I saw Andrea. Knowing exactly where she was and wondering whether she'd be glad or sad I didn't show was slow torture. I wanted to call Rod or Chef, or even Meg and Sue, and beg for little scraps of information. How is she? How did she look? Has she been eating? Is she happy? Does she seem hopeful about her future? *Does she miss me?*

I hear people beginning to fill out the security floor, and others, the overnight guys, heading out. Reaching over to my laptop I do the secure entry and then do what I do every morning and check in on Xavier's, Dauphine's, and Madam's cellphones. I need to issue a phone to Josie now that she's almost part of the family.

As expected everyone is where they are supposed to be. I send a secure message to the security team contracted in Charleston, South Carolina, and request an update of the family's plans for the week ahead. I'm about to close the page when I hover. The crew list is below the family list, though I don't normally even look at them when they are off the boat for the season. Except Andrea's. I always watched hers, looking for anything that would indicate her husband found her, especially anytime Angus dropped off the radar in England. I even had her on the top-tier family list for a while until I moved her almost two months ago. I don't have to worry about her husband anymore. And besides, if I scrolled down, the line with her entry would be grayed out. Not that I was looking. I purposely avoided scrolling down the page to where I could see her name. I promised myself weeks ago not to look. And only twice I caved, but it was pointless. She had changed phones and there was nothing to see, nothing to click on because she obviously left her Pascale Company one in a drawer somewhere.

I quickly close out the page before I cave. Then I stalk to the staff kitchen to get more coffee.

Pete steps off the elevator, backpack hanging off one shoulder, hair slicked back and freshly shaven.

"You got a date later or something?" I grumble.

"No, hotshot. I just shave like a grown-ass man and wear nice clothes. Something you could stand to get back to."

"I'm trying something new."

"Caveman look?"

True. I've ditched the suits at the office, favoring my

comfortable tactical trousers and hoodies, but that's because I've started handing over more responsibility to Pete and getting the guys used to coming to him with all the day-to-day issues. And I only shave every three days instead of every morning now. I want to experiment with a beard, but as soon as I hit day three, I have to get it off my face. I made it to day four once, but only until lunchtime. How Rod is growing in a beard is beyond me. It feels hot and itchy and unruly, and okay, maybe those are my neat-freak tendencies coming to the fore. The truth is I just don't give a fuck about much these days.

"So, when are you leaving," Pete asks me.

"I was thinking tonight."

"Are you going to try to see her before you go?"

"What's the point?"

"I hate to still be the broken record, but," he starts signing the words as he says them, "to tell her how you feel."

"We've been over this."

"Yep. And you're still being an ignorant fool."

Fuck you, I sign back.

"Glad to see you're keeping up with your languages."

I stalk over to the coffee machine and make a shot of espresso. Then I ignore him and head back to my desk, pretending he's not sharing my office right now. I had him move his desk in weeks ago as part of the transition to him taking over.

I have reports I need to categorize for the class in corporate security I'm due to start teaching at the London School of Economics on the first of January. Before that I'll go spend Christmas with my parents. I've been approached about being a guest lecturer for years from various institutions, including Scotland Yard. For a long time I never let myself see a life not revolving around Pascale Company. And as much as I feel loyalty to Xavier, I have lived and breathed this company and the family without pause. And I'm realizing now it was almost entirely to do with Andrea, in case she needed me. And she very clearly does not. I feel like a fool. She's been getting on her feet for almost two months, and I expected at least a text.

Something.

Anything.

I'm feeling really fucking shitty today. It's a good thing I'm taking a long sabbatical. Whenever I took time off before, it was brief and I usually went to see my mom and Sam. Xavier has been my best friend since we were teenagers when my dad had a job with *his* parents. But even before he left for Charleston, and before Josie, Xavier and I didn't simply hang out anymore. For one, his late wife, Arriette, and I never really got along that well, I never trusted her with my friend's heart. And after she passed away, Xavier retreated into himself and his work, and the days of me being around him in any other capacity than security dried up.

I miss Xavier, my friend, today more than I have in a while. Especially with Pete riding my ass. Though I doubt Xavier would be any different.

Over the years, Xavier never made me feel like he was leaving me behind when his business took off, he only paid me more, and in stock options, which are entirely too generous. I used to joke with him that they were golden handcuffs or he was buying my loyalty, but I realized recently it was his way of giving me the financial freedom to leave if I wanted.

I just never did.

Because of her.

I've been smart and lucky with what I've earned and increased my wealth at least tenfold. I've built the security arm of his business to the point we train and consult with other firms, and I often get headhunted. I have an amazing team, headed by Pete, and I know I could have left at any time. You could say I'm independently wealthy now. I don't actually need to work. But something has to keep my mind occupied.

I slap down another report. I can't concentrate. I'm determined to leave tonight and drive to at least one of the little villages past *Lyon* by midnight so I avoid the commuter traffic in the morning. With any luck, I'll be in London by the following day after spending a night in Calais. I toyed with doing the *Eurostar*, but I love the sea crossing to Dover. It's a beautiful thing to be an Englishman and to have been gone so long because seeing those white cliffs is an almost religious experience.

Immediately, I'm reminded of Andrea telling me how much she misses England. I sigh. Why hasn't she gone back then? At least to go and deal with Angus' estate.

"I swear to God, if you don't stop sighing and slapping bits of paper around, I'm going to call her myself and tell her—Hey, up." He frowns at his screen. "I thought Andrea wasn't using the company phone anymore."

I'm instantly alert. "What?"

"You checked everyone's locations this morning?"

"Not the crew." I'm out of my seat and rounding his desk to peer at his screen.

"Why would her phone suddenly be on and pinging from," he clicks the link to a map and zooms in, "the farthest tip of the cliffs at *Saint-Jean-Cap-Ferrat?*"

My heart plunges down through my body, and my knees almost buckle.

I frantically grab my cell phone and call her number. It goes straight to voicemail. "Fuck."

"What are you thinking, Evan? Talk to me. You look pale as shit." Pete gets out of his chair and in moments he's literally holding me upright.

There's a roaring in my ears, and I sway. "What would she ... why would she. Maybe someone has her. Or she's ..." I trail off. She's not suicidal. Right? God I don't know what if she's ben depressed these last few months. She went through a lot. It's hard to be a survivor.

"There's no way she's standing on a cliff edge. That is not Andrea. There's never been any indication—"

"Stop, I can't think." I shrug him off.

"Listen. She wouldn't hurt herself. Not after fighting for so long. You need to calm down so you can think about this rationally."

"The girls," I yell at him as I start dialing her number again. "Call Meg and Sue. Ask them if she was okay last night." The ringing goes to voicemail again. "Fuck!"

"Maybe the phone was stolen," he reasons. "You could go check it out."

"No." I'm shaking my head, heart pounding. I need to think. Or go there. Yes, I need to go there. I round my desk, grabbing my keys.

"Okay, or ... *maybe* she turned it on. On purpose."

"Because she's in danger," I immediately realize and slam open my bottom drawer and grab my sheathed knife and strap. I miss guns.

"No, dipshit! Because she wants you to come find her."

"What?"

"*Jesus*, I didn't realize you were going to freak the fuck out so badly. I never would have gone along with this."

I still. "What the fuck are you talking about? Gone along with?"

He scrubs a hand down his face. "I'm sorry. I actually thought it was romantic. She wanted you to wonder why the phone was pinging and to go find it and then she'd be there and …"

"And what?" I growl.

"She'd tell you that she loves you because you're too chicken shit to tell her first. And you're a dumb motherfucker," he adds.

Air is heaving in and out of my chest as my adrenaline fades, and I process what he's saying. "That's the worst fucking idea I've ever heard. I thought she was about to *die*."

"I know that *now*! Jesus. You're a freak show. You know that, right? Please, for the love of God, go and get her and tell each other you love each other and get on with your fucking lives."

"Wow. Thanks for the pep talk."

"You're fucking welcome. Now, what are you waiting for?"

FORTY-TWO

Andrea

OKAY, so making elaborate grand gesture plans at midnight without really thinking it through wasn't the best idea.

Even if everyone was in on it.

And hiking alone about an hour around the peninsula to a lighthouse in December with the windchill as dangerously low as it was, knowing I was going to have to wait at least another hour for him to see I'd turned the phone back on and come to investigate was nothing short of idiocy.

And what if he didn't come? I'd corralled Pete into helping too, just in case Evan didn't see I'd turned the phone back on. I hoped that was a solid back up. Because despite the GPS pinging away into the ether, I had no cell phone service to speak of.

At least Chef had packed me a backpack full of food,

including a thermos of hot coffee and one with his legendary *vichyssoise*.

I had good hiking gear now too, thanks to my newfound hobby. I'd shopped with Marianne several weeks ago and bought sturdy boots, proper hiking pants with all the little zipper thingies, which made my little girl's heart sing, thermals, a fleece, and a windbreaker I was supremely happy with right now.

What had seemed like a romantic gesture last night of luring him to a picturesque spot by turning my location permissions back on seemed flimsy and ill-thought out in the very cold light of day.

At least the sky was blue and the sun was shining, even if the wind felt like it was coming straight out from "Beyond the Wall." I'd been bingeing Game of Thrones, and when Robb Stark was killed, I'd sobbed like a baby because he reminded me so much of Evan. If Richard Madden had hazel eyes, they could be brothers.

I shivered and hunched up against the cold as I continued on my way along the pebbled and rock-strewn walkway. At least it was a walk and not a difficult hike. Below the waves crashed wildly against the rocks, the wind blasting the spray up even higher.

There hadn't been even one other person on the trail because everyone else was too smart to walk out to the end of a massive, rocky peninsula on a windy day in December.

As I got close to the lighthouse, I could see the gate was closed and not open to the public. I stopped and stared up its sturdy light stone walls. Even in the bright sunshine, the beam never stopped slowly rotating. It had originally been built in the

1700s to replace an even older structure. And this one had been rebuilt again after the last world war. It felt pretty symbolic that one could keep building and rebuilding, new over old, studier and stronger, with each new iteration.

I found a bench that had a small windbreak built over it set a few feet down from the path. It faced toward the ocean and the beautiful *Villefranche-sur-Mer* coastline, and I breathed it in with a deep sigh to dispel my nerves. I couldn't see the lighthouse behind me from here, but I could just about see the walkway approaching if I leaned forward occasionally, and it offered a little bit of protection from the cold bite. Below me, the water was a deep clear sapphire blue as it swirled and broke into white foam over the rocks.

Pulling out the thermos of coffee and a book, on the off chance it would actually distract me from said nerves dancing in my belly at what I was about to attempt, I settled in to wait.

Time crawled. Eventually my fraught nerves got tired of jumping and settled a bit. The story, about two astronauts stuck in Antarctica on a Mars training mission, began to suck me in. I swiped page after page on my kindle, grateful I'd had the wherewithal to bring a book and pushing away the awful creeping feeling I'd sorely miscalculated and Evan was never coming. I wouldn't blame him, in the end. I'd been a mess when we last interacted. Not everyone wanted to sign up to deal with the kind of baggage I carried. And I understood that.

But the things I could never get out of my head were how in tune he'd been with my needs. The things he'd say to calm me. The way he'd been with me for years, quietly making sure I was protected. How he'd instinctively known when to touch me and when to wait. And the careful and sensual way he did it. My heart ached in remembrance. Even in the throes of passion—I closed my eyes and relived the moment on my couch with me astride him, the angle making it so deep, and so, so good, his hands gripping my hips, waiting for me to beg before driving himself up into me and losing control—

I gasped and snapped my eyes open as the need ripped through me, bringing me right back to the way it felt in that moment. I was wet for him, and he wasn't even here.

A sound emerged over the crashing of the waves, and I shook my head and leaned forward to check the path.

Like I'd conjured him, there he was. He was running.

My heart pounded and my mouth dried up.

Did he look mad? He looked mad.

I'd just tell him quickly how I felt before he could say anything. Then the chips would fall, and I'd know one way or the other. God, he looked good. He was in flack pants, molded to his muscular thighs as they pumped, and a dark green hoodie. He was squinting against the sun. Maybe he hadn't seen me. Quickly I leaned back out of sight to collect myself before standing and stepping out from the small windbreak.

My pulse was pounding in my whole face as I realized he saw me and kept coming, not slowing a fraction. Then he was just yards away, and then feet, and then …

I took a breath. "I love y—"

His body crashed against me, mouth covering mine as his hands cupped my face.

I grabbed his wrists, holding on for dear life as his lips molded to mine and his tongue pressed in, demanding entry. I gave it and melted against him.

He tasted of coffee and Evan and salt and sea and the rest of my life.

My hands slipped past his shoulders to cradle his head, sliding through the beautiful brown tresses and raking over his scalp.

An agonized sound ripped out of his chest and carried away on the wind. He broke away. "Is this okay?"

"God. Yes," I gasped and kissed him back with every ounce of longing and love I had in my body.

Heat flared between us as the kiss picked up even more urgency and need. I needed him. God, how had I been surviving without this for so long? How had I survived without touch for so long? Without *his* touch?

He stepped forward, mouth never leaving mine, stumbling us backward out of sight between the windbreak and the bench. The temperature sky-rocketed as we stepped out of the wind. His kisses broke off to land frantic smaller ones over my face, my cheeks, my eyes, my throat, and my mouth again. "Sunflower," he croaked in my ear before his tongue slipped over the lobe, and he sucked it between his teeth.

Fire raced over my skin, and I arched against him. "Evan," I gasped. "I missed you."

He tipped my head toward him and leaned his forehead against mine for a moment, eyes made green in the winter light, searing into mine. "I love you. I *love* you," he repeated. "I love you so fucking much. I've loved you since the very beginning. I didn't want to. I tried not to. I'm sorry if how I felt ever held you back. I want ... I wanted to be able to let you go. But I wanted you to come back to me too. I think," He swallowed. "I *know* you were always supposed to be mine."

"I love you too," I whispered, blinking back tears through my smile, and slipped my hands under his hoodie to feel the heat of his skin. "And I *am* yours. If you want me."

His forehead creased at the contact, his throat bobbing, and his lips found mine again, coaxing, the pressure demanding, his tongue seducing. "God, I need you."

"And I need you too." I broke off breathily. "Please, Evan. I need your touch, I need you inside me. I need you."

"Here?"

I nodded. "Yes."

"Fuck." He groaned the word, and his mouth took mine again. His hands swept under my windbreaker and fleece only to hit my thermal underwear layer. "How many fucking layers do you have on?" he rasped and ripped the thermal layer upward from where it was tucked into my hiking pants, only relaxing when his skin touched mine.

"I was trying to be prepared."

"To avoid sex?" He chuckled.

"I didn't think we'd do this here. Or that you'd even want to."

"I guess you learned nothing in the short time we spent together, Sunflower. I crave you. I can't see anyone but you. If you'd said the word, I'd have had my hands on you every second of every day." He chuckled against my mouth, and then his hand slipped up and over my breast.

Damn me for wearing a sports bra. He growled and pushed it roughly out of the way. Both hands swept up and cupped me.

"More," I gasped, and his thumbs pinched the tight buds of my nipples. His eyes watched me closely as I breathlessly arched into his touch. "Yes."

Finally I reached for his waist and worked at the buttons before frantically reaching in to cup his hot, hard cock, the skin stretched silkily under my touch.

"Baby," he rasped, and his lips found mine again.

I wrapped my fingers around the thick shaft, making a fist, and dragged up and over his length.

His breathing grew ragged, his jaw becoming slack, and his throat working to swallow.

Before I could second guess, I dropped to my knees and sucked him into my mouth.

"Fuck," he managed, and his fist banged hard against the wood windbreak behind me and he leaned forward. "This is not … you don't need to … oh shit." His other hand sifted gently into my hair, and then skimmed down my cheek and my jaw so softly I felt a burn of tears. He remembered my fear.

I swirled my tongue around the tip and then drew him deeply inside again, my hand wrapping around the shaft to mimic the movement as I started a rhythm.

He let out a choked sound, his breathing ragged and shallow and increasing in pace, the sound of it flooding liquid heat between my legs.

The hand at my cheek fisted like he wanted to grip my face but remembered he couldn't. Knowing that no matter how far we went he'd always think of my needs almost broke something inside me. I loved him so damn much. I wanted to bring him so much pleasure, to show him how much I loved him. "Shit, stop. Sunflower." His hips rocked forward once. Twice. Then he pulled roughly out of my mouth with a pop. "No. Not like this." He dragged me upward, his mouth finding mine again.

Then he was spinning me to face the bench. I grabbed at

the back of it as his hands reached around and snapped my pants open and dragged them down my hips. His mouth was hot at my ear in the cold air, sending prickles racing over my skin. "This okay?"

"Yes," I gasped and pressed backward. "Please."

"God. Baby," he rasped and kneaded my butt before dragging my underwear down to join my trousers at my knees. "Fuck, you look good." His touch danced down my ass cheeks then up my inner thighs.

"Too slow," I panted. I could feel his hard wet length against my thigh. "Please. I'm ready."

A finger sank into my wet heat, earning a deep moan from both of us. "You're so wet for me."

"Please, Evan," I begged, rocking back against his hand.

Then he was gone and in the next second he was on his knees behind me, his hands holding me open before his scorching hot tongue landed on my clit in a long lick.

Oh, fuck. My skin was on fire, arousal robbing me of sense, of breath, of any ability to talk except to moan and pant and whimper and beg. I pressed against his mouth, wishing I could widen my legs as his tongue flicked over my clit and dipped into my center, over, and over, and over. My moans had grown louder, and I was thankful we were alone out here because I wasn't in control. Prickles raced over my skin, tension coiling tight inside me. I was freezing and burning up from the inside at the same time.

And then suddenly he stood and his thick length drove into me.

The sound that ripped out of my chest was practically feral.

"Shhh, baby." Evan chuckled breathlessly into my ear as he

dragged his length back and plunged in again, forcing another moan from my throat. "You're going to get us arrested." His hands roamed up under my layers and squeezed my breasts, using the grip to drag me back and meet him stroke for stroke.

"You feel so good," I sobbed.

"Too good. It's so tight like this. I can't last much longer." The guttural sound of his voice in my ear made goose bumps arc down my arms. "I've missed you," he rasped. "I love you." His mouth closed over the skin at my neck.

"God," I cried at the emotion in his voice at my ear and the feel of him all around me, over me, behind me, inside me.

"What took you so long?" he demanded, his voice raw, and he plunged in deeper.

I wanted to laugh and ask the same thing. "I-I don't know. I didn't know."

"Are you with me?"

"Yes, Evan. Please."

He drove in again, and I whimpered at the feel of it. I'd never known it could be so fierce but so pure and beautiful and safe all at once. Tears iced my cheeks, and the fire of need and love coiled tight and hot.

His hand found mine on the bench back and pried it loose to guide it between my own legs. "Rub yourself for me, baby. I want to come inside you. You. Are. Mine."

FORTY-THREE

The wind blew through the pine trees and over the rocks, and the waves crashed relentlessly below. But still we sat, Evan on the bench, me cradled in his arms as we stared out to sea.

After we'd cleaned up, and righted ourselves, and Evan had looked around to make sure we hadn't drawn anyone our way, least of all the lighthouse keeper, we settled on the bench and enjoyed the food Chef had prepared.

Even though it was getting warmer from the sun, and certainly our exertions had warmed us up, I still crawled onto Evan's lap and let him hold me as I burrowed into his neck, inhaling the woody clean scent of his skin.

My heart had ballooned so large in my chest, my ribs felt they might crack.

Every now and again he would bury his nose in my hair and inhale deeply.

"You scared the shit out of me with this stunt, you know?"

"I know. You told me. I wasn't sure if you checked my location anymore since I switched phones. And I thought if it was going to work to lure you, then it needed to be somewhere unexpected."

"You didn't need to lure me, you sweet dork." He pressed a kiss into my hair. "One word. One text. Jesus, one ring on the phone before you chickened out and hung up, and I would have fucking been on your doorstep with my heart in my hands."

I blinked at the sudden flooding in my eyes.

"Not true." I nudged him with my elbow.

"So true." He inhaled and then lowered his voice. "I was giving up on you," he whispered. "I just needed one sign."

"I needed the time, I think. But I think you knew that, didn't you? But hearing you were giving up on me—" My throat clogged.

He continued quickly. "Not giving up exactly. But I was going to go to England and really give you some space. And hope to fuck you didn't do something utterly stupid like agree to go out with Christian Fuckface because then I would have had to have Xavier fire him and quietly ruin his life. Kidding, obviously. I don't do that kind of thing."

"I know you don't." My lips quirked at his attempt to bring humor to the awful thing that had happened to him at the hands of Angus. "But anyway, more than time, I think it was hard for me to believe you might have feelings for me after I knew you'd given your heart away a long time ago. That there couldn't possibly be space for me. I had to reconcile that with still wanting any piece of your heart you had left over."

His exhale was half laugh, half moan. "It was you, Sunflower."

"What?"

"*You* are who I gave my heart to a long time ago." His gaze pierced me with its brilliance, and with its vulnerability. "I was so scared when we were making love that day, that you were going to see right through me. That you would see how much you mean to me. And I wasn't ready to show you. I didn't think you were ready. I didn't know if you ever would be."

I gulped, my throat thick. "So, when you said you'd given your heart away, you were telling me ... I thought about that later. I hoped. But I didn't know."

We sat quietly as I absorbed the enormity of all our admissions. Our lips found each other in slow, languid kisses before we lapsed into a still and quiet embrace.

"How is everything going with the estate?" Evan asked eventually.

I sighed. "Fine, I guess. I have his pension, though I can't spend it without feeling ill. Luckily, I have enough of my own savings at the moment. That's why I'm still working at the gallery even while I'm studying."

"I heard about you getting a degree," he whispered. "I'm so proud of you. I think that's absolutely incredible, and you're going to be brilliant at it."

I turned and leaned my face toward him to capture his lips with mine in a long, soft kiss. "Thank you," I said when I peeled my mouth off him, looked up at him through my lashes, and licked my lips.

He grew hard under my ass. "Careful," he said and nipped my ear with his teeth. "We might not be so lucky at not getting caught next time."

Laughing, I squirmed a bit just to mess with him before burrowing in again to his warmth. "I'm too cold to pull my pants down again, sorry."

He chuckled. A seagull flew down to hop around and stare at us sideways to see if we'd dropped more crumbs from our lunch since the last time he'd flown in.

"Sorry, buddy," I said. "We put it all away."

"What about the house?" Evan asked after a few minutes.

"Actually, I want to ask you about that. I was thinking, maybe I could donate it, like," I nibble my lower lip, suddenly nervous, "like to your mother's network? I mean, only if you need more places. Safe places, as it were. You may already have something there. But it's set back from the road a bit, and if it hasn't changed much, which it doesn't seem to have from the pictures Neil sent me, it's pretty private and has a very pretty backyard. At least it does in spring. It used to be one of my favorite places to sit and garden when Angus was out. I could find peace out there. It could—" I broke off, embarrassed. "I don't know, maybe it's silly. I don't have a house of my own, but I could never live there again. Even selling it and using the money, I just can't."

Evan's arms had pulled me in closer as I spoke.

"No. It's not silly," he said. "It's amazing. Are you sure?"

I nodded. "Very. I can't think of a better future for that place than to help provide safe refuge for women and children in need."

He dropped his head forward, resting his cheek on my hair. "Fuck. I love you so much, it actually hurts. No one tells you that."

"Love songs do."

"Oh yeah, some hairband Sam and my mom used to listen to had that song. I should have paid closer attention."

"But it's a good kind of hurt, right?"

"It's terrifying and good at the same time."

"Are you scared?" I whisper. I knew I was. Especially when I looked at his beautiful, rugged features, hard jaw, soft mouth, and mesmerizing eyes. He was so damn beautiful. And it was hard to believe I could be getting my happily ever after. It didn't seem real.

"Yeah," he admitted.

"Why?"

"I still can't believe this is real," he said, echoing my exact worry. "Like you're going to wake up one day and realize you haven't had a chance to meet anyone else because I kept you on the damn boat and away from everyone."

"I could have left, Evan. But I didn't want to."

"Because I made you so dependent on me."

"No. You didn't. I put up with it because I wanted to stay close to you. I understand that now. I orbited around you when we were at sea, coming up with ridiculous errands to get under your skin, and I counted the days on land until we could be near each other again. For a lot of years it wasn't conscious. But now, after this time apart, I'm even more convinced."

"Letting you completely go the last couple of months, trying to prove to you and to myself that I wasn't a controlling bastard, has been the hardest thing I've done."

I kissed his temple. "Do you know why I chose here to tell you I loved you?"

"To scare the shit out of me so I'd realize I *had* to tell you how I feel?"

"Is that what happened?"

"Kind of."

I sucked my lips together to keep from giggling at his affronted look again. When he'd told me about what happened with Pete this morning, I'd had a hard time not laughing then too. But I'd apologized profusely.

"I chose it because it's symbolic. I called you my lighthouse before. Because you were always there, no matter how hard the sea raged and how hard the rain beat down. No matter how hard I snapped at you or how much I pushed you away. You were always there. Quietly and steadily there. And I suddenly realized the lighthouse is immoveable. The lighthouse can show the way to safety, but it can't force a ship into safe harbor. I had to do that myself. You did that for me years ago when you had your mother plaster flyers everywhere I went." My voice wobbled under the onslaught of the memory and love crawling up my throat. "And you've done that for me the last few years as I slowly healed. And you did that for me the last few weeks when you waited patiently for me to process everything that happened with Angus and find my footing in this new world where I'm not looking over my shoulder all the time."

"Sunflower," he breathed.

"And you waited for me to realize *you* are my home." I swallowed over the ball of tears. "Because you are, Evan. You are everywhere I want to be. You are my beacon. My lighthouse. And wherever you are, I know I'm safe."

"Fuck, I love you."

I smiled. God, it felt good to say. "I love you too."

"All those things you said. That was the same for me. My heart was a magnet pointing to wherever you were, spinning me around, driving me fucking crazy. Xavier saw it."

"Chef saw it. Josie saw it."

"My mum saw it."

"Pete saw it," we both said at the same time.

He whipped his head toward me. "What? When did he tell you that?"

I kissed his cheek. "Yeah." I laughed through my tears. "He told me this morning."

"Fuck, really?"

I nodded. "He wanted to make sure I was on the up and up. He also said to tell you, you're a dumbass."

Evan laughed. "Yeah. I guess I was. Hey." His tone softened. "I really was going to England. I was leaving tonight, but I can wait a bit. But I'd really like you to come with me and spend Christmas with me. With my mom and dad."

"Someday I won't be crying around you all the time," I said, garbling through yet more tears that stung my cheeks in the cold.

"Happy crying?"

"Yes." I sniffed. "I'd love to spend Christmas with you and Abby and Sam."

One of his hands wrapped around me came up and wiped my tears. "Good. There's nothing I want more than to wake up with you every morning forever, but Christmas morning, surrounded by love and family especially."

The vision of what he described undid me. I clutched his shoulders and hugged him so, so tight. "It's been such a long time. I haven't even dared to hope for such a beautiful thing," I whispered.

"As long as I can give you those moments, I'll give them all to you for the rest of my life. I love you, Sunflower. I love you with every cell in my body and every piece of my soul. I'll keep you safe and loved as long as I have breath to do it." He kissed me softly.

Then I leaned back to meet his emerald eyes. "And will you take me to Skyfall?" I sniffed.

"What?" He chuckled.

"Your secret James Bond hideaway. Will you take me there?"

He chuckled. "Yes. I will. It's your getaway too now. Probably always was, if I'm honest."

"What do you mean?"

Someone shouted. A women's voice rang out. "There they are! He made it! Thank God."

"I told you we shouldn't have come," Rod grumbled.

"What if he hadn't shown up?" Meg demanded. "Who would have been around to pick up the pieces then?"

"Andrea! Evan!" She jogged the last little bit. "Fuck, it's cold out here. So you found her," she directed at Evan. "Thank God." She held up a bottle of tequila. "This was Plan B."

"Because walking on a cliff path shitfaced above crashing waves is such a solid Plan B." Rod rolled his eyes.

"You would have saved me," Meg sang.

"Anyway, I told you," Rod said, flustered at Meg's tone. "You didn't have to worry. Of course Evan would go get her. He's only been in love with her for fucking ever. Right, mate?"

Evan and I stood up and caught each other's eyes. "Rod saw

it too," we both said at the same time and burst out laughing. Then Sue and Chef materialized to join us.

"Are you engaged yet?" Sue called.

"Sue!" I admonished.

"Pregnant, at least?" She pressed with a cheeky wink as she and Chef reached us.

"Maybe," Evan smirked.

"Oh, give over." Rod bellowed a laugh. "There's no way you two buttoned up tossers did it out in public."

"Of course not," I said, trying to keep a straight face.

Chef stamped his feet and blew into his hands. "It's colder than a witch's tit out here for sake. So it worked then, did it?" he asked me.

"How many people were in on giving me a fucking heart attack this morning?" Evan grumbled.

I slipped my arm through his and gave him a kiss on the cheek. "Are you mad with how it turned out though?"

"No." He smirked. "Obviously."

"Well, since we're here, and you're not pregnant," Sue sang, "let's all have a quick shot to ward off this nasty, slice-you-to-the-bone wind, and then head back."

I grabbed the bag Chef had packed and dug around, producing two plastic glasses and the screw cups of each thermos that I quickly rinsed out with the rest of the water. "These will have to do."

Meg poured four hefty shots. "Evan, you better share with Andrea." We held the cups together. "What are we drinking to?" Meg asked.

"Love," Rod said irritably. "Obviously."

"Love," Meg agreed.

"Love," Evan followed.

Chef held up a small bottle of mineral water. "Love," he echoed and gave me grin.

Love that was freeing, not caging. Love that was euphoria, not fear. A love that was a quiet and joyous song and not a bruising touch.

"Love," I stated and closed my eyes, sending everything in my heart out into the universe as if I were a unicorn spreading confetti and sparkles on literally every dark corner where there was fear and pain and hurt. Love.

Evan drank, then gave the cup to me and I did the same, feeling the burn of it scald down my throat and into my chest. Immediately my nose stung and my eyes watered. "Wow, that was strong."

Evan fumbled in his pants pocket and pulled out his phone. "Xavier's calling. X?" he asked, answering it. Then his shoulders eased. "I guess you were in on it too?" he asked his friend. Evan sighed, shaking his head with a grin. "Yes," he said. "Yes, it's good news." He caught my eye and winked. "Okay. Hang on." He turned the phone toward all of us. "We're on video."

Xavier's voice was faint over the sounds of the ocean, and I didn't hear his response. We all stepped closer to see and hear better. Xavier and Josie sat next to each other on the tiny screen. "Hi, everyone." Josie waved, the light catching her stunning engagement ring. They were both grinning.

"Josie, this is Meg and this is Sue." I pointed to each of them.

"Hi guys! Nice to meet you! So, Andrea, are you and Evan officially done dancing around each other now?" she asked me. "Pete called Xavier to tell him what was going on."

"I guess so." I laughed.

We all caught up for a few minutes. Then we said our goodbyes, my heart full. I promised Josie I would call her later, and we left Evan and Xavier chatting and finishing up the call.

"How was my picnic?" Chef asked me.

"Amazing," I said. "You should open a restaurant," I added.

"Actually," Meg said. "After you left last night, we persuaded Chef to talk to the bistro owner who's selling, and Chef made him a verbal offer, and he accepted!"

"Stop," I gasped with a huge grin. "Are you serious?" I asked Chef. "This is amazing!"

He smiled sheepishly. "Dead serious. Still a lot to work out. But after you and I chatted last night, I realized the only person holding me back was ... well, *me*."

Rod clapped him between the shoulder blades.

"Evan!" I called. "Tell Xavier, Chef is going to open his own restaurant!"

Evan's eyebrows shot up, and his smile widened as he relayed the info to Xavier.

"All right," exclaimed Rod. "We're all having another drink to that, and then we are getting the hell out of here. My ass cheeks are starting to freeze together."

Sue cringed. "Ew."

"It's true." Rod shrugged.

Evan appeared at my side, warm and solid, and slung an arm over my shoulders and placed a kiss at my temple. "You want to go somewhere and warm up?" he whispered in my ear.

"Yes, please."

"Ew," Rod said. "Save it for later, you two."

"Come on," said Meg. "Let's go."

The six of us began the long walk back along the cliff path. The sun was higher, the sky cloudless and blue. And I breathed in deeply, my heart feeling as though it could inhale the joy of the whole world it felt so big.

Evan linked his fingers through mine and we followed the path home.

EPILOGUE

4 weeks later
Andrea

THE RANGE ROVER rounded another bend on the narrow country lane, hugging the low stone fences. The air was thick with mist shrouding the deep green of the British countryside. Through the windshield, the road shone slick and wet in the headlights we'd had to put on even though it was only two in the afternoon.

"We're almost there," Evan said. We'd left the cute little village where we'd had a ploughman's lunch about ten minutes before. Under my hand, his thigh, wrapped in expensive butter soft denim, flexed as his foot eased off the gas. He'd long had to take his hand back from where he'd been holding mine, to hold the steering wheel on the winding lane. But I honestly couldn't bear not to be touching some part of him. I was an addict. And so I was leaning close to the center console, my arm resting over it.

I peered ahead, as we took a sharp right at a gap in the stones and then eased up to a tall wrought iron gate. There was nothing but field and mist ahead.

"Skyfall," I breathed.

"It's not a ruined Scottish castle, you know. Besides we're at least an hour from even reaching the Scottish border."

"Skyfall wasn't a castle, it was a stately home." It had been amazing being back in England. I'd been quite emotional every time I let it sink in that I was back after so long.

"Well, this is a cottage."

I laughed. "I'd love it if it was, but I know you, Evan. Little stone cottages are not your style."

"I think you'll be surprised."

I tore my gaze off the gate in front of us and turned to him.

He was staring at me fondly, a crooked smile on his lips.

"I think..." He swallowed, a flicker of vulnerability flaring in his gaze. "I *know*," he amended. "I always had you in mind as my future. And if there was no you, there was nothing else. I think I bought this place like throwing an anchor into my future. I think I bought this place for you." He took his hand off the wheel and closed it over mine pressing it into his thigh before bringing my palm to his mouth for a soft kiss.

"You're just saying that." My heart grew big in my chest and pressed against my ribs.

"Sadly, I'm not."

"It's not sad. It's—God, I can barely talk with the swoon bubble currently growing in my chest." I laughed and gazed at him in wonder. He was everything so familiar and so new all at once.

His hair had turned darker without the constant sun since we'd been in England. It curled softly around his ears and brushed over the corduroyed collar of his Barbour jacket. Underneath, the crisp of his white button-down shirt added to the English gentleman look that I was fast growing to adore. Although there'd been nothing gentlemanly about the things he'd done to me before we got out of bed this morning at the small inn in Hampshire where we'd escaped after the whirlwind Christmas festivities with Abby and Sam.

I flushed in remembrance, my body aching in delicious ways, and wet my lips.

"Hold that thought," he growled, so in tune with me it was ridiculous. "We're almost there." He pulled his hand away and got out. A blast of chilled damp air replaced him as he stalked to the gate and undid the large padlock. Then he opened each side with a loud whine.

He hopped back in and pulled through before repeating the process to close it.

"I'm surprised you're not more high tech," I said. "Very unlike you."

"Like I said, I think you'll be surprised. But truly, it draws less attention to have a rusty old lock than some fancy security system that tells people you have something to hide. Doesn't mean there isn't a perimeter set up and cameras all over." He shrugged with a wink.

I swallowed. "So it really is a safe place. And you would have brought me here, wouldn't you? If Angus *had* gotten close."

"Yeah." His eyes snapped to mine briefly before pinning back on the slick road. "That was the half-baked plan."

I grinned. "So we were always destined to fall in love in a little stone house. It just happened in France. But it a thousand percent would have happened here too."

"It happened nine years ago for me. No stone houses necessary."

I held my breath. Evan had alluded to the fact he'd loved me a long time, but he always evaded my questioning when I dug for details.

Then we were crunching over the gravel and a damn manor house rose out of the mist, grabbing my attention. "Told you." I laughed, momentarily distracted. It was January, so obviously things looked a bit gloomier, especially in weather like this. But there were vines around the front door and I knew they'd be bursting with color come spring.

"Roses?" I asked.

He nodded.

From the leaded pane windows there were clearly at least three rooms either side of the front door and a second story. "Cottage, my ass," I said. But it was old and pretty and I simply loved it.

"That ass needs to get inside."

I smiled and reached for the door. "Don't need to ask me twice!"

INSIDE, Evan snapped on lights, revealing a cozy and inviting interior with wood floors and simple antiques and linen covered or wood furniture. I'd been worried everything would be heavy and drab in a house this old, but Evan had clearly had design help.

"I had someone who works for me come by and stock the fridge, pull the dust covers off, and make up a bedroom. It's a couple that live on and tend to the property. You'll meet them tomorrow."

I nodded and blew into my chilled hands.

"And turn the radiators on," he added. "But they only came this morning. It's going to take a while to warm up, we should build a fire in the meantime."

We left our bags in the hall and he led me into the kitchen first through a door he had to duck through. I sat at an old farm table and watched him fire up the AGA and fill the kettle. I gazed around me, noticing the cabinets were new, though they fit perfectly, painted a pretty light blue. Above me an iron chandelier cast light on the table and small modern spotlights were set in the old wood and plaster ceiling. There was a shelf of copper pots under the mullioned window to my right. "Have you ever stayed here before?"

"Once or twice while it was being renovated and a few times since. But not really. I didn't want to be gone too long."

Once the kettle was warming, he motioned for me to come through to another room, and we entered a sitting room that was cozy and small. It had a bookshelf built into one wall. I imagined it was a lovely spot to curl up with a book by the windows in summer, like a cat lying in a sunbeam.

Evan walked over to the bookshelf that honestly had quite a disappointing lack of books on the shelves. He reached over to one small stack and pushed the grouping to the side, and all of a sudden the shelves moved back and swung to the side.

"What the ...?" I managed, startled.

Evan smirked. "Secret room."

"You *are* James Bond," I said gleefully and darted forward.

I followed him through the opening into a library.

"I had them make the ceiling in here taller and turned the room that's above us into a storage area. What do you think?"

I gazed around me, feeling like Belle. There were floor to ceiling shelves, and since the ceiling was so high, there was a ladder on wheels and a track that ran around the room. I clapped my hands together. It wasn't crammed with books—there'd be space for me to add some too. The center piece in the room was a large stone fireplace on one wall with tall windows either side that would flood the room with light on a sunny day. Someone had already laid the fire. Evan reached for a box of matches on the sill and struck a flame to a crumpled piece of newspaper under the logs. "It's gorgeous," I breathed. "You know, you could have led with this and I would have come with you on day one."

Evan chuckled, flicking the match into the opening. "Maybe you can help me pick out furniture for this room. I didn't quite get that far."

There was a plush rug on the floor but that was it. I stood in the middle of the room and twirled around, my arms out. When I stopped, dizzy, Evan was smiling at me softly.

Yellow flames licked small but insistently in the fireplace, and the smell of burned paper and pine logs began to fill the room.

"I always remember you reading," he said. "You sometimes said you couldn't wait for off-season just to read a book. I figured you'd love this."

"I do. I love it. I love it so much."

He slipped his fingers in his front pockets. "What do you love so much about reading?"

I lowered my knees to the ground and knelt in the middle of the room. "It saved my life," I said. "In my darkest moments, I could always escape to another world and live there for a while. It made life manageable. For a while, I sought out difficult and heart-breaking stories."

His brow furrowed as he approached. "Why?"

I lifted a shoulder. "Ways to make my own situation not feel so hopeless, I guess. Recently, I'm really into happy endings."

His eyebrows lifted, a saucy look on his face. "How happy?"

"You're a dirty boy, Evan Roark." I looked up at him from my spot on the floor. "One step closer and I guess you'll find out."

Air left his chest and his cheeks flushed, eyelids lowering. The kettle suddenly screeched in the kitchen, making us both jump, and then laugh.

"Don't move," he said. "Not a muscle. I'm coming back to this."

I bit my lip and nodded.

"Good girl," he growled and turned on his heel.

Well, that was hot. I pressed my hands to my cheeks marveling that I'd found myself in this place with this incredible man. A man who made me feel so treasured, so safe to be myself, so beautiful, so sensual. And most of all, so necessary to his survival. He was the same for me, I realized.

"Hey, Evan," I called.

"Yeah?"

"Thank you for bringing me home."

I looked around me. The fire warmed my back as it spread its heat through the room. In minutes Evan was back with two steaming cups, handing me one.

"You're welcome, Sunflower."

"I mean back to England. And I mean back to you. And to your family. And of course, here."

"My mom and dad adore you. Honestly, I think they might prefer your company over mine."

I giggled and blew on the top of my tea. "I love them too. Thank you. I feel like I've known them forever. I feel like I have a family again. Is that ... too intense? Too soon?"

"There's nothing too soon when it's the rest of your life." He gazed at me as he settled on the floor cross-legged, our knees almost touching.

I swallowed, overcome with the intensity of staring into his beautiful eyes.

"You can feel any way you want to," he went on. "The good and the bad. But I know you also need to take it slow. So all I ask is that you share with me however you're feeling. I never want to hold you back, or rush you. Being with you and being able to love you is the best thing that's ever happened to me in my life. All I want is to watch you live yours. However you want to live it." His throat bobbed, and I could almost hear what he wasn't saying.

I reached for his free hand with mine and interlinked our fingers. "As long as I'm living it with you. I know deep down you doubt us. You think I haven't had enough time to know what I really want. But Evan, I had ten years. I had ten years that *you* gave me and you never asked for anything in return. You've been there as I healed. As I grew comfortable in my own skin. As I learned new skills and took on more responsibility. You were there as I confronted my fears. You were there and never pushed me. You never took from me. No. Listen," I pressed as he gave a tiny head shake. "From now on we're emotional equals. You're having a bad day, you tell me. We have to trust in our love for each other. Storms and rain and bad winds, even other people, might cause ripples or waves on the surface but underneath our pool of love is just the same. Vast and deep. It's so deep, I can't see the bottom. You need space, you tell me. You need me as close as possible, tell me. The pool is big enough for that. Same for me. But Evan, I've never felt more like myself. More like I know myself and know what I want. And it's you. I want life with you. I would live inside your soul if that was a thing. Everything else is inconsequential."

I exhaled and blinked. Evan's mouth was open like he was dazed and slightly winded. He closed it. "You do." His voice was grit.

He set his cup down and reached for mine to do the same. Then his warm palm slid up my face and into my hair where he closed his fingers and tipped my face back. He leaned up on his knees and came forward until he was staring right into my eyes from centimeters away.

I inhaled the woody scent of him, my eyelids slipping down to half-mast.

"You do live in my soul," he said. "You have since the moment I set eyes on you. I should have fought for you. I should have saved you from ever knowing him. You were mine. You were always meant to be mine. I'll never forgive myself for letting that monster take you. But when I got you back is the day I fell in love with you. You opened your eyes in that hospital bed, and stared right at me, right into me. And my heart was never the same. It's why you had to come with me to France. Why you ended up working for Xavier. I stole you. Because I was too fucking selfish to let you go. Not again. Not when the last time I did, you went through hell."

"Evan," I breathed and my eyes closed, lips seeking his. His warm mouth molded over mine. I brought my hands to his soft rain-damp hair and closed them over fistfuls of it as I opened my mouth to his and our tongues slid together." I moaned at the feel of him. The languid way his tongue stroked and his mouth took gently and reverently, lips moving and closing and pulling, and opening again for more. The taking and drinking and seeking the love from the depths of me, which I freely gave. He pulled back but only to push me onto my back so he could settle in his weight on me. I groaned at the feel of him. His hips pressed into mine and I opened my legs to cradle him.

Leaning up on his elbows, he gazed down at me. "I don't want to ever let you go. But my love has grown from that small selfish beginning into something so big, I'd let you go if you needed me too. I would hate it. And I would pray for you to return to me. But I would let you go if you needed me to."

A wet lump of tears formed in my throat and I blinked. "Please don't ever let me go," I whispered. "I've never been more true to myself than with you. And you do fight for me. You did fight for me. And please always fight for me. For us. I know *I* will. But—" I bit my lip.

"What is it?"

I swallowed. "What if I can't give you children? What if I don't want to." I didn't know if I did.

"Why do you think that has anything to do with how much I love you?"

"How can I deprive Abby and Sam of that joy too?"

"We'll give them a baby goat." He shrugged, forcing a laugh from me through the tears about to fall.

"I'm not saying I don't, I—"

"Shh." He nipped my lips with his.

I tried again. "It's just that I don't know—" His mouth closed over mine in a growl, his tongue and the shift in his hips shutting me up. His kiss turned feral, fingers threading through mine and pinning my hands to the carpet. His hips bucked, his long thick erection hitting me in just the right spot.

I moaned aloud around his kiss, back arching, heat pooling low and achy.

"Nothing matters except loving you, Sunflower," he whispered hot and wet into my ear, making prickles race over my skin. "Everything else is inconsequential."

Those words, my words, delivered back to me did me in. I whimpered, my hips pressing up to his, my hands gripping his fingers where they pinned me down. Suddenly he raised up onto his knees and began unbuttoning his white shirt, before pulling it apart, revealing his beautiful strong body. My mouth watered watching him rip it back off his shoulders, his muscles tensing. That was a mental snapshot I wouldn't forget any time soon. Skin burning bronze in the half light from the fireplace and backdropped against a library. He should be a magazine cover. Or a book cover. The swoon balloon billowed up my throat again, cutting off my air.

Fingers finally free since he'd let my hands go to remove his shirt, I danced them down his abs and trailed them over the quivering skin above his jeans. I loved the way his breath labored when I teased the hard ridge beneath his jeans and toyed with the button, before snapping it open. He went still, eyes glittering on mine as I opened his jeans and gently pulled his cock out. It was steel. A small pearl glistened at the tip.

"Do that thing I like," he growled.

I blinked innocently. "This one?" I asked, before reaching out a finger and swiping the small bead of moisture pearled at the tip, and then sucking it into my mouth.

"Fuck." His length bobbed, and his cheeks flushed dark. "Why is that so fucking hot?"

I grinned wickedly.

"Turn over," he said. "Both of us get to have a favorite thing."

My eyebrows pinched together, but I did as he asked, his legs moving to allow me to roll onto my belly.

The carpet was rough, but thick, and smelled clean and new. I leaned up on my elbows, not sure what Evan was thinking, but he pressed between my shoulder blades encouraging me down. Straddling me, he pushed up my sweater so he could reach the top of my leggings and began dragging them and my knickers down over my butt. "I still have my boots on," I protested. The warm fire was doing its best, but the air in the room sweeping over my exposed flesh, still made me shiver. Or maybe that was Evan.

"Your arse is so fucking decadent, I want to bite it," he said, and gave one cheek a small smack.

I gasped and laughed. "Is this another of *your* favorite things? Or did you think that was mine?"

"I know what you like, trust me. I've been paying attention."

Two warm hands closed over the cheeks smoothing and kneading. More prickles raced over my skin, though not from the cold. My sweater was pushed up farther, and Evan's hot mouth instantly made contact with the top of my spine and began working its way down. The combination of his hot breath, and the cool air and his warm tongue, made my breathing shallow. It began sawing in and out. He snapped my bra strap open and licked down my spine.

"You see?" he whispered. "You love this." Kiss, lick, lower. "And the closer I get to your arse, the more you whimper. And the wetter you get. Baby, you have one long path of erogenous zones right here."

My back arched, then my hips. My stomach quivered and my core clenched. And yes, I whimpered. My leggings and my boots prevented me from widening my legs. I tried pressing myself back. It was useless. "You're driving me crazy," I gasped.

He chuckled. "I know. Fuck, I love your body."

I turned my head, grabbing a vision of him kneeling over me, shirtless, jeans undone, his long, thick erection bobbing free, and I almost doubled over under the force of need that ripped through me. Especially with the look of worship on his face. "Please."

We locked eyes, and he knew. Grabbing my hips, he yanked me onto my knees. Then he was behind me and in one swift thrust he drove himself all the way inside me.

I screamed. It was a wave of completion, knowing, and bliss, sweeping up my body as he filled me.

One hand on my hip, the other reaching forward curling around my hair, he pulled me back onto his length in another strong thrust as deep guttural sounds emanated from his throat.

"How do you do this to me?" he asked, breathing labored, words staccato between hard won inhalations. His hips pumped, filling me. "I had plans. Plans to take it slow. God. Fuck, you feel good. To undress you. Seduce you. To make love. And all I want to do is fucking depraved."

"Later, we'll take it slow," I gasped, and I pressed back, needing even more, pulling my head forward, so his fist in my hair tightened. God, that felt good. "Just give me everything now," I begged.

It was like when we were at the lighthouse, I couldn't open my legs wide and the pressure of the tight fit was like suddenly finding yourself at the top of the cliff ready for the freefall, stomaching bottoming out. There was no slow climb up. It was all pounding nerves and adrenaline and then I was airborne, the wind and the world rushing past my skin, making my insides weightless. Every time we made love—and it was making love for me, no matter what he was doing to my body, every dirty and sweet thing—it felt new. And every time, I had the thought that I'd never known it could feel like this. It was like nothing before had ever existed. My insides coiled tight in a dizzying, painful rush, before exploding outwards with such force that I jerked and shuddered and went rigid.

"Jesus, baby," he gasped, but he wasn't far behind me. "Oh fuck." He hauled my body up and pressed his front against my back, arms wrapped around my waist and neck as he rode out his orgasm, hips still jerking, breath sawing in and out and into my hair.

Our panting gave way into chuckles.

"God, I'm useless around you." He nuzzled into my neck and pulled down the neckline of my sweater to kiss my skin.

"Didn't even manage to get our clothes off. I had plans. Sweet plans and dirty plans. But plans to take my time."

"We still have time for all of those plans," I assured him.

He gently drew my pants back up and then tucked himself away. Turning me into his arms we flopped back onto the rug. He kissed my temple. "I'm sorry, I made a bit of a mess down there. I have a lovely big Victorian tub upstairs, and I'll run you a hot bath and bring you a glass of wine."

I moaned.

"That sounds good?"

"It sounds like heaven, Evan Roark. You must be a god."

His laugh was deep and throaty. "I hope you think that forever, Sunflower."

"Just keep being you." I kissed his throat then his jaw, the stubble rough on my lips.

We grew sleepy in front of the fire, my head in the crook of his arm.

"What are some of your favorite *non*sexual things?" I murmured.

"You first."

"Hmm. Libraries. Books. Rainy days. Sunsets. Christmas trees. Stone houses. Dirty talking lighthouses."

His chest shuddered. "Is that me? Am I the dirty talking lighthouse?"

I smiled, nodding.

"Well, I'm glad I cracked your top ten, at least."

"It wasn't ranked." I let out a soft laugh. "And you? Give me some of your favorite things."

"Sunflowers," he said and then lapsed into long even breathing.

"Sunflowers," I repeated. "That's it?"

"That's it."

I smiled.

"Come on." He kissed my forehead. "Let's go get you into a nice warm bath."

Another Epilogue

SIX MONTHS *later*
Evan

"HURRY UP, babe. We're going to be late," I call out and check my watch. I slip my fingers into the starched collar of the shirt I put on for the party tonight, pulling it away from my neck. I'm not used to much formal wear anymore. At the back window of our private *gite* at a hotel near *Ramatuelle*, I look toward to the forecourt of the main building and see the car and driver I booked. He also checks his watch.

"Coming. I promise," Andrea calls back.

"I'm sure you look perfect." I turn just as she comes out of the bathroom and does a twirl, stopping my breath in my throat. "Well?" she asks.

"Wow," I manage.

She cocks a hand on her hip, the pale periwinkle blue silk making her eyes glow.

"Turn around again," I order.

She does and I almost swallow my tongue at the dip in the back of her dress that almost bares the top of her butt. Her smooth back has a thin gold chain running down her spine, to join another that circles low on her waist and disappears inside the dress. It's so fine that it's only visible when it catches the light, which it is now. "Does that stay on when your dress comes off later?" I whisper.

"Yes, if you'd like it to."

"I'd like it to."

She smiles. "As long as you give me time to remove the extremely unsexy contraptions that are keeping my boobs in place under this dress. Absolute nightmare." She rolls her eyes, and I chuckle.

She's curled her blonde hair into loose messy waves. It's grown darker and richer during our winter in England. "Ready, Professor?" she asks, her teeth catching her bottom lip.

"Don't start that now, we'll never get out of here."

Ever since I started teaching at the university in London, Andrea has started calling me Professor and sometimes—a lot of times—we get a bit carried away.

"Yes, sir. Of course. Shall we go?"

"Minx," I complain.

"You're safe, don't worry," she assures, slipping a lip gloss into her evening clutch. "I'm so excited to see everyone, I don't have the heart to detain us much longer. I haven't seen Josie in almost a year. And I'll hardly see her at all tomorrow while she gets ready for the wedding. I'm glad we're doing this tonight."

Both our phones buzz as we exit the cottage and make our way down the stone path. The smell of lavender wafts over us from the field to our left.

"Group text?" Andrea asks, as she pauses and takes a moment to drink in the gorgeous sight.

I pull out my phone.

Rod: *Whose bright idea was it for Chef to cater Xavier and Josie's party at his new restaurant? The guy is about to lose his ever-loving mind. Normally I'd give someone a shot of whiskey and tell them to calm the fuck down, but you know.*

I smile. "Chef's losing it with nerves, says Rod." I take Andrea's hand as we keep walking, and she uses her other to hold up the silk of her dress so as not to catch it on her heels.

"Tell Rod to remind Chef about the breathing techniques he learned," she says. "Shut him in the freezer for three minutes if he has to." Andrea had persuaded Chef to go with her to some three-day meditation retreat a few months ago, where they ate vegetarian food, chanted, and meditated. They didn't even drink caffeine.

"That's a bit high-handed, don't you think?" I say.

"I'm sure he won't mind if Rod shuts him in with Gabriel. That should concentrate both their minds." She laughs.

Chef had hired a young Mallorquin chef who he'd thought was a man. Instead, a fiery, raven-haired beauty with a genius hand in the kitchen and a chip on her shoulder the size of the Verdon Gorge showed up. It had set light to a powder keg that was definitely going to blow up sometime in the very near future. "I think that's more likely to short circuit the entire port," I mutter. "God knows what would happen if they were locked in a room together."

"You think there's something there too?" she asks.

"I do. But she's, like, fifteen years younger than him."

"And? The heart wants what it wants." She slips a hand up my chest and rests her palm flat against me.

"Not judging," I assure her. "But I'm sure he's insufferably condescending to her. Anyway, I don't think it's anything to do with the heart for either of them." We reach the gravel of the circular driveway, and the chauffeur jumps to open the back door of the black sedan.

"Well, Chef is a catch," Andrea says. "He's attractive,

grounded, owns his own place, and has good friends. He also has a good heart. She could do a lot worse."

"You might be right," I answer as I help her into the back seat of the car and thank the driver.

"And I think he's learning how to keep *her* grounded," she continues as I climb in the other side. "It's a match made in heaven if you ask me."

Inside the back of the car we lapse into comfortable silence. The car sails out of the gates and winds down toward the port in *Saint-Tropez*.

I lift her hand up for a kiss. "I meant to tell you, since I lost my tongue earlier, you look exquisite."

She smiles at me. "So do you. Oh, I forgot to tell you, I'm having coffee with Marianne tomorrow morning."

Tomorrow, I would be busy with best man duties, and Josie had two of her friends from America as her bridesmaids which definitely left Andrea at a bit of a loose end for part of the day. But I had very exciting secret plans for later in the day I needed to check in with Josie about.

"That's great. Tell her I say hi. I was going to book you in for a spa day so you didn't get bored."

"You can do that too, please. I love it when you spoil me."

"Good, because I did already." I grin.

The car rolls to a stop, and I'm barely opening the door before Josie comes flying toward the car and pulls Andrea into a hug. "Andrea! You're here! You have to meet Tabs and Mer. God, you look incredible," she adds pulling back and holding Andrea at arm's length.

"So do you." Andrea smiles and they hug again.

"Hi Evan," Josie says.

I raise my hand. "Hi. Good to see you."

"Come on, thank you so much for getting here early. It's going to be nuts later with me meeting a bunch of people I don't know." She takes both of our arms and walks us to the restaurant. The place is awash in flowers and fairy lights and lanterns that will turn on later. For now, there's carpet laid on the cobble stones, and silver buckets of champagne everywhere. Waiters trot back and forth straightening and polishing and setting things up.

"I sent Meredith and Tabs to find Chef. They found him and Gabriel in the walk-in fridge. Can you believe it? Thank God, we found them. They would have died."

I catch Andrea's eye on the other side of Josie and wink at her. She sucks her lips between her teeth.

Inside we're greeted with stone walls and old oak furniture and soft modern lighting twinkling like stars from the ceiling. On one side were floor to ceiling wine racks, and at the back a plate glass window to see into the kitchen. It's so different than the rowdy bar I remember frequenting with the crew in years past. Chef emerges and Andrea walks straight to him, folding her arms around him in a massive hug. "It looks incredible," she says. "I'm so proud of you."

"Great job, man," I add, and clap him on the back.

"Thanks. It's been a lot of work. But good work. I'm so proud of it. Now, if I can just find some good help ..."

"Gabriel not talented enough?" Andrea asks.

Chef clears his throat, the tips of his ears going pink. "She's talented. But, damn, does that woman make me want to dive straight back into the bottle."

"Hi, you guys!" Josie walks up with two women in tow. One

is an absolute knock out, tall, with dark skin and gorgeous natural curls that are a statement in and of themselves. The other, also pretty, is a willowy brunette with pale skin and sleek shoulder length dark hair.

"So this is the infamous Evan," the dark skinned girl says with a bright smile. "I heard you finally told Andrea how you feel." She turns to Andrea. "Andrea, I presume." We both shake her hand. "I'm Tabitha, I run the nannying agency that sent Josie over here. And this is Meredith."

We all say our hellos as Chef melts back into the fray of the kitchen.

"The bodyguard, right?" Meredith asks.

"He's more of a professor these days," Andrea says without a trace of nuance and refuses to catch my eye. I'm not a professor, I just teach a couple of classes. I smirk.

Josie comes up on my other side. "We're all ready for tomorrow," she whispers. Andrea has turned away to lead Meredith and Tabitha over to a painting she helped Chef pick out for the restaurant.

"Are you sure it's okay to do tomorrow? It's your day. We can wait. I was going to do it next week. But honestly I want to do it as soon as possible."

"No way! We are all so excited we want you to do it when we can all be together to celebrate."

"Are you sure X is okay with it?"

"Yes, I promise you, Evan. Just show up tomorrow night engaged. That girl deserves her happily ever after."

"She does. And she'll get it. I'm ready. I've been ready. Patient as a bloody saint. I just didn't want to overshadow your day."

"There's nothing that would make X and I happier than seeing you happy too. You know that, right? More than his best friend, you're like a brother to him. Chef has the picnic prepared and Xavier has pulled his strings and booked a private tour of the lighthouse, and you'll have the lookout to yourselves for two hours until we show up for a quick champagne toast."

My pulse thrums with nerves. "Thank you."

"Well, we appreciate you being willing to jump the timeline. I'm so freaking excited."

She smiles at me and squeezes my arm, just as a huge crash and a scream comes from the kitchen.

"*Puta di Madre!*" a woman yells, and suddenly she appears like a hurricane, ripping her apron off and her dark auburn hair out of its bun. It tumbles over her shoulders. "*Ya he terminado!*"

"Fine," Chef's voice yells out from somewhere we can't see. "Go!"

She runs past us, chin trembling, and eyes on fire.

We all stare in shocked silence as she leaves out the door of the restaurant.

"I guess that was Gabriel," Andrea says.

Rod exits the kitchen. "Should have locked them back in the freezer," he says, with a shrug. "Champagne, anyone?"

∽

The end.
Sign up for Tasha Boyd's Romance Newsletter , or by going to natashaboyd.com
To get a simple TEXT alert when I have a new release or a sale, please text NATASHABOYD to 31996

You can also listen to the STOLEN ENGLISH playlist on Spotify

AFTERWORD

Domestic abuse comes in many forms. Sometimes it's violent, yes. But sometimes, it's mental which can be even harder to identify. It often starts slowly and so insidiously, it's hard to spot, it's hard to admit, and easy to explain away if you're experiencing it. Angry outbursts, belittling comments, gaslighting, separation from friends or family, financial control, those and *many* other things start small. If you feel that you or someone you know may be at risk, I encourage you to reach out to free resources for advice.

In the USA please call the National Domestic Violence Hotline at **1-800-799-7233** For anonymous, confidential help, 24/7.

In Canada, you can contact WAVAW Toll free: **1-877-392-7583**

In the UK, you can call Refuge free at **0808 2000 247**

And in Australia, call RESPECT at **1800 RESPECT**

On a personal note, I had a close brush with a manipulator

and 'gaslighter' in college, and I have no doubt it would have turned violent. It can happen to anyone. More recently, I had two close friends go through the most heart wrenching situations with their partners. One is lucky to be alive, and her partner was arrested and sentenced, but he got out after an infuriatingly short amount of time due to 'good behavior'. He has a new girlfriend in another state. I pray she is okay. The other friend, would hate to even be mentioned here, and she is, thankfully, finally divorced, but misplaced shame and humiliation kept her silent for a long time. And still does. But abuse recognizes no gender, no zip code, no race, no nationality, and no income level. It can happen to anyone.

You deserve to be respected and not belittled, loved and not hurt. Please seek confidential help, especially if you have children.

With love,

ACKNOWLEDGMENTS

Thank you so much for reading STOLEN ENGLISH. I fell in love with Andrea and Evan in BROKEN FRENCH and just knew they had to have their own story. It's not in the glamorous setting of a mega yacht, but their story was no less beautiful and compelling.

Thank you so much for the critiquing skills of Al Chaput on a chapter by chapter basis, the critique reading and cheerleading skills of Karina Asti (as well as her proofreading https://www.karinaasti.com), beta reading skills of Brenna Leigh, and exceptional plot hole spotting and encouraging WhatsApp Voice Memos from Brenna Aubrey (what would I do without you?), the editing of Judy Roth www.judy-roth.com, the support of my amazing husband Stephen Boyd, the cheerleading of my mom, the patience of my kids, the gorgeous cover by Julie at hearttocover.com, and the cover critiquing and feedback from bloggess extraordinaire Natasha Tomic (www.natashaisabookjunkie.com).

So, I struggled hard with how to deal with Angus. The first edition of this book had him dying of cancer. But people really wanted him to be vanquished ON THE PAGE. I did too, to be honest. But the mental and emotional place I was in when I was writing this book simply didn't allow it. I couldn't get there. I should have waited before publishing. But the pace of publishing these days and Amazon preorders mean that you don't really have that much time to marinate and change your mind on something. There are a lot of people out there who read the original, and they may never read these new scenes at the cliff with Angus. But I believe it's a stronger story for the new scenes. And the good thing about publishing these days is that *you can change it!*

Thank you to all the readers, bloggers, bookstagrammers and TikTokers who have picked up BROKEN FRENCH over the last year and kept me sure that you all wanted Evan and Andrea's story. Your support and enthusiasm has been epic!

With love and thanks from the bottom of my heart,

Tasha xxx

NEXT

If you would like to know more about my romances and not miss my next release or sale, let's keep in touch by visiting my website www.natashaboyd.com and signing up for an infrequent newsletter
Or in the US text 31996 to NATASHABOYD

Read where it all began:
BROKEN FRENCH
Blurb
Josie thought she was getting a promotion at her architectural firm, but instead her career implodes. She impulsively takes up her roommates' offer to nanny for a little girl on a mega yacht in the South of France. Even though she can't stand boats, this seems like fate giving her an opportunity to lick her wounds in a bucket list paradise while she figures out how to get her life back.

But this little girl she's arrived to look after has a daddy. A widowed, hot, billionaire of a daddy. And if there's anything that Josie needs less than having to be stuck on a yacht, no matter how luxurious, it's an inconvenient and highly-combustible attraction to her new boss. A man who, for all his wealth, is grumpy, conceited, and utterly closed off.

Xavier Pascale is on an emotional island of his own making. It's just him and his daughter and he likes it that way. He works hard, his shareholders are happy, his best friends are his body guard, and the people who work for him. What's wrong with that? But then he meets Josephine Marin. Her arrival in his life is like a deep ocean tremor along a catastrophic emotional fault line. And now... well, now, he's very, very aware of his isolation and his very human need. But he can't be distracted. When he gets distracted terrible things happen.

He should send the nanny home.

He really should.

But what if he just takes what he wants, just this one time ...

This is a standalone, contemporary romance. It includes luscious scenes of sparkling blue ocean, and tantalizing, seductive food, was well as a smoking hot, dirty-talking Frenchman. If traveling scares you, or sexy times scare you, then this book is not for you. But if you're looking for a decadent armchair vacation--a story that will make you laugh, swoon, fan yourself, and cry--then this one is for you!

ALSO BY TASHA BOYD

The Butler Cove Novels
Eversea (Eversea #1)
Forever, Jack (Eversea #2)
My Star, My Love (An Eversea Christmas Novella)
All That Jazz
Beach Wedding (Eversea #3)

The Charleston Series
(Romantic Comedy)
Accidental Tryst
Irresistible Beau
Sunshine Suzy
Keeping Tabs
Very Merry

standalone contemporary romance :

Deep Blue Eternity

Mediterranean Series
Broken French
Stolen English

ALSO: Ever wished your favorite romance author would write a "bookclub" type book? Well, I did! **The Indigo Girl** a historical fiction (or should I say, *herstorical* fiction?) novel is available now in hardcover, ebook and audio. It's based on a true story and it's a woman's story you don't want to miss. I am so incredibly proud of this book, and the honor of being able to tell this incredible young woman's story. I do give talks about it at libraries, museums and schools and bookclubs via zoom. So contact me via my Website www.natashaboyd.com

ABOUT THE AUTHOR

Natasha Boyd (writing romance as TASHA BOYD) is a USA Today and Wall Street Journal bestselling and award-winning author of both historical fiction and contemporary romance. Her historical fiction novel THE INDIGO GIRL was long-listed for the Southern Book Prize and was a Southern Independent Booksellers' Association OKRA PICK. She holds a Bachelor of Science in Psychology, and lives with her husband, two sons, and her dog in Atlanta, GA.
Text NATASHABOYD to 31996

facebook.com/authornatashaboyd

instagram.com/authornatashaboyd

tiktok.com/tashaboydwrites